# Frozen Notes

## FAY LAMB

Write Integrity Press
*Frozen Notes*
© 2017 Fay Lamb

ISBN-13: 978-1-944120-45-0
ISBN-1-944120-45-9
E-book ISBN: 978-1-944120-46-7

This book is a work of fiction. Names, characters, places, and incidents are either products of the author's imagination or used fictitiously. Any similarity to actual people and/or events is purely coincidental.

All quoted Scripture passages are taken from the KING JAMES VERSION (KJV): KING JAMES VERSION, public domain.
Published by Write Integrity Press;
PO Box 702852;
Dallas, TX 75370
Find out more about the author,
Fay Lamb at her website www.faylamb.com
Or at her author page at www.WriteIntegrity.com

Printed in the United States of America
Library of Congress Control Number: 2017944754

# Praise for the Amazing Grace Series

Fay Lamb really has a knack for tension. If *Frozen Notes* doesn't keep you up and chewing your nails past your bedtime, nothing will!

~Anne Baxter Campbell, author of
*The Truth Trilogy*

STALKING WILLOW is not what I expected. It is heart-pounding scary at times, and tear-inducing sweet at others. Certain parts of the story—such as part of "who-dun-it"—I had figured out. Other parts of the story—such as "Bear"—didn't turn out as I expected. Ms. Lamb is an absolutely stellar romantic suspense author, and if this is the type book that Write Integrity puts out, I will be looking at more of their books. To be honest, the small press books I've read recently have been better written and more engaging than some put out by major publishers. I will definitely be looking at more of Ms. Lamb's books. If you like romantic suspense and don't mind a little terror and blood and gore, then you will love STALKING WILLOW. Great book. Great read. Great author. Don't miss it. 5 stars.

~ Laura V. Hilton, author of
*The Amish Firefighter* and other popular stories

The Amazing Grace series by Fay Lamb has so many "can't put the book down" qualities beside being well-written: suspenseful, romantic, good plots, believable characters, and descriptive settings. Each book builds on the one before, which brings in suspenseful tension from page one. You won't want to miss reading any of these wonderful books.

~Jennifer Dison Hallmark, Contributor to
*Not Alone: A Literary and Spiritual Companion for*
*Those Confronted with Infertility and Miscarriage*
and the Writing Prompts blog founder and editor-in-chief

Each book in the Amazing Grace series is a wonderful combination of suspense, romance, intriguing characters, and underlying story of God's love and forgiveness that I thoroughly enjoyed. This author certainly knows how to write a story that keeps the reader engrossed from the first pages, and she is definitely one of my favorite authors of Christian suspense.

~ Ann Lacy Ellison
Reader and Reviewer

Engaging characters, suspense that grips you tightly and won't let go, and an ornery villain you'll love to hate—things I've learned to expect from Fay Lamb's Amazing Grace series. Lamb's strong narrative and characterization brings the story to life. If you love a mystery with a strong element suspense and enough romance to make it interesting, you've come to the right place. I've read two books in the series (more than once) and eagerly await my return to Amazing Grace for another installment.

~ Betty Thomason Owens, author of The Legacy Series
*Amelia's Legacy* and *Carlotta's Legacy*
and the Kinsman Redeemer Series
*Annabelle's Ruth* and *Sutter's Landing*

The Amazing Grace series written by Fay Lamb is loaded with well-formed, complex characters who are both funny and sad, witty and confused, and so realistic they could be your neighbors and friends. The story plots are believable, with excellent rising and falling action that kept the storylines moving forward, and with enough romance to start the embers smoldering. My favorite part of these stories is the little town of Amazing Grace that comes alive between the pages. I know it's on the map somewhere, and one day I'm going to visit. I just adore these books!

~ Elizabeth Noyes, award-winning author of The Imperfect Series: *Imperfect Wings*, *Imperfect Trust*, *Imperfect Bonds*, and *Imperfect Lies*

# Dedication

This one's for you, Dad. Oh, how I wish you were here to read my dreams come true.

Thank you for being a harsh critic to a young writer. I mean, that letter to the Beatles really didn't work when I spent half the correspondence telling them how to get to where I lived. I appreciated my first critique from the man who taught me how to read and to write and to love words before I turned five years old.

Even though you were absent for most of my life, you were always in my heart. I really do believe that God plants seeds into the souls of those who belong to one another and that, despite all, if we only tend to the garden, the love will bloom.

I have learned that I'm definitely your kid. I sense you in the things I do and definitely in the way I think. I see you in the eyes of my sons and in the faces of my grandchildren. They certainly are a legacy for a man who never wanted to be a father, but I'm so glad you did become one.

The longing ache of a daughter for her father never truly goes away no matter the circumstances: choice or death. Many people think a lot of things about you, but I'm the only one who knew you as a daughter, and Herbert James "Doodle" Thompson, I believe that only God (and Grandma Fay) could love you more than your only child.

I'm clinging to the God-given, God-reminded faith that I will be seeing you again one day.

# 1

A hush fell over the small crowd loitering outside Lyric Carter's house as paramedics placed the bodies of the two men, both encased in body bags, onto separate gurneys and wheeled them to the waiting ambulances. The sheriff's deputy had completed the gun residue test, and Lyric backed away from the woman. She fell hard into the chair at her kitchen table near the open front door and stared at her still bloody hands, not knowing what to do next. The winter's cold air gusted into the home, but the chill had set in the moment her husband, Braedon, had returned to the house, brandishing his handgun.

Lyric fought to keep her tears at bay while investigators plundered through her home looking for shell casings, additional bullet holes, and other evidence. But a murder-suicide was pretty cut and dry. The investigators wouldn't search for much else.

Her body lifted with her sobs. If Braedon had only looked at the documents he couriered from Raleigh, he and

Matthew Roberts would still be alive. He'd left them unopened on their table before a phone call sent him out. Before he returned, Lyric opened and then hid the evidence where no one would find it, prepared to face Braedon's wrath should it come to that.

"Which one do you think she's crying over?" Joe Johnson from the *Amazing Grace Gazette* said from somewhere outside her home. She'd recognize his haughty voice anywhere. He wouldn't be so close to her now if Braedon and Matthew were alive and not stretched out on the gurneys ... or if Balaam was here.

No. She stilled her thoughts. Braedon deserved more respect than that despite what he had done. Balaam had no place in her thoughts—not tonight—not ever.

The flashes of several cameras pulsated from outside and through her windows and doors. The blossoming migraine delivered pinpricks of pain behind Lyric's eyes. She ran her tongue over the cut on her lip, felt the mass of swelling beneath the surface of her skin, then wrapped her arms around her to stave off the cold.

A stomp at the front door announced a new arrival. Lyric turned in her chair and bit her lip to squelch a rising panic attack.

Sheriff Daniel Dixon pointed toward the newshound standing in her doorway then toward the street. Johnson ducked around the sheriff and scurried off behind the paramedics. Daniel moved around the crime scene, ignoring his investigators. He'd look in her direction soon enough. She strengthened herself for the interrogation to come.

Everything she'd struggled so hard to redeem or protect—her reputation, her son, her vulnerable heart— they were all in danger.

"Lyric, what's going on here?" The chair beside her scraped the floor. Daniel sat. "Did Brae do that to you tonight?"

She started to speak, found no words, not even an emotion to send them forth, just this rising sense that she needed to do something or that something needed done by someone, but what? The inability to latch on to the reason for her all-consuming fear cycled in her, raising the terror level.

"Lyric?" Daniel questioned.

She closed her eyes and bowed her head without betraying her dead husband. Braedon had been unable to live with the one truth everyone in the town knew, although he'd promised her he could. They'd never been happy, even before she gave birth to her son.

Her son? Where was he?

"Lyric," Daniel pushed, "two men died in your house tonight. I need to know why."

She forced herself to stay focused. "Braedon loved me. I know he did." But had she loved him or simply used him as he'd proclaimed within the melee preceding his death.

The moist and sticky blood of both Matthew and her husband stuck to her skin, its touch making her colder there than the rest of her body. The smell, similar to rusty iron, invaded her senses. Tremors consumed her entire body. "No!" she screamed. "This isn't happening."

The sheriff's strong arms encircled her. "Don't." She pushed him away in a futile, insane effort to keep his clothes and his soul clean.

He always protected her with fierce determination. Not just her—all of them.

Lyric started to swipe at her tears but stopped, holding her trembling blood-soaked hands out in front of her instead. For a second, she imagined the beat of Matthew's pulse as she'd pressed against the open wound in his stomach torn by the bullet that exploded from her husband's gun. Before the impact thrust her and Matthew to the ground, another shot sounded, and Braedon's faceless body had fallen toward her.

The warmth of Daniel's arms released her, and shock returned to replaced his hold. He reached over her sink for a paper towel and handed it to her. "They've gathered most of their evidence," he said. "But the place will be off limits for a day or so."

She looked down at her fingers and rubbed the paper over them. The red stain remained. She rubbed harder and faster, wanting to free herself of the smell, the sight, and the memories it evoked. The napkin left white lint stuck to the blood. Lyric grew frantic in her attempt to cleanse herself.

"Here." Daniel pulled her toward the sink, placing her

hands under the faucet and turning on the water. He unfurled more paper towels from the roll. The water turned red as it fell into the sink and slowly washed down the drain. When her hands were no longer covered, Daniel led her back to the table and helped her to sit. "Tell me what Braedon and your momma met about tonight." His whispered tone was meant for Lyric's ears only. Green eyes held her firmly in his gaze, and his hand pressed against her shoulder, an unspoken warning to keep her voice down.

"Momma?" Lyric blinked. "She called here. Braedon left right after. I don't know why she called." But she did know, and her mother knew; Momma had always known. The secret belonged to Momma, and Lyric had hidden the proof where no one would find it.

Daniel sat once again. "She and Braedon met at the Backslide Tavern. Willis called dispatch because he saw the gun Braedon tucked in his belt. He overheard him threatening to kill someone. Appears he followed through on his threat." He cleared his throat and leaned close. "Did Braedon have a reason to kill Matthew?"

Daniel's words slapped at her vulnerable heart. If he knew the truth, he'd never ask that question. If Momma sent Braedon to kill anyone, it hadn't been Matthew. But no matter the target of Braedon's anger, Momma had done the unspeakable. She'd consciously made a choice that screamed of her hatred of Lyric and cost Matthew his life.

Lyric lowered her head and stared at the still-wet

11

bloodstains on her shirt. "Matthew thought if I left Braedon it would force him to get help."

Should she tell him Braedon hadn't taken aim at Matthew? He'd just gotten in the way.

"I'm sorry, but these questions are going to come sooner or later." He clasped his hands and stared at them before giving her a sideways glance. "You and Matthew weren't having an affair?"

She forced herself to look into Daniel's eyes and hold his gaze. "Matthew and I were not having an affair. Now or ever. We're friends. We've always been friends. All of us." Even that wasn't the entire truth, but the reality of who they were would catch Daniel in a storm that would rock his neat little sheriff world. The truth would utterly undo him—give his long-time enemy an edge.

Braedon had been working with that enemy, though he'd lied, telling her he had nothing to do with Jessup Roy.

Daniel gave a slight nod. He stood, turning his back on her and staring out the kitchen window. "Do you want to tell me what led to this?"

Lyric took a deep breath and released it. "Braedon was gone most of the day."

"When he did get home, he got a call and left?"

She nodded.

"What was his behavior like when he first arrived?"

"He was agitated and short with me, but he wasn't violent. Still, I did feel uneasy. I don't know why. I sent Cade over to a friend's."

"And when Brae returned, he found you and Matthew?" Daniel continued to stare out the window.

"Matthew showed up while Brae was gone. He said something was up. I needed to come with him. We'd stop and pick up Cade. He said he'd keep us safe." Anxiety ratcheted up a notch more at the thought of her son, but being with his friend was better than being here.

"He didn't tell you why he was concerned."

"Before Braedon came back, Matthew told me he'd heard a rumor—one he said he knew was true, but someone was telling Braedon something different. He said Braedon wouldn't handle it well. He didn't tell me what the rumor was. He wanted to talk about it later when we had time." Those rumors had been confirmed in the papers Braedon left behind before going to the tavern. She'd wanted to tell Matthew she had the proof, but she never got the chance. "How long before Braedon killed Matthew?"

"That's what doesn't make sense. He came in without a word—started swinging at me. He was so angry. He was crying, and he hit me two or three times before Matthew could get to him. Then he lashed out at Matthew, accusing him of ..." She closed her eyes and fought against the nausea.

"He accused Matt of what?"

"Of sleeping with me. He said Momma confirmed ..." Lyric stood and rushed to the sink, releasing the contents of her stomach. She clutched the counter for a moment to make sure she wouldn't vomit again. Then she rinsed out her mouth, grabbed another paper towel, and turned back to him. "Daniel, why would Momma lie to Braedon?"

Daniel's face hardened. He heaved a heavy sigh. "Who knows why your mother does anything. She loves to see others struggle. Maybe it gives her peace to know her life isn't the only one in shambles."

"But this—she's destroyed so many lives." Lyric held her stomach and bent forward then straightened, no longer able to deal with the emotions. "I have to make funeral arrangements."

"Let him rot in the morgue. What do you care?"

"He loved me. Someone needs to tell Braedon's brother. He won't come home, but he needs to know. And there's Matthew's mom and dad. Oh, Lord, what do I tell them? Their only son is dead, and I'm the reason."

A crash from the living room spun Lyric in that direction. The clamor caused her insides to feel as if her body were being torn apart. She needed Cade, but she didn't want him here to see this mess she'd made of their lives.

Lyric stumbled and braced herself against the table.

Daniel didn't seem to notice. "It's okay." He picked up the picture frame his investigator had knocked over and handed it to Lyric. "I remember taking this."

Her hands shook as she reached for it. She covered her mouth. Fresh tears sprang to her eyes. Through them, she stared into the photo taken so long ago—five young children, four boys each toted a fishing pole, and the girl in the middle held up the string of trout. Braedon and his brother, Balaam, were on each side of her, their arms draped over her shoulders. Quinn, her brother, stood beside Braedon. Beside Balaam, his hand resting on Balaam's shoulder was Matthew Roberts.

Matthew. His death would forever be on her hands.

If they'd known life would have come to this, would they have been so close all those years ago? Thick as thieves, the five of them—and they had not been beyond thievery back then. Yet, Daniel always maintained a careful watch over all five of them.

"Lyric!" As if summoned, Quinn ran through the door. "Oh, Lord, thank You." He stumbled toward her, grasping her hands in his. "Are you hurt?" He stared at the blood covering her clothes.

"Braedon killed Matthew." She continued to clutch the photo. "He killed ... Matthew."

Quinn reached up and pushed the hair from Lyric's eyes, and she saw the sorrow in his, though he'd never speak of it. "Did Braedon do this to you?"

"Yes, he did," Daniel answered for her.

Quinn turned toward the sheriff. "You killed him?"

"He killed himself, Quinn. I'm sorry. I know he was your best friend." Daniel's jaw lifted as he clenched his teeth.

The muscle in Quinn's jaw flexed as well, and he seemed on the verge of losing his composure. Clearing his throat, he nodded. "He saved me from doing it. I told him one more time, and I'd—"

Lyric placed the frame on the table and started to step away from the two men, but trembling took a hold of her. She paused, catching the scream and forbidding it to leave her throat. She pushed it away, along with all other emotional agony.

"Where's Cade?" Quinn questioned. "He didn't see this, did he?"

"Cade's with my mother." Daniel patted Lyric's shoulder and gave her a gentle squeeze, as if he knew her son's whereabouts had not been far from her thoughts throughout all of this.

His touch settled her nerves.

"I caught him outside," Daniel said. "I didn't want him coming in. Lyric, you're going there tonight. Mom will take good care of you. She'll help with the arrangements."

"I'll make the arrangements." Quinn dropped into a chair at the kitchen table. He slumped forward. "Matthew's parents will take this hard."

"I'll go to them after we get Lyric across the street to Mom's. I'll also go see Zeke. Braedon's death is going to be a blow to him as well, especially with Balaam not around," Daniel said.

"Balaam? I wonder if he'll want to come home for the funeral. How can we find him? Do we know where he's playing?" Quinn looked to Lyric.

Quinn had washed his hands of Balaam Carter long ago. Why did he care now? Did he really think she'd followed Balaam's career after all these years—that she would hurt Braedon like that? That she would let Balaam have an ounce of thought now after what he'd done to her and to their son.

"Los Angeles, for three final shows on his tour, starting tonight." Daniel nodded.

Daniel's knowledge of Balaam's whereabouts knocked the wind out of her.

Lyric shared a look with Quinn. "I need some clothes." She made her way toward the living room, her teeth biting into her bottom lip to quell the anxiety that, again, rose in her like a spiking temperature.

"Won't be possible, ma'am. You'll have to borrow something to wear until our investigation is complete." A deputy blocked her way.

Lyric hesitated, but it didn't matter. They could search all they liked in the house. She'd hidden the dirty little secret that Braedon had dug up for Jessup Roy, and no one would ever know. She heaved in a deep breath and pivoted. One foot, then the body would follow—along with the fear.

Her legs wobbled. Waves floated before her eyes, turning to pinpricks of light floating toward her. Then a sea of darkness billowed. "Quinn." She caught the back of her brother's shirt and fell forward into Daniel's protective embrace, crying out and burying her head against his chest when he lifted her into his arms.

The speed of the gurney made him want to puke his guts out. Maybe that's what they wanted. He'd lose the pills and live, but Balaam Brasher the rock star didn't want to live. He wanted to die.

Balaam Carter on the other hand ...

He wanted to live. *I do, Lord. I do.* Would God heed his cry for mercy?

He could hear the medics and nurses talking around him. "Maybe too late. Too bad. Guy had a lot of talent."

*No, Lord.*

He struggled to open his eyes. He'd done this to himself. One did not always commit suicide with deliberation. He'd popped one too many pills and swigged too much bourbon. Within him, his body begged for release, but his soul clung to this world. He had apologies to make to Lyric. Braedon needed to know how much he appreciated him for what he'd done.

His brother made everything right. Balaam wanted to say thank you.

Balaam craved the sight of his son. Did Cade look like him or like his mother? Even in weightlessness, the successive beeps told him his soul was losing its grasp. *No! God, please don't do this to me.*

In an instant, the bountiful field of bluebells surrounding Shepherd's Rock spread out before him.

Confusion reigned only for a moment until he spied Lyric running toward him, the wind catching her mane of luscious raven curls. Heaven looked a lot like the place where he'd proclaimed his undying love for her—such a cruel joke to play on him at his death.

She had naively believed him, and he had stupidly thought his words a lie. How could he ever know that he'd miss someone who'd always been a part of his life until separated from her by his blind ambition? To live his dream, he'd stolen hers. Only two reasons could make him return to life in Amazing Grace, and he had forfeited his right to both.

"I've missed you for so long." Lyric's slender arms wrapped around him, and he buried himself against the familiar softness, no longer caring that Braedon's kindness made Balaam's actions unforgivable. When she pulled away, they both knelt beside a small boy, his face a blur. "Bay, this is Cade," Lyric's voice sang out.

She'd always been the one with the voice and with the talent for writing beautiful songs. The remorse for what he'd done by leaving her overwhelmed him, but Balaam smiled and pulled the boy close. A strong wind blew, ripping his son and Lyric from his embrace.

The air swirling around him rushed into his lungs. The pills and alcohol spewed out. "We brought him back." He heard the triumphant voice. Whether it was an angel, or a paramedic, he couldn't tell.

## 2

Balaam opened and closed his eyes several times before he grew accustomed to the light in the room. The constant beep he'd heard earlier now came every few seconds. He tried to lift his hands, but they held fast. Turning his head, he watched the heart monitors. Had God really given him a second chance? He struggled to sit up, but the bands restraining his wrists prevented him. His gaze followed a clear tube at his side to where it ran into an IV that dripped fluids into his veins.

"Mr. Brasher?" A nurse stood over him.

Balaam blinked.

"Mr. Brasher, everything's okay."

He tugged at the straps tying him down. "Why?" His throat ached as the word scratched their way to the surface.

The nurse placed a hand on his shoulder and offered him a sweet smile.

He stopped fighting.

"We'll take these off once the doctor gives the order.

You gave us some trouble last night, the drugs you know. Now, you lay here and try to rest." She brushed his forehead with the palm of her hand. His long blond hair clung to his arms, moist with his sweat. Why then did he feel so cold?

Tears sprang to his eyes. The old man said he'd come to this. He hated it when Poppa's old country-boy wisdom proved right.

"Can I get you anything?" the nurse asked.

"Cold." He couldn't get his trembling body under control.

The nurse held up her hand. What was that supposed to mean? He pushed his head back against the pillow. She left his room and returned with a blanket. As she laid it over him, the warmth brought blessed relief. She touched his shoulder. "Rest, Mr. Brasher."

"Carter." His teeth chattered. "My—my name is Ca— Carter."

Balaam Brasher the rock star had killed himself, and in his place laid the resurrected man Brasher had killed. Balaam Carter had returned from the grave where Brasher had tried to keep him buried.

Lyric sat on the stool at Grace Dixon's grand piano and plucked a few keys from memory. She'd written the song so long ago, and she hadn't played since Balaam abandoned her. Yet, the tune never left her memory.

Another sign that Braedon's inability to accept Cade was her fault. Though she tried so hard not to mention Balaam, somehow, she always managed to hurt his older brother.

A knock on the screen door brought Granny Grace from the kitchen, the soft patter of her orthopedic shoes fell upon the old wooden floor. As she crossed the living room's threshold, she waved her hand up and down, silently indicating that Lyric should remain where she sat.

Mumbled voices, one of them Grace's in an unusually angry tone, floated around the corner. Okay, maybe not angry, but as close as Granny Grace would ever come.

The screen door opened then shut, and a heavier pair of shoes sounded after Grace's steps.

The stranger followed Granny Grace to the living room's opening. "You wait right here, young man. Badge or no badge, you ain't talking to her until I've notified my son."

Lyric stood, facing the man she'd never met before. "What badge would you have?" she asked.

"My credentials. I'm a federal agent, Mrs. Carter. Name's Ethan Goodman."

She remained silent. Miranda rights and all. Though they'd never been read to her—not yet anyway—she'd been with the Carter boys and her momma long enough to be able to recite them from memory.

Ethan Goodman was tall. His dark hair was cut short, but not too short. He dressed in jeans and a black pullover, the kind of shirt with the seams on the outside. He wasn't wearing a jacket, but angry or not, Granny Grace would have offered to hang it on the coatrack by the door. If he hadn't announced himself as an agent, Lyric would have guessed he was part of Jessup Roy's drug cartel.

The roar of silence had stretched on since he'd introduced himself. Now, he looked at his wristwatch.

"Agent Goodman, I haven't done anything wrong. You have absolutely no reason to be here on my neighbor's doorstep. How did you find me anyway?"

"In this town? I just asked the first person I met." His lips curved into a pleasant enough smile, but she hadn't been wooed by a man's pretenses since Balaam's departure and Braedon's declaration of undying love for her and for Balaam's unborn child.

"I came to ask you some questions about your husband," he offered.

Lyric's firsthand account would never change, though the tidbits of truth she'd kept for herself would forever play in her mind.

The fact Braedon had actually wanted to kill her was beside the point. Why open that to scrutiny? Nothing about Braedon's behavior made sense. Whether he killed Matthew or had managed to murder her, the crime was senseless. For some reason, Momma had told Braedon a horrible lie. He obviously hadn't learned the truth, though he'd held it all in his hands before leaving it on their table to rush to the Backslide.

"Just a few questions, Mrs. Carter." Goodman raked a hand through his hair.

"That's what every investigator says." Lyric remained sitting. No use to encourage his entrance into the room.

The agent gave a soft chuckle. "Yes, I guess it's a habit. We know your husband acted as courier for Jessup Roy on a number of occasions. Did he tell you anything about his job?"

This agent cared nothing for her husband or for Matthew. He wanted Jessup.

Foolish man. It would take more than the federal government to nail the professor. Jessup was too good at subterfuge. His recruited minions were too loyal to him. No one who met him would suspect him of being a major drug trafficker. Daniel had been trying to bring down the man for years. And Braedon had been working with Jessup after all, lying to her when she'd asked him for the truth.

"Did you hear me, Mrs. Carter? Do you know anything about your husband's job as a courier for Jessup Roy?"

"Not firsthand, no." She closed the cover over the piano keys the way Granny Grace had taught her during those lessons so very long ago—given to Lyric for free because Momma never bought anything that didn't have a bottle cap and a label. "But I suspected as much."

"Our informant tells us Mr. Carter picked up a parcel in Raleigh on Wednesday afternoon. We can account for his movements, and there's no indication he spoke with Roy or any of his people. Would you know anything about the package?"

She couldn't face him and lie to him. She turned to stare out the window onto Granny Grace's front porch. Then she shook her head.

"No? You didn't see the package?" Goodman asked.

"Young man," Granny Grace returned, "Sheriff Daniel Dixon said for you to stay right where you are. He's across the way. Saw you pull up, and he isn't happy that you're here."

Agent Goodman grimaced.

"You know him, do you?" Granny Grace snickered. "He said as much."

Lyric studied her hands, fighting at the smile and surprised that she even had one left inside her.

Sending Cade off to school that morning had been difficult, and she'd forced a few grins onto her face and into her voice. She shouldn't have bothered. He was sullen and too quiet, almost angry. She'd worked so hard to keep her son happy, no matter what Braedon did and said. Until now, she thought she'd succeeded.

Despite Granny Grace's lingering presence, Lyric stared up at the lawman. "Why should I tell you what you already know?"

"You didn't see him with a package at any time?" Agent Goodman broke into her thoughts.

"I already answered you."

"I understand you have a lot on your mind. You need to bury your husband and your ..."

Lyric stood, crossing her arms over her chest, daring him to say the lie.

Goodman fumbled with his notes for a moment.

"My friend," she goaded. "I need to bury my husband and my friend. You can say it." She pushed her curls from her forehead only to have them spring back into place, exasperating her even more. After Balaam's departure, she'd cut her long hair because Balaam had liked it long, said he hoped she'd never cut it. He'd challenged her that he could grow his as long as hers.

Based on the glimpses of pictures she'd seen of him in videos and on the Internet, he'd won the challenge because she'd forfeited the stupid games of childhood.

And she had been a child back then. If only she'd behaved like a childhood buddy instead of a love-struck teenager, all of this could have been avoided. She'd have been on the road with Balaam and his band right after high school, but Nathan Roy, Jessup's son and Balaam's self-declared manager, convinced Bay that a pregnant girlfriend, and eventually a kid, would have been trouble on the road. And Balaam wasn't about to give up his dreams for anyone, not even her. Not even their child.

"Are you okay?" Granny Grace came beside her, slipping a comforting arm around her waist.

Lyric nodded to the dear woman and then turned toward the man. "Did anyone in this town say he was anything more to me?"

Agent Goodman continued to write in his notebook without answering.

"Because if they did, they're lying," Lyric said a little too loudly.

Granny Grace's hold tightened. "They won't dare say it—at least not where I can hear it. Daniel either."

As if summoned, Daniel, wearing the brown uniform of the Amazing Grace Sheriff's Department and a heavy jacket, stepped around the agent. He carried his Stetson and another coat—hers.

Quinn had been across the street, having finally been given permission to go inside. He'd been cleaning up, refusing to allow her inside until he'd done his best. Lyric hadn't noticed Daniel anywhere near her home, but that was the only place he could have retrieved the coat.

She closed her eyes, searching for strength. No matter what life threw at her in the past, Lyric had never felt alone. She had always sought out Quinn or Matthew, and then Sheriff Dixon.

When Balaam Carter left her behind with Cade in her belly and her own dreams of being the keyboardist for his band dashed by motherhood, she'd run to Daniel because telling Quinn the truth had terrified her. She'd wanted to spare her brother the fact that the sister he had raised was no different from their mother. And imagining Matthew's disappointment had filled her with shame. And she hadn't wanted Matthew to be angry with her or with Balaam.

Now, Daniel and Quinn were all she had left to confide in.

Daniel brushed past the agent. "Goodman, when we spoke this morning, I asked you not to bother Mrs. Carter today."

"I'm just finishing my investigation."

"I told you she doesn't know anything about Braedon's side businesses with Jessup Roy."

"Well, she just confirmed that for me." The agent nodded in her direction, an eyebrow raised in a silent declaration that he didn't think he'd gotten enough information from her.

Goodman left, the screen door closing after him, and Daniel walk toward her. He placed her jacket on the stool. "There's a good reason, I think, for you to stay here and not at your place. Mom takes her guard duty very seriously, and Quinn's over there." He leaned his head in the general direction of her house. "He doesn't have anything to tell them unless you've told him something. He says you haven't."

"Protecting the pastor, Daniel? Too late. He's guilty by default. He's the son of Madga Moxley and the brother of Lyric." She'd never refer to herself as a Moxley again. She'd discovered the truth—or Magda's version of it anyway. Who knew the real truth? Everything she'd never known and had just learned could still be a mystery. Her mother's truths were always grounded more in booze than reality.

Lyric wished what she'd learned was booze-soaked lies and nothing else, but at the same time, she prayed they were God's honest truth. Her spirit had been crushed enough over the years by this very same issue. She didn't think she could take one more disappointment.

"I want to go home. Cade and I have a new life to settle into. The sooner the better, don't you think?"

"At the risk of hurting your feelings, darling, I'm going to tell you that I think that your new life has the possibilities of a lot more good in it than it had before." Daniel looked into his Stetson as he spoke.

"If I don't mess up again, you mean." Her words struck out at him before she had a chance to pull back the verbal punch.

Daniel leaned low, garnering her full attention and, as he stood, Lyric kept eye contact with him. "Those Carter boys did the messing up." He gave a slow nod. "They both missed out on precious much. You and that boy are treasures that one Carter abandoned and the other abused." He placed the Stetson firmly on his head. "Do you have anything to take with you?"

"They took my clothing for evidence. Quinn bought over these for me. He'd forgotten the jacket." She took it from him, but placed it on the bench. The desire to leave the safety of Granny Grace's home and the protection of Daniel ebbed from her. Maybe she could stay for another day. "Thank you for bringing it to me, but ..." She stared up at him. Unstoppable tears streamed down her face. "Do you think Quinny would mind if Cade and I stayed here one more night? I don't—I can't go home right yet. I'll go before Brae's service tomorrow."

"She'll be thrilled for you two to stay as long as you'd like."

"Quinn?"

"He'd rather you stay here. He's a good brother to you, Lyric. He made sure I had your coat before I walked over. I don't know anyone who loves you more."

Lyric nodded and turned. "The fact that I learned that lesson a little too late is a major mistake, don't you think?"

"Our mistakes sometimes give us the most precious gifts from God." Daniel turned his hat in his hand. "Beautiful, wonderful treasures." He swallowed hard, a fleeting shadow of remorse crossing his eyes. "Like your Cade."

Magda Moxley strolled about the vast living room of Jessup Roy's mansion. She stumbled on the carpet but managed to right herself. Maybe he didn't see.

The floor-to-ceiling windows showcased the town below. From here, on a good day, you could see everything. Today, though, the fog had moved in, and the dew it produced had prickled her skin with cold as she made her way in from the car.

Only the wealthiest lived up on the point where they

could look down at all the others. "Living where you can use the clouds as pillows." That's what Quinn's daddy said when he promised her they'd move up here one day.

The liar.

Last she'd heard, he was living in Denver, Colorado, running a big corporation. Another woman slept with her head on a pillow of clouds—his second wife—in a big house with their three kids. Kids he was putting through fancy schools and colleges. She'd made sure Quinn knew about it, too. No use of him pining after a man who didn't care about him. Quinn, Sr., left and he never looked back.

She closed her eyes to shut out the painful memories then turned on her heels to look at the man who helped to make her day-to-day existence bearable. He owned her because she needed what he had to offer. As silent partner in the Backslide Tavern, he kept her tab running. She didn't have money to pay for the booze, but Jessup did.

Her benefactor unbuttoned his suit coat. Placing his hand on his hips, he revealed the gun strapped to his side. An indication of his jealousy for Daniel Dixon. The sheriff had always worn everything better than Jessup, especially his gun. "You mean to tell me you can't find two little packages in your daughter's tiny house?"

Magda lifted fearful eyes toward the well-dressed man. She cursed the day she'd listen to his plans for her life. He'd destroyed her with them. Not that her life hadn't always been a train wreck, but the actions he'd convinced her to take shifted the tracks a little further apart, causing a lot more collateral damage than she'd ever thought they would.

Well, no use worrying about that now. She was up to her ears in it. If she could just stall for time, she could get him what he wanted. "The house isn't that small. She could have hidden them in a hundred different places." Her hands trembled, and she licked her dry lips. Why didn't he offer her some of his fine bourbon? Providing her something to quench her thirst was the least he could do since he'd awakened her from a deep sleep and it only being noon. She'd ask, but that would show her desperation.

As if reading her thoughts, Jessup strolled to the bar. He held up a shot glass and poured the brown liquid close to the rim. She kept her eyes on the prize as he started to put the glass to his lips. He stopped, looked at her, and sat the full glass on the bar. "And did you search each of those hundred hiding places?"

"I didn't have time. Daniel's watching. Quinn is in and out of the place. You don't want them to catch me there, do you? Daniel's already asked me about Braedon. He might figure it all out. Besides, if the crime scene investigators didn't find it, how am I supposed to know what happened to it?"

Jessup's fist hit the bar. Bourbon spilled from the glass. What a waste.

She fixated on the glass as Jessup picked it up again.

"What do I care if Danny Boy figures it out? When he does, he'll know I have the noose around his neck. Jessup ran a hand across his reddish-blond trimmed-to-perfection beard dotted with gray then through his hair of the same colors. Some called him Roy the Lionhearted. They didn't know him like she did. His face morphed. Anger seeped through those cold eyes of his. "However, Braedon had something else I need. If Daniel comes upon those…" He shook his head as if cobwebs had cluttered his mind for a second. "I'm afraid I'll have to resort to something I've never done before if I thought Daniel could get his hands on the second set of papers your son-in-law said he had in his possession—at least before you called him to meet you at the Backslide. Willis told me what you said to that boy. He was already on the ledge of madness where that girl of yours was concerned. You drove him over it." He shook his head in that slow way that said he pitied her, but he didn't really.

Jessup and her, they were alike. They had pain, and they covered it up. She used the alcohol. Jessup found his peace in watching others suffer. She'd seen his brown eyes flame with passion while some coked-up kid gave him a sob story about needing his next fix.

Jessup's daughter had been murdered out in Colorado somewhere. His son never came home, touring with that Carter boy that put Cade into Lyric's belly before running off on her. Seemed only fitting that Jessup should suffer, with Quinn's God and that "eye-for-an-eye" vengeance and all. She could add to his suffering, bring the big man tumbling down.

Yeah, she knew all about Jessup. Enough to destroy him. But why would she want to do that? He kept her drunk and blissfully numbed to her own pain.

"Just think what the voters will say if they get wind that our pious sheriff once had his hand in the dirtiest cookie jar in town."

Magda stood tall and straightened her ratty coat. What right did he have to say those things? She did have feelings after all, and they were exposed right now without the alcohol coating.

Jessup looked her up and down then laughed. "I don't think it'll happen, though. Daniel won't want anyone knowing the truth. He'll do as I ask. He hasn't got much of a backbone. I saw that with Desiree. Didn't even fight for her. Let me have her. Gave me two kids and, well, look what I took from him. He got nothing."

Magda was too sober for this. Jessup's mention of his kids never came with the truth. He still seemed to live in a land where they existed in all their perfection. Jasmine seemed like a good kid. Never got into trouble. Magda had been sad to learn she'd died. At first, everyone was told she'd committed suicide. Later, the town had been abuzz with her murder at the hands of an old college friend. Now, Jessup's son? Well, that boy was just like his old man. Meaner than dirt and sleazier than a down-and-out gambler in a Las Vegas trailer park. At least Quinn had turned out good, and he'd tried hard to make Lyric respectful. He might have done it, too, but Lyric was always drawn to trouble, and it was spelled C-A-R-T-E-R.

"I'm torn," Jessup held up the glass of bourbon and peered through it as if it held the deepest secrets of the world, "about telling Daniel the truth or letting him live out his days alone. Keeping the secret unless I have to use it for leverage isn't what I planned on doing."

Magda gulped down any sympathy she had for Daniel. He never had any for her.

"Magda, what I want is for you to get those papers—all of the papers. Do you understand?"

"Yes. I do. I will."

"I know you will." He lifted the glass full of the substance she craved. "And until you do, I'm instructing Willis at the Backslide to close your tab."

"Please." Magda moved toward him, holding her hands out for the drink. "I'll find it. I promise."

A smile crossed Jessup's face as she approached. He held out her prize.

She stumbled forward, her hands almost around the glass.

He tossed the liquid into her face. "Now, get out of my house, and don't let me hear of you asking Willis for a glass of water until I have all the papers I need."

Magda licked her lips, tasting the sweet liquor. She ran her hand over her skin then licked her palms.

"Disgusting. Have you looked at yourself lately? You're not even half the woman you used to be." He pushed her forward. "Get out and don't show up here or at the Backslide until I see you with those records, or I might tell Daniel that you as good as pulled that trigger on Matthew Roberts. Nadine!" he bellowed for his housekeeper. "Get this piece of trash out of my house."

Nadine entered the room far too quickly. She had to have been listening in on the conversation. The woman had worked for Jessup for quite a while. Something about her had never set right with Magda. She'd seen the woman in town buying clothes and jewelry at that fancy dress place, but here she wore a dress that reminded Madga of that old television show, *Hazel*. "That how he likes to dress you up, Nadine?" Magda couldn't resist. "You'd think he'd at least like some fishnet stockings or something." She leaned closer. "I saw you buying some in that fancy lingerie store in town. Were they for Jessup, or do you work for other rich folks up here in the clouds?"

Nadine tugged Magda's arm, opened the door, and thrust her outside.

Magda stumbled out into the chill. Sheltering her eyes with her hands, she looked around. Jessup wasn't much on the gentleman side these days. Oh, people said he was proper and kind, but they hadn't discovered the real man. He could charm the skin off a rattlesnake before stealing its rattle.

He had her driven all the way up to his estate, and now she'd have to walk back to town in the cold. Her coat was one she'd stolen out of the thrift store, threadbare and a little dirty. At least she could maintain a straight line.

Usually, she found herself walking two feet east, one foot north, maybe a step or two south, then about three feet west. A straight line would get her back to town more quickly, and maybe she could sneak into Lyric's place once again.

Since Lyric's teenage years, Magda failed to find anything her daughter hid from her. Quinn never got the hang of keeping her out of his stuff, but Lyric, she must have been part pirate. Her treasures always stayed buried. But Momma needed this one, or she would die.

Yet, therein was Magda's quandary. If Lyric had the package, she knew the truth, and if so, the girl would add a pound more of hatred to their relationship. If Lyric hid the package, and if Magda couldn't find it, Lyric wouldn't despise her for much longer. Magda couldn't survive a week without a drink.

Magda lifted her chin and started walking. She'd get those papers one way or the other. Jessup wouldn't let her rest until she did. He needed the proof. No one would believe the word of the town drunk—and the other party to the secret, he wasn't about to tell anyone.

He'd sold his soul to Jessup, and Magda knew for a fact, he'd do anything to purchase it back. Well, almost anything.

What if Lyric took a hit, got hurt by it all? She was alive. Matthew—he was gone. Her plan had backfired. She'd been drunk. Hadn't thought it through.

She couldn't think of that now. The pain would about

kill her, and she had nothing to drink to take the sorrow away. She started walking.

"Magdalene."

Had he changed his mind? Would Jessup give her a drink and a ride into town? She spun around, almost falling.

"Just in case you're thinking something bad might happen to you, it might. But if you don't give me what I want, it'll be your grandson, Cade, that gets hurt. Do you understand?"

Magda shivered. She didn't care about many people, but Cade—she loved him. Sometimes, when she looked at his little boy face, she was reminded of Quinn and how he was before his daddy left them, and for a moment, she'd bask in hope. After what she'd done to Quinn, she couldn't let Cade down.

Magda looked to the cloudless sky. Not a breeze stirred around her, yet she shivered from the cold and the lack of alcohol. She needed a drink. The edge that kept her from sentimentalities had long faded.

Whatever it took, she'd get those papers to Jessup.

**FAY LAMB**

# 3

Balaam's hands shook. His head pounded. One moment he was hot. The next he froze beneath the blankets. He'd do anything to make this torment stop.

And the hospital reeked of alcohol. When you were a moonshiner's son, like a bloodhound on a trail, you knew that scent. He'd drink it straight if they'd leave a bottle near him.

The aides wheeled their carts by the door. He could see the cups of medicine. If he could stand, he would snatch a few pills. Didn't they keep them more secure these days? He didn't care what, though he could pretty much identify the medications that made him feel the best—Vicodin, Xanax, Klonopin, Loritab. Too bad he was too weak to walk. The nurses even had to wheel him to the shower.

He burrowed underneath his blankets once more, the tremors uncontrollable though the sweat built on his forehead.

Someone entered, feet scuffing against the waxed

floor. Balaam lifted the covers from his face.

"Man, you look awful." The band's manager, Nathan Roy, pulled up a chair with the back facing Balaam, and straddled it as he sat.

"Shut up." Balaam's teeth chattered as he spoke. He didn't bother to sit up. He needed the warmth of his blankets.

"All things in moderation." Nathan lifted a brow. "I've never seen you so loaded. Look where it got you."

"I said shut up." Balaam glared at him. "I don't need you telling me the obvious."

"When can we spring you out of here? You still have two dates on the tour. Trying to keep the band sober enough to play when they're bored isn't an easy job. We'll need to reschedule if you aren't out of here soon. Then there's the next album."

"I don't care about the tour." The touch of his waist-length hair, wet from his earlier shower, was too much for him. Balaam pulled it off his shoulder and his back. He pulled the covers tighter around him, pressing the edge to the cloth against the bridge of his nose. "I'm entering rehab tomorrow."

Nathan's brown-eyed stare bore into him, but he said nothing.

"And I'm leaving the business," Balaam continued. "I'm going home."

Nathan rose from his seat and moved closer. "Will you be quiet? Everyone's asking, and someone will tell.

Reporters have ears everywhere." He dug into his pockets. "Look, I brought you something to hold you over. I knew it'd be rough."

Nathan hadn't been careful with his words when he'd entered. Why would he? In the illusive land of rock 'n roll, surviving an overdose was like a badge of honor. And he'd never let them pin that on him. Getting sober, though, could ruin a career. He prayed to God above that his career was trashed beyond repair.

Still, Balaam couldn't turn his stare away from the three Klonopin in Nathan's hand.

"Go on, Bay. Take them."

Balaam reached out his hand.

"Mr. Carter, are you doing okay?" A nurse looked in at him from the door—the sweet woman who'd been with him when he'd first awakened. She'd convinced the doctor to take away his restraints.

Nathan closed and lowered his hand.

Balaam put his own hand back under the cover. "I'm fine. Thank you."

Warmth returned to his body, and as had been the routine, soon he'd be so hot he could barely stand the thin, humiliating gown he wore.

"Can I get you a Ginger Ale, maybe some graham crackers?" the woman asked, stepping inside, watching Nathan, then casting a steely brown gaze upon Balaam. She went about straightening the bed.

Balaam pushed the covers off and sat up. "Some

Ginger Ale with ice. Thank you." Again, he lifted his long hair away from his back. It made the hospital garb wet and uncomfortable.

"All right." She looked Nathan up and down. "Mr. Carter needs to rest. You have two minutes." She walked out, the soles of her shoes squeaking against the floor.

Nathan wasn't as likeable as his father, Jessup. Balaam never trusted either of them, but Nathan had pulled him out of Amazing Grace and into the spotlight. Balaam had sold himself to the devil, and until three days ago, he hadn't cared. Now, he wanted out of Satan's grasp. Satan needed to leave his room and stop with the temptation.

"Here." Nathan held the pills out again.

"Keep 'em." Balaam clutched the blankets, anything to stop him from reaching for his greatest desire.

"Balaam, if you could see yourself. What if some nosy reporter sneaks through? Your face, looking like this, would be all over the tabloids."

Nathan's pretense at caring for anyone other than himself sickened Balaam. The mirror shining back on himself was a little too much to take. If Nathan could have gotten a reporter past that nurse's eagle eyes, he'd have already done so. The report would have made Balaam a hero for surviving. His survival had nothing to do with him. God had pulled him away from death's edge, and Balaam had no desire to ever step to the precipice again.

Balaam looked from his manager to the bright blue California skies beyond his hospital window. When had he last seen daylight? For nearly nine years, he'd been a creature of the night. No more of that. Somehow, he'd find a way to give someone an honest day's work in the sunlight, and he'd sleep at night—if he could toss aside the nightmare of all those people falling into hell because they'd followed him.

He turned back to Nathan. "Are you afraid they'll discover I'm a mere mortal?"

"In this business, you either stay high and unpredictable or you die and leave fans clamoring for anything you've ever offered. Going sober doesn't sell, Bay, not in our business." He shook his hand. "Take them." The pills danced in Nathan's palm like a desirable woman.

Balaam didn't dare reach for them. He swallowed hard. "Planning on killing me for the money that will come from my martyrdom into ungodliness?" He pushed away Nathan's hand with the little strength he had left. "I don't want them," he hissed and hunkered down beneath the blankets once more, fighting to remember why rehab was so important to him.

When God allowed him to live, he'd promised to go straight. The part of him that was Balaam Brasher was the conman, the liar, the one who went back on his promises. Like with Lyric and the promises he'd made to her when he'd held her close.

The long-ago lies belonged to Balaam Carter, but Balaam Brasher had caused them. Nathan had created Brasher, and he kept Brasher in line with the promises of fame, the drugs, the alcohol, and the out-of-control life that had kept Balaam from thinking straight for far too long.

Time had come to right his own failings. He looked square into Nathan's waiting gaze. "I've had enough. After rehab, I'm going home."

"And the two nights left on the tour?"

"The tour ended when I nearly died." Balaam's entire body shook beneath the covers.

"I have a contract. The band has contracts with those venues and vendors." Nathan slammed his fist down onto the railing. "You can't do this."

"Let the boys play. Find a new front man. I'm done."

"You're the ticket, you fool. Look, take the pills. One won't hurt. Spread them out. You'll think straight then. We can wrap up the last two dates, and you can make your decision from there."

Balaam turned to look at Nathan. Why had he never noticed that the man's eyes were always clear? Nathan drank a little, nursed a Solo cup or a glass, but Balaam couldn't remember him ever taking one pill. He'd also never shot up with the others in the band. At least Balaam had refused that as well.

Nathan was a manipulator like his father. He didn't partake in the drugs himself. He was the one who got people hooked on them, on fame, on anything that would help him make a buck off them.

"It's over. I'll pay off the vendors. I'll reimburse the venues, pay everyone for their time, but I'm not going back. I'll never take anything you or your father offer. You've made all the money you're going to make off of me."

"If we're sued for breach of contract, this falls in your lap."

Again, Balaam pushed to a sitting position and threw off the covers. He was soaked with his sweat. He could smell the alcohol oozing from his own pores. "Get out of here, Nathan."

Balaam's hiring of a secretary had been the only thing he'd done right in all these long, wasted years. She'd been the one who insisted he needed a competent personal attorney and an accountant, separate from the snakes that represented the band and Nathan Roy. He'd called her to ask her to make arrangements for rehab, and she'd worked with the hospital and the rehab before visiting him with the information. He could have kissed her when she winked at him and said she'd talked to his attorney who, in turn, had contacted the promoters, the venue organizers, everyone involved with the last two tour dates. That man was slick. According to his secretary, he'd carefully phrased his requests to allow the band to perform without Balaam fronting them saying, "Due to the unfortunate circumstances of what occurred, we want Mr. Brasher to recover now, don't we? The least we could do is take this burden from his shoulders and let him help his band."

Help his band? He couldn't even help himself. Balaam had led them astray. What if he had brought a pregnant

Lyric with him on this wasted journey? She might hate him for leaving her behind, but truth be told, his selfishness had probably saved her life and given their child a better chance. Nathan would have gotten her into drugs because when that gal got riled, she was a handful—a delightful, sweet, head-rush of a handful, but a bother for Nathan all the same. And with the problem her momma had keeping sober, Lyric would be a mess by now.

Of course, he didn't know. She could still be a mess. Magda Moxley hadn't needed to leave town to fall prey to Nathan's dad.

Nathan snapped his fingers in front of Balaam's face. "Where'd you go? Did you hear me? Any loss or litigation comes out of your pocket."

Nathan obviously didn't know that his secretary and attorney had bested him. Balaam had directed the accountant to write his girl Friday a sizeable severance check, thanked her for her diligence and for watching his back, and then he'd sent her on her teary way, promising a glowing recommendation if she needed one.

Now, all he had to do was decide what to do with all his ill-gotten millions.

Nathan started toward the door but stopped. "Something to think about, Bay. When you've grown tired of sitting around a nowhere place like Amazing Grace, the fans will have forgotten you. Isn't that why you left that hole? To be somebody, to show them you could make it, to have people falling over you for a touch or a moment of your time?"

"Maybe I did back then, but idols aren't real, and I don't want worshippers. All I want is peace in my life. I can't have that on a stage, sending young kids and immature adults into a frenzy." Balaam picked at the hospital bed sheets.

"Are you sure? This is the end of our business relationship? No more events, no tours, no special appearances? Balaam Brasher has just walked off into the sunset? You'll never have anything better."

"Balaam Brasher walked into hell."

In the door, the nurse stopped, not entering. Nathan couldn't see her, but her gaze stayed on the band manager's back. If looks could launch a ballistic missile, Nathan would've been obliterated.

"You go on back to Amazing Grace. You'll be eating out of my father's hands. The only job you'll get is running courier for my old man." A slow smile crept across Nathan's face. "Well, he is looking for a new guy. The one he hired when you left, he's not there anymore." He walked back toward Balaam and laid the three pills on the sheet. "You may need these. I forgot to tell you that Quinn called. While you almost killed yourself, your brother murdered Matthew Roberts then offed himself."

"What?"

"Enjoy rehab, man." Nathan laughed on his way out the door, pushing past the nurse.

"What did you say?" Balaam screamed after him.

The nurse entered, her gaze falling upon the pills beside him. She opened his Ginger Ale and poured it into a cup containing the ice he'd requested. "Mr. Carter, why don't we make a call and find out if what that evil little man said is true?"

"I—I don't have the numbers."

"Give me the names and location. I'll see what I can find for you."

"You'd do that?" How long had it been since he received even the simplest kindness from someone not wanting something from him? When had he ever been kind to another without expecting something in return? "Amazing Grace, North Carolina. My brother, Braedon, B-R-A-E-D-O-N, Carter. Or you can try Quinn Moxley."

"I'll make you a deal."

Here it came. Either she wanted an autograph or one of her family members was a big fan and wanted to meet him. He waited for her to ask.

She pointed at the pills. "You pick those up, hand them to me, and you tell me if your guest gave you anything else. You do that, and I'll move heaven and earth to find out the truth for you."

Balaam could barely grasp the medication, but he managed to pick them up. He clutched them in his hand. One move and he could get them into his mouth, let them take all the tremors and the sweat away—soften the pain if Braedon had ...

No, his brother wouldn't do something like that. But

Balaam had to know for sure.

The nurse didn't move.

He opened his hand, and when she lifted her own, he let them fall out of his grasp. "This is all he gave me."

"You didn't take anything else?"

He shook his head, surprised at the tears gathering in his eyes. "I promise. Please ..."

She placed a warm hand on his shoulder. "Lie down."

He obeyed, and she covered him.

"Give me a few minutes." She stopped in the doorway. "Am I right in assuming those pills weren't part of a prescription—one with your name on it?"

Balaam shook his head. He had never had to have a prescription filled. Nathan's supplier was fully capable of developing a very credible imitation of any drug. "You assume correctly."

She gave him a curt nod. "I need to report the fact that he tried to give them to you."

Balaam didn't care.

"But I won't ask you his name unless he returns. I'll leave strict orders you're not to receive any other visitors, and if he does slither back here, his name will be gotten, and I'll testify at his trial. It will be the biggest mistake of his miserable little life."

Balaam could have laughed at her if he wasn't so worried and feeling so terrible. Instead, he nodded his understanding. He didn't want visitors anyway, and Nathan in jail? That thought was a pleasant one.

He closed his eyes. If the tremors, the chills, the headache, and the alternating sweats would leave, he might make it, but the cravings were the worse. What he wouldn't give for a jar of Poppa's white lightning.

The world drifted away, and he found himself in the holler where his poppa hid the still. He moved around it slowly, examining the furnace and following the copper wiring to the thump keg. One more step, and he stood in front of the worm box and its protruding tap. That old still had been Poppa's only inheritance from Grand Poppa.

Balaam reached for one of the mason jars Poppa always kept stored nearby. He was so close. He'd been ten years old when he'd first sneaked a jar away from Poppa's inventory. His face had heated with the first whiff. When the liquor hit his mouth, it seemed to warm on its own accord. When he swallowed, the stuff heated up like a radiator pipe running through his system.

He'd stood there, his eyes wide as he stared down. The warmth bleeding through him made him think he'd peed his pants.

Braedon had laughed so hard he'd fallen to the ground.

He'd have never taken another drink after that if the old-timers hadn't always claimed that Poppa's was the best shine in several states. Sure, it was premium. Poppa used the best corn mash, from the corn grown on the farm. As Balaam acquired the taste for it, he agreed with the experts.

Now, if he could just get the jar under the tap, but it seemed some unseen hand held him back...

"Mr. Carter?"

He stirred at the soft voice of the nurse. He opened his eyes. Her hand rested on his, and Poppa's secret hiding place was gone.

He didn't like what he saw on the woman's face as she stood over him.

Pity so deep he could drown in it.

"I found someone at your brother's home. I have him on the line for you."

He must have been out cold. He hadn't heard her place the call. Balaam reached for the phone and stared at a large envelope she held in her hand. "Brae!" Balaam's heart lifted. Nathan had pulled a cruel joke on him.

"No, Bay. It's Quinn."

"Quinn?" Balaam swallowed. Lyric's brother hated him. At least that's what he'd said the day Balaam left town without her. "Tell me it's not true."

"I'm sorry you had to find out in a message, but Nathan wouldn't let me through to you." Quinn cleared his throat. "It's a mess, and Lyric's right in the middle of it. I've been trying to get to you."

"I'm in the hospital." Balaam struggled to speak. "How's—how's Lyric? How's the boy? I know Larry and Bernice must be devastated over Matthew. Poppa?" Stupid questions all, but he had to ask.

"Lyric's not doing well, but she's pretending she is just the same. Cade understands only enough to realize his father's gone. He's grown sullen."

Balaam pressed his palm hard against his eyes, but he couldn't stop the flow of tears. The boy's father was right here.

"Larry and Bernice are struggling. Matthew was their whole life, and they're blaming Lyric."

"Matthew," he breathed his best friend's name. "How did it happen?"

"Brae shot him. Then he turned the gun on himself."

"Did he hurt Lyric?" Balaam choked out the words. "My son?"

"Braedon started beating Lyric almost as soon as Cade was born. I tried to help, but Brae couldn't handle knowing the truth."

"The boy knows about me?" Balaam took a deep breath and felt a new rush of emotion. He brought his knees up and leaned his head on them.

Quinn didn't speak for a moment, then he said, "No, she hasn't told Cade."

He couldn't blame her. He'd left her with her belly swollen with his child after he'd worked so hard to convince her of his love.

"Did you want your son to know you abandoned him?" Quinn's words were sharp, and they cut. They were also telling—Quinn wasn't faring well through all of this. Of course not. Growing up, Braedon had been Quinn's closest friend.

Balaam took a quivering breath. "Was she hurt in the shooting?"

"He beat her up pretty badly beforehand, and she went into shock."

Balaam lifted his eyes to the ceiling and uttered a silent prayer of thanks to God that Lyric and Cade had been spared. "The funerals?"

"Your dad asked Lyric to forego a service for Braedon. We'll bury him beside your mother on Monday around two o'clock."

"And Matthew?" What would he do without Matthew in his life? His best friend's compass always pointed north. Balaam's tilted south. When Balaam followed Matthew's leading, things went well. When Balaam went in his own direction, well, things went south with him.

"We're burying Matthew the day after." Quinn's voice shook. "I know the Roberts are hurting, and I agreed to officiate ..."

"Officiate?"

"I'm their pastor. I'll preach the funeral, but Larry and Bernice asked Lyric not to attend."

When had Quinn become a pastor? What else had changed since he'd left town besides the fact his brother had turned into an abusive husband and a murderer?

"We've taken a lot from the people in this town, but this blow has crushed my baby sister."

And Lyric and Quinn were too close for this not to defeat Quinn as well.

Balaam shook the thought away. "Matthew has always been a part of us. Why would they treat Lyric that way?"

"The Amazing Grace rumor mill," Quinn ground out.

That rumor mill must have circled double time after he left and Braedon married a noticeably pregnant Lyric. Now that her husband had killed Matthew, he could imagine the vindictive accusations being bantered around.

"Can you be here?" Quinn asked.

The urge for something to take the edge off his emotional torment grew stronger by the moment. How could he not attend the funerals of his brother and his best friend? But, then, how could he do so in the shape he was in? He lifted his head. The nurse had not left his side.

"Balaam?"

"I'll be home, Quinn, but not for the funerals. I need a little while."

Quinn gave a short snort. "Typical."

"What?" Balaam demanded.

"It's always about what you need, isn't it? When have you ever thought about Lyric and Cade? What about your dad? He's eaten up with grief."

"Quinn, do you think Lyric needs a strung-out rock star on her doorstep right now? What about Cade? Do you think he needs to see me trying to find my next high? And Poppa, he'd rather I'd have died." He balled the covers in his fist and yanked at them. If he could find something to throw, he would. He'd break it into a million pieces—like the many lives he was responsible for shattering.

"Mr. Carter." The nurse reached for the phone.

He turned away from her, keeping the phone to his ear.

"Quinn, if this was only about me, I'd be home tomorrow. I'm waiting for release from the hospital and going straight to rehab, preacher."

Quinn's sigh was audible. "I apologize."

Lyric's brother always had a way of disarming a person by failing to return anger for anger.

Balaam calmed. "If I were you, I'd have assumed the same thing. I've voluntarily committed myself. They're transferring me on Monday. Once I arrive, there's no getting out. I agreed to have no visitors or outside contact of any kind for six weeks. Another stipulation is that once I've entered, I don't leave until they give me the go ahead." He doubted he'd ever see the outside world again.

"Is it that bad, Bay?"

Balaam chanced a look at the nurse. She'd stepped back, still holding the envelope in her hands. "I nearly died. God got my attention."

A clamor came from the other end of the line. "Uncle Quinn, I'm home."

Balaam longed to see the boy's face. What color was his hair? Did Cade have his blue eyes? He had to. Lyric's eyes were the same color. Did he have his parents' ears for music or was he more stable and levelheaded like his Uncle Quinn? *Dear God, don't let him have my streak of rebellion.*

"Cade, go see your mom. She's at Granny Grace's. I'll be right there," Quinn said.

"Yes, sir," the young voice answered, and Balaam cast

another glance to the heavens. "He's how old now?" Shame filled Balaam. Years had passed without him counting.

"Eight, almost nine."

"Why is Lyric with Grace?" Balaam asked.

"I told you. She went into shock last night. Grace looked after her, and Lyric's staying there. I'm trying to get things cleaned up." Quinn sighed again. "It's a real mess."

Balaam nodded though Quinn couldn't see. "I wish I could be there for her and the boy."

"I'm counting on you to be here when you can. Something's going on. Lyric isn't telling me everything. Your brother left us with a load of trouble on our hands."

"Quinn, I'm sorry for all of this. I placed myself above everyone. Matthew and Brae are dead because of my selfishness."

"I wish I could blame you." Quinn cleared his throat. "Truth is, I think this had nothing to do with you and everything to do with my mother."

"Magda?" With her name came the memories of a drunken beauty so incapable of love she made his Poppa look like a loving 1960's sitcom father. But Poppa wasn't really all that bad. He loved Braedon. He'd loved Momma, cared for her when she took sick. He tolerated Balaam. He hated and mistrusted the federal government. What moonshiner ever completely trusted anyone?

Quinn cleared his throat. "I can't talk about it now. Maybe when you get home I'll know more, but don't carry that burden with you to rehab."

"The name of the clinic is Shepherd's Rock outside of Malibu. Would you send me a picture of Lyric and Cade? I'll sweet talk them into letting me receive it."

"Shepherd's Rock?" Quinn said. "God has a sense of humor, huh?"

If He did in this instance, Balaam didn't quite get the joke.

"I think the first time we experimented with the drug and alcohol thing was in that field," Quinn said. "I wish I could go back to that time and take it away from all of us."

Shepherd's Rock was the place where Balaam had wooed Lyric, told her he loved her, taken what wasn't his. How many wondrous days had they spent in the tall grass, holding to each other, filled with lust? Two stupid kids— two desperate teenagers—clinging to what they thought real, dreaming of life on the road in a band.

Shepherd's Rock was also the place he'd chosen to tell Lyric he couldn't stay, and she wasn't welcome to go. She was on her own. She'd have to raise their kid by herself. He'd send money, but he couldn't be held back by her or a baby. Nathan had convinced him of that, not that the man had to work that hard to get rid of Lyric. Back then, a baby was the last thing Balaam had wanted.

He'd sent money, though. Braedon had refused it. Balaam set up a college fund for his son instead.

Maybe a place called Shepherd's Rock wasn't the place for his rehab. He wished he could take it back and turn the memories into good ones, like his dream of holding Lyric and Cade in that field.

But he had to go somewhere.

"Don't tell Lyric I plan to come home. When I can, I'll give you the okay." Why now, was the woman he'd abandoned the one he wanted to see more than anyone in this world?

"Balaam?"

"Yeah."

"Can we pray?"

Balaam again covered his eyes with his hand. "Yes." He gripped the phone in his other hand.

"Father, we pray for Balaam. Give him the strength and the courage to see his rehabilitation through. Give him counselors of wisdom, not the world's wisdom, Father, but those who know Your truth. Watch over him and over Lyric and Cade. Lord, bring Balaam home safely to us, and help him to see Your great goodness in his life."

Balaam wept through Quinn's prayer, great heaving sobs as he agreed with each request.

A warm hand touched his back, steadying his resolve. With a deep breath, he began, "Oh, God forgive me for ever making anyone think of me as better than You. Forgive me for ever forgetting that You are the one true God. Take that life away from me, and give me the life You've always wanted me to live—the life I threw away so long ago."

"Amen," Quinn said. "I'll be praying for you. Good night, Bay."

"Take care of Lyric and Cade," Balaam said.

"I've failed miserably, but I've always tried." Quinn hung up before Balaam could argue.

The nurse took the phone from him. She put it on the bed stand. "I'm sorry, Mr. Carter."

He nodded and wiped his eyes. "You threw those pills down the toilet, huh?"

She smiled. "Yeah, I did." She lowered the bed rail and sat beside him. Her dark brown eyes bore into him. "You can do this."

"How can you be so sure?" He looked away, unable to bear her scrutiny.

"Because you handed me those pills. You want sobriety. It's the ones who don't that fail. You also seem to have something a lot of folks don't when they go through something like this." She placed a firm hand on his shoulder, an action he was beginning to realize meant she cared about him—and others.

He looked at her.

She pointed upward. "Psalm 105:4, my life verse. You can share it with me if you want. It says, 'Seek the Lord, and His strength; seek His face evermore.'

God is mightier than any trial you're going to go through, Mr. Carter. Seek His face and find His strength. I'm going to be praying for you and for your friends and your family. My church folks will be praying, too, if you don't mind me adding you to our prayer list." She fingered the envelope she'd been holding the entire time. "Now, this came for you. Your secretary brought it, said it was there when she went to check your mail for you. With your permission, I'd like to open it and make sure no one's tried to smuggle in contraband."

Balaam nodded.

She peeled the clasp back and lifted the flap, handing him the papers and turning the envelope upside down. Nothing more fell out. She stood. "Do you feel like looking at it right now?"

The tremors were less pronounced since he'd slept even for the few minutes before the call. He nodded. "Nurse, thank you."

"You're welcome, angel." She winked. "I'm a big fan."

"Don't be. Balaam Brasher is a fraud."

"Not of Brasher. Never heard of him before they brought you in here. I'm a big fan of Balaam Carter." Her shoes again squeaked on the waxed floor as she started out. "You still have your Ginger Ale," she called behind her.

Balaam picked up the cup and took a drink. He turned the envelope over in his hand and read the return address before he leafed through the papers.

What was it Quinn said? Brae had left them with trouble. Seems Quinn wasn't the only one thinking the same thing, but why had the damning evidence been sent to him?

# 4

Lyric walked down the hall of the ranch home built by her husband's hands, his sweat, and what she once thought—before Cade's birth—was Braedon's love for her. The heels she wore clicked on the hardwood floor. Entering the living room, she brushed her hand over her black dress and stared at the floor. The pine planks where Matthew had fallen were now brown and discolored from whatever Quinn had used to clean them. He shouldn't have wasted his time. When she closed her eyes, she could see Matthew's and Braedon's blood pooling over and around her.

Braedon had slammed down upon her and Matthew, and when she'd managed to untangle herself from his faceless body, the blood not left on her, ran onto the heavy throw rug. Quinn must have gotten it out of the house and to the dump.

She shuddered. She should sell this place. Maybe she and Cade could leave Amazing Grace and start a new life.

She bit her lip. That was one dream she'd never give in to. Quinn was here.

Footsteps sounded on her front deck. Her visitor pounded on the door, and Lyric leapt at the force of it.

She pushed the living room curtains aside and parted her blinds. Why today of all days? She took a deep breath, letting it swirl through her body and down into her feet before she released it. She leaned against the wall by the door and counted to ten.

Leaving on the chain, she opened the door until the latch held it in place. "What do you want?"

"Is that anyway to talk to your mother?" Momma looked clean. She'd whacked off her long hair. No longer reaching down her back, it was cropped around her face, uneven strands falling in perfect proportion at the edges. Only Momma could make herself a mess and still look beautiful. Even the dark circles under her eyes did nothing to take away her striking beauty, and she stood straight. Was she giving up the booze?

"Spit it out, Momma. I need to get Cade ready for his father's memorial." Lyric bit her lip. No need to accuse her mother now. What good would it do? Braedon was gone. Matthew—well, Momma would just have to live with that one.

"Cade doesn't need to go. Why don't you let me watch him?"

The fury coursing through Lyric's veins vented with her short laugh. "Are you kidding? Let you watch my son?

For a moment, I thought you were sober. Excuse me." She pushed the door to close it.

Momma slammed against it with such force Lyric stumbled backward. The chain broke. Lyric fought to regain her hold on the door, but Momma blocked her from slamming it shut. "Missy, we need to talk, and I'm not playing games here. You need to give me a few minutes to come inside and tell you something important."

"You haven't said anything of importance to me since I turned fourteen, and you told me it didn't matter who my daddy was, every man in town thought they were, and that suited you just fine."

"You still letting that eat at you? I was drunk."

"I've never known you when you weren't drunk. That's your excuse for everything. When you'd scream at Quinn and me, you'd cry into someone's arms saying the booze made you do it. Funny how you never got rid of the cause. You liked living with the result. Now, please go away. This isn't the day to bother me with your petty problems."

"Lyric Kay Moxley—"

"Carter," Lyric corrected. She'd never been a Moxley; the man abandoned Quinn, and he'd been long gone when Lyric had been conceived. And Lyric had the proof of it.

"Lyric, I need what Braedon gave you the day he died."

Lyric stepped outside and closed the door behind her. Now she understood why Daniel wanted her to stay under the protection of his mother. She should have remained across the street with Grace Dixon. For Momma, Grace was like holy water to a vampire. She didn't dare cross that dear older woman.

"Are you going to give me those papers?" Momma pushed.

Lyric blinked back to the reality of her life. "What makes you think Braedon gave me anything except this black eye, busted lip, and a broken heart?"

"Because he went to Raleigh to retrieve it, and he didn't have it with him when he came into the Backslide."

"When you called him there, you mean. What was he supposed to have? Tell me. What did he have that was worth Matthew's life?"

Momma opened her mouth to speak then closed it. She shook her head then swallowed before speaking. "You, girl, caused his death. Couldn't stay away from him. Always had to have him near. You were married to Braedon. Your husband was jealous enough of his own brother. Couldn't you see hanging out with Matthew was asking for trouble?"

Momma knew what she'd done, and the woman was so dead in soul it didn't seem to bother her. No. Cast the blame elsewhere. That was the way Magda Moxley worked.

"Get away from my house! Get away from me! Don't you ever come back!" Lyric screamed the words with such force her throat ached. "I could kill you, Momma. I could put my fingers around your neck and squeeze the life out of you." She leaned forward. "Matthew was my friend, and whatever you made Braedon believe—whatever that sick, booze-soaked brain of yours made him think—that's what killed Matthew."

Momma leaned back, her face absent any emotion. "Jessup Roy wants those papers, missy, and you best come up with them."

"You can tell Jessup I don't have what he's wanting, and he can stop trying to get to me through you. I stopped caring anything about you years ago."

"What did Braedon do with them? I need to know."

"So you can ruin someone else's life? I think not."

A light of recognition flashed in Momma's eyes. "Whose life we talking about, missy? Yeah, you got those papers, and you got the truth you've always wanted, didn't you? Was it worth it?"

The truth would have been worth it if Braedon had learned it before he needlessly murdered Matthew. Her mother's secret was more important than Matthew's life. Why then did she seem so bent on destroying Daniel with it? If Jessup got his hands on those papers, everything would come out, and Momma had set herself up to lose more than anyone. One little word from Daniel or Lyric and the woman would die in prison. She'd set it up to have her own child murdered.

Lyric couldn't dive into those emotions now. She needed to tread the surface until she could find time to be alone. "Besides never seeing you sober, I've never known you to say one word of truth." She buoyed herself with her anger. "Just because it was officially recorded doesn't mean you didn't lie. If you want those papers so bad, you can get certified copies."

"Those aren't the only documents Jessup wants, you little idiot. One gives him what he desires; the other keeps him out of trouble and offers him an edge over his competition, and you're in the middle of it all. Jessup may be the least of your troubles if you don't turn the information over to me. You're in the middle of something dangerous, and you don't want to be there. Believe me."

"Since when did you start to care what happens to me?" Lyric crossed her hands over her chest, waiting for one conciliatory remark from her most-hated enemy.

The right side of Momma's lip curled upward into a smirk. She tilted her head and narrowed her eyes. "Since Jessup told me your precious son might be the one to pay for your foolishness."

Lyric gasped. "You brought Cade into this. I can't believe even you would hurt him. He's been through too much already."

"You get those papers and give them to me now, or you'll be sorry."

Quinn pulled into the driveway.

"I don't know what you're talking about, and I want you to leave us alone."

Quinn closed his car door and stood for a moment

before walking toward them.

Lyric leaned close to her mother. "You tug at Quinn's heart as if it's never been broken and glued back together. I'm the tough one, Momma. He's the one who still has hope you'll love him. Since that won't ever happen, why don't you just leave him in peace?"

Quinn stepped onto the deck.

"Lyric, this ain't about me." Momma's voice rumbled like thunder in the distance. "You got a little boy to think about. You don't hand over those papers, and something bad could happen to Cade."

Quinn rushed forward and grasped Momma's shoulder. "What are you talking about? What could happen to him?"

Momma pulled from his hold. "I don't want that, and I know neither of you do. We can settle this all right now. Lyric needs to give Jessup what he wants."

"Jessup Roy will never get anything from me. I hate the man." Lyric opened her door. "He and his son took everything from me."

"What does Jessup want?" Quinn asked, his gaze on Lyric.

"Nothing," Lyric said. "Quinn, I'll tell you what she's done later."

Quinn stepped around Momma. He opened the door and ran his hand along the doorframe where the chain had been forced from the wood. "Did you do this?" He turned back to Momma. "You've upset Lyric. She doesn't need this today, and if Jessup wants to settle anything, you tell him to look for me and not an innocent little boy.

Lyric pushed into the house and slammed the door in her mother's face. She turned the bolt lock before hurrying through the house to check on her son. "Cade?"

Cade sat on his bed holding the picture of Braedon, Balaam, and Matthew she'd given to him the night before when he'd asked. He had hardly spoken to her since he'd run into her arms when Lyric had walked into Grace Dixon's house with the sheriff the night everything had gone down. Cade had held to her for a long time before pulling away and sitting on Granny Grace's couch.

Grace had given Lyric a sad nod, telling her Cade remained otherwise emotionless.

Lyric sat on his bed beside him. "We're going to all be missing them for a long time, but I promise it'll get easier with each day that passes." She took the picture from his hand.

For years, she'd begged her mother for the truth about her father. Momma's silence sliced deep wounds into her soul. How could Lyric ever tell her young son his real father smiled up at him in the photograph he held, and he was very much alive?

She slipped her arm around her son. He held so much inside.

Balaam never wanted him, and that truth stung her still today. Braedon tolerated Cade, taking his anger out on her, but Cade would never know Balaam walked away from him without looking back. She'd never let her son feel that pain. She'd seen the effect of it her entire life. All she had to do was look upon her brother. Quinn longed so badly for a father's touch.

She kissed the top of Cade's head.

"Hey, buddy." Quinn sauntered into the room.

Cade looked up at his uncle.

Quinn messed his hair.

Cade smiled.

"Ah, that's the welcome I've been missing." Quinn pushed him playfully to the side.

Lyric stood, fighting emotion. She kissed her brother's face. "If not for you ..."

"And for you."

The familiar phrase gave her comfort. No matter what, Quinn would always love her. Together they had survived so much. Lyric laid a loving hand against Cade's back. "I guess we need to go. Grandpa Zeke might be waiting for us at the cemetery. Grab your coat."

Quinn walked with Cade to the bedroom door. Cade pushed around his uncle, but Quinn looked back at the picture Lyric left on the bed. "I talked to him ..." Somehow her brother could always read her thoughts.

"And?"

"He's sick, Lyric. Very sick. He won't be here."

Like a dry twig under a heavy foot, Lyric's hopes snapped. "Sick?" She managed to get the question out.

"Like Momma." Quinn nodded in the direction Cade

had taken. "He's seeking help."

She understood, yet her heart still didn't release the hurt. Balaam left her in the middle of her pregnancy. He'd dashed two of the only real dreams she'd ever had, turned them into dust as he drove away from her in the van filled with his manager and his band, including the new keyboardist Nathan Roy had hired to take her place.

Balaam never called to see how she was. He didn't return when she gave birth, and now he couldn't even be here to help her survive this nightmare.

She was right in never telling Cade the truth. Braedon wasn't much of a father, but he'd been here, and with Quinn and Matthew, her son had most of what he needed.

Cade had dug out both their coats from the closet to the right of the front door, a separation from the kitchen and living room.

Quinn led the way.

Lyric locked up before following him, thankful Momma was nowhere in sight.

Lyric's body ached. She was tired, and standing on the hard, uneven cemetery ground only added to the weariness. In the cold, her swollen lips and her black eye throbbed. She wrapped her coat tightly around her and checked Cade to make sure he'd done as she'd asked by zipping his jacket. At least it hadn't snowed yet.

She pushed the dark sunglasses up to shield her eyes from the bright sun. Yesterday, she might have cried for her husband. Today, the well had run dry, or maybe she didn't want to drop the bucket into her heart and pull them out. She wanted to go home and fall into a deep sleep.

Behind them, Daniel parked his car at the edge of the cemetery road. Then he walked around to the passenger side and opened the door for his mother. Grace looked up and waved to her. Daniel and Grace waited for Zeke Carter to step out of his old Ford, a truck he'd most likely purchased new thirty years before. With patience born of taking care of Grace, Daniel walked between the two. Grace was nearing eighty-five, yet Braedon's father, at sixty-three, appeared years older.

Lyric shared a sad smile with her brother before turning her gaze upon the simple coffin she had chosen for her husband. Then she fixed her stare on one of the nearby granite monuments to the life of a stranger. Braedon would have only a simple marker beside the tiny little marker of his mother's grave. Lyric couldn't afford much else.

One autumn, the full moon shining upon them, Braedon had perched himself atop an old gravestone while Quinn walked around in the darkness, inviting a ghost to visit them. Balaam had wrapped his arms around her as she shivered from her own silly fear of ghosts and goblins. Matthew had gone off hoping to scare Quinn. "Wonder how many people will come to my funeral?" Braedon had asked.

Not too many.

Braedon had killed his brother's best friend, a man the town of Amazing Grace loved, the town's best veterinarian, a man for whom Lyric never understood the depths of her love until her husband had taken him away.

Matthew would have many more mourners, but she'd been asked not to attend. This open wound of rejection would never heal. Larry and Bernice knew the truth. They had to know.

Cade left her to meet up with his grandfather. Her young man walked beside the old one. Zeke's trembling hand was barely able to rest upon his grandson's blond head. As Zeke neared, he thanked everyone for coming. Shaking Quinn's hand, he nodded and wiped an uncharacteristic tear away.

Quinn stood at the head of Braedon's casket, his head bowed. Lyric looked to the heavens. Her brother needed the Lord's help, but she wasn't the one to ask for it. God wouldn't hear her prayers. She'd never trusted Him with her soul, so why would He care to listen to her? Quinn was on his own.

"Thank you for coming." Quinn gained her attention. He mentioned their youth, and the fact he and Braedon had known each other since infancy. Beyond that, Lyric's mind wandered. Local history would not record Braedon as a good man. Many good men had flaws, and by accident, Lyric had found her husband's weakness. Braedon could not accept someone or something that he couldn't absolutely possess. He had tried, but her heart had never been completely his, and her son would always belong to Balaam, whether Balaam wanted Cade or not.

The guilt wilted her. Despite the cold, Lyric wiped her forehead with the back of her hand. Quinn stopped, and she rolled her hand, motioning him to continue. Then she stepped away. She needed a tree to lean upon. Daniel started to follow, and she waved him off.

The guilt followed her like a swarm of bees buzzing around her head. She'd tried to be a good wife to him, but Braedon reminded her often of her failures. Why couldn't she look at him the way she used to look at Balaam? How often did she think about his brother and wish for his return? Didn't she realize how much it hurt to know he'd received Balaam's leftovers?

Brae never seemed to remember he'd begged for Balaam's seconds.

The leafless dogwood took her weight as she leaned against it. Eventually, she'd given up on trying to appease his hurt and pain. They'd talked about divorce, but Braedon wouldn't let her go. What Balaam had left behind belonged to him, and no one else would ever possess her. If only she could have made Braedon understand the love she held for him. They'd been good friends long before he grew to hate her.

His last act toward her and toward Matthew had been one of unspeakable cruelty. Why then did she grieve?

"I'm sorry. I'm sorry," she whispered to the wind. "Braedon, I'm so sorry." Yet, in her apology, she betrayed Matthew, and that disloyalty sickened her.

A handkerchief was pressed into her hand. She took it and covered her face for several long moments. The tears refused to come, but the guilt would not abate.

"Don't take the fault for this, Lyric. It belongs to me."

Lyric closed her eyes, afraid it was only a dream—her desires creating a mirage in her parched soul. If she looked, Balaam would disappear.

She took a deep breath, lowered the handkerchief, and opened her eyes. "Bay?" Again, her heart played the ultimate traitor, beating at a rapid tempo.

He leaned against the other side of the dogwood, keeping his eyes on Quinn as her brother continued to expound on Braedon's goodness. His long blond hair hung down over the crisp, dark suit he wore. His blue eyes were clear, but he did not look well. "He has always been able to forgive easily, hasn't he? I could almost believe he's forgiven me for what I did to you."

"He has a tremendous heart," she whispered.

Over nine years. She'd like to say they'd been good to him, but he struggled to stand. His hands shook, and his forehead beaded with sweat. Dark circles formed under his eyes. Balaam was not wearing sobriety quite as well as her mother. He leaned closer to her, his back braced by the tree, his shoulder touching hers. "Forgive me, Lyric? Someday?"

She took a minute before speaking. Quinn would admonish her for what she held in her heart, but she wasn't ever going to allow Balaam Carter to get away with hurting her so easily. "Someday could be a long while off. You'll just have to take civility from me right now, because I wouldn't do anything to hurt my brother."

At the grave, Quinn asked the mourners to bow their heads while he prayed.

Lyric stared at her brother.

Quinn paused for a moment and lifted his gaze in her direction. "And for the young man Braedon left behind, Lord, may he always find love and know that he is loved. In Jesus' precious name. Amen."

"He is loved, Lyric. I've never met him, but I love him."

Lyric huffed out a breath. "Your brother may have treated Cade with indifference, but he stayed here. He allowed Cade to call him Daddy. Brae put a roof over Cade's head, and we've never wanted for anything we needed. That's a lot more love than you ever showed to your child."

Zeke's aged blue eyes turned toward his only living son.

Balaam pushed from the tree and ran a hand through his hair, pushing it out of his face. The heavy, always luscious, strands fell down his back. "Time for this musician to pay another piper."

Lyric nodded. "Your dad needs you."

Balaam nodded, but he did not move. "Lyric, if you have an ounce of compassion left, would you help me? I can't walk that far on my own."

She slipped her arm under his jacket and around his waist. "The compassion is for Zeke." Lyric allowed Balaam to lean upon her, supporting nearly his full weight. His sweat coming through his white shirt and black vest dampened her arm. She took heavy steps with him.

Quinn closed the space and took Balaam's hold from her.

"Boy, I'm surprised you made it." Zeke walked past.

"Poppa, I loved him, too, as much as anyone."

Zeke stopped and turned to face Balaam. "He carried a pretty big burden for you."

"Poppa," Lyric admonished, reaching for her son.

"A good burden, too, but a burden nonetheless." Zeke reached out and touched Cade's head once again. "I love you, young 'un."

"I love you, too, Grandpa." Cade's monotone response sent slivers of dread through Lyric, but her son held out his hand to Balaam. "I'm Cade. You're my—you're Balaam."

When had her son become so mature?

Balaam's gaze flickered to Lyric then back to Cade. He pulled from Quinn's hold and held out his hand. "Cade, I've wanted to meet you for a very long time."

"Uncle Quinn and Uncle Matthew told me all about you." Cade's words remained flat, indifferent, mimicking the way Braedon had often spoken to him.

78

Lyric started to embrace Cade, but Balaam fell to his knees in front of him. "Those two guys, your uncles, they've always been something special."

Cade stood for a moment. Tears pooled in his eyes.

Balaam bent down, arms wide. "Come here…" His whispered words held magic.

Cade threw his arms around Balaam's neck, reminding her of the child he was and not this pseudo little man he'd been portraying.

"Let it all out. A cry is good for the grieving." Balaam held to Cade.

Cade leaned into the embrace as if Balaam were his lifeline and he a drowning swimmer.

Lyric and Quinn both reached down to keep Balaam upright.

Balaam closed his eyes tight, holding the sobbing boy against him. "Thank You." He mouthed and looked upward. "Thank You, God."

Lyric caught the cry in her throat and swallowed hard. Not here. Not right now. Later, when she was alone, she'd find time to free herself of this swirl of emotions.

**FAY LAMB**

# 5

Balaam leaned back in the old familiar swing on Grace Dixon's porch and looked across the road to the home Quinn said belonged to Lyric. Love built a home so complex in detail the art was lost in the appearance of simplicity. Quinn told him Braedon bought the lot, paying it off by the sweat of his brow before building the home for Lyric and Cade. Something had gone terribly wrong with a mind that could build so much affection into a home and then commit such atrocities behind its doors.

"I keep thinking I'm going to wake up, and this will all be a dream." Quinn faced him, leaning against the porch post. "But I know this is just one more of those nightmares conjured up at will by our loving mother."

Lyric peered at Balaam through the screen door. He gave her a slight nod. As if the moment between Balaam and Lyric hadn't happened, Quinn changed his course of conversation. "So, you take a plane out tomorrow?"

Lyric moved out of sight. Did she not want to face his

answer, or was she desperate to get rid of him?

Balaam nodded. "When I changed the arrangements, I wondered if I was doing the right thing, but even with you and Lyric here, I think my boy needed someone else to share his pain."

Quinn pushed from the post and took a deep breath. "I'm glad you came, too. I've been praying for something to strengthen me for this journey. God sent you. If you can travel here in this condition, I can hold on until this storm passes."

"We both lost our best friends." Balaam studied his hands clasped in front of him.

"I hate to disparage your brother on the day we buried him, but Brae stopped being my friend the moment he threw my sister against a wall. A picture frame fell and gashed her head."

Balaam looked again at the house across the street. "Were they ever happy? He built her that house."

"Took him about two years after they married to get it paid for and built. The house was his obsession. He said he was building it for his family, but no matter how hard Lyric tried, his emotions ran hot and cold toward her and always frigid with Cade."

Balaam rubbed his hands together then balled them into fists. "Did he hurt my son?"

"Only with his indifference." Quinn turned away, leaning on the railing, his palms resting against the white wood. "Matthew and I wrapped Cade with our love."

"Brae must have had his moments. He built that house." His brother's labor with wood and concrete was Balaam's only anchor to the loving brother he'd known.

"I think he dealt with his pain by taking some of the drugs I suspect he trafficked for Jessup." Quinn raised his brow. "Are you a mean addict like your brother, Bay?"

"I don't think so." Balaam shook his head. "I function better with them than without." He held up his trembling hands.

"Don't tell yourself that. We need you here. Lyric and Cade need you clean and sober."

"I think your sister would disagree." Balaam pushed to his feet. The world tilted, and he grabbed for the chain of the porch swing. Missing, he prepared for a fall. Instead, Quinn's firm grasp took hold of his wrist. Staring into the preacher's eyes, Balaam nodded his thank you.

Quinn pulled him forward into an embrace. "I need you clean and sober. There's rough water ahead." He patted Balaam's back and leaned away, his hold never leaving Balaam's wrist until Balaam could stand steady on his feet. "You're staying at my place."

"I'd like to, buddy, but Daniel asked me to stay with him. Bunking at the Amazing Grace Inn was okay, but I'm not sure I could ignore the call of the Backslide or Poppa's moonshine, not that Poppa was happy to see me."

"He's hurting. Give him time."

Balaam nodded, but he doubted his father would ever come around to loving him.

"You're staying with Daniel, huh?" Quinn switched subjects again.

"Yeah, go figure." Balaam smiled. "The outlaw and the lawman."

"Ba—Balaam?" A shy voice came out of nowhere.

Balaam looked to where the porch wrapped around to Grace's kitchen door.

Cade stepped forward.

Balaam's heart caught in his throat. How could he have walked away from seeing this kid with the dimples and the impish face? He had Balaam's blond hair, but the eyes—they didn't belong to either him or to Lyric. They were the deepest green, and both he and Cade's mother had blue eyes.

"Granny Grace sent me out to get you. Dinner's ready."

Balaam messed the boy's hair and watched it fall back into place the same way his had done when he wore it short. How many years ago had it been since his hair was above his ears? "Thanks, kiddo. Tell her I'm on my way in."

"I'll walk in with you," Cade insisted. "Will you stay here and not leave town?"

Was that expectation in the boy's voice—the first change in tone Balaam had heard in Cade's speech?

Balaam hated to dash his hopes. "Give us a minute?" he spoke to Quinn.

Quinn went inside, and Balaam sat carefully in the chair next to the door.

"I want you to stay." Longing lingered in the boy's words.

"Cade, I want to stay here with you more than anything in the world, but after Uncle Matthew's funeral tomorrow, I've got to go away for a few weeks."

"If you really wanted to stay, you could."

Balaam reached out a trembling hand and brushed the boy's shoulder with it. "I'm not feeling well. I need to go to a hospital."

"Are you dying?" The boy's eyes rounded, and Balaam hated that he'd added to the boy's misery.

Balaam swallowed. How close had he come to never having this conversation with his son, of entering the hospital only to have his family notified he'd not made it? "Nope. I'll be gone for a while, but I'll be back, and when I do, I'll be much better."

"Do you promise?" The mature child was showing his true age now.

"I'm going to do my best to get back here as soon as possible so we can throw a football, go fishing, or whatever you'd like to do."

Cade nodded. "When you come back, I'd like you to tell me about my—my dad, when he was a boy."

A second or two passed before Balaam could respond. He cleared his throat. "I'll tell you everything you want to know about him and about his brother, too."

Cade's lips pressed into a hard line.

"Something wrong?" Balaam asked.

Cade shook his head. "Just thinking about what you meant. You'll tell me about both of you. I'd like that."

"I look forward to it. In fact, I'm going to write it down as a promise, and I'll look at it every day until I get back here and keep it."

If that didn't get him back to Amazing Grace, nothing else in the world could do it.

# 6

The next morning, Lyric plunked out a few chords on Granny Grace's piano and stared out the window. Thunder rumbled as the rain lessened for a few moments, allowing just enough time for Quinn to jog out to his car with Cade in tow.

Quinn had wanted to arrive at the funeral home early so that Balaam and Cade could have a private moment to say their good-byes to Matthew. She wouldn't have sent her young son if she didn't think he needed the closure the service would bring.

Grace sat beside her, dressed for the funeral but wiping her hands on an old dishtowel. She laid the cloth beside her and placed her aged hands on the keys. With skill, Grace played "Blessed Assurance."

"Honey, you play it for me," the older woman said when she had finished. "You used to add something to it that this old soul couldn't find in her to put into the music."

Lyric shook her head. "I'm sorry, Grace. I lost

whatever that was a long time ago."

Grace placed a hand over Lyric's and remained silent. Lyric looked to her.

"Are you sure you ever had it?" Grace asked.

The mojo? Oh, she'd had it all right. She used to play the piano—any song in her own style. Grace had been a wonderful teacher, encouraging her to feel the music inside, to let it move her as she played.

"I'm not talking about the ability or the style," Grace said. "I'm talking about that blessed assurance the song is about."

Quinn thought she had, but Lyric knew without a doubt that she had no assurance of anything in this life or the next. And she wasn't sure she really wanted it.

"Honey, you and I both know that you're not staying away from that funeral home. Quinn told you he'd arrange it for you to stay out of sight of Larry and Bernice."

"They're hurting…"

"And so are you, and if Bernice wasn't burying that precious son of hers, I'd tell her so. No one's gonna get hurt. Daniel's picking me up in a bit. Why don't you hurry across the road and get ready, like Quinn asked? He needs you."

Lyric looked up into the woman's sympathetic green eyes as tears filled her own. She used the back of her hand to swipe them away. "Why'd he leave me here, Granny? Why'd he drive off and forget about me and his baby? He never called. He never wrote."

"Is that what's hurting you now, or is it that he came back to say good-bye to his brother and his best friend?"

Lyric nodded and leaned to sob against the woman. "Don't you see? His coming back here now means that he loved me even less than I thought he did. The lies he told me to get me to do what he wanted, they meant so much to me. I couldn't imagine him not loving me. Even all those years since he's been away, I wondered if he ever thought that leaving me had been a mistake." She lifted her head and covered her face. "I was less than a mistake to him. The words he said, the child he left me with, didn't even give him an afterthought."

"Oh, honey, I can't speak for the years he's been away, but from what I saw when Balaam was with Cade yesterday, if he never thought of the horrendous mistake he made in all the while he was gone, the truth's haunting him now." Grace stood and placed a hand on Lyric's shoulder. "You need to say good-bye to your friend. Let's let thoughts of Balaam rest for today, and you go do what needs to be done."

Lyric stood and hugged the older woman. "If not for you…" she said the words she always spoke to her brother.

Grace placed her aged hands on Lyric's wet cheeks. "Honey, you have been a blessing to me for so long, I don't know what I'd do without you." She kissed Lyric then turned her toward the door. "I'll see you in a little while, and you know my heart is always open to you."

Lyric nodded and walked out the door.

The sun had shone brightly for Braedon's small service, but today, for Matthew's funeral, the weather had turned colder, wet, and miserable."

As she stepped onto her porch, a truth crashed down upon her. God hadn't cried yesterday, but for their loss of Matthew, He and everyone else mourned.

Mr. Parsons, the aged funeral home director opened the door before Balaam and Quinn reached the threshold. "Pastor Moxley, Mr. Cade." Parsons shook Quinn's and Cade's hands then looked down his long hawk-like beak at Balaam.

Yeah, all right. He'd seen better days. Everyone would know it by the end of the day. So much for returning home a celebrity. Balaam pinched his lips together. He'd given up stardom. God had better things ahead for him. That's what Daniel said last night when the sheriff had reworked every plan Balaam had made since his hospital stay. He also said Balaam needed to stop worrying about what the town would think. They never thought much of him anyway.

Daniel was always one who could deliver the cold, stark truth.

Balaam held out his hand. "Mr. Parsons."

"Balaam Carter." The old man's frigid hand felt like

sandpaper, and his tone reminded Balaam of the time Parsons scolded him for breaking the funeral home's stained-glass window with a baseball. Balaam had lied about it being an accident. He'd tossed that baseball high into the air and with bat ready, when it fell to exactly the right spot, he'd hit that hard leather orb so hard, the window shattered into a million tiny pieces.

If he hadn't have wanted stardom so badly, he wouldn't have been a bad baseball player. Matthew, with that north-pointing compass, had encouraged him to play Little League and high school ball. Balaam had shrugged him off, declaring Matthew needed to let his talent shine. And as in all things Matthew did, there was light and goodness. The town celebrated four years of state championships. Even as a Freshman, no one had a better batting average or an earned run average than Matthew. He'd gotten a scholarship to college, though he hadn't needed it. As the town's county attorney, Larry Roberts and his wife were not without means to pay Matthew's way to any college who'd accept their son—and Matt hadn't been turned down by any of the ones he'd applied to. Matthew hadn't gone too far away from home. He'd never had Balaam's wanderlust.

Quinn had called Balaam this morning, asking if he'd like to say his good-bye to Matthew in private. Then Quinn had picked him up from Daniel's place. Cade had come with his uncle.

"We'd like a minute alone." Quinn motioned for

Balaam and Cade to follow him. To the left, they entered the room Balaam had always known as the "parlor." His mother's funeral had been here—how many years ago? The same year he'd broken the window, angry with God for taking her away from him.

Two rows of pews afforded a center aisle. Balaam kept his head down but started forward with Quinn to the open coffin.

Cade, with his hand in Balaam's, tugged back and Balaam stopped. The boy shook his head. "I don't wanna see him dead. I wanna remember him when he was alive and spent time with me. Please don't make me go up there. Please."

Balaam tilted Cade's chin upward. "That's a mighty good idea for you to do that. Why don't you go find us a seat? Grandpa will be here shortly. Save us both a place. I'll say good-bye to Uncle Matthew for you."

Cade's lips trembled. "Tell him… tell him I love him, and I'll miss Tuesday nights."

A vise held Balaam's heart. He could barely breathe. Finally, he was able to nod. "I'll do that." He had no idea what was important about Tuesday nights, but he hoped Cade would share it with him.

Cade turned and made his way to a row of seats at the far back of the parlor. Balaam nodded and gave him a reassuring smile.

Balaam approached the coffin and forced his gaze upward onto Matthew's frozen face and closed his eyes just as quickly. Why hadn't he taken the cue from his kid?

Deep within, he'd kept a memory of Matthew, and he pulled it out now, remembering the smile on Matthew's face as Balaam drove away from Amazing Grace never again to see his friend alive. Matthew had waved his farewell. "Don't forget us when you're rich and famous."

Balaam opened his eyes and looked around. Had those words, spoken so long ago, floated from his memory? Matthew's voice sounded so close, so real.

"You okay?" Quinn asked.

Balaam swallowed hard, nodded, then shook his head. "No. I'm not all right. This is my fault, every bit of it."

"Balaam Carter."

He turned when Larry Roberts slapped a hand on his shoulder. Behind him, Quinn braced him against the unanticipated weight. He could barely hold himself up let alone anyone else.

"Sir." Balaam shook the man's hand. "I'm so sorry. Both you and Mrs. Roberts were always kind to us. I don't know why this happened."

The older man stared down into the lifeless face of his son. "Our boy always had a heart for the less fortunate. Maybe that's why he wouldn't let Lyric go." He ran a hand over his balding head.

Larry had a tell. Balaam had recognized it from his youth. He was like a politician, and he lied with ease when he needed to compromise. The brush of his hand over his receding hairline spoke volumes.

The father's eyes spilled over with tears. "Bernice blames Lyric."

"No, sir. The fault lies with me." Balaam straightened. "From what I understand, Matthew was protecting Lyric from my brother. If I hadn't left Lyric the way I did, if I'd given her some kind of hope to cling to, we wouldn't be standing here today. But I didn't. I just walked away. I should have known Matthew would take over the responsibilities I ran from. Don't blame her."

"I don't. And I don't blame you either. Matthew loved you like a brother."

"I almost wish he'd married her."

Larry shuddered, shaking his head. "No. That would have been wrong. Terribly wrong."

Balaam bit down on the inside of his mouth. He wouldn't spew his anger at this grieving man, but Lyric wasn't a piece of trash to be denied.

Balaam caught Quinn's gaze. Lyric's brother studied him, and Balaam could almost read Quinn's thoughts. Both he and Larry had shot arrows through Quinn with their careless words.

Balaam looked down at Matthew. "Yes, it would have been terribly wrong, but only because I love Lyric. I'm sorry he died at the hands of my brother, but Lyric isn't to blame, and we both ought to mind the way we speak about her. Matthew loved her very much, too." Balaam reached out and touched the lapel of the expensive suit Matthew's parents had chosen to bury him in. "Cade says he loves you,

Matt. So do I, and whatever you two did on Tuesday nights, Cade says he's going to miss. Thank you for whatever it was that made it special to him. That's an awful lot of love you showed to me when I never returned it to you."

Bernice Roberts walked down the aisle with a determined gait. "We've put the blame squarely where it belongs. If Lyric had released her claws from him, Matthew would have gone away to attend college, not stayed at a school so close to home. He'd have met a nice young woman. He'd be married."

"Mrs. Roberts," Balaam nodded toward his son, "Cade isn't guilty in any way."

Bernice looked in the direction Balaam indicated. Her shoulders fell. "No, he is not. That poor boy."

"And, Bernice, Lyric has done what we've asked. She's stayed away from the funeral. We agreed to let the matter rest," Larry soothed, taking out a handkerchief and wiping his teary eyes. Balaam doubted he'd stopped crying since he'd heard of the tragedy.

"Again, Mr. Roberts, Mrs. Roberts, I'm sorry for all of this," Balaam said.

"And again, Balaam, this is not your fault. You haven't been here for years. I hear about your exploits often. Seems you've made something of yourself."

From whom would Larry hear anything about Balaam? He wasn't the type to follow the tabloids or the gossip magazines. Balaam shook the nagging question off. Besides, he was embarrassed that anyone knew of his behavior over the last nine years.

"This is all Lyric's doing," Bernice whispered as she leaned over the casket and brushed back a strand of Matthew's dark hair from his dead, pale face.

"Bernice, honey, now is not the time to discuss this," Larry calmed.

Bernice covered her face with her hands. "Matty. My little boy."

Larry put his arms around his wife, and they hovered over the coffin. Balaam stepped back, and Quinn joined him, greeting others as they came forward. Today's funeral would be a large affair in contrast to Braedon's lonely memorial.

"Poppa," Balaam whispered to Quinn.

His father walked with slow and unsteady steps to sit in the pew beside Cade. In Balaam's weakness yesterday, he hadn't noticed how much Poppa seemed to have aged. He was only a few years older than Daniel, but in comparison, Daniel seemed as healthy as a twenty-something man.

Poppa nodded at him and sat. He patted Cade's knee then lowered his head and did not look up.

Balaam started toward them but stopped when he came face to face with Jessup Roy.

"Balaam, I heard you might be back for good." Jessup held out his hand. "Looking for a job, too, I hear?"

If he had the strength in him, he'd punch the man, but Poppa had taught him differently. He'd get even with

Jessup soon enough. "I'm leaving today." Balaam sidestepped him and took the seat by his father.

It didn't take long for the "parlor" to fill up. As Quinn started with a prayer, Balaam put his arm around the back of Cade's chair and bowed his head. How could Quinn get through the service without showing his emotion? Daniel said Quinn was cried out, that all this hit Quinn pretty hard, but he was trying to be strong for everyone else. Maybe that was the key. Think of someone who needed you more than you needed to grieve.

With his own head lowered, the tears poured from him.

"Here, boy." Poppa slipped a tissue from the box across in front of Cade and into Balaam's hand.

Balaam, head still bowed, looked to his father. "Why'd you come, Poppa?"

"Braedon was a good boy. Matthew was better. I don't know what all went on, but I owe my respects. You?"

Balaam wiped his eyes. "I loved them both." His words, meant only for his father's and son's ears, shook the quiet room, and his sobs shook his soul as his father touched his shoulder and at the same time embraced Cade. "What have I done, Poppa? What have I done to everyone who ever loved me?"

At Balaam's outburst, Lyric ran from the funeral home

where Mr. Parsons had allowed her to stand in a room off to the side where no one but Quinn could see her during the service. Her heart echoed Balaam's cries, but no one would understand. How could they? They didn't know the truth—but how could Larry and Bernice not know? And why had they punished her so terribly?

Her heart had broken when Cade asked her why she couldn't go with him to his uncle's funeral. How did you tell a little boy Uncle Matthew's parents hated his mother?

"Mrs. Carter?"

Lyric came close to cursing at the sound of his voice. "Not today, Agent Goodman."

"Let me drive you home. You're too upset." He matched her stride.

"I cannot endure one more question from you, not today."

"I'll keep my mouth shut, and I'll take you wherever you want to go."

Lyric picked up her pace as she neared her car. "I need to be alone."

"I'll drive you to the cemetery, drop you off where you can't be seen, and I'll pick you up later."

"I'd rather drive myself. Now, please, leave me alone. I need to go before Mr. and Mrs. Roberts see me. I don't want to add to their hurt." She opened the door and sat inside, hands on the steering wheel, heart in her throat. Agent Goodman opened the passenger door. "I'll ride with you then, and I'll still keep my mouth shut."

What else could she do without causing a scene? She started the car and pulled from the parking lot.

True to his word, he remained silent. She drove straight to the cemetery and allowed him to get out near the gravesite. Then she drove from the place where they would lay Matthew to rest, parked her car, and stood where she hoped no one would notice.

The hearse arrived first, followed by Larry and Bernice. Lyric put a fist in her mouth to keep from crying out.

And there was Daniel again. He walked between Zeke and Balaam to the gravesite, a steady arm out for both of them. Grace followed behind. Balaam had a flight out in less than four hours, and she'd probably never see him again. Sure, he'd promised Cade he'd return, but Carters never kept their word.

The pallbearers carried Matthew's closed coffin to his grave. Quinn followed, holding his Bible close to his heart, a sure sign of his anguish. He waited for the mourners to gather before giving the final eulogy. Bernice's mournful wail reached Lyric's ears, and Lyric fell to her knees, the pain shooting through her own heart. Lyric wanted to be angry with the Roberts, but how could she? They'd lost so much—their only son.

Still on her knees, Lyric leaned against her car. "Matthew, did you know? Is that why you never left me alone? God, I'll never know the truth. How could You do this to me? I hate You for this, God. I really do hate You."

But she didn't. How could she hate God when her actions had caused all this sorrow? God wasn't to blame. "I'm sorry. I didn't mean it," she whispered the words to Him. Did He hear? Did He care?

Time passed, but Lyric wasn't sure how long she sat against her car until a gentle touch on her arm startled her. "They've all left. Do you want to say your good-byes?"

Quinn. How had he known?

"That Agent Goodman took my car. Daniel and Grace took Cade. I'll ride back with you." He helped her up and led her forward. "I made it through today because I saw you there and here. Thank you for that."

"Larry and Bernice?"

"They never suspected."

"How's Balaam?"

Quinn pointed to where Balaam stood alone on the Astroturf beside the expensive walnut coffin still sitting on the sling attached to two golden cylinders, which would lower Matthew's body into the ground.

Balaam held out his arm as she approached, and she allowed him to pull her close. "I've missed him all these years, but despite what I did, I always thought there'd come a day when we'd sit around and relive our childhoods—all of us, together, laughing about all we survived."

Lyric remained silent.

"He missed you, too." Quinn said. "How'd he get mixed up with us kids from the wrong side of the track?"

"Deliberately." Sarcasm laced Balaam's laugh.

Lyric nodded. Matthew had sought them out. He was the kid with privilege who'd rather hang with the four brats from the wrong side of town.

Quinn's hand touched hers, and he entwined his fingers with hers. "If not for you ..."

"And for you." Lyric stared down at the coffin. "And ... for ... you, Matthew."

A soft breeze tickled Lyric's ear and caused her to lift her head.

Momma stood in the distance, as Lyric had done earlier. Why did she come? She hadn't even bothered to show her face at Braedon's funeral.

"Magda," Balaam said her mother's name.

"It's hard to believe Matthew's funeral would bring her out of the bar." Quinn exposed his frayed nerves with the words he chose.

"She, more than anyone, needed to say good-bye," Lyric murmured.

"What do you mean?" Quinn asked.

*Hush*, the soft whisper of wind spoke to her, and Lyric backed away from the entire truth. "Whatever she said to Braedon that night at the Backslide sent him home angry with me, and Matthew died as a result."

"Good-bye, old friend. I love you, and I'll miss you until we see each other again." Balaam turned away. "And now I know what Matthew meant when he'd say, 'But for the grace of God and Daniel Dixon.'"

Quinn gave a short laugh. "You're just now

understanding that? If Daniel hadn't rounded us up and carted us to Sunday school, we wouldn't have a hope of seeing Matthew again."

"Rounding us up was the easy part. The trick of making us behave and listen is one I've never figured out." Balaam tilted his head and winked at Lyric. "I did listen, you know. I surrendered my life to Christ—again. I plan to be a better man, to help raise Cade, if you'll let me."

Lyric said nothing. Balaam had to work a lot harder to prove he'd changed, and she wasn't concerned with his walk with God any more than she wanted to think of her own.

Quinn led the way, both men taking Lyric by the hand. Lyric would have pulled away if she didn't think Balaam would fall.

Together, they climbed the hill toward Lyric's car. At the top of the hill, Lyric looked back. For an instant, she imagined Matthew there, his hand raised in a final farewell. As she sat in the passenger's seat, she raised her hand to the empty field. Catching Balaam's gaze, she forced a smile. "You seem stronger today."

"*Seems* is the right word for it."

"Balaam, I do hope you'll come back. A little boy is looking forward to your return. Whether or not I allow you to help raise him depends on whether or not you get rid of the drugs and alcohol. I've had enough of it."

"Can I see him before I leave?"

Lyric studied him. "He'd like that."

"I have a few minutes. I'd really like to spend them with him."

"They'll last him a lifetime." They probably had to. They'd most likely never see Balaam Carter in Amazing Grace again.

Balaam found Grace's porch swing more agreeable each time he visited, and now with Cade beside him, he didn't think he'd ever want to leave.

"When will you be back?" Cade broke the silence.

Cade hadn't even referred to him as his uncle. That title seemed reserved for those he was closest with—Quinn and Matthew. Would he ever hear the boy call him Dad? Did he dare try to take that title from Braedon's memory? "I hope to be back in about six weeks, but it may be a little longer."

"But you are coming back?"

"I told you I would. We're going to talk about things, remember?"

Cade nodded.

"Something wrong?"

"I miss him."

"You will miss him, for a long time. He was your dad."

Cade turned his gaze to Balaam. "But ..." The boy shook his head. "Uncle Matthew ..." he swallowed. "I miss Uncle Matthew. Today is Tuesday. We always went for ice cream on Tuesday night. Just him and me."

That's what the boy had meant. Balaam hadn't even noticed the significance of the boy's request because he hadn't even remembered today was Tuesday.

*Constant.* If one word described Matthew, that was the one. Short of his death, he'd never let the kid down. Balaam leaned forward and fought against a new barrage of emotion.

"Uncle Matthew said Tuesdays were made for ice cream and nothing else."

Balaam nodded. They certainly shouldn't have been made for Matthew's funeral. "I think he might be right. When I come back what do you say to going every Tuesday, and you and I will eat ice cream in Uncle Matthew's memory?"

Again, Cade gave a simple nod.

"Something else is bothering you?"

"I don't miss my da—dad as much as I miss Uncle Matthew. Is that because of what he did?"

So, the kid knew. Kudos to Lyric and Quinn for not keeping the truth from him. "That might be the reason, or it might be your memories of Uncle Matthew are ones you'd rather keep. What do you think?"

The question was a tough one to throw at a little guy, and Cade only shrugged in reply.

"Hey, kiddo. It's okay. Don't over analyze it. Miss Uncle Matthew without shame, and miss your dad when the time comes around for you to think about him. No one knew him better than me. Believe me. No matter what he did, he was still a good guy. He just had a lot of hurt, and it kept him from always loving you like he should."

"Can I ask you something?"

Balaam nodded. "Anything."

"Grandpa Zeke tells me I remind him a lot of you. Do you think we're alike?"

Poppa would try to put the notions in the kid's head. Had he not let Braedon forget the truth? Is that why Braedon made life so difficult for Lyric? "What do you think?"

"I don't know you that good."

"Well, we'll remedy that soon enough."

The screen door opened, and Quinn stepped out, a glass of Grace's sweet iced tea in his hand. "You need to get going, or you're going to miss your flight."

Looking at Cade, he thought of telling Quinn the truth—there would be no plane ride today. He forced himself to stand on weak and trembling legs.

"Please remember to come back." Cade dug into his pockets, pulled out a folded piece of paper, and handed it to Balaam.

"What's this?"

Cade stood silent.

Balaam opened the paper and sank to his knees in front of his son. He hugged Cade to him, staring at the picture in his hand, a pretty good rendering of a man and a young boy, their fishing rods dipping into the lake, "Home" scrawled across the top in a child's penmanship. "You drew this?"

Cade nodded. "Mom says I'm good at it."

"Mom's right. I'd say we need to get you some lessons at the art league. And nothing could be better for me to take with me."

"You ready?" Daniel stepped outside.

"Are you sure you don't want me to take him?" Quinn asked.

"It's okay, Quinn." Balaam struggled to get back on his feet. "I suspect Daniel wants to interrogate me a little— like old times. He must miss all the trouble I caused."

Daniel gave a half smile and tilted his hat down, a sure sign Balaam had spoken the truth. The old cowboy habit was hard to break, but Balaam had learned what it meant long ago. He'd been interrogated by Daniel Dixon more times than he wanted to remember—and he'd left town soon after his nineteenth birthday.

"I'm ready." Balaam bent to pick up his bag, but Quinn hoisted it on his shoulder, leading the way.

With each step down the path, Balaam waited to hear Lyric call to him. As his hand touched the passenger door handle, the old screen door squeaked then it smacked back against the frame.

Balaam turned.

Lyric ran toward him. She stopped just out of his reach. "Bay, take care of yourself."

He nodded. "I'll do my best."

"Your best isn't good enough." She placed her hand on their son's shoulder. "You need to be as determined to come back to Amazing Grace as you were to leave."

Again, he nodded. "Cade, will you write if Sheriff Daniel will agree to send the letters to me?"

"Yes, sir."

"I'll be back." He looked into Lyric's eyes. "I promise."

"A Carter's promise doesn't mean squat to me. It's what they do that I can believe in—or not."

Tough, but true. Lyric had grown as hard as nails, and why not, after all he and Braedon put her through? "Cade, take care of your momma, your Uncle Quinn, and Grandpa Zeke."

"I will."

Balaam winked at him and ducked into the car. Daniel sat in the driver's seat. "You ready for this?"

"Whatever you say, Daniel. I've got to trust you." Balaam touched the window, peering at his son. The tears streaming down Cade's face brought tears to Balaam's eyes, and the narrowed eyes of the woman he should have never left, amped up his anxiety. "Get me out of here, or I won't be able to leave."

# 7

Lyric took a deep breath and stared out the windows of Saved by Grace Antique Shop and Ice Cream Emporium where she'd worked for years—even before Balaam left her. Agent Goodman was heading her way, clad in jeans and a nice dark blue sweater that somehow still showed off his physique. Dark sunglasses covered his eyes.

The store wasn't busy today. The two young girls Grace had hired to run the ice cream and dessert counter in the unique store were doing some cleaning and, from what Lyric could hear, doing some whispered gossiping about her.

She smiled as Daniel stomped his way across busy Main Street, holding up his hand to stop Monday afternoon traffic. He sidelined Goodman before the man could enter the store. The agent took his sunglasses off and stood listening to whatever gruff Daniel was giving him.

Would Goodman ever give up? For a week, since they'd buried Matthew, he'd pestered her daily.

Lyric continued to price the items Grace had procured from an estate sale in nearby Jackson County. Lyric spent Sunday afternoon appraising everything from a heavy, wooden nineteenth century dining room set to Lennox china and then overseeing the movement of several large pieces and also redecorating the large store.

The door creaked open.

Lyric turned to look, anxious to see Granny Grace walk in with Cade. Grace was going to walk him home from school and let him play in the park.

Instead, Momma peered inside. "Lyric?"

Like chalk squeaking against a blackboard, the sound of her name on her mother's lips grated Lyric's last nerve.

"Lyric, baby, I need a drink." She stepped inside. "Can you get me a drink? Fred, he says Jessup promised to kill him if I got another one from him. Fred, he was helping me when Willis wasn't around." Magda licked her dried and chapped lips. Her hands trembled.

"I can't help you. You need to leave."

Magda slapped her hand on the glass top of the display case. Items inside rattled and one fell. Lyric checked it quickly and found it in one piece.

The two girls at the ice cream counter straightened and watched.

"Missy, I'm in this situation because of you. If you'd only give me those papers I want."

Lyric bit into the inside of her mouth to keep from saying something no one should overhear. Her mother seldom dared to approach her in a public place—and never, ever, in Granny Grace's store. Lyric leaned forward. "What'd he promise you for them? Because you never wanted those papers or anyone they pertained to. You threw away good people because they were the last thing you desired. The taste of the whiskey and the cheap thrills of men in bars, that's all you ever cared to have. Tell me. Why'd you keep Quinn? Why'd you hang on to us when you'd thrown so much away? If something happens to Quinn and me, will you stand in the shadows at our funerals, too?"

"Just give me what I want." Her mother's voice deepened. Her fingers clutched the display case; a wild demon stared back at Lyric. Not for the first time in her life, Lyric wondered at the foresight of some dead grandparent who'd named this oppressed woman Magdalene years before Lyric's birth. Had Quinn become a pastor to exorcise those things from their mother's life that kept her at a distance from him?

Lyric shook her head. "You won't get anything from me." She cast a wary glance out the window where Daniel had Goodman pinned against a bench, his finger pushing into the agent's chest as he spoke.

The primal scream and the crash of glass spun Lyric toward her mother. Her mother had sent the pricey china to the floor. Before Lyric could stop her, Momma, with all her might, pushed and toppled the glass display case on top of the china.

"Magda!" Daniel brushed past Lyric. "Why in the world did you let her inside?" He glared.

"The back door was unlocked." Lyric backed away from the fury in Daniel's voice, pushing into a warm body. With strong hands, Goodman pulled her out of the way as Daniel, with deft motions, yanked Magda's arms, pinned them behind her, and clasped handcuffs around her wrists.

Momma screeched in fury then in pain. "Let me go, Daniel."

"What's gotten into you?" Daniel held to her. "Hasn't Lyric been through enough? Why'd you have to come in here causing trouble?"

Lyric allowed her breath to release. Daniel wasn't mad at her. Had she gotten so used to Braedon's beatings that a man's voice raised in anger would frighten her so badly?

"You okay?" Goodman held her in a protective grasp.

Lyric turned and looked into caramel-colored eyes dripping with concern. She'd never noticed the kindness in them before.

What in the world was she thinking?

She pulled free. "Yes. Thank you."

"Lyric, Grace will be pressing charges. What do you say to that?" Daniel asked.

"I think she should, and I think Quinn and I should move to have her sent to the mental health facility for a three-day mandatory stay."

"Lyric, honey, come on. I'm sorry. You know how hard it is for me when I don't have something to drink."

Her mother's voice turned childlike.

"Momma, you need to go to the center. They can help you. Quinn and I will never give you alcohol. We want to see you sober."

"I'm sober now. Look at me. I'm a mess."

Bitter laughter sprang from deep within Lyric. "You've always been a mess. I think it's time to clean you up."

"Missy, if you let Daniel put me away, you'll have more trouble than you want."

"Are you threatening her?" Daniel pulled back on Magda's arms. "Don't you threaten her, Magda."

Lyric touched Daniel's arms. "I'll call Quinn and let him know. It's pretty late now. They won't have her in court before tomorrow morning at the earliest." She raised a brow. "If the sheriff's office makes sure she's held and not released on her own recognizance, she'll go before the judge." She and Quinn had done this before. Her mother was no stranger to the court.

Daniel let up a little on her mother's arms. "Lyric, you okay?"

"I'm fine," Lyric assured.

"How touching." Her mother smirked.

Daniel tightened his hold once again.

"You—"

"Not one more word." Daniel pushed Momma through the store and out the door. "Goodman, you've been warned," he called back over his shoulder.

"Yes, I have." Goodman laughed and placed his sunglasses to the top of his head. "I came here to ask you to have lunch with me, and I get accosted by the local sheriff."

Daniel led her mother across the street. In the past, Lyric had suffered every emotion at the hand of that woman. Now, she had none to offer.

"It's gotta be tough having a parent with an addiction," Goodman offered.

She didn't want to talk about it. "So, Agent, you came to ask me to lunch?" Lyric walked to the back of the store and retrieved a broom, a dustpan, and a large garbage can.

The girls behind the counter stood and stared. Lyric didn't want their help anyway. Her hearing was good enough, and their whispered words had hurt her.

She returned to find the agent down on his knees, gathering large pieces of glass and putting them in a pile for her. "Why don't we get rid of the title. Call me Ethan."

She bent beside him. "I repeat. You came to ask me to lunch? Is that a new tactic to your third degree, Ethan?"

"I ended my investigation yesterday. You have no papers, have absolutely no idea what I'm asking about, and you're in the clear."

"Since the investigation is over, might I ask what it is you think Jessup gave to my late husband?"

"I'd tell you, but Jessup or others might kill you if he suspected you knew."

What she had wouldn't turn Jessup into a murderer.

The professor was too smart to bring death into his repertoire of ill-doing—unless you counted the drugs that had taken numerous lives. But drug dealers didn't usually go to jail on murder charges, unless a gun or a real weapon was involved. "Why hasn't he come after you?"

"He doesn't know who I am or that I'm looking, not unless you, Daniel, or Quinn told him."

"Undercover but not undercover." She balanced herself, elbow on knee, and studied him. Impressive.

"Well?" Goodman asked her.

"What?" Lyric shook her head to clear her thoughts.

"Have you had an occasion to put my life in danger?"

Lyric smiled. "No, not that I haven't wanted to take such an occasion."

He laughed now, a short sound laced with doubt.

"So, Agent Goodman, if your investigation is over, why are you still here?"

"Again, the name's Ethan. Feel free to use it. Unless you really do want to get me killed." He stood to drop a handful of busted glass into the garbage can.

Lyric swept the tiny shards into a pile.

Ethan held the dust pan as she filled it with the demolished inventory. "I had a heck of a lot of vacation time accrued, and I said to myself, 'Ethan'—that's what I call myself. I said, 'Ethan, Amazing Grace is such a beautiful little mountain town, why don't you hang out here? Where else do you have to go? You have no wife.'" He cocked an eyebrow as if waiting for a reaction from her.

She gave him none.

"I continued the debate with myself, and I said, 'You don't even have a cat that misses you.' After a long conversation with myself in which I pretty much laid out my sad, pathetic loneliness, I decided a month in Amazing Grace was just what I needed."

"A whole month, huh?"

He stooped and held the dustpan as she continued to sweep up the mess her mother made. "A whole month."

"And they let you take a month-long vacation with an unsolved case on your books?" Why couldn't she just believe him?

Because since Balaam's betrayal and Braedon's inability to live with the truth, she really only trusted Quinn and Daniel like that. Had once trusted Matthew in the same way.

He leaned close to her. "Why not stay in case something happens here in relation to my case? This is as nice a place as any. I hear the skiing is great."

"So, not a vacation?"

"Very much so, as much as I can abide. I'm a doer. At least I'm not on a clock or answering to anyone. If trouble does show itself, I'll take myself off leave."

"Very diligent, I see." She smirked.

"My partner and I solved a few big ones before this little one came along. They owe me."

"Partner? Since you've been here, you've been alone."

"He thought I was chasing unicorns. Seems he was

right to stay in Raleigh and work the case from that angle."

Lyric gave one last sweep into the pan.

Ethan stood to empty it.

She turned her attention to the overturned display case.

Ethan stood beside her. "You know, righting it is going to make an even bigger mess."

"I'm sure this won't be the last mess my mother will cause." She bent at her knees and grasped the corner of the rack, taking care not to cut herself on any remaining slivers of glass.

Ethan bent to grasp one side. "One, two, three."

She followed his lead, lifting when he did.

The feel of something like a hot poker burned in Lyric's lower back, and she cried out in pain. The heavy display crashed back to the floor.

His arms fell around her as he helped her to straighten. "You okay?"

She winced and pulled from his hold. "It's been a little painful since the shooting, but the pain hasn't been anything worth mentioning. I wrenched it when I pulled up. I think my back wanted to remind me. Now look what I've done. Daniel will ask the state attorney to seek restitution, and I caused a bigger mess than Momma. Granny Grace is going to fire me."

"Granny will do no such thing." The elderly lady stepped into sight, her hands on her hips. "These are just things, child." She pushed past Ethan and placed her warm, rough hands on each side of Lyric's cheeks. "After all these years, you haven't learned you're more important to me?" She turned back to Ethan. "Daniel called me. He asked if you'd wait here and help him with the case."

"It'll be my pleasure."

"Grace, where's Cade?" Lyric pushed past her.

Cade stood in the back doorway looking longingly outside. "Cade," she called him to her.

He scrunched up his nose and pursed his lips the way Balaam used to do when they were kids and his mother asked him to do something. "Can't I go play in the park until you're done? My friends are there."

Cade had noticed his mother hovering over him like a hen with her only chick. "Didn't you and Granny Grace just come from the park?"

"We needed to come back," Grace said. "Someone arrived, and I didn't like the looks of him."

"Have you heard from Ba-Balaam?"

"No, but I think he's somewhere he can't call us for a while. Have you given Sheriff Daniel a letter to send to him?

"Yes, but he hasn't written me back."

She wouldn't remind him that Balaam had only been gone one day shy of a week. "Then we'll both have to believe he'll write, and he'll come home when he can. Meanwhile, I don't want you outside without an adult. Got it?

He shrugged by her. "Wow! What happened?" His eyes lit up for the first time since before the murder-suicide.

"Would you believe a big tornado came through that door?" Ethan teased.

A smile curved Cade's lips but disappeared just as quickly. "Was it Grandma?"

Lyric spun toward him. "Why do you ask?"

"She came to our house this morning when Granny Grace was with me, and she looked mad when I told her you weren't there."

"Grace?" Lyric questioned.

"This is the first I heard of her visit." Granny Grace raised her hands.

"Mom, I think Grandma needs some help. She looked mad like Da—Dad did when—"

"When what?" Ethan leaned forward.

"Before he killed Uncle Matthew."

"Oh." Lyric covered her mouth and turned from him. Her son's words punched air from her gut.

If he saw Braedon before the shootings, there was no telling what Brae had said to him. In the man's state of mind, he might have said things Cade shouldn't know. He might have seen Brae shoot Matthew. He'd know that the man he thought was his father had actually aimed the gun at her.

She bent forward trying to get the images from her mind. No. Cade played at Timmy's house. Daniel had picked him up when Cade walked home. *Keep saying that. Maybe you'll convince yourself, but your son won't be able to cope with it.*

"Cade, how do you know what happened?" Ethan's voice floated through Lyric's mental shock.

"Don't!" She sprung toward Cade.

"I saw it all." The four words fell from him without quivering emotion.

Lyric wrapped him in her arms. "I'm so sorry. Daddy was sick. He wasn't feeling like himself."

Cade wiggled in her hold, and she let him go. He narrowed his eyes at her. "He wanted to kill you. He pointed the gun at you, not Uncle Matthew. Uncle Matthew tried to make him stop. He ran in front of you, and Da-Da-Dad shot him."

Now, Granny Grace's gasp filled the shop, and one of the girls at the counter dropped something heavy.

She had to hold onto her sanity, and to do so, she reached for her son. He stepped away from her.

"Hey." Ethan rested a hand on her shoulder.

She reached out for Cade again, but he didn't move. The trembling of his body was the only outward sign that he was in emotional pain.

Lyric's gaze met Ethan's. He stood and held out his hand to Cade. As if looking into another world, Lyric watched her son take Ethan's hand and move away from her. "Cade, my name is Ethan Goodman."

Cade nodded.

Lyric stepped back to find a shelf that would hold her upright. Her gaze met with Ethan's kind stare.

"I think Mommy's worried about you seeing what

happened."

"I know. I didn't want to tell her, but Grandma, she looked like Da-Dad. She might hurt Mom and Uncle Quinn."

When had Cade started stuttering? She'd never known him to do it before. The horror of the shooting had to have brought it on.

"Daniel took your grandmother to get some help. So, you don't have to worry about your mommy or your uncle." Ethan continued to console him.

Cade nodded. He turned toward her. "Are you okay, Mom?"

He didn't hate her. That had been her worse fear, that he'd blame her for Matthew's death. Blaming herself was a heavy enough load to carry, to think that Cade believed it, too, was more than she could stand, especially now that he confessed he knew the truth.

"Mom?" Cade asked again, a little more worry sounding in her name.

She wouldn't lie to him. Lyric shook her head. How could she ever be okay? "But I'm going to get there because I have you."

Ethan released his gentle hold on Cade's shoulder.

Lyric held out her arms.

Cade didn't seem to notice. He walked past her and to a shelf of antique toys, feigning, she was sure, his interest in them.

"About that lunch, Lyric. Why don't we change it to

dinner, and let me take you and Cade?"

Lyric hesitated.

Cade turned to them, seeming to anticipate the distraction offered to them by the agent.

Still, she had to establish her boundaries. "We'd like that very much. Not tonight, but maybe before you leave town."

Cade's shoulders fell.

"We'll set a day later." The smile that spread across his handsome features vanished as Daniel opened the door to the shop.

"Thanks for staying." Daniel gave him a curt nod.

"No problem, Sheriff." Ethan pointed to the disaster. "If you'll help me get this up for the ladies, I'll be on my way."

Daniel and Ethan lifted the case. Daniel held out his hand and shook Ethan's. "I appreciate it."

Ethan nodded, placed the sunglasses over his eyes, and headed out the door.

"Cade, look what I have for you." Daniel produced an envelope. "I found it on my desk at the station."

Cade took the envelope and held it in his hand like a prize. "He wrote back, Mom. Look."

Lyric smiled. "Maybe Granny Grace will take you into her office, and you can read the letter."

"I have a better idea." Grace touched her shoulder. "Why don't you and Cade take a break and read the letter together?"

Lyric raised her brows at Cade.

He hesitated and then nodded.

"Go and wait for me. I'll be right there." She pointed.

Cade took off for the office, a secure place in the back of the store. Lyric stepped beside Daniel. "Cade saw everything." The tears she'd held off now sprang into her eyes. "Daniel, he saw everything." But most of all—he'd heard it all, and yet, he wanted to protect her from the truth. What had she taught her son?

Daniel lifted her chin with his finger. "I know he did. I found him running down the road. He told me everything. That's why I took him to Mom's. Lyric, he's as strong as his mother, and if you fold on him, he's going to cave, too."

Lyric closed her eyes and took a very deep breath. "But he needs to let it out. Why would he hold it in like that?"

Daniel placed his hand at the side of her face. "To protect you. And all men are little boys inside. Your little boy happens to carry things like a man. Give him time. I have all the faith in the world that the rascal in him will return soon."

Lyric pulled from Daniel's caring touch. "Granny Grace, I'll be back."

Grace narrowed her eyes and looked at the two gawking girls behind the ice cream counter. "Honey, you're my most reliable employee. Now, go be a reliable mommy to that hurting little boy."

Lyric walked away, her head down. She found Cade

sitting in one of the two chairs in front of Granny's old metal desk. The store's owner had so many wonderful antiques to choose from, but she said she preferred the desk her husband bought her new in 1960. The furniture was now an antique in its own right.

Cade stared at the envelope.

"Cade, I know you saw everything that happened. Did you hear what your dad... what was said?"

"I know he called me a bad word, but I don't know what it means."

She caressed his cheek. "You're never to use that word. It's hurtful and it demeans people who have no control over how God allowed them to come into this world. And, Cade, I'm sorry he said that about you. Truth is, baby, he could have said that about me, too."

Yes, she had made the choice, but God had created her son, just as God had created her without a father to show love to her. Maybe the fear of him growing up without a dad was the reason she'd taken Braedon up on his offer to raise Balaam's child as his own.

"He said things about you and Uncle Matthew." Cade's eyes filled with tears. "And I know they weren't true. Why did he say them?"

"Because someone lied to him." She brushed his blond hair from his face. "And thank you for your faith in me. I'm happy to tell you it is well placed. I loved Uncle Matthew, but I loved him like I love your Uncle Quinn."

How she wished she could take the pain from him, but

Braedon's words would always pierce Cade the way her mother's careless words about Lyric's lack of a father still stabbed at her. "Dad—"

He blinked and his body shuddered. "I don't want to call him that anymore. He wasn't my d—ad. I heard him say that. He said that Ba-Balaam was my father."

Those weren't the exact words he'd said. Cade left off the terrible cursing, things Braedon had called her and Balaam. She sat silent for a long moment, reasoning within herself. Part of her said that she was about to betray that man who'd kept her and Cade in a nice home with food on the table. Then she thought about the word he'd used for Cade. The man had never thought of himself as Cade's father. He'd been nice enough to let Cade think so, but he lacked emotion toward the boy. Cade's behavior of late showed that he'd learned well from both her and Braedon. She held in the secrets, and Braedon had held back the love.

"Why didn't Ba-Balaam stay? Why did he go away and make ... you know, make d-dad take care of me?"

"Let's call him Braedon," she offered. "He did a lot of things wrong, and he did something terrible, but Cade, baby, I knew him when he was different. He wasn't that man you lived with. I would never have thought he would really do what he did. He wasn't always a great guy, but he cared—a little—for us."

Cade shook his head. "He hated me."

Lyric lowered her head and let the curls fall forward. She pressed her lips together. No more lies. With a deep breath, she looked up. "No, he didn't hate you. I promise. What he hated was not knowing how to love you." The truth kicked her in the gut. Maybe, if she'd talked to Brae, her son might have had a father who showed affection toward him.

Cade swallowed hard. "Why did Ba-Balaam go away and forget about me?" he repeated.

"We were young. Balaam had dreams. Mommy didn't want to keep him from doing what he wanted even if it meant raising you alone. And when Braedon asked me to let him be your father, to raise you, I thought it was for the best. I was wrong."

"Does Ba-Ba-Balaam know?"

She nodded. "Couldn't you tell, buddy. Why do you think he came to the funeral?"

"To say good-bye to da-dad and Uncle Matthew."

She pushed his hair from his forehead, a habit she had when talking to him. "He came to make sure you were okay and to see you. He longed to see you. He told me so."

"Will Ba-Balaam let me call him Dad?"

She could answer for Balaam right now, but she bit her tongue for a moment. "Why don't you ask him when he comes home?"

"Can I write him and ask him?"

She drooped forward again. How could she answer him?

With the truth.

Looking up, she held his gaze. "You know what's

wrong with Grandma, don't you?"

Cade nodded. "She drinks lots."

"Well, your dad—Balaam…"

His lips pooched just a bit when she used Balaam's given name.

"Okay, here's the deal. You and I know who he is to you. So, let's call him your dad."

Cade sat up straighter, a little bit of the rascal Daniel mentioned returning.

"You can ask him, but I want you to know that I'd never let you do it unless I knew he'd tell you yes. But here's the deal. Your dad has lived a different life away from you and me. He's been drinking lots."

"Like Grandma."

"But there's a difference. You can see the way Grandma gets, what she does when she's drinking. Your dad has gone away so he can stop doing the things that keep him from being a good father to you. I'm trying to believe him when he says he doesn't want to drink any longer, that he wants to come back here to you."

Cade smiled and fidgeted. "He said that?"

Now she'd done it. She'd open a door to a world of hope that Balaam would probably close and never enter. "Yes, he did. I'm going to be honest because you're a little boy who doesn't deserve to be hurt anymore. Mom isn't going to let him be around you unless he never ever takes a drink again. Do you understand?" She'd take the blame off of Balaam if it would take the hurt of rejection away from Cade.

Cade gave her a big nod. The eternal optimism of a child was something she had always lacked. Somehow, Quinn still held to it. She was thankful for that, because Cade had to have learned it from somewhere.

"Can we read his letter now?" He kicked his legs back and forth.

Lyric roughed his hair and opened the envelope. She slipped the letter out.

Cade settled back in the chair as if waiting for a magical story.

She smiled at him then turned her attention to the letter. "You want me to read it?"

He peered over at it and then up to her. A mischievous smile parted his lips "Can you?"

She giggled. Balaam spent hours writing songs. In high school, she'd been the only one who could decipher the penmanship that had a style all its own—much like the writer.

"Then I think when you write him, you should ask if he writes back to you to make it more readable. Of course, be nice in your request."

"You don't think he'll write me if I send back a letter?"

She sighed deeply and huffed out a heavy breath. "Don't mind me. I'm thinking of the boy he used to be and not this guy…" She waved the letter like a flag. "… who actually wrote a letter. He sure wasn't the student you are when he was in school." She winked. "I'm surprised he can write at all."

Cade laughed. "I'm gonna tell him you said that."

"Hey, he can't deny it." Lyric reveled in this mother-son conversation, the first lighthearted one they'd had since the incident. "Okay, here goes." She straightened the letter. "'Dear Cade, I'm so glad I got to meet you. I've wanted to for so long. You asked me a question when I was there last week, and I've been thinking you deserve an answer. Yes, Cade. I think you and I are a lot alike, but we're different, too—in good ways that I've just begun to thank God for every night and every day. You don't know this, but I heard you over the phone. You were talking with Uncle Quinn, and I was so proud of the respect you showed him. He's an awesome guy. Different from Matthew, but I bet you he does special things for you all the time—the way Uncle Matthew did—the way Uncle Quinn used to do for your mom. Respect is important because it leads to another difference between you and me. Obedience. When Uncle Quinn told you to do something, you didn't hesitate.

"'Cade, my heart overflowed with ...'" Lyric leaned forward and pulled a Kleenex from a box in front of her. She blew her nose and wiped the tears. Her lips trembled for a long moment, and she couldn't speak. She gathered herself and smiled at her and Balaam's child. "Cade, my heart overflowed with love for you, and here's the deal: when I do come home, I want you to remind me to be respectful to others and obedient to God and to people like Sheriff Daniel. By the way, he thinks a lot of you and your mom and Uncle Quinn. He jawed all about you when I stayed with him and when he drove me away.

"'Well morning light is beginning to peek over the mountain, and I need to get to work. It sure is cold here. I'm trying hard to get back to you as soon as I can. In fact, I have a calendar in front of me. I've picked a date when I think I can be ready to come home. I'm not telling you when because I don't want to return until I'm supposed to, but I plan to mark the weeks, Tuesday to Tuesday. But whatever day I arrive, we're going to have ice cream at Granny Grace's store, and we're going to talk about whatever it is you want to talk about.

"'Thank you for the picture. I have it folded in my Bible, and I take it out when I first wake up and just before I turn out the light each night as a reminder to pray for you and for your mom. And by the way, tell her I said hello."

"Dad says hello." Cade smiled and a bit of the chasm in Lyric's heart closed.

"There's one more line." Lyric lowered the paper for him. "Can you read it?"

Cade looked down where she pointed, and he didn't look up for a very long time. When he did, his eyes were brimming with tears. His lips trembled, and he couldn't speak. Finally, he swallowed hard, sat up straight, and with tears streaming down his cheeks, he recited, "I love you... son." He lowered his head and splashes of tears fell onto his jeans. "He really wants to be my dad." He hiccupped the words, and Lyric enfolded him in her arms while he cried against her.

If only she could be so forgiving.

**FAY LAMB**

# 8

Lyric hated the courthouse. She especially loathed being in the courtroom where most everyone knew her mother was the woman in the orange jumpsuit on the other side of the glass, awaiting her arraignment for vandalism.

Momma was fidgety. Her glance kept cutting beyond and to Lyric's right. Lyric chanced a look and elbowed Quinn. "What's Jessup doing here?"

Quinn leaned toward her, his mouth close to her ear. "I bet those two arrested with Momma are in his class at the college. The kindly old professor gets his students out of trouble and puts them right to work trafficking his drugs."

She turned her head to speak into his ear. "He never bailed out Balaam."

Quinn bit his lower lip, but he couldn't keep the smile from showing through. "Balaam was no student, and whatever trouble he got into, he was good at getting himself out of. He didn't need any help."

True enough.

Lyric sat back. "I'll tell you one thing," she whispered. "If Bay doesn't come back here for Cade, no one will be able to keep him out of trouble."

"Agreed."

The bailiff came through the courtroom's side door first. "All rise."

A clamoring of chairs and shuffling of clothes filled the room as the small crowd of people stood. "Court is now in session. The Honorable Edwin Stowe presiding."

The judge, a man about Daniel's age, walked up to the bench and sat.

"Be seated," the bailiff said and took a chair by the door.

Judge Stowe surveyed the defendants behind the glass. "We are here for arraignments. If you have been arrested on a misdemeanor charge, the court may entertain the waiver of counsel and a plea of guilty or *nolo contendre*. However, I am under no obligation to accept your plea. If you plead not guilty, it does not guarantee your release without bail. This court may release you on your own recognizance or remand you to custody with bail. If you have been arrested on a felony, or if your crime is a misdemeanor and you wish counsel and do not wish to enter a plea at this time, the court will discuss representation with you and will schedule a second arraignment."

"She could plea out." Quinn sighed.

"If she does, we can't get her committed to the mental health facility for seventy-two hours. The only other possibility is if he gives her jail time."

Quinn turned to look at her. "I don't want her incarcerated, Lyric. You can't either."

Someone tapped her on the shoulder. Apparently, they'd touched Quinn as well. They both turned.

Daniel put a finger to his lips, correcting them as he had when they were kids in Sunday school class. Daniel had picked them up on the church bus and in Sunday school and church, he sat between Balaam and Matthew every Sunday without fail.

Lyric slipped down in her seat, feeling quite reprimanded. Beside her, Quinn did the same. Neither of them ever liked being called out for anything, though the odds were always in their favor that they would be—right alongside Brae, Balaam, and Matthew.

"Magdalene Moxley."

Momma stood and shuffled with her chains to the podium set up for the defendants to stand behind. Once there, she turned and looked out into the crowd. No mistaking it. Her gaze rested on Jessup Roy.

"Ms. Moxley, I'm here. I need your attention please," Judge Stowe said.

Momma's stare slid from Jessup, to their side of the room, then to the judge.

He looked through the court file, lifting papers, and reading for a long moment. "You've been charged with

135

vandalism and disorderly conduct, both misdemeanors, Ms. Moxley. Are you sober enough to understand the charge?"

"Too sober." Momma snickered. "I know what I did."

The crowd laughed.

Lyric gripped Quinn's arm. Warmth climbed up her cheeks.

Quinn lowered his head. "Please, Lord, make her behave."

Judge Stowe leaned forward. "Ms. Moxley, do you think this is a joke?"

Momma leaned against the podium. "No, I don't. I think it's revenge."

"Excuse me?" The judge shook his head.

Quinn tensed. Lyric felt it under her touch.

"Yeah, Sheriff Daniel. He's a sore loser. That's all." Momma stared in their direction.

"How do you wish to plea?" The judge closed the file and leaned back in his seat.

"I guess I did it. My daughter, she's hard to get to some times." Momma narrowed her gaze at Lyric. "You have to do things to grab her attention."

"I hate her," Lyric breathed.

"So, your plea is guilty, but you're offering an excuse for your behavior." The judge swiveled his chair. "And your excuse is you busted up property not belonging to you to gain your daughter's attention. Is that an example to set for a child?"

The judge was toying with her, and Lyric knew it. Judge Stowe was no stranger in this town.

"Lyric ain't no baby. She's a grown woman. You know that, Eddie."

The judge's face reddened. "And the items you smashed belonged to her employer, didn't they, Ms. Moxley? Someone who has the right to fire your daughter for your actions."

"Grace ain't going to fire the little missy. She's cooed over her since the girl was in diapers."

"Well, Ms. Moxley, here's what I'm going to do. I'm not going to accept your plea. I don't think you really have a grip on reality at the moment." He handed the file back to his clerk sitting beside him. "I'm remanding her to the custody of the sheriff's department and ordering that she be transported to Seraphim Mental Health Facility for a seventy-two-hour mental eval. Should the facility deem her unstable or a danger to herself or to others, they are to notify me. We will re-evaluate her bond at such time that she is no longer deemed as such."

"No!" Momma screamed.

Quinn jumped.

Lyric held to his arm to keep him in his seat. "This is what we wanted."

Quinn settled down and nodded.

"Quinny, baby. Get me out of here." Momma ran to the glass, the chains around her hands and feet rattling. She placed her hands against the window. "Please, Quinny.

You know your momma can't survive in that place."

Quinn shook his head.

"Daniel Dixon, you buzzard!" Momma screamed. "Ask him, Quinn, why he has it out for me."

The female bailiff grabbed Momma's arm.

Momma pulled away. "Ask him what he did. What the judge here did. You look up to Daniel like he's someone special. He ain't no different from the rest of them. Tell him, Daniel. You took just like all the rest." The bailiff yanked her hard, and Momma struggled. A second bailiff tugged her out of the courtroom.

Quinn turned in his seat, looking up at Daniel, who now stood behind them.

"Quinn, I—" Daniel started.

Quinn pulled from Lyric's hold. He stood. "Excuse me, please," he said to the lady on the aisle seat. Then he walked from the courtroom without looking back.

Daniel started to push behind Lyric.

She reached for his arm. "Let him go," she said. "You and I know he'll be ready to talk about it in a day or so."

Lyric sat in Quinn's car staring at her house in front of them.

Quinn gripped the steering wheel so hard his knuckles were whiter than white.

"Quinn, I know how you think of Daniel. He's like a

138

father to you, but you had to know he has flaws." She put her hand on top of his. "Let it go."

He released the wheel. "It's not that simple."

"I don't think he was sleeping with her when we were in church with him. I think it happened years before— before I was born—maybe when you were too young to remember he was around."

"How could you know that? Anyway, it isn't that simple. I never knew. I never thought he would do something like that." He slammed his fist into the door. "I need to leave." He started the car.

"You could say the same thing about me. You never thought I could sleep with a boy and get myself pregnant."

"No, I didn't. And I was angry with you and with Balaam when it happened. Listen. I really do need to leave."

"For what? To pray and ask God if you should forgive Daniel? I can tell you the answer to that one, and I'm not a pastor."

"I need to ask Him for the strength to forgive Daniel. I know what I'm supposed to do." He stared at her for a long moment. "Have you ever asked God to forgive you?"

She shook her head, surprised he would ask. His mistaken belief that she'd placed her trust in God had been her only consolation. She never wanted to cause her brother worry. She heaved a deep sigh and released it slowly. "No, Quinn. I haven't. I won't. This isn't between Him and me. This is between Balaam and me."

Quinn remained silent, his cheek dented in. He was sure to be biting down real hard. He didn't argue about faith. He said often enough that God knew better what people needed than he did, and if they didn't want to listen to Biblical reason, he'd leave them to God's hands. He'd left their mother's salvation in God's hands, too. Look where it got her. And now, Lyric had placed an even bigger burden on her brother. He would worry over her relationship with God.

"Did you pray to forgive me for what Balaam and I did, too?" She needed to get his mind off of her and back to him.

"Not then. I was a different person. I hadn't surrendered my life to God, hadn't been called to the ministry. But I did eventually—at seminary. I had to make things right with God, and my anger with you was one of those things I had to take care of."

His words wounded her in the way only betrayal could slice someone's insides open—the way Braedon must have felt when Momma lied to him that day at the Backslide.

"I gotta go." She opened the door and slammed it shut, running for her house.

"Lyric, wait!" Quinn caught up with her. "I know I hurt you. I didn't mean to."

She swung toward him. "I want you to remember one thing, Quinn Moxley. Daniel Dixon has treated us well. He watched over us while Momma drank away what little money she had for food. He's probably the only reason we

140

didn't end up in the system. Think on that when you're asking your God for strength to forgive the man."

"He's your God, too." Quinn grabbed her by the shoulders. "God didn't run out on you like Balaam. He didn't harm you like Braedon. He hasn't failed you like I have. He loves you, Lyric, and all He wants is for you to realize that so that you can come to a place where what He's done for you matters."

Lyric gasped. "You can't really believe you've ever failed me?"

His shoulders drooped. "You missed the most important part of what I said." He pulled her against him. "Time and time again. Every time I let Momma belittle or scream at you or when Braedon hit you. When I turned my head and allowed Balaam to wrap you up in promises of love-ever-after and when I watched him walk away from you without looking back, I failed you. But God hasn't."

"I appreciate the fact that you have loved and cared for me in ways Momma never has, but I'm not your responsibility."

"You're my baby sister. It's always been my job to protect you."

Lyric buried herself in his embrace. "If not for you..."

"And for you." Quinn kissed her hair. "Don't be distant with God—at least not for too long, and don't make any decisions about your life without making things right with Him. I can only try so hard to keep you out of trouble, you know."

141

She laughed, if only to soothe him. "And what decisions do you think I need to be making?"

He held her at arms' length. "What is it that you have that Momma wants?"

Lyric tugged from his hold. "Papers Braedon couriered for Jessup."

"Turn them over to Daniel."

She shook her head, and her curls bounced into her eyes. "I can't. They involve him."

He pushed her hair away. "Then he should have them."

She hadn't thought of it that way, but how would Daniel react to the information she had. Lyric hated to admit it, but she feared for her mother once Daniel saw the truth as Momma recorded it. "I need time to think it through."

"Jessup was in that courtroom for her." Quinn looked to the heavens. "Momma said Cade is in danger. Is it over what you have? I want to see it." He started toward the front door.

She grabbed at his arm. "No. I have it hidden. No one will find it until I'm ready."

"You'd risk Cade's health—maybe even his life."

"Momma said Braedon carried two parcels for Jessup. I have a feeling the package I have isn't what will protect Cade. If I hand it over to Jessup, he'll demand the other one, thinking I have them both. Braedon only left one, and the information inside simply gives Jessup a leg up on Daniel by blackmail. I think the other parcel is much more important. Jessup isn't one to threaten. It's not the way he usually does things. I think he's running scared."

"Mom!" Cade called from Granny Grace's porch across the street.

She looked at her watch. "I didn't realize it was late enough for him to be home from school. I need to go get him."

"And I need to go pray." Quinn kissed her cheek. "Make the guest bed for me. I'll be staying with you for a while. I'll bring over my stuff tonight."

Lyric nodded. "I appreciate it."

He winked and ducked inside his car.

She ran to his door. "Please think about what I said. Daniel cares for us. I saw his face when you left the courtroom. He didn't care a lick about his reputation, but he cares that what he did years ago hurt you."

**FAY LAMB**

# 9

Balaam stood at the door of the old wooden building, letting the cold air chill the sweat that had poured from him while working in the small blacksmithing enterprise his host operated. He stared out at the mountains surrounding the peaceful, secluded valley located about an hour and a half from Amazing Grace but a world away from the life he'd been leading for the last nine years. He'd been in big cities on crowded stages. He had barely been able to move without tripping over someone or without a fan hounding him for an autograph—or much more than he wanted to offer. He liked this solitude. Others lived on the mountain, but a lot of acreage separated the homesteads.

Jim Maynard, the pastor with a ministry to those with addictions, had ordered him to take a break.

The retired reverend had a keen eye, and he'd been reading Balaam from the moment, three weeks before, when Daniel had dropped the man off at the peaceful farm owned by Jim and his wife, Constance.

Balaam gulped from the jug of water with his name on it. Keeping hydrated in the forge was important. He hated for anyone to recognize that he'd grown weak, though. Poppa used to work him like a mule before Momma died. After that, the old man didn't seem to care much what Balaam and Braedon did as long as they fed the stock and were around for breaking the ground and harvest. Otherwise, they ran free.

Daniel had stayed for less than an hour after they'd arrived, having some coffee with his old friends. On the ride up here, he hadn't interrogated Balaam. Not one question about his brother, about what he might know about Jessup Roy's various and sundry activities outside his life as a well-liked and revered college professor, not one word of disdain over Balaam's treatment of those he'd left behind on his way to stardom.

When Daniel had gotten up to leave, he'd hugged Balaam as if he were a father dropping off a son at camp. He'd told Balaam to hurry home.

Behind Balaam, in the building Jim used for his blacksmithing, the older man pounded hot steel into shape. The first week of his arrival, Balaam's chore list consisted of feeding the stock and helping Constance with housework. Halfway through last week, when Balaam's tremors had subsided, Jim told him to bind up his long hair and invited Balaam out here. For the remainder of the week, after the 4:00 a.m. wake-up call for devotions and prayer, Balaam helped Constance with breakfast and the morning chores and joined Jim in the afternoon. He'd been given the job of cutting wood for the various tools. Getting his hands back into hard labor was painful, but the pain was a reminder that he still lived.

Balaam stared down at his hands. The blisters that had formed were turning into hard callouses. He hadn't complained about the pain. They were a badge of honor—that and the genuine surprise that Jim showed at Balaam's ability to work with wood. Jim's only complaint had been the amount of knife, saw, and axe handles Balaam stockpiled, taking up space in the small outbuilding.

But Balaam had known that fast work would let him get his hands on the forge. Jim wanted to finish up one last project before dinner, and he promised that on Monday Balaam could start his training in actually making the knife blades, the saws, and the axes.

He suspected his skin might be sporting third-degree burns on Monday evening, but Balaam couldn't wait.

The process fascinated Balaam. Jim had explained that he could tell the temperatures by the colors of the heated steel. After he forged the steel into blades, he would attach them to the wood, and sharpened the tools to perfection.

The pounding stopped, and Jim moved around behind him.

Balaam continued to stare out at the mountains surrounding the small valley. He'd memorized Psalm 23 since their devotions and the discussions that followed had centered on the depth of the verses.

Jim had taught him about the real Valley of the Shadow of Death where Israeli shepherds had led their sheep—a dangerous place, where sheep could be picked off by predators.

Jim had showed him how David, who'd been a shepherd, was speaking of the true Shepherd, and that every part of that Psalm described a shepherd's care over his sheep.

Combined with Balaam's memory of the shepherd leaving the flock to find one lost sheep, Balaam was comforted. The Shepherd had gathered Balaam in His arms, and Balaam was the lamb whose leg had been broken to keep him close to the Shepherd so that he could learn to trust Him and not stray.

God was good to piece those pictures together. Balaam had always been big on symbolism. Of course, his symbolism had always been dark and captivated by death.

God was showing Balaam the exact opposite: symbolism of the Light and Life, and being able to envision Christ holding Balaam in His arms sustained him through long nights of cravings, of wanting to walk off the mountain and to the nearest bar. Though Jim had told him the nearest bar was in another county. Where he lived was dry. Not a drop of alcohol sold within the county lines.

Balaam doubted a rehab in California would have done this for him. Instead, he'd have attended therapy sessions and talked about how all the wrongs in his life had turned him to alcohol and drugs. They'd have psychoanalyzed him and blamed his addictions on everyone but himself. He'd still be looking for his creativity in drugs and alcohol.

Daniel had been right when he suggested this alternative.

Instead of psychobabble, here on the Maynards' farm, he found nourishment in God's Word and from good country cooking like he'd known in his youth. Instead of the talk being centered on him and his ills, the Maynards kept Balaam centered on Christ.

Balaam was learning to seek God first thing every morning, a very early morning, and the last thing at night, a very early night. For the first time in years, he found himself sleeping without the use of something to bring him off the high of another drug. In fact, nearing the end of the third week of his stay, he couldn't remember waking up at all during the night. The tremors were gone, and he was feeling mighty good.

The pastor and his wife weren't holding him hostage. They told him he could leave anytime he liked but encouraged him to give it at least two weeks. By then, he'd have a feel for when he should leave. They had been right, and if he'd left before he was ready, they warned he'd probably fail again. He was welcome to stay as long as he wanted or needed. On his first day here, he'd set a goal and shared it with Jim and his wife, Constance. They'd smiled and encouraged him, even told him he'd been sensible in his planning, but they wouldn't push him out until he felt he could do it—even if it took longer than he planned.

That's why he hadn't given Cade the date. He didn't want to disappoint his son.

Balaam wiped his brow. Even with the lengthening time between now and his near death, the craving still haunted him from time to time. He wouldn't leave.

"You okay?" Jim came alongside him.

"I'm fine."

Jim leaned his heavy frame on the opposite side of the door. "I think Constance probably has some nice cold lemonade for us. Working in this shed gets mighty hot."

And Balaam suspected that this building, with the sweat it produced, was not here on happenstance. Sweating out the impurities he'd long used to abuse his body had to be good for him.

Constance's lemonade could cure any ill. Balaam swallowed at the thought of the tart flavor sweetened by just the right amount of sugar. But the sun wasn't heading down behind the mountains yet, and they'd never quit their work this early, and Sunday was their only day of rest. They attended worship services in the morning and the evening, and in between they rested. Jim had encouraged him to reflect on the pastor's messages and to catch a long afternoon nap. "You sure. I know Constance hasn't gotten dinner together yet."

Jim patted him on the back. "The truth is, we usually quit early on Saturday nights around here. We kept you busy for the first two weeks because idle hands and the devil, you know. You're ready for the break, and we have some time to do personal things. I know you've scratched a letter or two off to Cade since your arrival in the few spare minutes, but Constance and me, we like to just rest and take some real time for things that interest us. Constance reads a book. I check the television for the news. Maybe you have something you'd like time to do." He started toward the house.

Jim was right. They'd left him barely any time to do more than take a shower and to fall into bed. He'd wolfed down some mighty good lunches and hurried off before Jim was ready to get back to work so he could write Cade, or he'd found a minute in the early mornings to pen something to his son.

"Tuesdays were made for ice cream and for nothing else." Cade's quote from Matthew crashed over him like a wave. "Can I have a minute before I come inside?"

Jim nodded. "Sure, son." Jim didn't even look back, which said a lot. He trusted Balaam.

Of course, there was really nothing he could do, but he'd seen men so desperate for alcohol, they'd drink rubbing alcohol to feel better.

The screen door at the side entrance into the kitchen slammed shut behind Jim.

His son's voice rang over and over in Balaam's mind, torturing him until he dropped to his knees. "Dear God, my son needs Tuesdays more than I need to see him and his momma again. Take this craving from me, and let me get back to them. Now that I've learned that you're my heavenly Father, I want nothing more than to show You to him through Your example."

"'My grace is sufficient for thee: for My strength is made perfect in weakness.' Isn't that what the Good Book says?"

Balaam looked up into eyes of deep compassion. Eyes he'd never seen before. He nodded at the man who stood before him.

"That doesn't mean you don't need to follow through to be the best that you can be. Even the best fail when we forget to lean on the Lord in our weakness. Sometimes, we begin to think that the strength He has given us is produced by what we have done. We fall harder then. Even as He gives you strength, remember where it comes from, and continue to seek Him to add to it daily."

Balaam bowed his head and nodded, embarrassed that he'd been caught like this but glad for the words of truth spoken to him. "Thank you, sir. That's wisdom I'm going to follow."

"Balaam, you okay?" Jim said.

Balaam looked up and blinked.

Jim was alone, standing in front of Balaam. "Did I interrupt a prayer? I'm sorry. Constance has an early dinner on the table."

"Did you see a man? He was just here talking to me. An old man, kind of haggard looking, but he made sense. I was just crying out to God about Tuesdays—"

Jim stepped back and peered across his acreage. "I didn't see him."

"He was just here." Balaam grasped the doorjamb and stood. "Or maybe I'm hallucinating."

Jim patted his back. "Or maybe you weren't." He winked. "Now, what's this about Tuesdays being made for ice cream? Did you know Constance had churned some on the back porch for dessert?"

Balaam shook his head, walking beside the older man, searching the perimeter. Had he been an old hobo who had stepped out of sight, not wanting to be caught by the pastor? No. A hobo wouldn't come up here in the cold of winter. No vegetables to pick. He might steal a chicken, but that was a long way to travel. And that man didn't seem likely to steal a thing.

"So, Tuesdays?" Jim broached again.

"My son, Cade, he mentioned that Matthew would take him for ice cream every Tuesday."

"A precious memory for him—and for you."

"I plan to do the same when I can."

They stepped into the house from the back porch. Constance looked up from putting the bowls of food on the table. "Lemonade's in the refrigerator, boys. Fix it yourselves."

"Is there anything else I can help you with?" Balaam asked.

"No, Darlin'. You are so sweet. We've worked you plumb near to death since you've been here. Your only break has been Sundays, and we still have you working with the livestock. You look a little peaked today, and we're going to get back into our Saturday afternoon relaxation from here on out."

"I'd say you've made that a necessity." Jim laughed. "If we fit all the blades to the tool handles before I reach planting season, I'll be mighty pleased. Come spring, Constance and I do some shows at festivals and such to sell what we've made during the winter. Constance's canned goods and her jellies are well known in these parts."

Jim and Constance were treasures. With their talk, their hard work, their love for the Lord, and their care of the land, they seemed generations removed from the present. They were both good, honest people. In them, Balaam saw his father—minus that whole moonshine thing.

"What ya thinking on, Bay?" Jim poured two glasses of lemonade and handed Balaam one. They sat at the kitchen table. Constance came over with the last dish of food, placed it on the table, and sat between them.

Balaam had learned the old man believed moments of pondering should be shared so that Christ could be brought in to straighten things out for them.

For the first couple of days, the intrusion bothered Balaam, but now, he knew his soul needed cleansing. "I'm thinking about Poppa. He's as rough as they come. He has the old still on the mountain, but he and Momma, they worked the land. They worked real hard to raise Braedon and me. I fought against him." He sat in the chair near the window and looked out at the mountains surrounding the lonely valley farm. "I hated him for naming me Balaam."

"He ever tell you why he called you by that name?"

"He told me he knew I'd sell my soul to the devil someday. He said greed and worldly pleasures would take me away. The truth I discovered is, I'm named after a great-grandfather on my mother's side." Balaam gulped down his drink. "I've been thinking about what he said, though. He never spoke about God or the Bible, but he knew more about the Balaam in the Bible than a lot of people who go to church every Sunday."

"A name is just a name," Jim said.

"Did Daniel tell you anything about my music, about how I got in this condition?"

"Daniel wouldn't betray your trust, and I wouldn't ask him to do it."

Balaam ran his hand down the glass, wiping away the condensation. If only he could wipe his desires away as easily. "I've probably led a lot of kids straight into hell, Jim. They followed me as if I represented a god to them. At some point, I came to think of myself as a god. When I took those pills that night, I betrayed them all. You see, I might have doubted a lot of things in my life, but I never doubted the day I got down on my knees, Daniel at my side, and prayed for God to love me and to forgive me."

"I'm glad you can mark that day, that through it all you didn't lose that assurance of God's love."

"The day before I received that assurance, I had the fear of God put in me. Poppa had beaten me within an inch of my life after I broke out a window at the funeral home."

"Playing baseball," Jim laughed. "Every kid has one of those stories."

Balaam shook his head. "No. I actually took a ball, tossed it into the air, and with a steady eye, I took clear aim at that window, thinking I was getting back at God. The last time I saw my momma was in that place, and I blamed God for taking her away from me." Balaam slumped back at the sudden memory of the scene depicted in the stain glass: Jesus carrying a lamb in one arm and walking with His staff in the other.

Balaam swallowed down the mix of remorse and utter disbelief. Then the joy was added to the concoction of emotions. Back then, this very moment of contemplation had been known by Christ. He'd been watching over Balaam all of his life.

And Balaam had taken Him into some very dark places.

"You ever tell your dad this?" Constance helped herself to a bowl of mashed potatoes and passed them to Jim.

"No, ma'am. He didn't care to hear it anyway."

"So how did a moonshiner's boy end up in Sunday school where God could touch his life?" Jim asked.

Balaam took a stuttering breath. "If you'd asked me two seconds before this, I'd have said Daniel had done it, but I've just realized that Daniel is the person God used to bring me to that moment." Balaam leaned his head back, took a deep sigh, and looked back at Jim. "Daniel rounded us all up on the bus, and he hauled us there. Then he stayed, and he made us behave. Good thing, too, or I'd have acted up so much I wouldn't have listened to the story of Peter denying Christ. The story kind of spoke to my anger, how Jesus knew how Peter would behave, but He still loved him. I was so sure I'd pushed God too far with breaking that beautiful window and all. If God was anywhere near as mad as the funeral home director or Poppa..." Balaam shook his head. "I knew I was in trouble." He stood and poured himself another glass of the smooth lemonade and sat back down. "I went to Daniel's place that night. He and I talked about it, and he showed me how much God loved me." Another deep sigh heaved its way to the surface, and Balaam blew the air out. "And look what I've done with His love for me. I've harmed people—people I love, and people I don't even know."

Jim leaned forward, his hands cupped around his own glass. "Sometimes God allows us to walk a course, Bay, because He knows when we get to the end of the rough road we've paved, we'll be stronger for the job He has for us."

"Well, some good-meaning person told me soon after I got saved that I could live like the devil because God would never turn me away, and the more I lived like Lucifer, the more convinced I became I was living in the wrong place. I knew God had His hand on me, and I struggled against Him all the way—just like I struggled against Poppa."

"When did you turn your life back over to the Lord?"

"The night they resurrected Balaam Carter and left Balaam Brasher to the devil."

"Have you made it right with your daddy?"

Balaam shook his head and brushed back the hair that had escaped its clasp.

"Don't you think with your relationship to the Heavenly Father mended, you should mend the relationship with your earthly father?"

"I don't know how."

"Start with a letter, even with one line. 'I'm sorry' and a closing that says, 'I love you.' Don't you think your daddy's hurting? He's got one son dead and another gone from him. Give him some hope."

"Yes, sir."

"And read Daniel, chapter four, if you ever decide you want to be a god again."

"Daniel four. Yes, sir."

"Notice what the man who wrote that chapter did at the end of his rough journey. He praised God, giving Him the glory. Pray about something for me, will ya?"

"Sure." Balaam paused from taking a heaping of the mashed potatoes.

"Ask God if He desires for you to use your talent for Him? Specifically, your voice and your ability to write music. The song you said was swimming in your mind and you shared with me the other day while we worked was a mighty praise to our God."

"I'm not going back on stage. No, sir. Not unless God pushes me there. I don't ever want anyone staring up at me like I'm more than I am. Those faces will haunt me forever."

Jim smiled. "Spoken like a man who thinks he knows the direction God's sending him. Sometimes God defies our assumptions about Him. Maybe pray and ask God if He wants you to write the songs that those who haven't stood before others as a god can sing in your stead."

Balaam sat back hard in his chair. He'd never thought of it. His heart soared at the thought. "I will pray, Jim. Thank you. I have an old buddy I haven't seen in years. He's from back home, but everyone in the business knows his name. He's written a lot of award-winning songs."

"Just watch your associations," Jim warned. "If the buddy doesn't have any godly wisdom, I'd find someone else who does."

Balaam nodded. "Shane Browne. He quit the band. Well, his brother put a stop to his going on the road."

"Was he related to Beau—Beau Carmichael?"

"Yeah, his cousin. How'd you know?"

"Some things aren't for the telling," Jim said, "but I'm beginning to see that God might have a plan for you. When you're ready, and I mean really cleaned up and sober and not before, I bet you Shane can give you a lot of godly wisdom."

Balaam wouldn't pry, but he would trust Jim.

"One other thing."

Balaam looked up before he could sink the tong around a piece of Constance's fried chicken.

"Mull this over for me, and get back to me tomorrow morning. Are you holding on to that long hair for a reason? Seems to me that it goes with the rock-star persona. Since you don't plan to go back there, maybe you should cut it off."

Did Jim know how long it had taken him to grow his hair? It was his trademark.

Jim studied Balaam for a long moment. "I don't often pry. I like to let God work, but I've been praying, and God has placed this on my heart. Who in the Bible is noted as having long hair?"

Balaam thought back to all those lessons Daniel taught him.

"David's son Absalom had long hair."

"Do you remember how he died?" Jim leaned forward, hands clasped in front of him on the table.

Balaam had loved that story as a kid. In fact, he loved everything about King David. "He rebelled against his own father."

"You have a good foundation of the Bible," Jim complimented. "Tell me. What did Absalom do with his hair? Do you remember?"

Balaam shook his head.

"He weighed it. Does that tell you something about

him?"

"I thought he was a real jerk when he burned down Joab's land to get his attention like a spoiled brat."

Jim and Constance both laughed.

"Yeah, but Joab wasn't a nice guy either. We'll get there in a minute. Here's a question for you. Why'd you grow your hair out so long?"

Balaam smiled. "I wanted to look like a rock star. I even bet Lyric I could grow mine longer than hers."

"So, you wanting to look like a rock star and Absalom weighing his hair—what is that about?"

Balaam tried to swallow the truth down, but it flowed out of his lips. "Pride."

"What happened to Absalom because of his pride?" Jim questioned.

"He got hung up in a tree and... and Joab killed him even though David didn't want his son to die."

"And there you go."

Balaam pondered the thought for a long moment, trying to remember others with long hair. The Nazarites wore it long, but they were set apart by God to do good things.

Except for one. God had separated him as a Nazarite, but he'd thrown the blessing away. "Samson was full of pride, too."

"Samson was a judge of Israel," Constance added. "God had put him in place. His hair was clearly a part of his God-given strength, but his pride caused him to be taken in by a woman, and Samson reaped dire consequences. Did God ask you to grow your hair?"

Balaam didn't have to think about it. "No. I came up with that all on my own."

"There you go," Constance said as though the matter was finished.

Balaam continued to think about their words. Maybe his hair had been his pseudo-strength while he put himself up as an idol.

*My grace is sufficient for thee: for My strength is made perfect in weakness.*

Balaam didn't need his own strength. It had never done him any good. He needed Christ's strength in his weakness.

"God's Word tells us that it's a shame for a man to have long hair. I'm not so convinced that it has anything to do with the length of the hair as it is with the size of the pride that goes with the length." Jim shrugged. "And the decision is all your'n."

Balaam stared into his glass of lemonade. "I'd like to have that haircut as soon as I help Constance finish with the dishes, if you don't mind giving up a little of that time you set aside for yourself."

Daniel looked through the small window of the room in the mental health ward. Magda wasn't faring well. They had her strapped down. They'd been able to keep her here because of her own actions, but Stowe was running out of laws that could keep her safely tucked inside the facility.

Well, she wanted to see him. He owed her that much. "Daniel."

Daniel jumped as the hand fell upon his shoulder. "Quinn." He leaned against the door. Quinn was another one he owed so much, and he couldn't remember going this long without talking to him.

"You didn't need to come." Quinn held up the Bible in his hand. "I thought maybe reading some Scripture to her would soothe her a little."

"Could make her angry." Daniel placed his hand on the doorknob. "She asked to see me. Any reason she'd want to do that? Your momma hasn't sought me out in years." He winced. *Wrong choice of words there, Danny Boy.* He could almost hear his mom's voice.

Quinn shrugged. "I never knew she sought you out."

Daniel hated to see the pain in Quinn's eyes. Since the boy was old enough to realize the truth, he'd known what others thought of his mother, how men in the town used her. Daniel had used her like that. He shook the thought from his head. No, it hadn't been the same. Magda had been different with him. She'd been happy. They'd fallen together to forget, and for a while, they had.

And then it was over. Magda's depression returned. Back then, she hadn't been a drinker. The depression seemed to swallow her up at times, made her impossible to deal with. She'd lash out at everyone and everything. When

Quinn, Sr., had left, the town's consensus was that he'd done it to save his life, but if that were so, the man had a lot to prove to him. Why would he leave his son? Magda had not gotten over Quinn's father leaving her like he had. Daniel understood. He still struggled with losing Desiree.

The weight of the shame weighed on him like an anchor. He'd apologized so many times to God for letting his anger and his sorrow rule his actions. Nothing good had come from them, and now, the young boy Daniel had wanted so badly to become his was now a grown man without a father to lean upon. Daniel had completely failed Quinn.

Quinn cleared his throat, and Daniel stared into the eyes so filled with pain they almost bowed him over.

"Go on in. I'll make a visit or two. Some of these folks could use someone who'll listen to them," Quinn offered.

Daniel nodded and opened the door. "Quinn," he stepped back. "Where's your sister?"

"With your mother."

Daniel entered the room and shut the door. "Get me out of here," Magda growled.

Daniel stayed clear of her bed. He sat on the arm of a chair, putting distance between them. "You wanted to see me?"

Her eyes followed him like a frightened animal who wanted only to escape. Her dark hair laced with stands of gray, lay moist against her sweat-soaked brow. Her face was red, and her hands were white as she struggled against her bonds—the ones the court ruled the facility could use if necessary—the ones that allowed the judge to keep her inside the facility, on pretense that she was a danger to others.

"This will all go easier if you just relax. They'll give you something to help you. You haven't been sober in years, and your body is just going to have to go through this long stage of withdrawal for you to get better."

"I'm going to die in here, Daniel. They're trying to kill me. I need a drink. I can't live without something to get me by. The shakes are too bad."

"The medication will help you with that, but you have to get through this. Wouldn't it be nice to be free of that demon?" He edged closer. "Your children need you clean and sober. They need a mother like the one Quinn had when... when ..."

"When you were doing me!" she screamed. "Say it, Daniel."

"I don't think of it like that. I was wrong, so wrong." He lowered his head. "But I wasn't in my right mind. We were two lonely people. I would have ... I would have made it right, but you walked away. You stepped back into the darkness, and I couldn't pull you out of it." He moved closer. "Magda, we could have had it so good, you and me. I didn't care about the things you'd done. I wanted to shower my love and devotion on you and Quinn."

She sat up as best she could with the straps holding her down. Her dark eyes narrowed, and a soulless creature stared at him. "I have something you want, something you've wanted for a long time. I can give it to you, but you have to get me out of here."

"There's nothing I want more than to see you free from the alcohol, to see you and your kids happy. Your daughter lost her husband and one of her best friends."

Magda's face took on a vacant look, as if she'd gone somewhere else in her mind. Then she blinked and her piercing scream hit the air.

Daniel stumbled backward.

"Can't you see? Can't you see that's why I need the alcohol? I need it to deaden the pain of what I've done."

"You hinted to Braedon that Matthew was seeing Lyric, didn't you?"

"I did. I had to. Lyric couldn't be with him. Braedon needed to break it up."

"Well, he did. With a gun. And it shattered your little girl's heart."

She grunted and turned from him. "Get me out of here, and I'll give you your heart's desire."

What did she know of his heart's desire? She'd flamed the ashes after Desiree's abandonment but left them to smolder out and die. He slammed his fist down on the metal stand at the side of the hospital bed.

Magda jumped and whimpered.

Daniel raised his hands and retreated a step. How many men had treated her with this type of anger? He didn't need to add to the pain of it. He brought his raised hands together in front of him, shaking them back and forth. "Please, dear God in heaven, cure her of this need for alcohol. Take away her pain. Forgive me for adding to it."

Magda laughed. "God has never had any use for me."

"That's not true, Momma." Quinn walked through the door. "God loves you."

"Only fools believe in a God of love." She spat at her son.

Quinn blinked as if she'd slapped him. "Well, I'm no fool. The Bible tells me fools don't believe in God."

"I'm no fool either, Quinn." She leaned her head back against the pillow, calm compared to only a moment before. "I believe in Him." Her voice deepened, as if it weren't her at all. "I hate Him."

"I'm going to go now." Daniel started past the young preacher. He placed his hand on his shoulder. "Quinn, you're no fool."

"Daniel," Magda hissed his name. "If you don't get me out of here, you'll never discover what it is I have for you."

"Momma." Quinn shook his head. "Don't."

"That's not what I'm talking about." Magda licked dry lips and pierced Daniel with her stare. "Though you're not a stranger to that either, are you, Sheriff Dixon?"

"Magda, please."

But Quinn's eyes bored into him.

Daniel dropped his gaze to the floor. "Not like that, Quinn."

"Just like that." Magda's laughter was as wicked and

as frightening as her earlier scream and the change in voice. "Yeah, boy, the good sheriff took what I had to offer just like all the others."

Daniel dared to seek Quinn's gaze. The younger man's face was flushed, his eyes pain-filled. He stepped past Daniel and out the door.

Daniel moved closer to the demented woman in the bed. Her laughter cackled through the room. Maybe alcohol wasn't the true demon inside of her. What if the alcohol tempered her true psychosis? "Nice work. Your son may be the only person who ever truly loved you. I thought I could try, but you pushed me away."

Magda fell silent, and Daniel turned to leave.

"Good-bye, Daniel."

He turned back. "Do me a favor. If the court releases you, stay here until you can get out from under the spell of the drink, where you can talk to the doctors about what drives you to do what you do. I'll be there for you. Not like before. I'll show you what true love looks like. Love cherishes and doesn't take. I'm so sorry for what happened between us before, but I did want it to be different. Back then, I would have done anything for you and Quinn. Now, I'll do anything for you and both your children. I wanted you to know someone cared about you and about them." He pulled the door open and stepped out into the hall.

Quinn was nowhere in sight.

## 10

Lyric leaned back in her seat and listened to the two men talk, straining to hear what they said above the noisy pizza place. How could she have been so wrong about Ethan Goodman? When she'd opened her front door and found Quinn standing beside him, she had breathed a sigh of relief. If they'd gone anywhere alone, everyone would talk, and she couldn't blame them.

"I hope you don't mind. My invitation was friendly enough, Lyric, but I don't want to give anyone reason to talk about you. I invited your brother." Ethan had leaned toward her so only she could hear.

Quinn had stepped through her door with one of his what-were-you-thinking stares, the same look he'd given her when she told him she was pregnant with Cade.

The latest letter from Balaam that Cade had shared with her also brought conflict into her agreement to step out with Ethan. But the concern wasn't for Balaam's feelings. She didn't want her boy confused, and even the appearance of a relationship could do that for him.

Not that she ever planned to give Balaam another chance with her. She'd placed him in that section of her heart where her mother remained. Quinn's love for her was the only reason she pretended to care. Likewise, Cade's love for Balaam wouldn't allow her to hurt him with the hatred she held for his father.

These days, Balaam was the only one who brought out the happiness in her son.

"Mom?" Cade tugged on her arm, bringing Lyric back to the moment to the clanging of the games, the whirl of sirens, and the laughter of children running about the Pizza Palace. "Can I go play in the game room?" He ran a napkin across his lips, leaving half of the pizza sauce on his face. He tried again. This time his face was clean.

"Sure, let's go."

"Let me take him." Quinn stood. "Racing or skee ball?"

"Racing." Cade slammed his chair against the table and followed after Quinn.

"He's a good kid, Lyric." Ethan drank his tea.

"You sound surprised."

"Well, I am. Most kids his age aren't as mannerly. I have nephews and nieces, and not one of them sit as still as Cade. You never once had to prompt him to say please and thank you to the waitress."

She'd misjudged him once again. "I'm sorry if I sounded upset at your comment. Brae and I lived on the wrong side of town, and people in Amazing Grace never let us forget where we come from. Brae and Bay's mom was the salt of this earth. She taught us manners—well, she and Daniel Dixon. Brae's father Zeke, he's had his trouble with the law. He's a little self-righteous about what the government thinks is legal and what rights the citizens really should have. My momma, well, you saw her. She's been the talk of the town since she was a teenager. From what I understand, Quinn's daddy was a good man until Momma's demons ran him off. I'm both sorry and thankful that he left Quinn behind."

"What about your father? Your last name was Moxley. Quinn's dad wasn't yours?" Ethan leaned in.

Lyric shrugged. "Magda once said every man in town thinks he's my daddy, and she liked it that way."

He winced. "I'm sorry."

"Nothing to be sorry about." Lyric forced a smile. Besides, Momma had placed another last name on her birth certificate, but she'd kept Moxley later when other paperwork had been drawn up. "Quinn and I are made of stronger stuff than Momma. Braedon was made tough by his father, but he also had a soft side to him. He won't be remembered for it though."

"What about Matthew? What kind of life did he have?"

Matthew. Why did he have to ask about him? Lyric ran her finger around the lip of her glass. She closed her eyes and breathed in, releasing the air slowly, hoping to contain her emotions. "He had a good life. Larry and Bernice loved him very much. Everyone loved him. He always had a passion for animals. That's why he went to veterinary school. Top of his class."

"I was very insensitive to you that day at Grace Dixon's house. I'm sorry if I insinuated anything about your relationship."

She allowed one tear to fall. "Matthew was not my lover, but I loved him with a depth that only comes when two people are united in some way. He was a good man, and he saved my life, but I would rather have died for him, because when they put his casket in the ground, most of my soul went with him." She leaned toward him. "Please don't ask me about Matthew again. What's left of my heart can't take it."

His eyes softened. "I won't, but if you'd ever like to talk to me about him, I'll be happy to listen."

Lyric searched the gaming area until she saw Quinn and Cade. A smile crossed her face as Cade raised his arms in victory.

"May I ask about Balaam?"

She turned her attention back to him. "Is this bureau investigating or just friendly curiosity?"

"Friendly curiosity. He seemed very sick."

"I don't know much about Balaam. He left here before Cade was born, and he didn't look back. I guess God didn't send that donkey to talk much sense to him like he did to Bay's namesake."

172

Ethan laughed a little at her sarcasm. She hadn't meant to be funny, but she let it slide.

"He's a very rich and famous man. He had to get out of this small town to do that. Would you hold it against him?"

"What I hold against him is the fact he didn't take me and his unborn son." She nodded toward the gaming area. "I thought I was the most important person in Balaam's life, that he loved me more than he loved anyone. I found out real quick how little he cared for me. He was no better than Quinn's daddy, running off for greener pastures. I put Balaam behind me as best Braedon would let me. As soon as I'd have myself convinced that Balaam Carter never existed, Brae would accuse me of still loving his brother and having nothing left for him." She took a drink. "Wasn't so. When I'd see news about Bay, it turned my stomach. I couldn't stand to see him living the life that was meant for both of us and living it as if his crushing my dreams meant nothing to him."

"You mean to tell me you never read about him, followed his career, even a little?"

"Only what Brae went on his tangents about, or what I'd see in glimpses on the Internet. Looking for the news was too hard for me."

He opened his mouth to speak but sat back instead. Lyric stole another glance at her son and brother.

"I'm sorry, again." Ethan caught her attention. "The investigator in me always asks questions like an interrogator. I didn't mean anything by them."

Lyric ran her hand down the glass, feeling the coldness beneath her fingers. "You know, the heart is infamous for wanting to reach out for the things we know are best not to have. Balaam's leaving us behind was the best thing for Cade. As you said, Balaam was sick. The band's manager is Nathan Roy. If I'd have gone with them, who's to say I wouldn't have ended up like Balaam. I might have completed Momma's cycle of unwed mother, but Cade always had father figures in his life. Now, he knows the truth about Balaam. I can't trust the man who abandoned me to not leave our son behind. I will hurt Balaam if he ever hurts my son. If I do, you'll have to arrest me. I don't want Sheriff Dixon to have to do it. So long as Balaam does what's right by Cade, he'll be safe from me."

"Do you think he'll come back?"

She shrugged. "I'd like to hope he will. Balaam knows I can be a handful when someone I love is crossed."

Ethan nodded.

"Would anyone like dessert?" The waitress came to the table.

Lyric shook her head, and Ethan did the same. The young girl left the ticket on the table. Ethan picked it up, read it over, pulled out a credit card, and left them both on the table.

"Thank you." Lyric lowered her eyelashes. Receiving gifts had always been hard for her. "This has been a nice escape. I appreciate your sensitivity to my position."

The waitress breezed by and picked up the ticket and credit card.

"Lyric, I'm not here to make life hard on you. I had a job to do. Job's over, and I'm treading in unfamiliar territory. I'd like to spend time with you."

"That so?" she baited. "I saw your ears perk when I mentioned Nathan Roy. You know who he is and what his father does."

He took a minute. Then he nodded. "Yes, I do."

"And I bet your gears are turning at about a notch a millisecond."

He laughed. "You caught me."

Honesty ... she could live with that. And she'd return the favor. "I have not given anything to Balaam for safekeeping. I don't know Bay's current relationship with Nathan Roy, but breaking free from Nathan wouldn't have been easy. Either he fought hard for his freedom, or he bargained his way out of it. If the boy I once loved hasn't changed, he wouldn't do anything to put the people he cared about in jeopardy. He was pretty good at getting himself in trouble, but he was awful good at keeping others out of it."

Ethan pressed his lips together so hard that they turned downward, almost into a frown. "Thank you for telling me what I didn't ask. While I am on vacation, my head doesn't always clock out."

"Well, here's a little more info for you. There's a lot about my life I'll never share with anyone, but it can be pretty dangerous for a federal agent if he expects to advance in his career."

"Your reputation?" He raised his brows. "All I saw in our files were things you had no control over, so why don't you let me deal with that, and let's decide to be friends? That's all. For now."

She leaned forward. "Before that brain of yours clocks out of FBI time, would you mind telling me what is it you think Jessup believes my husband had?"

"I've told you before. If you knew, it could probably put you in danger."

"Magda says Cade might be in danger. Just like you, Jessup thinks I have something he wants."

"He threatened your son?"

She nodded. "So, I'd appreciate knowing just want he thinks I have."

Ethan sat in silence for a long moment, only moving when the waitress brought back his card. He filled in the amount of the tip, totaled the receipt, and signed it, handing them back to the waitress and pocketing his credit card.

"You're not going to tell me, are you?" Lyric pressed.

He stared out to where Quinn and Cade played the games. "I've given it a lot of thought. You've told me you don't have anything." He cut his eyes to her. "Which I don't believe is absolutely true, by the way. I think you got your hands on something, but it's possible what you have isn't the document Braedon had picked up as an informant for the bureau. That's the document that has to be of great concern to Jessup."

Lyric slapped her hand down flat on the table. "Are you telling me Braedon was playing courier for the FBI as well as Jessup?" Her back stiffened. So much for honesty.

"Your husband played both sides of the fence. The agency had him dead to rights on some drug trafficking charges, but we were looking to get some bigger fish on our hook."

Lyric stood, almost upsetting her chair.

"Lyric?" He caught her arm. "Sit down. If I'm going to give you confidential information, at least have the decency not to give me away right here and now."

"Braedon wouldn't traffic drugs. He wouldn't do that," she whispered, regaining her seat.

"From what I've learned, his father is a crafty old moonshiner. Braedon killed a friend, he beat you, but you can't believe he'd run drugs for money? I know your house is paid for, Lyric. Clean and clear. No credit card bills. He didn't make that kind of money as a carpenter. The profile doesn't fit, and you know it."

"You didn't know my husband. He would never—he was set up. The drugs were planted. You needed an informant with something to lose. I can believe he couriered information for Jessup, but I'll never believe he trafficked the drugs for the man."

"Okay, whatever you want to believe. However, it happened, and this is what I know. Braedon was good at what he did. With incentive from the bureau, he worked hard to get on the good side of one of Jessup's rivals in the Raleigh area. This man had some key information on Jessup's business associates. Braedon pretended he wanted to move in on Jessup's business, get the associates to side with him. Then he'd turn over a large percentage to the rival. He convinced Jessup he was going after the information so that Jessup could move in on the rival's territory and cut him in on his business. These papers had names, addresses, phone numbers, and more importantly, the trafficking information needed to bring Jessup and all his rivals down. Without that paperwork, we can't make an arrest."

Lyric's mind sorted through the information.

"And you're still telling me you've never seen anything like that?"

Lyric leveled her gaze with his. "Agent Goodman, I don't know what you're talking about. Braedon did not have that information on him when he came home."

"But ..." Ethan pointed at her, "He did have something else?"

Should she lie? If she trusted him and told him she had something, but nothing like the documents he needed, would he abuse her trust? Would he get a search warrant and tear her house apart?

"Why so serious?" Quinn touched her shoulder. "You okay, Lyric?"

She forced a smile. "I'm fine. It's getting late, and Cade has school tomorrow. We should go."

Ethan stood, and she followed. They walked to the door together, and he opened it. Cade and Quinn stepped ahead of them, and Ethan touched her hand. "I'm worried about both you and Cade. Braedon's sure left you in a precarious situation. You're vulnerable, and it appears the drug lords in this state think you have information they need that will keep them out of prison and gain full power over this region."

Lyric's body involuntarily shuddered, and she wrapped her arms around her. Dealing with Jessup and the information she controlled was one thing; having a second drug dealer thinking she could ruin him or make him even richer was another. "I don't have those papers. I never saw them."

He grasped her arm. "Let me see what you have, Lyric. I'll do my best to protect you and Cade. I promise."

She shook her head. "I've told you. I have nothing that concerns trafficking in drugs."

"But you do have something." He shook her.

Lyric fought to get out of his hold. If he hit her ...

"Hey." Quinn pushed him. "You don't touch my sister like that."

Ethan raised his hands in surrender. "Sorry. I got a little carried away."

When Quinn opened the two-door car for her, Lyric pushed up the seat and sat in the back, with Cade, leaving the front seat for her brother.

As Ethan drove, she stared out at the night passing her

by. She allowed one single tear to fall. *Balaam, I need you.* How many times had she laid awake after a beating from Braedon and cried for the only man she'd ever really love with all her heart, all the while trying to convince herself and everyone else that she'd shut the door on him? She'd lied to Ethan. She may have done her best to keep from following Balaam's career if only to protect her own heart that he'd crushed, but the longing for Balaam Carter had never ebbed.

Not once.

At times like this, it seeped through her soul like a raging river.

And Braedon had always known the truth.

## 11

The darkness told Balaam night had not yet ended when he opened his eyes. He lay in bed trying to repress the desire for a cold but warming glass of good Kentucky Bourbon over ice and the pill he'd swallow with it.

He brought down his fist hard onto the feather mattress. Jim told him each night would get easier and easier. Why, when he'd slept so good for the last couple of evenings would the demons seek him out now? Forty days and forty nights. Jesus had been tempted by Satan directly for this long. The sweet nurse from the hospital—she'd been a true angel, a messenger. Balaam had taken her life verse as his own. "Seek the Lord, and His strength: seek His face evermore." He quoted the scripture. "In Your strength, Lord, I can overcome."

He sat up and turned the key of the old lantern-style lamp, which sat on his bed stand. The room glowed in soft light. He pushed himself up and crossed the room, opening the drawer on the small desk by the window. He clasped the Bible, but his hands touched the envelope he'd received while in the hospital in Los Angeles. He pulled it out along with the Bible and moved back to his bed.

Balaam read for a few minutes, unable to concentrate on God's Word. The envelope beckoned to him, and he opened it, pulling out the multiple pages of names, addresses, and pertinent information about some pretty heavy drug dealers. Most of them he knew or knew of. He almost laughed at the irony of his situation. Here he sat with information at his fingertips that would give him all the drugs he desired.

He had no idea what he was expected to do with the data.

Balaam spread the papers in front of him, trying to find rhyme or reason. "Why me?" he whispered. "Why would you trust me?" He picked up sheet by sheet, tucking them back into the envelope one at a time. One name caught his attention, and he laughed. Someone who was really a "bad man" would never let anyone call them that. Had to be an alias. He shook his head and continued to read.

When he came to the second to last sheet, he realized he'd missed an attached Post-It. He pulled it out and read it.

Sweat broke out on his brow as he folded the paper and slipped it into his wallet laying on the bed stand. "Oh, Lord, help me to trust and to know what needs to be done." He'd talked to the note's author since receiving the package, but neither had mentioned the evidence. Balaam had wondered if it had come his way via that person at all. Now, he was sure of it, yet he was as perplexed as ever.

He picked up his Bible and allowed it to fall open where it may.

"'Jesus answered and said unto them, Verily I say unto you, If ye have faith, and doubt not, ye shall not only do this which is done to the fig tree, but also if ye shall say unto this mountain, be thou removed, and be thou cast into the sea; it shall be done. And all things, whatsoever ye shall ask in prayer, believing, ye shall receive.'"

Balaam slid from the bed and on to his knees. "I believe that You, Lord, can mend what's left of me. I believe that You have forgiven me even though I find it hard to forgive myself. I don't expect You to ever take away the images in my mind of those kids I might have allowed to slip into hell for my own gain, but Father, please use those images to strengthen me to do Your will and to save the lives of others. I believe that the papers in my hand are meant for good for others and not to tempt me. I believe, Lord, that You will protect my son and Lyric. Father, I believe that You have taken away my desire for alcohol and drugs, and I will rise from this closer to You and further away from self. And I believe most of all that You will move the mountain of pain built by everything I have ever done, and that You, Lord, will cast the hurt into the sea and return to me the treasure I tossed away so easily. Thank You, Father, for all that I have and will receive, what I deserve and what I do not. Please move these many mountains for me."

For some time, Balaam bowed his head in silence reverence. "I give you place, Father, as the one true God, and I thank You for Your mercy toward me when I thought I was more than this worm I have become. May I always exalt You and no other."

A sob that he'd struggled to press down caught in his throat and burst forth, breaking the silence of the home. He rocked back and forth, attempting to silence his desperation. So much belonged to God, and Balaam turned it over to Him. "My life, my talent, my dreams, my desires." He looked to Heavens. "My son. The woman that should have been my wife."

What had he done to Lyric? If not for him, Matthew and Braedon would be alive today.

Yet what were those verses Jim had asked him to memorize? Galatians? No. Ephesians. Ephesians 2, verses one through five. Balaam fumbled for the pages. He got off his knees and sat beside the bed, legs folded in front of him.

"'And you hath He quickened, who were dead in trespasses and sins; Wherein in time past ye walked according to the course of this world, according to the prince of the power of the air, the spirit that now worketh in the children of disobedience: Among whom also we all had our conversation in times past in the lusts of our flesh, fulfilling the desires of the flesh and of the mind; and were by nature the children of wrath, even as others. But God, who is rich in mercy, for His great love wherewith He loved us, Even when we were dead in sins, hath quickened us together with Christ, (by grace ye are saved;)'

"By your grace, Lord, I'm saved. There's no going backward. I need to march forward. The sooner the better. I'm going to sweat the desire for worldly pleasures away, and I'm going to serve You, and I'm going to start by memorizing these verses and distancing myself from the hell you delivered me from that I might pull others back as well."

Lyric held Balaam's letter to Cade in her trembling hands. Her son lay in his bed hanging to each word. "I know I've said this in each of my letters, but I can't say it enough. I'm so glad that you know the truth about me. I pray that we will have a lot of years together with you calling me Dad—that is an answer to prayer.

"I'm getting stronger every day, son. I can't promise you a date when I'll be home..." She stopped reading as the words pressed against her heart.

"Are you okay, Mom." Cade stared up at her, his eyes filled with questions.

Lyric nodded and cleared her throat. "And when I do get there, we can have that talk about me and about my brother. I want you to know the good things about Braedon and not what you'll hear from others. And just keep those Tuesdays open for ice cream, okay? I look forward to sharing that with just you. We can talk about Uncle

Matthew, and I can tattle on your mom and Uncle Quinn, too. Be good for them, Cade. I love you." She folded the letter and slipped it back into the envelope with her son's name written on the outside. Daniel must receive the letters in a proper envelope and hand them over to her. "A letter a week, Cade."

"He writes me back every time I write to him. He cares. He really cares about us."

She nodded without providing any other answer. If something better came along, some Hollywood starlet or another opportunity to get back on the road, Balaam would be gone, and her son would have a broken heart that would never mend.

Lyric was an expert on just how broken a heart could get. Cade's knowledge was a little too much, and she wanted Balaam to help her mend their child's brokenness.

"He'll be home soon, Mom. He said he would."

Lyric smiled. She stood and tucked the covers close to him. "'Night. Love you." She kissed his forehead.

He turned on his side, facing her. "I'm glad that when I go to sleep at night now I don't have to worry that Braedon will hurt you."

She knelt by his side. "I'm sorry you ever had that worry, but I promise, you'll never have to be afraid like that again."

He smiled so brightly that she saw Balaam as a child. "I love you, too."

"If not for you…"

"And for you. 'Night Uncle Quinn!" he yelled.

"'Night, Cade. See you in the morning," Quinn called from where Lyric had left him in the living room.

Lyric closed Cade's bedroom door and walked down the hall.

Quinn had stood from the kitchen table where he'd been studying for his sermon. Now, he stared out the kitchen window into the darkness. He turned and leaned against the counter, hands crossed over his chest. "You've avoided the subject for too long, Lyric. What is in those papers you mentioned, the ones Goodman asked you about?"

Her brother knew her all too well, and he'd been more patient than usual. Time had come to share as little as she could get away with. "They have to do with something Braedon brought home from Raleigh." She opened her refrigerator and held up a jug of sweet tea.

Quinn shook his head. "You've obviously not given him anything. Why is he still hanging around? As I understood it, he took off for a month, but he's still here."

If his story about a vacation was true, he should have left, but Lyric didn't say so. She poured herself a small bit of tea, enough to take the dryness from her throat. "He believes Braedon left me something the feds can use against Jessup and most of the kingpins all over this state."

Quinn pushed from the counter. "Braedon was mixed up with Jessup? I asked him to his face, and he told me he wasn't."

"Yeah, Balaam always said the same thing. Did you believe him, too?"

Quinn ran a hand through his sandy brown hair. "Yeah, I did."

Lyric couldn't help but smile. "Welcome to the club of people Balaam Carter lied to. Anyway, that's what Ethan told me. Braedon worked with Jessup. He was caught trafficking, and the FBI held that over his head in order to get him to work as an informant."

"Lyric, do you have it?" Quinn grasped her shoulders. "Please tell me you don't have what they want."

"I promise. I don't have what they want."

Quinn lifted his hand. "But you have something. What does Momma want from you?"

Lyric sat at the kitchen table. She allowed her gaze to wander to the living room then shut her eyes tight against the memory of Matthew's body falling into her.

"Lyric, what does she want?"

"Jessup is coercing her into finding all the papers Braedon brought with him from Raleigh, one set can harm him; the other information can destroy his operation and get him killed, I suppose. I think Momma's safe while she's in the mental health facility."

"Daniel, the assistant D.A., and even Judge Stowe are running out of ways to keep her inside. Momma's public defender, working on her behalf, has a bond hearing set early next week. She'll either be released without bond or if she's given a bond, sent to the county jail. Jessup can get to her there."

Lyric waved his words away. "Jessup is a lot of things, but an out-and-out murderer he is not. Too much entanglement. I don't even think he'd ask one of his puppets from the college to pull a trigger or slit a throat. But the information in the papers I've never seen apparently mean a lot to certain cartels in the state. Momma, though, isn't concerned for her safety. She just wants the booze that finding the papers will get her. She's not thinking clearly."

Quinn winced. "She is our mother, and even if she's going about it all wrong, I do think she cares for Cade. Doesn't that give you any compassion for her?"

"I'm sorry," she relented. "Quinn, I just don't care about her the way you do. She exhausted my love some time back."

"I understand, but I can't give up on her like you've done. I don't know why." Quinn kicked up his foot and pushed the heel of his shoe back against the toe of the other one.

"I'm beginning to understand the bond." She reached for his hand. "A son and his mother is a bond like a father and a daughter. There's some type of glue that bonds them."

"I'm sorry she hurt you the way she did when you asked her about your real dad."

She squeezed his hand in hers. "I thought if I ever learned the truth, I might be able to love her the way you do." She shook her head. "Well, that love never happened."

"At least I know where my dad is and…"

"You know a little of my pain. Let's leave it at that."

He nodded. "If Momma does get out, she's going to be desperate for a drink. You have part of what will get her that drink and back on Jessup's good side. She'll be relentless."

"And Stowe has to give her a bond. We'll know how desperate Jessup is, especially if Stowe believes he's made it beyond her capability to post bail. Jessup will get her out."

Quinn closed his eyes. "I don't want her in that jail. You can't either."

Lyric looked down at her hands. She couldn't hurt him with the truth. She'd be the first to testify to put her mother away. "I'm not sure what's more important to Jessup, the documents I do have or the ones that can destroy him."

"And you're sure you don't have the ones that the cartels could be after?"

"I don't. I've never seen them. If Braedon had them, he gave them to someone else. Maybe when Momma called him from the Backslide, he met up with another person. I don't know."

Quinn bent down in front of her. "What documents do you have?"

She shook her head. "What I have isn't important. What they want is."

"What you have may be the key to keeping Cade safe."

190

Lyric looked into his eyes, so different than hers. He apparently had his father's brown eyes, and Quinn's filled with love each time he looked at Lyric. Lyric had inherited her mother's blue eyes. Were hers growing as cold and indifferent as Madga Moxley's with each new day of dealing with the aftermath of Braedon's deeds.

"The news I have doesn't belong to you—not yet. I have to tell someone else first. I'm not sure I'll ever be able to do it, but if I do, I'll let you know."

"Why can't you tell this person?"

She stared into the depths of Quinn's gaze. "Because it will break his heart. We've had enough of that to last us a lifetime. I'm thinking of sparing him." And Quinn, most likely.

"So, it's come to this. You're placing a wall between us." He pushed up and paced away from her and back. "I guess the bed in your guestroom has my name written on it for a good, long while."

She nodded. Quinn had always been her protector. She was glad he had been staying with her. "I love you, Quinny." She stood and, on tiptoes, kissed his cheek.

"Will you answer two questions for me?"

She nodded without hesitating. After all that Quinn had done for her, two questions were the least he deserved.

"When Balaam comes back, are you going to tell Cade the truth?"

"He already knows." Her words came out in a rush.

"What?"

191

"Quinn, he saw it all. He heard everything. He was outside when it happened. He was running away from it. Daniel stopped him, took him to Grace's place. I learned it the day Daniel arrested Momma."

He sat hard in the kitchen chair, his face contorted. "He saw ..." As quickly as he sat, he jumped to his feet and walked down the hall. When he returned, he was pale. "Sleeping," he whispered the word. He paced between the kitchen and the living room then stopped in front of her. "He told you this. He said he saw it."

Lyric nodded, and it released the tears in her eyes.

Quinn's palm rested on the back of her head as he pulled her against him. "How, dear Lord, do we erase that from his tender mind? Help us, God, to protect his innocence."

She wouldn't remind him that God had nothing left for her because of her own stupidity. Maybe God would protect Cade because Quinn was doing the asking.

"Did he tell you he heard anything?"

"He heard it. He saw it. Brae screamed at me, accusing me of being loose, sleeping with Matthew like I'd done with Balaam. He asked me if I planned to have Matthew's child before I'd ever give him one. He called Cade Balaam's—"

Quinn put a finger to her lips before she could say the horrible name.

She buried her head against him. "I thought he loved me. I thought he'd love Cade like I love him—like he used to love and protect Balaam." She hiccupped and when Quinn didn't speak, she looked up at him.

Quinn's nostrils flared. His breath was uneven. "I should have kept good on my promise and killed him after the first time he hurt you."

"No, Quinny." She hugged him tight. "I know it's hard to believe, but Brae cared. Something got in the way of it, that's all. Something he couldn't get over—"

"Balaam."

She nodded. "He could never believe—probably because he sensed it—that I'd never truly let Balaam go. And he was afraid. Sometimes I would swear he was frightened. I'd ask him, but he'd never tell me. On occasion, he'd be so tender to me, as if he were afraid to lose me."

Quinn pulled from her. "I don't want to hear about it. He hurt Cade. That's all I need to know." He paced away and back once more. "Will you allow Balaam to see Cade?"

"Balaam's been really good about everything. They've corresponded since he left. Cade writes him a letter and gives it to Daniel. Daniel brings him a letter Bay's sent back.

"His writing a few letters doesn't mean he has the right—"

"He has the right to be the father he ought to be. What he did to me is between him and me. What he did to Cade is up to Cade to forgive or not, and Cade takes after you. He forgives very easily, and if Balaam keeps doing right by our son, if he stays away from the drugs, I'll give him every chance to provide Cade with what you and I never had."

"You're right. Let Balaam prove himself. He's a serious addict, and I'm praying he can lay the drugs aside, but until we're sure, we need to keep an eye on him when he's with Cade."

Lyric forced a smile for her brother's worried heart. "I agree. But you need to realize that Magda's pretty much a loser, and look how we turned out."

"Because we had each other." He stepped to her. "Balaam needs Cade. Make him work for his son. He'll be all that more precious to him."

"You had another question."

He smiled. "Yeah. You aren't falling for this Ethan character, are you? I'm not sure about him. When he grabbed you that way, I wanted to do what I never did to Braedon."

The warmth climbed from her neck up to her face. "I have a little boy who just lost the man he once thought of as his dad and one of his uncles. That happened because I've been careless most of my life. I trusted Balaam when he said he loved me. I did the same with Brae. I thought I could learn to love him, but the truth is, I never got over his brother. With my past history of choosing losers, I'm not falling for anyone."

"If Balaam pulls through this and wants to renew your relationship, what will you do?"

She walked away from him. "I answered your two questions. Now, I'm going to sleep. Your bed is made." She wiggled her fingers at him "Sweet dreams."

# FAY LAMB

## 12

Lyric paced outside of the Amazing Grace Sheriff's Department. The town had never incorporated, and since the town of Amazing Grace was located in the county of Amazing Grace, Daniel had been the sheriff for as long as she'd known him. No one could win against him. No one even tried anymore and probably never would unless Jessup Roy gave them reason. And getting Daniel out of his way seemed to be a mixture of personal dislike and good business sense on Jessup's part.

She kept a careful watch out for anyone sneaking up on her and slipped her fingers into the bookbag she held. Never one to carry a purse, she thought tugging out one from the inner depths of her closet and slinging it over her shoulder would cause suspicion.

She'd been a reader until Balaam left. Every novel seemed to have some element of romance, and when he'd left, she realized romantic love was truly fiction. She'd even made a trip through the library to complete here ruse.

197

She'd dug the papers out of their hiding place—under the back deck of her home, accessed via a wide entry used in case of plumbing or other problems. When Braedon left her on that fateful day, she'd hurriedly slipped the papers into a plastic bag, crawled to a far corner under the house, and buried the envelope containing the papers deep enough to keep anyone from easily seeing it. Now, plastic left in the trash at home, she carried the papers in her bookbag while she paced, trying to get the nerve up to go inside and face Daniel.

A deputy walked out of the building and tipped his hat at her before heading toward his patrol car.

Enough of this stalling. She needed to get a move on.

With a hefty push, she entered the familiar building with its open reception and half-wall, half-windowed rooms. Daniel's was to the right after she passed the reception area and the corridor behind it that led to the interrogation room.

There'd been a lot of Daniel-imposed detentions in that room. She and Matthew probably endured the least of them.

Matthew.

They were going on seven weeks now since the deaths. Either the town had lost interest in the melodrama, or Lyric had become immune to the stares and the gossip. Maybe with Magda still in the mental hospital, people were relieved to have her gone. Perhaps Quinn and Lyric had become heroes for a short span until the woman got out and spewed her venom again.

"Hey." Daniel stepped out of somewhere back beyond his office door. "You okay?"

She nodded, steadying her nerves. "Do you have a place we can have some real privacy? I got something to tell you."

Daniel stared at her for a long moment before nodding. Then he motioned her into his office.

She stilled and shook her head. "I mean private."

"No one can hear what we have to say," Daniel coaxed.

"But they can see."

He quirked his head to the side and chewed on his bottom lip as if deciding. Then he held up his hand, a silent way of telling her to wait where she was. He walked down the hall, peered into a room, and motioned her to him.

He stepped inside and turned on the lights to the breakroom. "Daniel, I don't…"

He tugged her inside, shut the door, and turned the lock. The he motioned for her to sit at the small table in the windowless room that contained a refrigerator, sink, microwave, and the chairs and table where they sat. He held out one of the blue scoop-like seats. She slinked down into the ugly thing.

He sat across from her.

A long moment passed before he leaned forward. "What's so important I have to separate my deputies from their coffee?"

Breaking the ice. Daniel knew how to do it better than anyone.

Lyric peered up at him from underneath the too-long bangs of curls, thankful they shadowed her eyes from seeing the pain she was about to dole out to him.

Bookbag plunked into her lap, she pulled out the envelope she'd kept hidden all this time. As she'd lain awake last night, she'd realized that the only reason she hadn't done this sooner is that she was waiting for a man to help her break Daniel's heart—not just any man: Balaam.

Though the letters to Cade had continued, he made no mention of when he'd be back, only that he would return. Even her son seemed to shed his optimism and crawl back into a shell of morose.

This was her job to do and no one else's. If the truth got out before Daniel knew, he wouldn't have time to answer for it, and there was a chasm growing between Daniel and Quinn that needed to be closed.

"Is that for me?" Daniel pointed toward the envelope.

"Daniel, I'm awful sorry that I've held on to these since Braedon left them on my table before he went to the Backslide. I hid them while he was gone even though I really think if he meant to give them to the person who wanted them, he would have taken them with him. When he came back, everything happened so fast. Agent Goodman began to demand things from me, and I realized that I don't have what the feds want. I have something that doesn't concern anyone but me… and… and… you."

Daniel seemed to breathe deeper and deeper with each moment that passed, but he said nothing.

"Jessup Roy wants these, but they belong to you." She bit her trembling lip then managed to find a way to speak around the emotion tearing up her insides. "Jessup suspects he knows what these say, but I don't think he can use them against you unless he has them. I wouldn't let that happen. No one has to know, if you don't want them to know. And…" She swallowed hard, her next words a lie that could rip her asunder. "And if you don't want anyone to know but us, I'll understand."

He started to reach for the envelope.

She pulled it back. "Let me finish. I've let this run through my head so much, I gotta say it."

He nodded.

She waited a minute, composing herself. When she gained the courage, she looked him straight in the eye. "There's something in here that's gonna hurt you bad, and I'm the cause of it. I want you to know right now how very sorry I am for my part in it. Daniel, I'd never hurt you for the world. You've always been good to me even when you didn't know—"

"Didn't know what? Sweetheart, there is nothing you could do that would make me ever not want to be good to you or to Quinn."

With her index finger, Lyric slid the envelope to him. Then she stood and faced away from him, arms wrapped around her like the cloth of a straightjacket to ward off the trembling her fear of his reaction caused.

Behind her, the envelope crinkled as Daniel pulled out the two single pieces of paper and the legal document that Lyric had memorized. The single papers shuffled and then the pages of the legal document were turned and then silence.

The tortuous emotions began deep within her, and she fought to hold them down. The sobs caught in her throat, and she battled against them to remain completely still, giving him time to absorb what he had in his hands. She lost the war within herself and put her hands to her face, deep, guttural sobs pouring forth, so strong that she had to gasp to breathe air back into her lungs.

Then she was turned and held tightly.

Daniel's body quaked as badly as hers as they cried together.

"Sheriff, you okay?" a female deputy knocked.

Daniel took a second to call out. "I'm fine. Tell everyone the breakroom's closed until I say otherwise."

"Yes, sir."

Daniel tipped her chin up to look at him. "I'm so sorry. I'm so sorry, sweetheart. I didn't know. I had no idea." He wiped the tears from her face and then off of his own. "You shouldn't have carried this alone all this time. Why didn't you come to me?"

"I was afraid you'd hate me."

"Oh, honey, no. I'm angry with myself." He led her to

the chair and bent in front of her. "I watched you both grow up. You all were so beautiful and smart and talented. He was such a good kid, handsome, smart, and talented like you."

"You had no way of knowing, and I'm the reason you'll never—"

He put a finger to her lips. "You're the reason for a lot of joy in this old guy's heart right now. That joy is drowning out a lot of sadness and anger that I'm sure will come later, but none of it will be caused by you." He pulled her to him again. Then he stood quickly and paced away, his back to her.

Lyric stepped as far from him as she could. If he'd realized what she'd cost him, and if he grew angry, she could scream for help. That would buy them time to help her.

Daniel turned and his eyes widened. He shook his head and smiled. "I'm not angry if that's what you're thinking."

"I don't know how you can't be angry with me."

"I just told you. You're not to blame in any of this." He hurried toward her and lifted her into the air. "What shocked me for a minute is that I'm not only someone's dad. I'm a grandpa, and Granny Grace, she's your real Granny."

He sat her down, and Lyric widened her eyes and covered her mouth with her hands. What had been terror and sadness now morphed into something akin to hope. "We can have the DNA testing."

Daniel's happiness seemed to ebb. "If you'd like, but I don't need any other proof than what you've shown me and what I see almost every day staring back at me."

"She could have lied on the birth certificates. How did she manage the adoption without you?"

Daniel closed his eyes. "I'm afraid that my old friend Larry Roberts is a crafty lawyer, and his friend, Edwin Stowe, probably thought he was doing at least one babe a favor, taking him away from your momma."

Why would Judge Stowe take Matthew away from Momma and not Lyric? "Matthew had a good life, but in the end, the fact that I was left with our mother is what eventually caused his death. Your daughter cost you your son's life."

"Did you have any idea that he was your brother?" Daniel bent down again, looking into her eyes.

"No."

"In hindsight, I should have seen it. You both had the same dark hair and the olive skin as your Momma. Maybe it was the fact that Matthew's hair was straight like mine—and Quinn's. You got those beautiful curls from your Granny." He seemed lost in thought for a second. Then he nodded. "Matthew looked like my dad—your grandpa's— side of the family. Thinking back, I believe he had Magda's high cheekbones. You both had your mother's eyes. But unless you were told, you couldn't have had any idea that Matthew was your brother."

"But I think we both felt something—a kinship.

Something ran deep between us. And he did say he wanted to talk to me. I guess I'll never know whether he knew or not."

"They say that happens to twins, even those who are separated."

Daniel was trying to placate her, but she detected no animosity in his tone, only love. Unconditional love. For her. For Matthew.

"I'm sorry that I waited so long to tell you."

"So am I." He mussed her hair as if she were a child again. "I would have liked to have been there for you. As it was, I didn't feel I had the right."

"And you're really not angry with me?" she begged for the answer.

"No, Lyric Kay. I love you. And I love Matthew. And you know who else I love?"

She looked up at him, shaking her head, the tears running like an erratic stream.

"Quinn. When I was with your momma, I had hope that the demons wouldn't return. You know, way back then, she didn't drink. She had some mental problems. I suspect something happened when she was a kid, but she didn't compound her sorrows with the alcohol." He seemed to think for a long minute. Then he nodded. "She left town for a long while. When she returned, she had you. Bernice had been pregnant, and she'd lost the baby late term. When Larry announced the adoption, no one asked any questions. That might have been around the time your momma started drinking. Before she left town—I guess when she was pregnant with you—I had confronted her about her treatment of Quinn, and I'd threatened her. Magda didn't take well to that. I suspect that her giving Matthew up for adoption, and having both of you in my presence, was her way of getting back at me."

"She never cared what my finding out would do to me or to Matthew either. I do believe something in her soused mind made her believe Matthew was more than a friend to me. So, she put Braedon up to ending it by killing me. Matthew wasn't the one he was aiming for. Braedon had the gun pointed at me. I had no doubt that he planned to pull the trigger." Lyric sat back hard in the chair and looked up at him. "I even wanted him to kill me. Brae would have to live with what he'd done to me, but I wouldn't have to live with what I'd done to everyone else. When Matthew moved to push me away, I was horrified. He was my twin brother, and Brae was going to kill him... and he did. I never got to tell him. By the time Brae shot himself and fell on me, and I pushed my way to Matthew, he was unconscious. I kept begging him to stay with me. I told him I was his sister, and I needed him." She took a deep, staggering breath. "I needed him. I needed him so much." She bent forward and then rocked back and forth trying to get the memory out of her mind. "And Larry and Bernice, they hated me, but I hated me even worse. I hate Momma for what she did, and... and I couldn't tell Quinn because you needed to know first." She'd worked herself into a hiccupping cry. "I want Quinn. Daniel, I want Quinn. Please get him for me. Please."

The breakroom door opened, and Lyric straightened from the slouched position she'd held since Daniel raced from the room. Daniel had returned to tell her that Quinn was on his way. She'd taken his hand, and held to it, still staring at the floor.

Quinn entered and shut the door. "What is it? Is she in trouble?"

Daniel released her hand and pulled up a chair beside her for Quinn to sit. When her brother sat, Lyric fell against him.

"Lyric?" Daniel asked.

He didn't need to ask. "I want you to please stay," she pleaded.

"What is it? You're frightening me." Quinn slipped his arm around her. "Is Cade all right?"

"Cade's fine." Daniel sat in a chair in front of them. "Mom's picking him up from school."

"Then tell me," Quinn urged. "Is it Momma?"

Lyric gave a half-laugh. "It's always about Momma, Quinn. Haven't you figured that out yet?"

"What's she done now? She wasn't released from the mental health facility. Judge Stowe's been pretty good about keeping her there."

Lyric shared a look with Daniel. "Momma's still locked down. I think if Stowe could keep her there forever, he would."

"So tell me. What's all this about? You both look like you've walked away from a funeral."

Daniel clasped his hands together and stared down at the floor.

"In a way, we have." She straightened and touched Quinn's face. "You're angry at Daniel."

Quinn's jaw clenched and released.

Daniel raised his gaze.

"I'm working on forgiveness. I want you to know that. You've been too much to us over the years for me to hang on to it, but your sleeping with her like every man in town, it hurts, Daniel."

Lyric had let Momma go a long time ago. Quinn never had.

But now he had someone better to hold on to. "Quinn, what if I told you that if Momma hadn't slept with Daniel, you wouldn't have me?"

Quinn looked from her to Daniel and back again.

Daniel leaned backward and carefully chose one of the papers he'd left there.

He showed it to Quinn.

Quinn's hand trembled as he read the truth, and Lyric placed her hand over his. "I've known Daniel slept with her since the day Braedon killed Matthew."

Quinn continued to stare at the birth certificate. Then

he turned to her. "Why do I feel there's more coming?"

"I'm not the only one who was here because Daniel cared about Momma. He said he did, and I believe him. He tried, and she's never been stable enough to understand that she deserves to be happy."

Quinn straightened.

"When I was born, Momma put Daniel down as the father on my birth certificate."

"I see that."

"Jessup wants the certificate to blackmail Daniel into submission or to get him out of his job, so Jessup can keep up his trade without Daniel's interference, perhaps back someone he can control."

"But Momma could have confirmed he's your father? That's all Jessup would need."

Lyric shook her head. "If she did, would anyone believe her?"

"You have a point."

"But Braedon came back with a couple more documents. I don't believe Momma realized that whoever provided the proof to Braedon had given him more than my information. Braedon didn't open the package, and if Momma had known what he had, she never would have done what she did to make Brae so mad at me."

Quinn stood and paced. "What did he find?"

"Another birth certificate and adoption papers."

Quinn startled and sat again. "We have another sister or brother."

Lyric shook her head, her time for mourning past. This moment belonged to Quinn. "I had a twin brother."

Quinn didn't move.

"Someone had to pull strings. I told you he was working both sides. Maybe a federal agent or someone. I don't know how those things work." Her hands trembled first then her body began to quake again. "It doesn't make sense, Quinny. None of it makes sense. Why would Momma endanger her own son?" She looked to the ceiling, willing her eyes to remain dry. "Matthew was our brother, and Momma sent Brae home to kill me, and he killed Matt instead."

Quinn's arms wrapped around her, cradling her. She sobbed against him now, her arms wrapped under his, her hands clinging to his shoulders. "I'm so sorry. I'm sorry for the pain I've caused you. But make it go away, Quinny. Make this all go away."

He held to her for a long time until Daniel cleared his throat. "Quinn, I've lost one son. My relationship with the other boy that I have long wished was mine is hanging in the balance here. Please forgive me for the pain I caused you, and let me love you and Lyric the way I was always meant to love you—as my own."

"But you're not," Quinn's whispered words cut through the room.

"I want to be."

Quinn stared at him for a long moment. Then he shook his head. "There was a time, a very long time ago, when that's all I ever wanted. It didn't happen." Quinn held out his hand. "But not forgiving you would be like saying you haven't given me the most precious thing in my life. My sister means everything to me. Thank you for that."

Daniel held out his hand and gave Quinn's a firm grasp. Then he hugged Lyric, kissed her on the top of the head, turned, and walked out of the room.

The next morning, Daniel leaned back in his high-backed office chair. He pressed his hands together and brought the tips of them to his lips. Lyric had stopped by and had a cup of coffee with him. She'd kissed his cheek before she left and said she wanted to check on Quinn since Grace asked Cade to help her out with some small chores at the store.

They hadn't told his mother or Cade about the news, wanting to give Quinn time to soak it all in.

Never had it occurred to him that conflicting emotions could tear you in two. His happiness at the discovery that he was Lyric's father battled with the sorrow of the two sons he'd lost—one his natural, flesh and blood, and the other the little boy he'd wanted to love as a father and had never gotten the chance.

If only he'd handled things differently back then. He could have had Magda put away. They'd have placed Quinn in his custody, or Mom would have cared for him.

The truth blew that self-composed idea right out of the water. Perhaps if he'd done more for Desiree—but no. Losing his wife to another man was what had thrown him into Magda's embrace, had shown him how much some of these kids in the town needed someone to look after them. Yet, Quinn had been so much more.

He closed his eyes and leaned back his head.

"Hi, Sheriff Daniel."

A smile crossed his face before he even took a look. When he opened his eyes, the little tow-headed boy was standing by his chair. He'd gotten that hair from Balaam's side of the family. Matthew and Lyric had inherited Magda's dark hair.

Daniel quirked his head a bit. Why hadn't he ever noticed Cade's green eyes? The boy had gotten them from his grandfather same as him.

Cade tilted his head a bit, mimicking Daniel.

Daniel laughed and ruffled the wispy locks. "What's up, little man."

"Granny Grace said we should come in and take you to lunch."

"Where is Granny Grace?" He pushed to his feet and stood beside the boy. His mother would learn the truth of his indiscretion. He'd see her disapproval of his actions, but Grace Dixon learning she was a grandma and a great-grandma, that was a gift Daniel never thought he'd be able to give to her.

His mother tottered through the door. "Hello, Danny

212

Boy. Cade told you we're not accepting no for an answer, didn't he? We're going to lunch. What do you say? Cade and I have a hankering for some pineapple upside down cake."

"Mom, that does not a lunch make."

"We'll finish it off with some soup or a sandwich, won't we, Cade?"

"Yes, ma'am."

Daniel grabbed his hat and his sunglasses from his desk and his coat from the coat rack. "Well, let's go then." They walked out into the main room of the station. He waved to the deputy on reception duty, pointed to his watch, and held up his finger then turned back to his mom. "Did Lyric go to the church?"

"Yeah, honey, she did," his mother answered. "She'd been gone a while, but Cade and I drove past just to check. They're both there."

"Did you happen to see a deputy parked nearby?" He gritted his teeth. She'd better have spotted one.

"We sure did. Joe Abner's on the job."

Daniel held open the door and let the two of them pass. Good for Abner—for a change.

"There was another car sitting back off the road, too." His mother raised a brow.

Daniel stopped.

"Agent Goodman." Grace nodded. "Lyric is well guarded."

And Goodman was going to hear about this. He should

have left town weeks ago. Daniel had tolerated just about enough from that guy.

Lunch first then he'd take care of the problem.

# 13

Ethan stared out the window of his car and up to the mountains to the east. Dark clouds lowered themselves to the earth, crowning the barren trees. He heaved a deep breath and blew it out quickly.

The airwaves crackled on the listening device. "Quinn, I'm sorry you had to learn the truth the way you did. You've had a rough time of it." Lyric sniffled when she spoke.

He'd accidentally, on purpose, run into her earlier when she'd bought two cups of coffee at Manna from Heaven. She wore a heavy jacket, and he'd slipped the device in one of her pockets.

He winced. If she had her hands inside the pocket, he'd be found out.

And Daniel Dixon might not kill him, but he'd make Ethan wish he had.

"Here," she said.

"Thanks." Quinn blew his nose, and Ethan winced at

the loud noise. "I'm going to see Momma again this evening. Do you want to come?"

"Why do you do this to yourself? She's never loved us. Isn't Matthew's death proof enough?" Lyric challenged.

"She must have thought you were sleeping with Matt. She wanted Braedon to separate you."

Lyric gasped. "I never... I would never have slept with Matthew. And your intimating that I would have slept with him before I knew the truth means that you think I'd have slept with any man who gave me attention—that I'd cheat on my husband. Quinn, that angers me.

A swooshing sound came through the device. Her jacket in movement, her hands brushing the outside of the pockets. Footsteps. Ethan grasped the steering wheel.

"Lyric, wait." Heavier footsteps sounded. "Lyric, I didn't mean it that way."

Lyric exited the church. The slamming door right in Quinn's face was proof she was angrier than a hornet sprayed by a water hose.

The deputy sitting close to the church took notice and flipped open his cell phone.

Ethan blinked. Sheriff Dixon would better be reached via the transmitter in the man's vehicle or the transmitter he wore on his shoulder, not a cell phone.

He jumped as Lyric slammed her car door, the noise rattling through his car. She started the car and roared away. Ethan started his vehicle. He'd have to get around the corner of the church in time to follow her.

She was racing down the side street when he caught up with her, staying a bit behind, out of sight. He didn't want to see her get hurt. Emotionally, she was a wreck. Physically, she was beautiful.

Her house wasn't far. She pulled into the driveway and rushed for the door. He pulled up, again keeping out of sight.

She stopped then began stepping backward, hands raised.

A man exited her home, a gun in his hand. A kid really. A green kid who'd blundered by not allowing her to enter the home—a kid with an overanxious look on his face.

The fellow motioned Lyric forward. Outside, it was one on one. Inside, it became a hostage situation. Ethan couldn't let that happen.

He slipped from his car, pulling his automatic from his holster. He dug for the cell phone in his pocket and dialed. "This is Agent Ethan Goodman. I need back up at ..." He turned to look for a sign. "Get me backup. Lyric Carter's place. Man with a gun on premises. Hostage situation."

Daniel's shoulder transmitter crackled. "Sheriff. Ethan Goodman called for backup at the Carter home—Braedon Carter's home. You copy."

"Copy."

"Says there's a man with a gun."

"Abner?" Daniel nodded to his mother and to the little frightened boy. "It'll be okay, Cade. You wait here with Granny Grace. I'll bring your mom to you. Abner?" he repeated the question into the radio.

"Got no idea, Sheriff. Goodman indicated it's a hostage situation."

"Get an idea." He ran for his car, flipped on the lights, leaving the sirens silent.

She lived only blocks away from downtown. Daniel swung his car into the drive and reached for his shotgun, pumping it as he stepped onto the concrete.

Goodman had a steady hand on his gun.

Lyric was by her car, hands in the air, her face stoic. The world had toughened her too much.

She looked at Daniel.

He raised a hand. Stay.

She nodded her understanding.

"Put the gun down, Bozo," Goodman barked the command. "This is the last time I'm telling you." His jaw worked pretty hard on a piece of gum. Probably a subconscious way to focus on the perp.

"Do as he says, Henry. You don't want to die for Jessup's ends, do you?" Daniel reasoned.

"Who said I'm working for Jessup?" The boy's hands shook.

Daniel hitched a look at Goodman. The man wasn't bluffing. If Henry Hoffman didn't surrender his gun or his hostage, he was going to meet the Maker... at one judgment or the other.

"Okay, Henry, so you were robbing the house. Mrs. Carter came home too soon. Put the gun down. Let's get you booked, and let your momma bail you out. She's done it before."

"Take the gun off of her, now." Goodman ordered, chomping harder on the gum.

Henry's hand shook. His finger played with the trigger. Not a good combination when the gun was pointed at Lyric.

His daughter stood straight as an arrow.

She'd been through this once before, only this time, it wasn't her husband with the gun.

"I'd do it, Henry. Drop the gun. This standoff is over."

"Henry," Lyric said. "Braedon died because Jessup Roy put him into a whole heap of trouble. My own husband tried to kill me, and he killed Matthew Roberts when no one should have had to die that day. Put the gun down and let Daniel take you in. You know as well as I do that he's a fair man. Jessup ain't a killer, but people who deal with him or work with him end up dead. Don't let him do that to you."

Henry tightened his quaking grip and lifted the gun's barrel. Daniel motioned Goodman off but didn't look to see if the agent obeyed his command. If the guy could get a shot and not hurt Daniel's daughter, he'd be okay. Goodman was taking a big chance because if Lyric had one scratch on her, Daniel would end the agent's career with a bullet placed somewhere that he'd never be able to work again. Still, they needed a bluff. He only hoped Goodman read it as such. "Henry, Jessup sent you here to find something you didn't come across. There's no reason for you to become a killer, spend your life in jail, that is if Goodman lets you keep your life. I'm taking my hands off the situation. Goodman, he's yours."

"Wait." Henry screamed, raising the gun into the air and firing off three shots before lowering the gun to his side and dropping it to the ground. With each boom, Lyric's body jerked as if she'd been shot.

She turned away, facing the car, hands over her face.

Goodman had good concentration. Even Daniel might have shot the boy. Goodman pounced on the kid, kicking the gun toward Daniel, and knocking Henry off his feet to lay face down on the ground.

Lyric crumbled to her knees. When Daniel wrapped his arms around her, she screamed and drew away. Recognition dawned in her eyes, and she fell against him hard. "I'm sorry. I'm so sorry."

"Nothing to be sorry for, darlin'." He helped her to her feet.

By the time Abner pulled in, Goodman had Henry handcuffed. The agent thundered past Daniel's deputy and stuffed him into Abner's patrol car. "Where were you? Your reaction time could have cost her life."

Lyric lifted her face to the agent but remained in

Daniel's hold. A question formed in the lift of her brow.

"He's been watching out for you." That was as good as she was going to get from him until he knew what the agent was doing. Goodman had declared his investigation was over. What purpose did he have for hanging around?

"Are you okay?" Goodman approached.

Lyric buried herself in Daniel's embrace once again, but she wasn't crying.

"She's fine, Ethan. You?"

"I'd be better if he'd given me a reason to kill him."

Lyric turned steely blue eyes in his direction. "He's a kid. Jessup has all of them wrapped around his fingers. He wouldn't have killed me. I'd have talked him out of it, even let him go on his way if you'd minded your own business, Agent Goodman."

Now, there was no doubt in Daniel's mind. This gal was his daughter.

The idiot, Abner, stood looking at them.

Daniel rounded on him. "Get him to the station, and you stay there." Not that he'd be there long after Daniel's return. The guy was a liability.

Abner ducked into the car and pulled out, barely missing Quinn who skirted death by jumping out of the way. Quinn drew close and stopped. He eyed Daniel then his sister. "What happened?"

"Jessup had one of his boys here waiting for her."

Lyric twisted from his arms without looking to Quinn. She started toward the door. Goodman ran ahead, barring her entrance. She stopped when he motioned. Goodman, gun raised, moved into the house. When he stepped out a few minutes later, he opened the door for her. They both went inside.

"What's going on between you and your sister?" Daniel asked him.

Quinn shook his head.

"No idea or a pretty good idea?" Daniel moved to his car and replaced the shotgun. He closed the door and leaned against it.

"Pretty clear idea." Quinn squinted against the bright Carolina sun.

"You're mad at me, boy. Don't take it out on her."

"I'm—I didn't mean to. The words just fell out."

Daniel pushed from the car. "What words?"

Quinn looked as ragged as Lyric. He didn't answer.

Daniel wouldn't press. "If you want to talk to me about any of this, I'll be available."

"She knew before I did." Quinn started toward the door.

"What do you mean she knew?" Daniel grabbed his arm. "About me?"

"I know I said I could forgive you, but the same thought keeps pounding at me."

"What thought is that?"

"You're the reason Matthew's dead. If you'd lived up to your obligations—no, if you hadn't have done what you did, none of this would have happened." Quinn's cheeks rose as he gritted his teeth. Then he sighed, and he slumped forward. "Then again, there'd be no Lyric. And I couldn't have made it without her. My insides are pulling apart. I don't know whether to love you or to hate you." He leaned back against Lyric's car.

"I've been feeling that tug myself about Magda, but I'm not going to apologize to you for my relationship with your Momma. I've asked God for His forgiveness, but as you said, amid this entire mess, something good and lovely came forth. She's your sister, Quinn. I know you lost a brother." Daniel thumped his hand against his chest. "But she's my daughter, and I've lost two sons."

"Two…? Your first wife?"

Daniel cuffed Quinn's face with his hand. "I lost you. I wanted to be your father. I tried. I did make a mistake. I handled something badly, but Quinn…" He placed his hand over his heart. "In here, I've always thought of you as mine."

Quinn stared down at the ground without speaking.

"We're all hurting now. So much death and trouble. I'm working on making things right, but God's in those details. Don't you forget that, Preacher." Daniel grasped Quinn's arm.

Quinn shrugged from his hold and walked into the house.

Daniel walked slowly to his car and sat inside. During the months he'd been with Magda, he'd taken Quinn everywhere with him. The boy was thoughtful and good.

He never gave Magda any trouble. But when the depression sunk its claws deep into her, Magda gave Quinn plenty of trouble. The poor kid could do nothing right. One day, Daniel had opened his door to find Quinn, teary faced and not old enough to be out alone. "Daniel, please be my daddy," Quinn had begged.

And that's when Daniel had made the biggest mistake of his life.

Daniel started his car and pulled down the street away from Lyric's house and his mother's home across the street.

He stopped the car. "Magda." Her name flew from his lips like a curse. "Why? What did you have to gain? What did Larry and Bernice give you for our child?" And why Matthew and not Lyric?

Daniel needed to find out.

"Sheriff," his transmitter sounded.

"Yeah."

"Officer down. Civilian reports Abner's car is off the road on Old Jericho Road."

"Old Jericho Road? I sent him back to the station. He was transporting a prisoner."

"I have units responding."

"I'm on my way." He signed off and picked up his cell phone and punched the number given to him, one he thought he'd never use. The phone rang three times.

"Goodman," the agent barked his greeting.

"Stay with them. I'll brief you later. I'm asking a deputy to escort my mother and Cade to the house. Keep them there until I return."

"Yes, sir."

Daniel ended the call and dialed his office to have his mother and Cade brought home safely. He wouldn't use his transmitter. Someone already knew too much. Something wasn't right. Jessup didn't work this way. Yeah, he was dirty and mean, but he didn't kill cops. Frightening young women and providing people with the drugs that would ruin their lives or kill them was more his style. A cold shaft of dread filled Daniel. He needed answers, and he needed them now.

Quinn narrowed his eyes at his sister. Lyric wasn't listening to him. She was hurt, and Quinn was lost. He nodded to Ethan and moved to the family room at the back of the house. He pulled out his wallet and his phone along with the sheet of paper with the name and number of Balaam's California rehab. He'd been gone longer than rehab should take. Surely, the facility would allow someone who'd been with them this long to take a call, especially from a pastor. "Yes, ma'am. This is Reverend Quinn Moxley from Amazing Grace, North Carolina. I have a friend at your facility. Balaam Carter. Is he allowed phone calls from clergy?"

The woman didn't answer, but he heard her nails clicking the keyboard. "Balaam? Could you spell that name for me?"

No use telling her it was a Biblical name about a guy and a jackass. "B-A-L-A-A-M Carter."

"Hold one moment, sir." Soft, smoothing music ripped at Quinn's last nerve while he waited to hear Balaam's voice. "Sir, our information is confidential, but I did check. We've never had anyone by that name here."

"Are you sure? I'm a pastor. He asked me to phone him when he could receive calls."

"No, sir. Balaam Carter has not been admitted."

"Thank you." Quinn ended the call.

"Everything okay?" Ethan stepped into the room.

"No. Our world is falling in. You're here harassing my sister over documentation she doesn't have. I've hurt her so badly that she'll never talk to me again."

Lyric leaned around the corner. "Ah, Quinny, never is a long time."

Quinn reached for her, and she came to him.

"I'm sorry, sis." He brushed her dark strands from her face. She reminded him of the freckled face little brat she'd once been.

"You know that nothing like that ever happened between Matthew and me. We didn't think of each other like that. Never. We were close. So close. Like you and me."

She was skirting because of Ethan.

"I didn't choose my words correctly. I never, not once, believed that about you." He pulled her head to his chest and held her there. "Why don't you go lie down? Cade will be home in a minute. I'll send him in so you can see he's okay."

She shook her head. "Dinner."

"We'll get more pizza. Cade will be happy, and Ethan will pay." Quinn winked at the agent.

"Gladly." Ethan chomped on his gum. "Go get some rest, Lyric. Quinn and I are on the job."

"I'll wait for my son." She paced to the front of the house and peered out the kitchen window. Then she went to the door and opened it.

Cade ran inside followed by a slower moving Grace.

"Daniel's instructions were for all of us to stay under this roof." She put her purse on the table. "Good thing I don't need the business."

"Grace, I'm sorry," Lyric said.

"Oh, honey. I'm not worried about that old place. I keep it for a hobby. Let those two girls learn a little about what you do for me in one day. It'll be good for them."

"Are you tired? Would you like to take a nap? Cade and I are."

"If I take a nap now, I won't sleep tonight. You go rest. You've been through an ordeal. Cade, take care of your momma."

"Do I have to? Can't I stay up with Uncle Quinn? I'm too big for naps."

"Do as your momma says, Cade," Quinn said. "We'll do something together later."

Lyric led him down the hall.

He started into his room.

"Hey," she said. "I know you haven't asked me to come sleep in your room for a long time, but could you come sleep in my room? Mom kind of needs to know you're safe."

Cade looked back down the hallway at Quinn.

Quinn gave him a slight wink and a nod. "Thanks," he mouthed.

Cade followed Lyric to her room.

Grace sat on the couch. "So, boys, you playing nice, or do I have to wallop both of you to get you to behave?"

How did that old woman know his every mood?

"We're playing nice." Ethan peered out the window then glanced at Quinn. "What do you know about that lame-brained deputy who works for Sheriff Dixon?"

Quinn smiled. That description fit Abner pretty well. "He's never been too bright. Easily swayed, a bully at times. Daniel uses him carefully and guides him every inch of the way. I get the idea he won't be Daniel's problem after his lapse today. Why?"

"He took his sweet time getting here when he was supposed to follow Lyric."

"And how did you get here so quickly?" Quinn sat beside Grace. "I should have been the first one here. She was with me."

"I was looking out for her. Good thing, huh?"

Quinn didn't answer nor did he argue. Ethan had done what Quinn had failed to do—protect his baby sister. He'd failed to protect his little brother, too. He rubbed tired eyes.

And to add to it, Balaam had lied to them. There was no rehab. He'd probably never come home again.

Cade would be heartbroken.

And despite every protest she'd given for it not being true, Lyric would never get over another one of Balaam's betrayals.

**FAY LAMB**

# 14

"Bay?" The light knock at his door silenced his dream.

Shepherd's Rock, Lyric, and Cade vanished as he turned over. "Yeah," he mumbled.

"Phone call," Jim said. "You decent?"

"Yeah," he said again and rolled off the bed and onto his feet. Jim opened the door as Balaam threw on his shirt. He ran his hand over his short hair and yawned. It'd been weeks, but he still wasn't used to it. "Who is it?"

"Daniel."

Balaam followed the old preacher down the hall to the only line of communication in the house. Picking up the hand piece of the old rotary dial phone, he fell into the seat of the antique phone desk. "What time is it?" he asked the sheriff.

"Early, if you're just getting up; late if you haven't gone down yet."

"Everything okay?" He yawned again. "Really, what time is it? Jim gets me up at 4:00 a.m."

"It's three, Bay. Can you let the time go?"

"Just wondering." Three a.m. What earthly reason ...?
"Daniel, are Lyric and Cade safe?"

"We had a scare here yesterday afternoon. Henry Hoffman was waiting for her at home. I didn't get a chance to find out why Jessup sent him, but I can imagine."

"Henry Hoffman? He's that old now?" Balaam remembered a gangly little weasel following them around when he was a kid. Balaam guessed he never changed, despite the fact they always sent him away from them. "He's a rat. He'll squeal."

"He can't, Bay. He and my deputy, Joe Abner, were found shot to death in Abner's patrol car not too long after he left to take Hoffman to the station."

Balaam cleared his throat. "How? Who? Not Jessup? Not his style. Unless he's grown desperate?"

"I've known Jessup Roy my entire life. Even if he was desperate, he wouldn't kill. He's too smart for that. Am I wrong in my assessment?"

The fact that Daniel could ask him such a question was a testimony to Balaam's past. Well, that and the fact that Daniel always knew what Balaam had been up to. Naturally, the son of a moonshiner would run drugs for a local drug czar. Jessup had paid more than Poppa. Actually, Poppa never paid him. "No. Jessup is a lot of things, but he isn't a cop killer. He'd be more likely to send Henry to Lyric to shake her up or to search her house."

"Exactly what I thought. Jessup's been as clean as a

whistle, but he's had others get caught. He never had to go to those extremes to protect himself. They don't turn on him." Silence filled the space between them. "But someone else with something to hide might not understand the loyalty those kids give to Jessup. They might also believe Jessup' close to getting his hands on the information that Braedon retrieved. Or already has it. If Henry turned on Jessup, they could imagine Jessup naming names to gain favor with the prosecutor."

This was the first time Daniel had spoken of the papers since sending them to Balaam. Daniel's thinking was sound. "Did Henry hurt Lyric or the boy?"

"He didn't have a chance. A federal agent, Goodman, was tailing Lyric. Kept a bad situation from getting worse."

*Goodman. Goodman.* The name rang in Balaam's mind, triggering something out of reach. He couldn't remember hearing the name or meeting the guy. Neither Daniel nor Lyric had mentioned an agent.

"Cade…?"

"Was at lunch with my mother. He's fine."

"He ain't fine, Daniel. His favorite uncle and the man he once believed was his father are dead."

"And his grandmother went crazy mad when Jessup cut out the drink. She's in the mental health ward."

"And his real father's in rehab. Poor kid. Does he have a chance?"

"Jim tells me you're doing fine. How you feeling?"

"Why do I get the idea you didn't call me to ask that

question?"

"Because I didn't. I called for Jim. I asked him what he thought of you coming home. We could use you. I'm no longer sure who I can trust in my department—one or two, yeah, but none of them think like you. I need an asset. That would be you. Are you strong enough?"

Balaam raised tired eyes to Jim. "The cravings don't come on as much as they used to, but here I have no temptation, and Jim keeps me busy. He's said the choice is mine. I can go, or I can stay until I think I'm ready. I'm scared I guess."

Silence stretched between them. Jim slapped his shoulder. "Your boy's worth every sober day you make it in the real world, Bay. You drink, and you stand a lot to lose and not just your sobriety."

"I'll find a way to get home."

"I'll take you home," Jim balked.

"No," Balaam said a little too loudly. "I have something else I need you to do."

"When can you come, Bay?"

"As soon as Jim can find someone who can keep their mouth shut and give a hitchhiker a ride to Amazing Grace."

Daniel chuckled on the other end of the line. "I always knew you were smart, boy. I just didn't know how smart."

"When it comes to keeping the people I love out of trouble, when I put my mind to it, I'm a genius."

Daniel laughed again. "See you in a couple of hours. You can't stay with me. Not this time. Not with what we need to plan."

"I'll hang out with Quinn. Think he'll have me?"

"You sure aren't staying with your daddy."

Balaam laughed now. "No, too much temptation."

"I'd hate to put him in prison at his advanced age, but you take one drink from that still, and I'll do it. And I'll bust that antique piece of finely tuned hardware to pieces. After I'm finished with the still, I'll haul him off to jail. You got me."

"You ain't found that still in twenty years, Daniel. You aren't likely to find it now."

"Whippoorwill Holler ring a bell?" Daniel asked.

Balaam swallowed hard.

"You tell him I know, and so help me..." Daniel allowed his threat to trail away.

"I won't tell him." Balaam sighed. "I suspect you've kept him from trouble the way you tried to do his sons."

"Glad you understand. He's only sold to the good old boys around here. Kept a few old-timers from drinking death in a bottle. His stuff is safe. No one needs to know but me and you."

"Thank you, Daniel."

"Balaam, Lyric isn't going to tell you so, and I have a feeling you aren't going to get back into her life easily, but she needs you. Her son needs a father. Do you understand?"

"I understand."

Jim held out his hand for the phone. "Go get packed.

I'll have a ride here in thirty minutes."

Balaam walked down the hall. He stopped before he went into his room and looked back at the preacher.

Jim kept eye contact with Balaam. "Daniel, you got to promise me, you'll keep an open communication with Bay. You listen to him. You don't put him off for one second if he says he's craving the liquor. You be there for him."

Balaam leaned his head against the doorframe. He'd never been this terrified in his entire life. He'd failed Lyric once. He never wanted to fail her again.

He pushed off the door and moved inside his room. He'd grown comfortable here on the farm. Hard work, clean air, no outside influence. Things were about to change. Like a chameleon, he needed to adapt, become whatever Lyric and Cade needed of him ... do whatever Daniel wanted him to do.

"How you doing?" Jim came into the room.

Balaam threw the last of his clothing into the only bag he'd brought. "The truth?"

"Yeah, the truth. Nothing else."

"I'm scared, Jim. Real scared."

"Good." A wide smile crossed Jim's face. "If you weren't, I wouldn't let you leave here. If you don't fear failure, how can you succeed?"

Balaam crossed the room and threw his arms around the big guy. "Pray for me."

"Constance and I are here. We'll be here for you if you need us. I'm a phone call and a car ride away." Jim patted him on the back. "Get into church. Read your Bible every morning. Start when the sun comes up this morning. Find some honest, hard work, and dig in. Write the music you started here, Balaam. Good stuff. Draws people to God and not away. Find Shane Browne and tell him I sent you."

"My ride?" Balaam zipped his bag.

"Got a neighbor putting on his pants now." Jim reached in his pocket and pulled out a twenty. "Fill up his tank, and thank him like you mean it. He's the salt of the earth, and that's all he'll want."

Balaam took the twenty. "I'll return it tenfold."

"Stay sober, and it'll be a hundred-fold return."

Balaam started to say he promised, but the first thing Jim taught him was never to make promises. A little too late for the promises he'd made to Cade when he'd been in Amazing Grace, but leaving this mountain was leading him to a place where he could keep those promises he'd already made. But promises led to expectations, and expectations, unlike goals, would result in failure.

Lights filtered through the bedroom window. A horn blew.

Balaam reached for the envelope he'd received, the one thing he'd brought with him other than his clothes and the picture Cade had drawn. "This is important to me. Will you hold on to it? Keep it safe? No one but Daniel knows where I've been and that's important. If I thought someone knew, I'd never ask you to do this. I'm pretty sure two people died yesterday because of it. Daniel or I will call if it's needed."

Jim nodded.

Balaam picked up his bag and walked to the front door. Constance stood there, a steaming cup of coffee in her hand. She put the coffee down and hugged him tight. "I'm going to miss you, Balaam. It's been a real treat having you here."

"Thank you, Constance." He looked at the couple. "One day soon, I'd like to bring my boy up to meet you, to see the farm. Would you mind?"

Constance's face brightened. "We'd love it. The sooner the better."

Balaam nodded and ducked outside. He threw his bag into the back of the old pickup, jumped into the cab, and waved at the couple who'd led him closer to the One who'd given him back his sobriety.

Daniel had fallen to sleep at his desk. He jerked awake, rubbing his eyes. He was too old for these all-nighters. The paperwork took longer than usual. Two deaths in a patrol car, no witnesses, and a federal agent on a separate crime scene involving the two murder victims—not a good thing.

Goodman had phoned. The agency had asked him to stay on it. They were sending his partner up from Raleigh. Somehow, Daniel sensed Goodman holding back information, but he didn't press. With the murder of a deputy, they'd be on the case anyway.

Maybe Ethan was meant to be here, though he thought the guy had a thing for Lyric, and Daniel didn't like it one bit.

A movement to the side of him made him jump.

"Wondered when you'd notice me." Balaam laughed and laid an opened Bible on the desk. His hair was cut short, and he looked—well—he didn't know when he'd seen the kid look this healthy.

"How long have you been here?"

"Just long enough to finish my reading and prayers and to know you wake slowly."

Daniel pointed to Balaam's head. "Looks good."

Balaam nodded and ran his hand over it a couple of time. The thick layers fell down in place—just like Cade's did when Daniel messed up his.

Daniel stood and picked up his coffee cup. He held it up. "Want some?"

Balaam shook his head and leaned against the wall, arms crossed over his chest. "I want to know what we're going to do about the situation. How are we going to keep Lyric and Cade safe?"

Daniel closed his door. "You put those papers I sent you in a safe place?"

"Jim has them."

"I thought that's what you were leading up to when you kept Jim from driving you in to town. Smart." He reopened his door. "Now, excuse me. I need my coffee."

"Do you have any theories on who would kill Abner and Hoffman?"

Daniel strolled down the hall past the window without saying a word. He needed his coffee. Then he'd talk. Stepping into the break room, he found a fresh pot, filled his cup, and headed back.

"What's going on here?" Balaam pressed.

"Did you meet Ethan Goodman when you were here last?"

"No, can't say I did. You said an Agent Goodman kept Henry from hurting Lyric."

"That's him. Not that I disagree with Lyric. She'd have talked the kid down. Goodman's here looking for something. His partner is on his way to town. Why don't we find out if what they want and what Jim's keeping for us is one and the same while we keep Jim and the paperwork our little secret?"

"Not a problem for me. I'm my father's son, Daniel. I don't trust a federal agent. Never have."

"You best not start trusting this one either, boy. I think Lyric has bewitched him without even knowing it."

Balaam peered up at the ceiling tiles. "And Lyric? She interested in him?"

"That girl doesn't fall in and out of love easily, genius."

Balaam smirked then sobered. "What was going on between her and Matthew?"

Daniel brought his coffee to his lips and peered over

the rim of his cup. "Not what you're thinking. And don't ask it again. Give her time, and Lyric will tell you all about it."

Balaam ran his hand along the edge of the old file cabinet in the corner. "She wasn't seeing Matthew behind Brae's back?"

"Did you lose your hearing on that farm? Don't ask me again. She wasn't seeing Matthew. She didn't cheat on Braedon."

"What makes you so sure?"

"Strike three." Daniel straightened. "Lyric is made of strong stuff. Maybe Magda slept with a man who in most situations is an honorable sort, and Lyric inherited his God-given sense of loyalty. You'll find out soon enough, and you'll have to make that determination."

"What are you talking about?"

"The gal you left behind with a broken heart, she still loves you. She tried not to, but I know she never could get you out of her system."

Balaam cleared his throat. "Her inability to discern the truth in the men she loves is something she gained from her momma."

Daniel blinked hard. The truth hurt. "One thing she'll never tell you is that your brother wasn't shooting at Matthew."

Balaam jerked his gaze, sharp and eagle-like on Daniel.

"He had her in his aim. Matthew jumped in front of

her. Saved her life."

"Brae—no, that's not true. He wouldn't hurt her." But he wouldn't have thought that he'd kill Matthew either.

"Magda planted that same thought you've been badgering me about into Brae's head. That's something I'm going to deal with Magda about, but you… I want you to play stupid unless or until Lyric tells you the truth."

"Okay." Balaam shrugged.

"Something else you ought to know." Daniel tucked his hat onto his head.

"I can't wait," Balaam whispered.

Daniel met his gaze. "Your son. He saw the whole ugly scene. When I found him, he was running down the street away from home. He thought Braedon had killed both Matthew and his momma. He saw Matthew leap in the line of fire. He saw Matthew's body slam into his mother, both of them motionless on the ground. That's how Cade learned he was your son. He heard your brother tell Lyric what he thought he was and who he really belonged to."

Balaam brought a fist down onto the filing cabinet. The pictures from Daniel's camping trip last year rattled. One fell. The glass broke.

"One more thing that no one but Cade and I know."

Balaam gripped the filing cabinet.

"Braedon looked right at Cade, put the gun to his own head, and pulled the trigger."

Balaam fell back against the wall. For a second he said nothing. Then he pushed past Daniel. "Take me to my boy."

Daniel grasped his shoulder and pulled him back into his office. "I thought yanking off the Band-aid quickly, by giving you all the painful stuff, we could talk, work it out. If you wade through all of that without a drink, you'll make it. There's some stuff you're going to be learning about Lyric. I want her to tell you. Only Quinn and I know. I suspect that if she tells you, you'll know she's forgiven you."

Balaam didn't move. "I think knowing what my brother did to Lyric and my boy while he was obviously drunk will keep me sober. If not that, then the fact that I set it all in motion will definitely keep me from leaving the rails again."

"One moment at a time." Daniel nodded.

"One deliberate moment after another." Balaam held out his hand. "Thanks for the truth. I'd rather Poppa never know. Braedon was his favorite."

"He'll never hear it from me." Daniel started out. "Let me take you to Lyric's so you can surprise your son and see how Lyric takes your return."

"Ha-ha." Balaam pushed Daniel from behind.

The sun peered over the mountains, and Jessup Roy watched it rise. Would he have many more of these left to see? With a finger pressed against his lips he heaved a sigh.

"Good morning, Professor Roy." His maid entered.

Jessup didn't answer. To do so would invite a wealth of conversation, and he didn't feel much like talking this morning.

"Have you heard?"

He should have known. Gossip set the woman to working her mouth quicker than a kid with a lollipop. "I heard, Nadine."

"Who do you think killed 'em, Mr. Roy?"

He had a very good idea, but he wasn't saying—not yet. "No telling."

"Joe Abner," she tsked. "And Henry, he weren't a good boy, but he wasn't the devil either. I talked to him recently. He said you were a professor in one of his college classes." She stopped and stared at him, as if looking to see him squirm.

He wouldn't give her the pleasure.

"I can't figure who'd want to kill them two." She shook her head. "Rumor is, they were coming from Lyric Carter's place. Trouble follows that gal. Always has. Now, there's a stranger in town. He follows her around like a hound dog picking up the scent of something. Got me wondering if it's a pleasant scent or something fouler. You know what I mean?" Again, she stopped, seeming to wait for his reaction.

Wasn't going to happen. She already knew too much of his business.

She fisted her hands and rested them on her hips. "And

Balaam Carter, he's done gone and left her again." She tsked. "Of course, both those Carter boys were faithful to you. And your son, he did right by Balaam. Made him a big star."

"Do you have something to do in here, or are you only wasting my time with your words?"

Nadine's face reddened and then set hard as flint. Something he'd never seen before. Usually she ignored his surliness. "No, sir. I wanted to share the news if you hadn't heard." She backed out of the room, closing the door behind her.

Jessup shut his eyes. Nadine was right. Trouble did follow Lyric Carter, but little of it had to do with her own foolishness. Her husband had been a bright man, brilliant maybe, but no one gave him credit for his smarts. Best carpenter in three counties.

Best courier he'd ever had.

Now, even he wondered if Lyric had the paperwork Braedon brought from Raleigh. The guy did his job, and he always left the packages sealed. Braedon was the one he trusted. No one else.

If Braedon had opened the one envelope, if he'd seen the birth certificates, he wouldn't have killed Matthew Roberts. Magda had panicked. She'd set the kid up to snuff out the life of a lifelong friend.

Henry Hoffman said he'd seen Braedon with the other envelope. Jessup had believed him. The kid tagged along after those Carters for as long as Jessup could remember.

But had the idiot made up the story to gain a position within his organization? Did he have someone inside his own organization who would have been gunning for Henry to keep him quiet, or did this new stranger Nadine had mentioned and Jessup had noticed in town have something to do with the deaths?

And who would gun down two men—one of them a deputy. Yeah, Abner was on the take, but no one knew that. Together, neither Abner nor Hoffman had a full brain. Abner was only to keep an eye on the situation, watch Daniel, see if the girl made any unusual moves. So far, Lyric had done nothing out of the ordinary.

Daniel, on the other hand ...

Daniel. He'd visited Magda at the mental health facility. He and his momma were with Lyric and the boy constantly. Had Daniel intercepted those birth certificates?

No. If he had, and if he realized why Braedon couriered them, Daniel would be knocking on Jessup's door. Even with Abner and Hoffman dead, Daniel had no probable cause to enter Jessup's home on official business. Now, to handle a personal matter...? No doubt. Daniel would arrive sooner rather than later.

Jessup was smarter than Daniel. Always had been. Daniel might have taken Desiree away from him for a while, but Jessup had won her back.

And he hadn't kept his job at the college and his side business running this smoothly for so long by being careless.

A light rap on the door made him turn.

Nadine stood on the threshold. "Professor, you have thirty minutes to make it to the college."

Jessup nodded. Wouldn't do to keep his students waiting. Where else could he enjoy watching the students, working to grow their trust in him, to root out the good recruits who then rounded up their fellow students as customers?

**FAY LAMB**

# 15

Lyric pushed up from the bed. "Braedon? Is that you?"

"You should have seen your face, Lyric." Braedon laughed, his lips turned into the full smile she hadn't seen in years. His handsome face glowing with glee, his blue-gray eyes twinkling behind tears of laughter. "We had you going, didn't we?"

Lyric looked down at her son, sleeping soundly beside her. Something didn't make sense. When she lifted her gaze, she saw the other man standing beside her husband, his face holding the exact opposite emotion of her husband.

"Matthew?"

Matthew frowned, looking to Braedon then back to her, his eyes giving her no inclination of his thoughts.

"Braedon, how could you do this to me? How could you make me think you'd killed my ... killed Matthew?"

Braedon's hand brushed against Lyric's face. "Forgive me, darling. Forgive me everything I've ever done and said to you and the boy. All I want to do now is to make it up to you."

Lyric leaned her cheek into his warm touch. "How can I be sure you won't do it again?"

Braedon sat beside her on the bed. "Lyric, God help me, but you weren't the one who made me angry."

"Then why?"

"I was mad at myself. I loved you forever, and I watched Bay take what you offered and throw it away."

"He was a dumb kid. We were all dumb kids."

"And I wanted what he'd taken from you, but I could never get it back." His warmth left her, and she blinked. This couldn't be. She had to wake up. Braedon was dead. He'd killed Matthew.

Matthew.

He was gone. Not a word—no message for her.

"Dad." Cade struggled beside her.

Lyric sprang upward.

"Dad." Cade fought the covers.

Lyric shook her head. Braedon and Matthew had been a dream—her dream. Braedon was no longer Dad to Cade.

Was she awake now?

"Cade." She leaned toward her son, whispering in his ear. He continued to fight nothing. "Cade, baby, Momma's right here."

"Don't kill my momma. Please don't kill her. Uncle Matthew!"

"I'm here, baby. Momma's here," she repeated.

Cade bolted upright. "No, Dad! Don't! Don't! Please

don't!" His eyes widened. "No, Dad. No!" His hands clawed at his face. "No," the mournful moan rose from deep inside a tortured soul and buried itself in Lyric's heart. He lifted another piercing scream; the sound sliced Lyric's soul.

Balaam shut his car door and walked with Daniel toward the front door of the home that Braedon built for Lyric. With each step, his heart grew heavier. Did he have the right to invade this sanctum that love had built, even if the love had soured?

"No, Dad! Don't! Don't! Please don't!"

Balaam pushed past Daniel to the front door. Locked. He banged.

The door opened and a man pointed a gun straight at his head. Balaam raised his hands.

"Goodman, put the gun down," Daniel barked, walking between Balaam and the angry looking guy.

"No, Dad. No!"

Balaam ran toward the cries, down a long hallway. He pushed open a door.

"Cade, baby, wake up. You're dreaming," Lyric pleaded.

"No ..." the boy's sorrowful denial tore at Balaam's heart.

"Hey," Balaam fell beside the bed. "Cade, hey."

Cade blinked.

Cade's upper teeth held his trembling lips. Tears streamed from his eyes. "You came home."

"And I heard my son calling for me. Are you okay?"

Cade threw his little boy arms around Balaam's neck. Great choking sobs fell from Cade as Balaam lifted him onto his lap and rocked him back and forth.

"I'm here, Cade, and I'm not leaving you like this again. Do you understand?"

Cade shook his head beneath Balaam's chin.

"I love you," Balaam cried, the words the most powerful he'd ever spoken. He'd never said them with any kind of meaning behind them—not even to Lyric.

Lyric. He lifted his face. She was no longer in the bed. He looked around the room. She'd gone, leaving him alone for this moment.

Cade held tighter, and Balaam let him cry against him. "I love you," he repeated. He'd never stop telling the little guy how much he cared for him. He'd never again let him feel the pain of abandonment.

"Dad?" Cade looked up at him.

"Yes, son?"

"I'm glad you're home."

Could it be so simple? What had he done to deserve such ready acceptance?

"I'm glad to be here."

Cade tipped his chin upward. A smile peeked into the corner of the boy's lips, faded, and then filled his face.

Balaam gave a playful growl and buried his face

against Cade's neck, tickling the boy with his early morning beard. Cade giggled, like a child younger than his almost nine years. When Balaam drew back, he tweaked Cade's nose. "I'm the luckiest father in the entire world to have you as a son. Dad's sorry it took him so long to realize it."

Quinn leaned forward and lifted the covers over his mother's thin body. Her worn, weary features seemed reposed. Her breathing lifted and lowered the covers. He couldn't remember ever seeing her look so peaceful.

He lowered his head. "Dear God, give her the peace she craves. Give it to her without the need for alcohol. Please, Father, let her feel Your loving arms wrapped around her tight."

When was the last time he'd hugged her or told her he loved her? Yet, he did love her. Something deep down inside of him refused to let go of the hope that she really did care about him.

Not even the day she'd taken the frying pan to him. Her rage had flown at him for no reason at all.

Momma turned the full might of her fury on him that day, and when she'd passed out, he'd hightailed it directly to Daniel's house. He'd been a very little boy who wanted a father to love him.

Daniel would say differently, but when Daniel had returned him home, Quinn realized what an unwanted orphan felt like. Yeah, Daniel had gotten food for the house, he'd even taken Quinn for a good lunch where he'd explained to Quinn how to dial his number. He'd tucked a napkin with that number into Quinn's pocket. When they arrived back at home after buying more groceries than Quinn could remember them ever having in the place, Daniel cleaned the house—all while Momma slept, never missing Quinn.

As he was going out, Daniel stooped down and chucked him on the chin. "Be a brave boy. When Mommy wakes up, if she's still mad, you call me."

Daniel had closed the door, and Quinn had lifted his shirt. He'd never shown Daniel the bruises, but he would have, if Daniel had acted like he wanted a son.

Quinn caught the cry in his throat. He leaned back and looked to the ceiling to quiet the emotions the memory always churned within him. "And all that time, Daniel was Lyric's father—Lyric's and Matthew's."

Momma had given birth to Matthew, and she'd as good as killed her own son with her vindictiveness.

"Quinn?"

"Yeah." Quinn couldn't look at her.

"What time is it?"

Quinn turned his arm to see his watch face. "Early. Seven thirty?"

"In the morning?"

"In the morning." He smiled. When had she last seen a morning? "How are you feeling today?"

"How do you think?" Her terse voice made him look to her. "I haven't had a drink in how long?"

"Then I'd think you'd be getting better day by day." He stood and paced away from her.

"You'd think."

"I see they took the restraints off." He walked back.

"I promised to be good." She ran her hand through her cropped locks then reached to the ceiling in a good, long stretch. In her time, she probably was a good hairdresser, but that was before his father left and her troubled world crumbled completely in on her.

"What you thinking about, Quinny?" She pushed the button on the bed, raising herself upward.

He shook his head. Now was not the time to go there.

"Thinking about the sins of your mother, no doubt."

He took the chair beside her again. He didn't want to fight. One good visit. That's all he asked. "My actual last thought was that your hair looked good. Did you cut it?"

She brushed her hand through it again. "Not since I've been in here. Scissors and all."

She was edging for a fight. Still, with the alcohol out of her system. He'd known forever that her real sickness wasn't the craving of the alcohol. Deep inside, she was wounded. If he hadn't seen Christ change lives, he'd think her psychological injuries terminal. "I hear the carts coming. Breakfast is being served. Are you hungry?"

She studied him for a moment. "This small talk doesn't work for me anymore than it works for you. Why don't you tell me what's on your mind?"

"I came to visit with you. I don't want to argue. Can't I just sit here while you eat breakfast?"

"You weren't ever much for confrontation. You'd think being my son would make you a fighter. I tried to toughen you up for this hard, old world, but you kept getting softer and softer."

A young woman entered with a tray of food. She set it on the stand beside Momma's bed.

"She's a pretty one, Quinn. You ever going to find a girl, or are you hiding behind your religion for another reason?"

Quinn's face burned as the girl sidestepped him and moved toward the hall. He followed her movement. When she got to the door she turned and offered him a sympathetic smile before leaving.

His mother giggled like a deranged child.

"Thank you." He stood and moved the stand so that she could reach the tray. "I don't know what I did to deserve that, but if it makes you happy ..."

She lifted the lid from the meal then slammed it back down. "Get it out of my face. The smell's enough to gag a moose."

"You need to eat."

"I said get it out of my face, Quinn."

Quinn started for the door. "You want it away, you do it yourself."

The loud crash turned him around. The aide who'd

brought the food ran into the room. "What happened?"

"I don't want that gruel," Momma screamed at her.

Quinn bent to help the aide pick up the mess.

"I'll get this." She touched his arm.

"I'm sorry," Quinn offered then stood. He cast his mother a stern glance. "Nice, real nice."

"You came here for more than a visit. Why don't you say what you came to say?"

The aide stood with the lid filled with a mess of food. "I'll get the nurse," she whispered as she stepped by him.

He reached for her and shook his head. "Have her on standby. I think it's time my mother and I have a little talk."

She nodded and left them.

He faced his mother. "Why did you?"

"I didn't like the food. It stinks."

He leaned over her, his hands grasping the bedrail. He shook it with all his might, feeling the rage build in him, remembering the beatings of his early childhood and the times he'd fought to protect Lyric from her ugly words. "Why did you keep Lyric and me and throw Matthew away?" he screamed. "Why, Momma? Why us and not him?"

She stared back at him. Then she straightened and smoothed her hospital gown. A smile crossed her face. "Lyric did have the papers. I thought she'd blundered when we spoke. Thank you, Quinn, for letting me know for sure."

"Why?"

Momma studied her ragged fingernails. "I kept you

because I loved your father. No one wanted Lyric; Larry Roberts sure didn't, and anyway, I had to have a story. A few people had learned I was pregnant. No one knew it was twins. I went to live out of town where Larry Roberts paid for me to see a doctor regularly. Had them in a hospital in that town. You took pretty good care of yourself when I went into the hospital as I recall. Near five years old and all grown up. Larry and Bernice brought their adopted kid home, and a few days later I showed up with you and my new baby girl. No one was the wiser, and Larry was willing to pay dearly for him."

Quinn released his hold on the rail and backed up, one step, then two. He lifted his hands in the air, surrendering. His mother had finally won the hard-fault battle to make him hate her. He took one step at a time away from her and the mess she'd made of her life.

Momma was wrong. She'd never wanted him and someone had always wanted Lyric—needed her—since she'd fallen into his life. Quinn had been the only father Lyric had ever known until she learned about Daniel, and Quinn loved her with all of his big brother heart.

Time had come to leave Momma to her own devices. His sister needed him.

Lyric clanged the dishes a little too loudly, and the three men and the little boy in the house watched her. She didn't have to see them to know it. Their silence spoke volumes.

"Here, let me help?"

She jumped at the voice and spun toward Ethan who pulled the dirty dish from her hand. He ran it through the sudsy water and handed it to her. She placed it in the dishwasher.

They worked in companionable silence until the last of the breakfast dishes was done.

"Did Quinn say where he was going?" Lyric asked Daniel, who sat on the family room couch on the other side of the counter from the kitchen.

"To the facility to see your mother. Care to tell me what's wrong?" he asked.

She gave a haughty half-laugh. "Wouldn't it be easier to tell you what's going right?" She slammed the dishwasher shut and leaned against the counter beside Ethan.

"He's a lot different than he appears in the tabloids and on stage, huh?" Ethan whispered and nodded toward Balaam who sat, playing a card game with Cade.

Lyric nodded. "I've never met Balaam Brasher. I've only known Balaam Carter."

"Carter seems like a nice sort. So, what's got you so mad at him?"

Balaam peered up at her from the game. He leaned and whispered into Cade's ear before planting a kiss on the top of their son's head.

"I'll keep Cade occupied." Ethan touched her arm before moving away. "Play nice, okay?"

Lyric smiled. He could be rather charming when he tried. Ethan pointed at something in the living room, a trophy or something, and Cade followed him there.

Daniel remained on the couch, a wariness seeping into the lines of his face.

Balaam sauntered into the kitchen. "Is it me that has you so fired up?"

She'd never get used to the hair. He'd only worn it this short when he was a little boy, but she had to admit he looked more handsome than words could describe. Younger. Innocent. Sober. His skin had a healthy glow, his blue eyes were bright and clear.

She took a deep breath, chastising herself for her weakness. All Balaam ever had to do was look at her, and she gave him whatever he wanted.

"Lyric, I ..."

"You hurt Cade, and so help me, I'll kill you." She leaned close, her whispered words meant only for him.

"I will do my very best never to hurt either of you again."

She planted her hands on her hips. "You aren't ever going to hurt me again. You took everything from me. Every hope. Every dream."

"And I'm glad that I did."

Her hand stung at her slap. She hadn't even realized she'd taken aim at him before she felt the pain of it.

His face bore the red mark of her anger.

She'd never struck out like that. She turned, clutching the counter. Daniel should come and slip the cuffs on her and haul her away for aggravated battery—or Balaam could return her anger, and he'd be arrested and thrown deep into the county jail.

"I guess I deserved that," Balaam said, not moving close to her.

She didn't turn. "Even if you did, I shouldn't have done it."

"Did you ever slap Braedon like that?"

The words squeezed her heart. She faced him. "If I had, I wouldn't have lived to tell you about it."

Balaam reached down for her hand. He held her fingers with a light touch, as if he knew anything more would be making a claim she would never let him stake. "Then I'm glad you weren't afraid of me. I did deserve it. I walked out on you and our child, and I didn't look back. You and I talked forever about the band and how rich we'd be. We saw only the glamor. I got to leave town and experience that life."

She pulled her hand from him. "And I stayed here experiencing nothing."

"Nothing?" He quirked a brow. "I'd give anything to have experienced the birth of that boy or to have seen him walk for the first time, to have heard him speak for the first time, to watch him play baseball, or even to look over his report cards when he brings them home."

She couldn't help but smile. "I don't think you'd have handled the sleepless nights or the trips to the doctor where he cried from the moment he arrived until we walked out the door, or the spitting up, or watching him stand up to a bully because you knew he had to do it for himself."

He lifted her chin. "I think you enjoyed those times as much as the ones I mentioned. I don't believe you'd have handled the sleepless nights hopped up on whatever pills Nathan Roy handed you to get you through the night or to bring you down when the gig was over, the endless line of people who wanted a piece of you, never seeing the sunrise or even the sunset for that matter."

Lyric stepped away from him. "Do you think I'd have let that happen to you?"

Balaam half-laughed. "Do you think I'd have allowed you to stop me? What makes you think that anything would have been different on the road if Cade hadn't come along? Or would you have wanted him to live that life?"

She closed her eyes. Hadn't she already admitted that to herself? Her heart was so hardened that she couldn't see a blessing. She kept clinging to the never-haves.

"Do you still play?" he asked.

"Not really."

"Not even for the church?"

She smirked. "I only go to church because Quinn wants me there. He has a pianist, and he's never asked me to play because I'm not a church member."

Balaam sucked in his breath. "You're not a member?

Why?"

"Because I wouldn't lie to him and tell him I've accepted Christ when I have not. I haven't felt Him near me, Bay. Quinn deserves the comfort. I don't."

"Well, I don't know where I'd be without that comfort today. He saw me through."

"Good for you." She stomped back toward him. "Let's get one thing straight. I'll never be fooled by you again. It ain't gonna happen. Our son, he does have that comfort you say you have. I'd never make light of it with him any more than I would with Quinn or Matthew, Daniel or Grace. You leave me alone. You enjoy your comfort, and don't try to get me to go there."

"With what I know, I'd think you'd be thanking the Lord—"

Lyric rounded on him. "What did Daniel tell you?"

In the living room, Daniel stood and stretched, throwing a wary glance in their direction and shaking his head. What was it he didn't want Balaam to say?

Balaam led her to the small kitchen table and pulled out a chair for her to sit. She did, and he pulled out the other chair. "It's not what Daniel told me, Lyric. We never had any secrets growing up. Your momma's heart was hard. You were tough, but you weren't calloused, especially against God."

"I didn't understand—I still don't understand."

"What don't you understand? How life could turn out the way it has? Matthew's death? How Braedon could have done what he did?"

"No, you idiot. I understand that life is motion. People live and they die. Matthew and Braedon are dead. They were important to me. Joe Abner and Henry Hoffman are gone, and they were important to someone as well. I'm not blaming God."

"Well, I'm no great theologian myself. But maybe if you share what you don't understand."

"Momma believes in God. She hates Him. Quinn believes in God. He loves Him. You believe in God. He comforts you. I believe in Him, but I don't feel Him. He's like an…" She looked to where Daniel stood, watching and listening. She was helpless to prevent the revelation she'd just had from rushing through the river of her emotions and flooding over the man whom she'd always recognized as a wall of protection, even before she knew he was her father. She kept her gaze riveted on Daniel. "He's like an absent father."

Daniel winced.

Lyric covered her mouth with her hand, her eyes wide. "I'm sorry."

Daniel winked and gave a slight nod in Balaam's direction reminding her of what she'd forgotten. How could he be so forgiving of her and her judgmental nature? Her words had to have hurt him.

Yet, only four people knew the truth of Daniel's fatherhood, and Lyric wasn't sure she wanted to cut Balaam in on the story, not just yet.

Balaam stood. "I'm sorry you don't have a father—at least one you know, but God's been pretty close to all of us. I'd even say God's placed a big, burly guy in all of our paths, a father of sorts. He's been a picture of Christ to us, so why don't you think on that for a bit. As great as Daniel's love and protection over us, God's is so much greater."

His words gave her pause. They stung like a hypodermic filled with the medicine of truth she needed, but she hadn't wanted the shot, hadn't asked him for it, and she trembled with the anger at the dosage he'd given.

She leaned in close to him so that Cade wouldn't overhear. "I don't need lectures on God and fatherhood from you, Balaam Carter. You've been back hours—hours out of our son's life—and you're lecturing me on God being a good father? You saw me standing in the road, tears in my eyes, my hand over my swollen belly, and you rode away without one look back." She stood and walked to the sink and smacked her hand down, the anger stewing in her like one of Granny Grace's soups in the kettle. She turned back to him, begging him for a fight so that she could vent what she'd held in all these long years.

Balaam didn't move. He lowered his head, and his words were almost too quiet for her to hear. "I hope someday that you can forgive me. I don't plan to leave you again. I want Cade to know the love of his real father."

She glared at him.

Daniel moved, and she looked to him. He offered her

a hint of a smile. "Get it out," he mouthed.

Balaam still stood, his gaze on the floor. Humble. Not the proud boy he'd always been, the one she sometimes had trouble getting through to because of his pride. "I mean it, Bay." The words were on the tip of her tongue. *I'll never love you. I'll never trust you again. You had your last chance when you left Amazing Grace nine years ago.* Instead, she straightened, took a deep breath, and let it out. She walked to him and took his hand in hers. "We've always been friends, you and me, even before our own foolishness pulled us apart. So, I'm giving you one chance—one chance—with our son's heart. If you blow it, you're out of his life."

He laced his fingers in hers. His ocean-blue eyes stared into hers, and even in her kitchen, in the home built by his brother's hands, for her, his brother's widow, being watched over by her father, she wanted to wade in the dangerous tides again, to feel reckless with Balaam one more time.

She wanted him to love her—not physically. For real this time. The way she had always loved him, even when she thought she could hate him—like now.

"I won't let you or Cade down this time. I'm not promising. It's a fact. I'm sorry for all I put you through with my lies, and following my own desires, even my lust after you was more for me than for you. But I know what real love is now. God's touched me with it over and over again in these long sober weeks that I've been away from you since Braedon's and Matthew's deaths. This love I have for you and our son is the best high a man could have. I'll cherish the chance, and I won't let you down. But you have to know that God has never abandoned you."

She smarted at his remark. The hypodermic of truth struck a nerve, but she didn't want to think about it. "You leave that between me and God. Quinn doesn't even step in between that. I won't let you either."

He nodded. "Understood."

She yanked from his touch. "I hurt when Cade hurts, because when Cade is broken, I'm broken, too." The tone of her voice climbed as the anger boiled to the surface. She had to make him understand. "The ghost of Quinn's still-living father haunts him today. I don't want that for our boy."

Balaam gave a quick look to where Ethan and Cade were out of sight. Then he shushed her.

She straightened. "Don't you tell me to be quiet."

He grabbed her hand and pulled her to the door.

"Oh no." Ethan ran from the living room to bar their exit. "You're not going outside."

"Get out of my way." Balaam glared at the agent.

"Bay," Daniel voiced his warning. "Ethan is here to protect Lyric and Cade. When his partner arrives, the three of us will work out a plan."

"We're still going outside to finish this conversation," Balaam insisted.

"You okay?" Daniel nodded to Lyric.

"I'm fine." She shirked from Balaam's grip yet again. "Give us five minutes."

Daniel motioned Ethan away.

Ethan hesitated for a moment then did as ordered. Balaam opened the door and pulled her outside with him.

She tried to shut the slider, but someone blocked it. Daniel stepped onto the deck. "I'll be right here," he said.

Balaam led her down the deck steps and near the back edge of her home. "Can't you see that I'm trying here? I don't know what it means to be a father, but I want to be one, Lyric. I want to help raise my son. I only shushed you because he's heard anger from at least one parent for far too long."

"Like you cared about Braedon's anger and what he did to us." She laughed, the sound of it filling her with guilt even as it rang in her ears. Her momma hurt people with her laughter and her harsh tone and the words to match. *Oh, God, what have I done? Don't let me hurt this man because of my bitterness. Help me to understand.* The prayer lifted in her, stopped only by Balaam's tight grasp wrapped around her forearms.

"Don't laugh at me, Lyric. Don't take that tone. I need your understanding."

She fought Balaam's hold on her, needing to free herself. All she could imagine was his holding her in place. Then he'd lift one hand from her and use it to pummel her face.

Daniel's footsteps pounded down the steps.

268

Balaam released her before Daniel got to them. "Lyric, I'm sorry."

She backed from him, falling against the house, rubbing her arms. She dragged her breath into her lungs. She kept her gaze focused on a stock-still Daniel, hovering over them like a guardian angel. He was her protection. He was her security. He was her savior.

"I'd never hurt you. You know that, don't you?" Balaam pleaded.

She nodded. She'd say anything to keep his anger abated.

He cast a quick, wary glance at Daniel and back to her. "Baby, I'm not my brother. I'd cut my arm off before I'd harm you or Cade. I still can't believe that Brae would touch you, but I saw the evidence the day I arrived for the funeral, and I see it now in the fear in your eyes."

What could she say? She didn't believe him, but she'd stay on his good side, keep Cade from seeing his real father brutalize her. Make sure she had Daniel around her.

Balaam walked to the corner of the house and stared down the street. "I don't plan to leave Amazing Grace—not like I did before—not to live that life. I've worked long hours, sweating out everything that took me away from here," Balaam said. "I talked to God about my desires. Everything boiled down to three things that I want, and I don't deserve any of them."

Lyric waited.

"I want to glorify God. I want to know my son, to show

him unconditional love—the same kind of love God has shown me, and I want to earn your respect and to one day love the mother of my child as she was meant to be loved—honored—treasured." He made his way back to her.

She didn't know what to say. Life with Magda Moxley taught her never to trust an alcoholic. She wanted to trust him so badly but how could she after all her mother had put her through?

"Say something, Lyric?"

In Daniel's presence, she regained her courage. "He's my son." She slammed her fist against her chest. "My son. You weren't here." The hurt poured from deep inside her, and it wasn't about her dreams of playing in the band. The pain welled up in her because she hadn't been enough for Balaam to give up his dreams and start new ones with her. He'd not only abandoned her. He'd left Cade, and that was the kind of hurt she was trying to get him to understand. She felt it to her very core, and she never wanted Cade to experience it again. "You left Cade here for Braedon to tear out his heart."

Balaam rushed toward her.

She backed away.

Daniel stepped between them.

Balaam stopped, holding up his hands as he moved around Daniel and toward her with slow, cautious steps. "Braedon did more than tear our son's heart out." He drew near, leaning close to her.

"Bay…" Daniel's voice held a warning.

From her vantage point, she could see the curve in her driveway.

Quinn pulled up in his car.

Balaam didn't seem to notice. "My brother looked our son in the eye, put the gun to his own head, and pulled the trigger, all while Cade watched. All I could think of when I walked into your room, hearing him cry, and seeing him claw at his face, was that I had to take that pain away. I wasn't thinking of you or me, Lyric. I was thinking of my boy. I'm sorry for leaving you both, for leaving you no choice except to live with my brother who clearly became a monster—and I caused that to happen."

Lyric fought for her breath. She opened her mouth to cry out, but Quinn was advancing on them, a scowl on his face.

Hearing his approach, Balaam turned.

Her brother pulled back his fist and brought it forward, knocking Balaam to the ground.

Lyric stumbled back from them.

A loud crack split the air, and a blast shattered the wood on the house where Lyric's head had been only a second before. She screamed as Daniel ran forward, pushing her to the ground, shielding her with his body.

Quinn and Balaam scurried toward them and helped them get under the deck crawl space. They pinned her behind them. Daniel had his firearm pulled.

Lyric searched each of them. No one had been shot. The glass door above them slammed open.

"Goodman?" Daniel said.

"Sir?" the agent was apparently ducking behind something. His voice was closer to the floor, but there wasn't much cover on the deck. "Anyone hurt?"

Daniel turned to look at them, his face tense like granite, but the love in his eyes for her more palpable than she could have ever imagined. She was his daughter. She felt it to the very core of her being.

*As great as Daniel's love and protection over us, God's is so much greater.* Balaam's words repeated, matching each beat of her heart. Her father had never abandoned her. He was right here protecting her. He hadn't been the one to save her. For some strange reason, God had brought Quinn along to punch Balaam in the face. If he hadn't, Lyric would be dead.

Daniel wasn't her savior. No. He was a gift from the Savior, a gift she hadn't been given until recently, exactly when God knew she'd need him more than she ever had. She had accepted him as a sought treasure now found. She bowed her head. *I understand now. And I'm ready, God. Will You forgive me and let me be Your daughter? I want it now more than I ever wanted my father's love.*

In a crawl space under the deck, after having been shot at, peace like no other she'd ever experienced cloaked Lyric... Dixon... Carter.

"Lyric," Daniel touched her shoulder, "are you okay?"

Lyric looked up at him. She couldn't prevent the smile if she tried, no matter the seriousness of their situation. She leaned close to his ear. "I'm fine, Daddy."

Daniel leaned his head against hers, then he turned to whisper in her ear. "I thank God He spared my daughter."

She slipped her arm around him. "I thank God that He saved your daughter—and His—too," she whispered.

**FAY LAMB**

# 16

Balaam had returned to make things right between them, but now his stupidity had nearly cost Lyric her life. If Ethan Goodman shot him one more annoying glance, he'd show him how a man raised by a moonshiner took care of federal agents.

Balaam sighed. And if he did that, he'd never be able to prove to Lyric he wouldn't harm her or their boy.

He had another problem. Quinn had decked him for no apparent reason, and from the flare of his nostrils, and the I'm-going-to-kill-you glower, Balaam wasn't getting out of this without a fight—verbal or otherwise.

Lyric didn't seem any happier with him than she had been outside. She sat at the kitchen table nursing what must be a long-cold cup of tea.

Well, he needed to get this over with. He looked to Daniel for support. The sheriff narrowed his eyes. His jaw rose with the clench of his teeth. Yeah, Daniel was a little ticked with him, too.

"Look, I'm sorry I placed Lyric in danger, but this is Amazing Grace, North Carolina. Who expects someone to shoot at them in broad daylight in this town?"

"Someone who tried to tell you it was dangerous for Lyric to be outside," Goodman raged. He leaned closer. "I believe you know two men were killed yesterday. Two men who'd just left this house."

"Let him alone." Lyric set her mug down a little too hard.

At least Lyric took his side against the agent.

"Bay's right. This is Amazing Grace. This stuff doesn't happen." She sipped her tea, made a face, and put the cup back on the table.

"At least not in this part of town," Daniel said.

Lyric stood. "The side of town Quinn and I came from wasn't that bad either, Daniel." She stretched and winced.

"Why don't you start dinner. I bet Cade's a bit hungry?" Goodman turned his watch on his arm and peered at the time.

Balaam didn't like the agent telling Lyric what to do with his son, but he let it slide.

"I know how to look after my kid." Lyric slid her chair against the table. She picked up her cup and put it in the sink. "But I suppose you're hungry or you wouldn't have asked."

Balaam bit his lip to hide his smile. Way to put the guy in his place. He worked his jaw. He didn't know what hurt worse, the punch from Quinn or the hard whap she'd landed on him. If Goodman wasn't careful, he might get that powerful slap she'd put on Balaam. Nothing he'd enjoy more.

Goodman smiled at her, either missing the jab or dancing around it. "You're a tough little cookie, Lyric, but I think you're about to crumble." Goodman looked at his watch again. "I thought suggesting something for you to do might alleviate your stress."

"If you have somewhere to go, you're welcome to leave," Balaam groused.

"You're welcome to do the same," Lyric said to him. "Ethan, if you have something to do, we'll be fine. Daniel's here, and so is Quinn."

And so was Balaam.

The silent sarcasm stung him worse than the dart she'd tossed the agent's way.

Quinn grunted and stood, making his way to the glass doors leading out to Lyric's porch. He parted the curtains to peer outside. A storm was brewing both inside the house and outside. Dark, heavy clouds pushed over the mountains.

"You going to tell me what it is that I've done to make you so mad?" Balaam asked.

Quinn continued to stare out the glass doors and to the yard beyond it. The sky had turned that shade of gray that only occurred in winter. Perhaps the snow would fall or the clouds would release it over another mountain range.

"Quinn, I need to know what I'm dealing with before I can apologize."

Quinn tilted his head back and breathed deeply, exhaling long and steady before turning. "Cade, do me a favor and give your dad and me a minute."

"I want to stay with my dad," Cade protested.

Balaam hadn't missed the kid's head moving to each of them as they spoke, and Quinn was right. Cade had heard enough heated arguments to last him a lifetime.

"Cade, do as I say," Quinn pressed.

"Do I have to, Dad?" The kid turned his green eyes to him.

Green? From what pallet did God paint from in order to give him a green-eyed son when both he and Lyric had blue eyes? He couldn't deny Cade was his. They boy looked just like him at that age. He shook the errant thought away. "Yeah, I think so. I can't overrule Uncle Quinn. He's been here longer than me." Balaam winked at him. "Go take a breather. I won't leave the house without telling you."

Cade smiled and started down the hall. Lyric followed him. Balaam didn't look away from them until they went into Cade's room.

"What happened to rehab, Bay?" Quinn said between clenched teeth. What was all that stuff you declared about Cade never seeing you drunk or high? Were those just words to you?"

"Quinn, you best stop before you have apologies to

278

make." Daniel lifted his sheriff's hat from his head and smoothed his dark hair.

"She's had enough." Quinn kept his hate-filled eyes on Balaam. "I don't want her turning out like Momma. If you hurt her, she might."

"Lyric's made of stronger stuff than your momma. We both know that," Balaam challenged.

"I don't know anything," Quinn clasped his hands in front of him. "I thought you were in rehab, but they've never heard of you."

"Do you think that this long in a glorified California spa for celebrities would have me doing this well? I went somewhere else, someplace close, and I sweated the drugs and alcohol out of my system. I worked hard, and I gained more wealth in those weeks than I did for all those years partying and playing."

"Mind telling me where you went? Otherwise, I don't want you around my sister and my nephew."

Balaam didn't miss the shake of Daniel's head. "I can't tell you. Not now anyway, but in time, when Lyric and Cade are safe."

Goodman looked at his watch again, moved to the living room window, and parted the curtain.

Daniel kept his eyes on the agent. No denying it. The sheriff didn't like the man, and he sure enough didn't trust him.

"What's up with you?" Lyric came from her son's room. "You act like you need to be out of here. We're not

279

holding you hostage."

Goodman offered a smile that didn't brighten his countenance as he let the curtain fall back. "I've been looking for my partner. He's never late, and right now, he's right on time." He pulled open the door.

The man stepped inside Lyric's home like he owned it. He slipped the glasses from his face and looked around as if sizing it up for something.

"Tom Pierce, I'd like you to meet my new friends," Goodman beamed. "Pierce is my partner in the agency."

Just what they needed, another federal agent. "Lyric, you mind if I spend some time with my son?"

Lyric shook her head, and he started down the hall. When he reached her, he stopped. "I'm really sorry I allowed ..."

She stepped out of his perimeter. "You had no way of knowing some fool was going to try to kill me." No missed touch had ever spoken so loudly. "Will you stay with him until we get back?"

Daniel straightened at the question directed at Balaam. "You aren't going anywhere," he said to Lyric.

Lyric tilted her gaze to her brother. "I want to see Momma. She knows some things, and I really just want to see her."

If she'd told her brother that an alien stood at the front door, Quinn couldn't have looked more surprised.

"I won't let Cade out of my sight." Balaam smiled as he turned away.

"That okay with you?" Quinn asked Daniel.

"Only if I'm driving," Daniel answered.

"Hey." Footsteps sounded behind Balaam, and he turned at the slight push on his shoulder. "Literally, don't let him out of your sight. I'm trusting you. Please, for the first time in your life, don't let me down."

He'd rather she'd slapped him again. The pain those truthful words caused almost made him double over.

Convincing Quinn to let her go into their mother's room without his warning Momma first nearly wore Lyric down, but she'd won him over with a promise that there would be no name calling or angry words spoken on her behalf.

Lyric slipped through the door and shut it.

Momma slept, curled up in a ball. She looked almost child-like. These long weeks in a controlled environment had done her mother good. She'd never seen her sleep so still. Even when drunk beyond belief, she grumbled and tossed and turned, calling out to something or someone tormenting her in her dreams.

Lyric picked up the heavy wooden chair and moved it around to the other side of the bed where her mother was facing. She took her time putting the chair in place, not wanting to rouse the sleeping woman.

Lyric sat. She studied her mother's face and tried to

remember a happy moment. Just one.

Grief sent a single tear down Lyric's left cheek. Momma had never been happy around her. Lyric had seen her laugh and cut up but always around the men she brought into the house, the men that Quinn guarded her against. Momma would throw her head back and laugh with such glee as she allowed the men to paw at her, some nearly ripping at her clothes.

That's when Momma would look up and see Lyric and Quinn. Her face would twist and contort with anger, and she'd yell at them to get out of her sight, to leave the house or to go to their room. Sometimes, to punctuate a point, she'd throw something in their direction.

Lyric swiped at the second tear, catching it with the first and wiping it away. Until this moment, she had always convinced herself that Momma didn't matter to her. Her hatred was something she could live with.

"Let her be nice to me. For once, please let her be nice," she mouthed the words.

A touch on her hand nearly brought Lyric out of her seat.

Momma raised up, crooking her elbow and resting her head in her hand. "You okay, Lyric Kay?"

Lyric took a shaky breath and nodded.

"How nice, you sitting vigil over me."

"That's not what I was doing. I wanted to let you rest. You looked so peaceful."

Momma turned and sat, bringing her knees up and

resting her arms on them. "I can't say I've ever had a moment's peace in my entire life."

Lyric's heart pounded against her ribcage. She could barely get air into her lungs. Her every nerve was taut, waiting for the mesmerizing cobra to strike out at her.

"Ain't you got nothing to say?"

Lyric swallowed hard. She braced her feet to be ready to move away from her mother in case her mood turned foul. "Are you feeling better?"

She fought against closing her eyes at the stupid, leading question. Had she done that to Braedon, too? Made it easy for him to goad her into an argument.

Momma stared at her for a long moment then she looked away. "I'd almost think you cared."

The breath Lyric released was ragged, as if riding a choppy wave on a windy day. "For the first time, I think I do."

Momma jerked her body so quickly that Lyric flinched, fighting to stay in her seat. "You? Care about me? Girl, I never wanted that from you."

Lyric's lips trembled, but they turned into a smile. "I expect you didn't."

Momma smiled. She actually smiled in Lyric's direction for the first time that Lyric could ever remember. "You're the tough one. Quinn got in the way of me hurting you plenty enough, but he couldn't save you from Braedon Carter. You owe that dead husband of yours some gratitude. Life's hard. Gets harder the more you go."

A thunder roll of words clattered in Lyric's brain, but she'd promised Quinn, and she wasn't going to let her brother down. She let the clamor in her head die down. Then she took another deep breath, this time steadier. "Braedon will always have my gratitude. I think he loved me. He just didn't know how to get over what I did, even though he wanted so badly to be the solution. He was a good man. And because of him, I understand something about you."

Momma lowered her head to her knees as if she had a headache. "What's that?"

"The pain someone leaves you with can make you act different from the person you really are deep down inside."

Momma turned to look at her, and a tear that had seeped from her eye, trickled toward her mouth. "There ain't nothing good in me, girl. Don't go fancying me as something I'm not. I'm gonna get out of this place soon enough. Stowe can't keep me in here forever, and when I do, I'm going to get drunk, and I'm going to live it up."

Lyric nodded, a curt motion. She understood.

"'Course, if I don't give Jessup those papers, he's going to make it hard for me to get my hands on a drink. Is that what you're betting on?"

"I'd like to ask you a question, and I'm not trying to start a fight. Are you talking about the birth certificates and the adoption papers, or are you afraid for me because of the other information I know you're aware Braedon had?"

Momma studied her so long that Lyric's skin crawled

with anxiety.

*Please don't let this end badly.*

"The only papers I care about are the certificates and the adoption papers. I want Daniel to hurt for what he's done to me."

"Daniel knows, Momma. Quinn does, too."

Her mother nodded. "I know he does. Quinn came here asking questions this morning."

And poor Balaam had been the punching bag for Quinn to exercise the anger out of his system. Quinn was probably already feeling the remorse, and he'd apologize to Bay later. He never went long without righting his wrongs. But she wouldn't let her mother know about Quinn's behavior. She'd revel in the fact that a preacher had punched a man who'd done nothing to him. "I suspect Jessup's schemes might pan out for him because you know deep down inside where that good part of you lives, that my daddy is an honorable man. He wouldn't lie about you and him, because he loves me and Quinn. I think he might've loved you once."

The tears that Lyric had never seen from her mother poured.

Lyric stood and plucked a few tissues from the box on the bed stand and handed them to her.

"You see, that's how you can know there ain't a good part of me."

"How's that?"

"I know he loved me. I might've loved him if I knew

how to love. Instead, I took what he wanted most, and I kept it in his sight all these years, and I never once told him."

Lyric stood. She'd bend down and kiss her mother's moist cheek if she thought the woman would accept it. "I think Quinny wants to say hello."

"Tell him I don't want to see him."

Another way to hurt an innocent person who cared for her. She'd make sure Quinn didn't come in for another visit today. She didn't want him to be hurt a second time. When Momma was sober, Quinn couldn't concoct an excuse for her mistreatment of him.

"I'll tell him. Thank you, Momma."

Momma lifted her head, her chin jutting out with that false pride she'd always shown. "For what?"

"So many things."

"I don't enjoy being laughed at." Momma raised her voice.

"No. No. I'm serious." Lyric stepped closer. "You didn't have to keep me. I can understand that your motives weren't all that pure, but without you I wouldn't have Quinn in my life."

"And Matthew?"

"He was there. Always. But not like you thought. We were always friends. I want you to know that."

"Braedon?"

"For that... I forgive you. Braedon didn't deserve to die, but Cade suffered at his hand."

"Braedon hurt Cade?" Concern lit Momma's eyes, and she clutched the bedsheets with white-knuckled fists that belied her declaration of pure evil.

"Only with indifference and with each fist he put against me. You may have lied to Brae, but he's the one who killed my brother and turned the gun on himself. A stronger man wouldn't have done that. I wish it had happened another way, but Cade is free of him."

Momma's eyes darkened. "I wanted him to kill you."

Lyric didn't bat an eye. Her mother's confession wasn't a surprise. "I know you did. I don't know how you convinced him to do it, but he was aiming at me."

"I told him that you'd never been shed of his brother. You loved Balaam, and you'd never let him go in your heart, that you were using Matthew as a substitute for that boy, and Braedon would never be enough. I told him that Matthew would have to live with the pain if Braedon killed you."

"And what would that have done to Cade?"

Momma stared straight ahead.

"You never thought it through, did you?" Lyric asked.

Her mother pressed her lips so tight that the fine lines around her mouth became ridges.

"I still forgive you, and Cade is the one reason I know that there's something redeemable deep inside. I do hope that when you're let out of here that you'll think about him. Cade worries so much about you." Lyric started toward the door. "If you'd take the first step and do something for someone other than yourself, you might find happiness. Maybe begin with Cade. He loves you."

"Does he know, Lyric Kay?"

"What?" She stopped, hand on the door.

"Does Cade know that I'm the one who got his Uncle Matthew killed and lost him the man he thinks was his father?"

Lyric had played the scene over and over in her mind. Braedon had never mentioned her mother's involvement. "No, and he'll never hear it from anyone who loves him." She nodded. "I hope that includes you."

Momma nodded. She'd never humble herself and show gratitude, but her acknowledgement of the kindness was another new direction for their complicated relationship.

"Will you be okay?" Lyric asked. "When you get out of here, will Jessup hurt you? The other papers he wants, they haven't turned up."

Momma waved her away. "I ain't afraid of Jessup Roy. If Daniel knows the truth, Jessup can spin it against him. That'll make him happy enough. Jessup doesn't need my help anymore. Things will go back to the way they were with us. I'll do his bidding, and he'll give me something I need in return. That pain you blabbered on about. It's deep in Jessup's soul, too. He loved his wife."

"The one he stole from Daniel?"

"The only woman Jessup ever loved. Truth is, he stole her back from Daniel. And he took care of her, too. She didn't live long after that little girl of theirs was born. Died of cancer. Pretty near killed Daniel, too. You'd think he'd have been angry with her, but Daniel hurt with her passing."

"Well, he's another reason I have to be thankful to you. Any man in this town could have been my father, but you gave me the best, even if it took years in the coming."

Momma turned over and curled into the fetal position again.

"I'd like to come see you again if you stay here. Do you think we could do this?" Lyric motioned between the two of them, but Momma didn't see. "I mean, can we keep the truce?"

"Don't come back here." Momma brought the pillow around and clutched it in the bow of her body. "Don't look for me when I'm out. Nothing's changed between us. I never wanted you, and I never will."

The words should have hurt, should have rendered her a sad mess. "Okay, Momma. You watch out for yourself."

"Always have," she mumbled. "And you keep Quinn away from me, too."

Lyric opened the door and walked out into the hall. Quinn started in, but Lyric put her hand on his chest. "I got all the kindness she can give for one day. She's tired. Let's let her rest."

Daniel, hat in his hand, joined them. "Quinn, let's give her a little time."

Quinn turned without a word, and they followed

behind him.

Lyric slipped her arm through Daniel's.

"How'd she handle your visit?" Daniel asked.

"Let's just say that I had the first talk in my life with my mother where tough issues were discussed and neither of us raised our voices. She doesn't want to see me, and I'll oblige her."

Daniel squeezed her toward him, a sheltering she'd never received from anyone other than Quinn and Matthew. A weight she'd carried her entire life lifted from her. She was free. Things with her mother were settled.

Lyric looked heavenward. "Thank You," she mouthed.

Magda struggled to free herself from the restraints again placed upon her. Lyric's visit had doused her like a pot of boiling asphalt. The reminders of Matthew brought back the anxiety and the need for a drink.

She cursed Lyric. Why did she have to come here and put her in this state, undo her plotting? She was still wily enough to sneak out of this place.

She threw her body back against the pillow. "Let me out of here, you pigs!" she screamed. "You can't hold me like this. I know my rights."

If Stowe wasn't careful, she'd tell the good citizens of Amazing Grace that their fine judge could be moved to rule when his palm was greased just right. Didn't matter that he'd made sure, as he signed the papers, that she understood he was doing what he'd done to save at least one child. He'd asked her to release Lyric to an adoption agency, but even the great big judge couldn't make her do that. Besides, Jessup would have killed her if she had. He was so eaten up with bitterness that he wanted Lyric to grow up in this town where Daniel would see her and never know the truth.

How long had she been in this prison? Edwin Stowe had no right to keep her here. She had her rights, and her rights included the ability to drink herself into oblivion. Without a drink, she was in hell for an eternity.

She pulled hard against the cloth binding her. Hell. That's exactly what she deserved.

"No," she grunted.

Hell was here on this earth, not in some place beyond death. God tormented her with her wrongdoing. Even in Lyric's peaceful face and calm conversation, she'd found no sanctuary. Maybe Quinn would come, even if Lyric had told him he wasn't wanted.

Thoughts of Quinn brought on memories of standing in the shadows and watching Matthew grow up. Funny, the one she gave away had been the most precious to her. And she'd allowed Jessup to do to her the same thing that he'd done to Daniel.

And when the pain became too much, he'd coaxed her to take the first drink, and the second, and the third, until she learned that alcohol could numb her from the pain.

She rolled her head back and forth, anything to keep the memories from eating her alive.

If Daniel had truly loved her ...

But she'd pushed him away, knowing he'd want his twins.

"Daniel." She let loose a small cry. He could never love her as much as he'd loved Desiree.

Like her, he was a loser at falling in love—they'd both found the wrong ones. And no one else could make it right for either of them—even each other.

She closed her eyes against the memory pressing in upon her. The boy babe, his small hands and feet flailing in the doctor's arms. "A boy. The first one is a boy," the nurse announced.

She couldn't look upon him. She'd made the decision. Larry Roberts made it easy for her. Paid her big for her little boy.

And though she wanted nothing to do with Lyric, she'd brought her home, no one the wiser for the scheme worked out between Jessup and Larry—not even Bernice knew who'd given birth to her precious adopted son—and no one knew better than she did how deep Larry was in Jessup's business. Making Magda give up Mathew wasn't the only favor Jessup bestowed on the then lowly attorney. He'd gotten Larry appointed county attorney. And Larry had moved up in the world, but he was still forced to live in the dark, unseemly world of drug trafficking. They might live in a nice place, and Matthew might have had everything he ever wanted, but Larry was dirt just like Magda.

And no one was more surprised when, Lyric, like a magnet pulling steel, had drawn Matthew's attention from the moment they'd met as very small children.

Larry had warned her to keep Lyric away, but Magda never had enough power to do that. As they grew older, she'd begged Larry to tell Matthew—and Bernice—the truth. Swear them both to silence.

Maybe God would give her credit for trying to save Matthew. Larry refused, of course, too afraid of losing his son, his wife, and Jessup's favor.

Look what that got him.

She'd never told Lyric. The girl asked too many questions, always wanting to know the name of her daddy.

A single sob escaped, and she yanked on her bands. "Let me out. You've got to let me out of here." This torment had to stop.

The door creaked open. Magda turned. Had Quinn come? Would he listen to reason, tell the judge he needed to let his momma out of here? She could be taken back to the jail, get a bond. She'd find a way to get Jessup to spring her, and now that Daniel could be targeted, Jessup would open that tab at the Backslide for her again.

The man took off his sunglasses as he made his way toward her, tucking them in his shirt pocket. "Mrs. Moxley," he said.

She needed to be careful. This guy might hold the key

to her freedom. "Who are you?" She settled back in the bed.

He held something behind his back. "Who I am is of no importance. You have information about something I want."

"Look, mister. I'm a little busy trying to get myself out of this hole. Maybe you help me. Maybe I'll help you."

"What is it your daughter has, Magda? Do you know?"

"Yeah." She nodded. "I know. You work for Jessup?"

He shook his head, moving around the bed, gliding his hand across the railing, then the foot of the bed, and finally the opposite railing to stand beside her. Something about him flamed a memory. Maybe she'd met him somewhere when she'd been smashed. She narrowed her eyes and tried to remember. He looked like someone she knew—may have seen.

He smelled of that expensive cologne all the dandies wore. His cold eyes peered into hers as he leaned forward. "I'm more powerful than Jessup Roy."

Magda blinked. Someone in this area more powerful than Jessup? No way. But she clamped her mouth shut.

"I want those papers. I'm willing to pay a good sum for them."

"For a couple of birth certificates?" She laughed.

Confusion flickered in his steely gaze then vanished. "I'm looking for a list of names. Your son-in-law brought it with him from Raleigh. I don't care about birth records."

"Braedon didn't mention anything else," she lied. "He'd gone to Raleigh to retrieve some birth certificates.

That's what Jessup wants from that stubborn girl. Braedon didn't even know what he had." She might be a drunk, but she wasn't an idiot. This guy wanted the papers that would undo her tab at the Backslide, take Jessup down and her with him.

"I beg to differ. Jessup wants something else. Something Braedon couriered for him. Between the time the idiot met with you and then killed himself, he did something with it."

Magda knew evil. It'd been a part of her practically from birth, and this guy stunk with it. "If he gave it to Lyric, she didn't say."

His expression didn't change. "You don't want to lie to me. I plan to get those papers, even if I have to have a few more people murdered to do it."

What did she care? He could kill whomever he wanted.

"I've already stepped into your world. You might want to make it easier on those you love—say that grandson of yours, that daughter and son."

Magda held his stare. "I don't care about any of them." Another lie could save Cade. "And even if I did, how can I get something into your hands I never knew existed."

He slipped the sunglasses from his pocket and back over his eyes, and a crooked, evil smile contorted his face. He reached into his back pocket, lifting his shirt. Keeping one hand behind him, he drew out a knife, opened it, and leaned down.

Magda winced. How long would it take them to find

her? The call button was too far for her to reach. She was bound. She would die.

She tugged her arms against the cloth, hoping to pull them free.

The smile never left the stranger's face. He'd enjoy killing her. The gleam in his eye told her so.

With a fluid motion, he brought the knife down and under the restraint on her right arm, freeing her. In his other hand, he brought forth a bottle of whiskey—not just any whiskey, the best Kentucky bourbon on the market, and though the lid was opened, most of the amber liquid remained inside.

"All the better for you to drink this." He held it toward her, turning the bottle around in his hand. Her tongue was parched, her head screaming for the brown liquid to flow down her throat and warm her insides, taking away the memories, the excruciating truth of her own failures. She reached for it.

He kept it out of her reach, shaking his head. "I need a promise from you. Do you understand?"

She nodded, licking her lips. "Anything."

"Get good and drunk. Enjoy yourself. Drink yourself right out of this place." He raised the bottle to his lips, stopping short of partaking.

"That's all you want from me? Really?"

"That's all I want?"

She giggled like a little girl. "I'll do it. I promise."

"That's what I like to hear." He thrust the bottle into

her free hand and lowered the sunglasses to the bridge of his nose. Then he closed his knife and slid it into his pocket. "Drink up, Magda. The nurses will break up your party soon." He walked to the door.

Through the bottle tipped to her lips, she saw him stop and look at her. He'd looked like a devil when he'd walked into the room, but leaving, he appeared to her like a pure angel. She'd do whatever it took to get on his good side, to work for him. Jessup never gave her the expensive stuff— not once.

And as the liquor brought sweet oblivion, a window of her mind was opened.

She realized why the nice fellow seemed so familiar. He had the same features of someone she knew and had never trusted.

# 17

Lyric was thankful for Ethan's aid in the kitchen. He'd actually made a trip to the grocery store, her list in tow. Then he'd returned and helped to make the salad and keep the prep dishes clean as she made the meatloaf, mashed potatoes, and the corn. For so many years, she'd cooked only for Brae and Cade. Now, with Daniel, Quinn, Ethan, and Balaam all staying in her home, meals had become more complicated, and the table more filled. When they'd returned home, Ethan's partner, Pierce, hadn't been here. He wasn't back yet, but he was expected for dinner. Did she have enough food for all of them?

"This will be plenty." Ethan must have read her mind. "And if it's not, we'll call Tom and tell him to bring some dessert when he gets back from wherever he went."

Lyric pushed her beaters into the old mixer and glanced over her shoulder at Balaam talking in hushed tones with Daniel.

Lyric poured a bit of cream into her potatoes then

turned on the mixer.

"Food looks and smells good. We don't get homecooked meals too often. Pierce isn't going to like it if he misses this." Ethan stepped near her, washing off a dish she'd left out.

A knock took Balaam away from Daniel and to the door. He peered outside, turned back to Daniel, again for a fraction of a second, before frowning and opening the door.

"We were just talking about you missing dinner," Ethan said. "Make yourself useful, Skipper. Set the table."

"Skipper?" Lyric laughed. "He definitely doesn't look like a Skipper. And you're not Gilligan."

"Well, my partner doesn't look much like a bad man, but that's what we call him." Pierce's smirk was neither friendly nor teasing. "Right, Badman?"

"You're right. Ethan can't be a bad man. Poor choice of nicknames, I'd say."

"Thank you." Ethan's smile was nicer, teasing. "That's what I've been telling him for years, since we were kids."

"You've known each other that long?" Lyric jerked back, surprised. "I thought those kinds of law enforcement friendships only happen on television."

Pierce narrowed his eyes at Ethan. "He exaggerates. We were sworn into the bureau on the same day. Feels like I've known him too long already."

"I know. He's confessed to me that he talks in first person," Lyric teased. "That would drive me crazy."

Beyond Ethan, Lyric didn't miss the sharp look Balaam cast their way. Jealous. Well, good. How many women had fawned over Bay in all the years he'd been on and off stage. How many had he…?

She flipped the switch on the mixer, sending it into liquify mode to drown her thoughts.

Potatoes pulverized, she turned off the mixer and pushed the eject button for the beaters. Ethan had his hand out, ready to take them.

She offered him a smile as she scraped the potatoes into a bowl. Ethan pulled out seven plates.

"Daniel, would Grace like to join us?" Lyric asked.

"Pinochle day," Daniel said. "The ladies are all at her house."

Lyric looked out her kitchen window. Despite the fact that the day had turned cold, dark, and gloomy with a sure sign of a storm, cars lined Grace's drive. Nothing would keep those older women from their weekly pinochle, not even a near hostage situation and a double killing.

Ethan handed the plates to Pierce then counted out the silverware needed.

Lyric pulled the meatloaf from the oven and placed it on a trivet to move it to the table. She set it in the middle and walked down the hall.

Opening the door, she stepped inside Cade's room. Quinn and Cade had a boatload of plastic building blocks on the floor and a town almost built—a gift Ethan had given him upon his return from the store. "Okay, boys, if I step on even one piece, I'm confiscating every last one of them."

They glanced up at her at the same time, Quinn looking like the young brother who used to sit with her and play despite the fact that he wanted to be anywhere else but attending a tea party with his lonely sister. Her heart filled near to bursting. Quinn had always worked so hard at giving Cade what had been missing from their childhoods. She closed her eyes and allowed the emotions to overtake her.

If she'd gone on tour with Balaam, Quinn would have been all alone. And Balaam. She'd have grown to hate the man he probably became. She'd seen a glimpse of it when he pulled out of town without her. Now that he was back—other than the death of Braedon and Matthew, Cade's presence, and the feds eating dinner in her house—things with Balaam seemed almost as they had been before they'd decided they were all grown up.

"Hey." The warmth of Quinn's hand caressed her face. "What are you thinking about?"

"About the long ago. Before Bay and I went and messed everything up."

"I'm sorry that I hit Bay earlier. It's just that he wasn't at the California rehab, and I got a little overprotective of my little sister. I let the anger get the better of me. I've asked the Lord to forgive me, and I'll ask the dummy out there for his mercy." He tilted his head. "Forgive me?"

"No need to ask." She pushed him playfully. "Ever."

"You hit Dad, Uncle Quinn?" Cade shoveled up the pieces that weren't used and dumped them into the box.

"I did, and I'm really sorry for it, Cade. That's not the way to solve issues. I should have asked him what I wanted to know, and I might have my answer to the question I need to ask him, and he wouldn't have taken the brunt of my anger, which is never right. It grows in you, and it causes you to commit more sin."

Cade nodded. "Dad will forgive you. I know he will." He smiled big.

She laughed at him. She wanted to tell him that his dad was a lover not a fighter. He got out of most situations with his quick wit and fast thinking, but she didn't want Cade to ever take after that part of Balaam. "Dinner's ready." Someone's phone rang, and she ducked out of the room.

"Lyric, Quinn." Daniel nearly slammed into her in the hallway. He braced her, keeping her from falling back. "We have to go to the hospital."

Lyric startled. "What's wrong?"

Balaam hurried to her side and drew Cade toward him.

Lyric touched his arm. "Wait here just a minute." She pushed out of the hallway and into the living room where everyone followed her. "What's going on," she demanded.

"The mental health center called. They're taking Magda by ambulance to the hospital. They want you both there," Daniel said.

Lyric shook her head. "What happened?"

"She's drunk."

Lyric gave a short shake of her head. "No way. She was sober when I left her. Could they have given her a different medication, something that caused a reaction?"

Daniel grasped her shoulders with a gentle touch. "One of her restraints was cut. Somehow, she got hold of a bottle of bourbon. Drank the entire thing, and the alcohol has a reaction with the medicine they have her on. You all go on ahead now. I have someone I need to meet." He released her. "Lyric, you and Cade go with your brother to the hospital. Bay, you're welcome to tag with Lyric or cross the street and play Pinochle with the grand dames. Starsky and Hutch can watch over them at the hospital." Daniel leaned back and looked at the two men. Ethan busily covered the food. Tom Pierce eyed them with keen interest.

"I'm sticking with Lyric and Cade," Balaam's voice was low and broached no nonsense. "Don't know why you'd think otherwise."

Daniel nodded. "Just a nice way of saying you aren't welcome to go with me. I knew you wouldn't leave them anyway."

Quinn grabbed three coats from the door: his, Cade's, and Lyric's. He left Balaam's on the rack.

Lyric took it down for Bay. "Give me just a minute, Quinn. We can eat when we get back, but I don't want Cade waiting that long. Let him eat something while I get ready." She headed for her bedroom.

"We'll hurry and eat," Balaam offered. "Quinn, you need to try to put something in your stomach, too. We may

304

be in for a long night."

Quinn followed Balaam into the kitchen. "I'll make you a plate, Lyric."

Lyric sat at her bed and stared down at her hands clasped together as if she planned to pray.

Many times in church, she'd bowed her head and listened to Quinn or the prayers of others. Daniel had prayed a lot in their Sunday school class.

She'd never once allowed the words to seep through her mind. Now, she knew why. God had seemed as absent from her as the father whose identity she hadn't known at that time.

She slid off her bed and turned to face it, hands folded and her head resting on top of them. "Are You there?" She looked upward then bowed her head. God was beside her. She couldn't see Him, and she couldn't describe it, but His arms encircled her. "I'm sorry," she whispered. "I'm sorry for everything I've done. I—I think I was trying to get Your attention. Please forgive me. Please love me. Please let me be Your child. Momma's not a bad person, God. She's probably trying to get Your attention, too. Will You take care of her? I haven't been nice to her, but I don't want her to die. Quinn will hurt so bad." She sat for a long moment, taking in deep breaths. "God, I'll hurt, too."

# 18

Daniel lifted his Stetson from his head and waited at the heavy mahogany entrance, swiping at the little bit of snow that landed on his shoulder, the cold in the air, keeping the flakes from dissipating.

He heard the footfall on the other side. The maid pulled back the door, scanning him from head to foot. "Sheriff Dixon, you're a good-looking man when you're wearing your everyday clothes and not that tired old uniform." Nadine Johnson smiled, but a wariness touched her eyes as she looked around him to the mansion's drive as if she expected someone to be with him.

"Thank you, Nadine. Is Jessup home?"

"You know, I've been off in the kitchen. He could've slipped by me. Come in, and I'll check for you."

The slender woman scampered out of the foyer and then reappeared. "Sheriff, come on in. Professor Roy's in his study."

"I know where to find it. Thank you." Daniel made his

way down the marble-tiled hall and turned to his right. He knocked and pushed open the door.

Jessup came around his all-too-neat desk. "Daniel, I've been waiting for you to make this call on me. But to what do I owe this honor?" He held out his hand.

"Ah, Jess, we've known each other too long and had too much pass between us to pretend I'd ever make a friendly call on you."

Jessup lowered his hand. "I thought maybe you'd become a better man, and let the past go."

Daniel nailed him with his deadliest glare, the one he practiced on every criminal he'd ever met, especially this one. "No. Not going to happen."

"Well, at least take a seat. We can be hospitable."

"I'll stand."

"Then tell me what it is you've come to say, and let yourself out of your misery." Jessup sat behind his desk, looking up at Daniel like the condescending academic Jessup had always been. Smarter than everyone—too smart to get caught whether it came to drug running or wife stealing. Whatever he did, Jessup considered himself the one in control.

Daniel turned his hat in his hand. "Tell me what makes you do the things you do?"

"Can't say I know what you mean, Danny Boy?"

Daniel smirked. Baiting him wouldn't work. Jessup had called him Danny Boy once in high school. Daniel had beaten the crap out of him for it. Only his mother got away with using that nickname.

"Do you care to speak in clearer language, or do I need to guess where your hillbilly train of thought is leading you?"

Daniel laughed. "Two days apart, Jess. We were born two days apart in the same hospital right here in Amazing Grace." He again turned his hat in his hand. "My mother once told me you were so scrawny you nearly died. If you only had passed on."

Jessup blinked.

"Yeah, you heard me. How many young kids have lost their lives because of your dealings? How many fathers and mothers have neglected their children because you've plied them with your filthy drugs? How many innocent families have been torn apart because of your trade?"

"Daniel, your accusations have fallen on deaf ears all these years. What makes you think anyone's listening to your babbling now? You've never proven a thing against me. You're here in my home without probable cause, and you know it."

Daniel lowered his hands, "I'm not here as sheriff. I'm a man concerned for some kids that I've always loved, always tried to look after. Two of them are mine. And one of my sons died at the hands of a man working for you."

"I can't begin to fathom what you're talking about. Care to speak English?" Jessup gave undue attention to a piece of paper in front of him."

Daniel clenched his teeth and brought his hand down

hard on Jessup's desk.

Jessup jumped.

"I have the papers Braedon was sent to retrieve. The ones he didn't give to you."

Jessup stared up. Daniel had his full attention. He could see the academic wheels turning. What papers? That was the question Jessup was asking himself.

"My daughter doesn't have them, nor does my son, Quinn. Matthew's dead, and I won't bring Larry and Bernice into this, but I'm sure that you had a hand in what Magda did. I've been thinking it over a lot lately. There's a reason I can never get to you. Larry's the county attorney. He's got no jurisdiction over my office, but he's got a pulse on this town. You know what he did. You probably helped him take my son away from me so you'd have something to hold over his head." Daniel paced away and back to the desk. He leaned forward. "Tell me. What is it that makes a smart man like you do the things you do? You don't need the drug business. The Roys are old money. If you needed to make a living, you could do it honestly. I thought your daughter's death would help you to see that your kids are more important. Didn't Jasmine mean anything to you? Desiree at least left a part of her here with you in them, didn't she?"

"You leave my daughter out of this. Jasmine left me long before she died."

"You couldn't handle her dating my deputy. I suppose you were probably happy when that deputy and your daughter ended up dead."

"I suppose you want to blame me for their deaths as well."

"No. Those are probably two deaths you haven't had a hand in. I thought it would shake you up, though, get you to seeing that other peoples' kids are precious to them, stop playing with lives and plying them with drugs."

"You've skipped from one argument back to another. Make sense, man, or get out of here." Jessup pushed from his chair.

"How'd Magda Moxley get a bottle of whiskey in the mental health center?"

Jessup stared then gave a half-laugh. "Who knows how Magdalene does anything? I haven't been near her. I had them stop her tab at the Backslide. She has a serious problem."

"Yeah, Jessup, she does, and plying her with booze inside that facility isn't helping her children or her grandson."

"Ah, now we come full circle. The other part of the conversation. Quinn and Lyric. Magda didn't want them to know. You never showed any interest in her after you found out what she's really like. She was a poor excuse for Desiree, wasn't she?"

The heat of anger rose up Daniel's neck, but he tamped it down. Jessup didn't know it, but his life or his freedom was running short. "I know about Lyric now, and both of them are my kids. Make no mistake. I've been denied my fatherhood way too long. And anyone who's put a hurting on them as long as you have, won't get away with it any longer. Their world was rocked by Braedon's actions. Those actions were a direct result of something you started. Lyric lost a husband and her twin brother." Daniel heaved in a deep breath. "Quinn's best friend killed his little brother. Help me to understand, Jess. How can you stand to see them suffer and not care about them one bit? What about Larry and Bernice? We've known them all our lives. They lost their only son." Daniel straightened. "Or is it always about having the edge? Those boys—best friends all their lives—dying like they did. That bothers you no more than your own daughter's death. While she was alive, while Nathan was here, I always kept an eye out for them. Kids have a way of finding trouble when someone isn't looking, but Jessup, if either of your kids ever found trouble, I'd have done everything I could to help them, including giving up my own life."

"Sure you would." Jessup leaned his head back and laughed. "The kids that Desiree wouldn't give you. The ones she and I had. You'd have given your life for them. That's rich, Danny Boy. Good thing you'll never have to prove it. Nathan won't ever come back here. Jasmine's already dead."

Daniel straightened. "Desiree was my life, and maybe I didn't see it back then, but her staying with me when she loved you, that would have made her miserable." He put his hat on his head. "I'm glad she knew you when you were just a skunk who stole another man's wife. She never would have left me if she hadn't loved you before she loved me. I don't hold that against her, but I'll tell you. If she were alive today to see what you've become, what you've done to the lives of others, she'd despise you every much as I do."

"She loved me more than she loved you, Daniel. Don't tell me that doesn't still eat at you. She spent more of her life with me than she did you. She had my children. Her dying days were spent with me and not with you." Jessup swiped at his eyes and turned away. "And you didn't waste too much time before turning to Magda, now, did you?"

"No, I didn't, but look what I just learned. I did a terrible thing without thinking of the consequences, and I'm reaping some pain, but in the midst of it, God has blessed me with a daughter and a son. And I know that my other son, he's in heaven. God gave me the pleasure of introducing Matthew to Christ. If I had to do it all over again, I would." He started toward the door then turned. "I don't think you answered me, but what would Desiree say to you today if she knew what you'd done to so many of the lives in this town?"

Jessup's silence was answer enough. The man turned his chair and stared out his office window at the swirl of snow in the air and falling onto the ground where it clung to the dead grass.

He stared at Jessup's back.

Jessup rounded on him. "Daniel, you're going to feel

313

the pain I felt at Desiree's passing—the grief you didn't feel—it's going to roll over you, crush you, the way her death crushed me. Maybe you owe me for taking that pain for you back then, but I'm returning the misery tenfold. Now that you've claimed those kids, I'll shout to the world that the town sheriff was friendly with the town prostitute. That'll end that career of yours. Break your momma's heart. She'll see what this scrawny kid who almost died can do to her precious only son."

Daniel pointed at the man. "You're going down. You may want to think about turning yourself in because those other papers—the ones I didn't come here to talk to you about—they give me probable cause to come knocking on your door again. I have a deputy and one of your gophers in the morgue. I know you didn't do it, but someone did, and I suspect they're close on your tail as well. They can't be happy about this door you've opened to expose them." He pointed his finger at himself and at Jessup. "I'll do my best to save your life as this plays out—albeit it'll only be so that I can see you behind bars. But if you make one more threat or try to entice any of those kids that I love, I'll kill you myself and produce the probable cause after I do it."

As he turned and walked out the door, he passed Nadine Johnson. Her skin was ghostly pale, and he was certain she'd been listening at the door.

He'd tipped his hand and hadn't been thinking about Nadine's propensity for gossip as he dug his heels into Jessup.

314

Daniel didn't care. Jessup Roy hadn't responded to him. He'd only stood there. The fear in Jessup's eyes was tangible, and that was something Daniel had waited to see for a very long time.

Balaam stood with his back against the wall by the waiting room door. He and Cade had just returned from the front door of the hospital where they'd watched the snow, which had been flurries, change into something more substantial as daylight gave way to night.

Cade stood beside him, trying to act mature but jumping with every move in his direction, waiting for word about his grandma.

"What's with you?" Goodman's sharp tone reached the hall from inside the waiting room.

Balaam winked at Cade and put his finger to his lips, asking the boy to be quiet.

"What's with me?" Goodman's partner shot back. "Since when do you help a woman with the cooking and the dishes, Badman?"

"Lyric's had a lot happen to her. Helping her was my way of making her feel she's not alone."

"That isn't going to work with her. Man, she has that hot-shot rock star, that good-old-boy sheriff, and her brother. She can't be duped by you."

"Dad?" Cade whispered.

Balaam shook his head and bent down. "Whisper in my ear?"

"Are you a rock star?" Cade asked.

"Nope. Not anymore." He spoke in Cade's ear.

"What are you then?"

Good question. What was he? Then it hit him, and he smiled. "Don't you know?"

Cade shook his head.

"I have the best job in the world. I'm your dad."

Cade beamed.

"Not that it's any of your concern," Ethan said. "I like Lyric Carter. She's got class, and she has something else I haven't seen in a woman in a long while. She's got morals. They're deep. She's learned from her mistakes."

"Yeah, right. Odds are she was sleeping with the other guy her husband killed."

"Pierce, shut up," Goodman warned.

They'd stayed one beat too long. Balaam pushed off the wall and walked down the corridor, motioning Cade with him. His son didn't need to hear anyone disparage his mother. Balaam passed a nurse carefully guarding a cart full of pills. His gaze strayed to them. He'd always been good with a slight of hand. How easy would it be to pick up the cup with the Xanax?

Then he'd be no good to anyone. He'd have to find a corner to crawl in and sleep, but the worries Cade's innocent question introduced would float away.

"Dad, are you really staying?"

Balaam pulled his eyes away from the pills. "How long you want me to stay, Cade?"

"I don't want you to leave."

"Well, I'm going to do my best to stay."

A scream pierced the air, and Lyric ran out of a room further down the corridor. Balaam started toward her, but she held up her hand and walked their way. "Bay, can you go in? Seeing me upsets her for some reason. Quinn can't handle her alone."

He walked down the hall. Before he even reached her room, he smelled the bourbon. He turned back to Lyric.

"Thank you," she mouthed.

"Okay, Lord. I need your help here," he muttered before stepping inside.

The color had left Quinn. He looked like a dried-up washcloth, too dry to crumble, but one more squeeze and he'd crack.

On the bed, Magda thrashed, her eyes wild, her words incoherent.

Balaam put his hand on Quinn's shoulder. "Let me sit with her for a minute. Go outside and take a breather. Get a soda or something."

The smell of bourbon was so strong, Balaam could almost taste it. Kentucky. Aged. If the nurse came by with her cart, he could take that Xanax and be satisfied. Just one.

"You okay?" Quinn asked.

Balaam shook off the thoughts. Cade needed him here. "I'm fine. Go on. Take a break."

"Matthew?" Madga stared at Balaam.

"No, Magda. It's Balaam Carter."

Magda didn't look away.

"She's fighting some demons the liquor didn't vanquish." Quinn didn't move.

"Matthew?" Balaam questioned.

"Matthew," Magda moaned. "My baby boy. I'm so sorry."

Balaam turned to Quinn. "Matthew?"

"Go with Lyric, Bay. I'll take care of Momma."

"What does she mean, Quinn? I didn't know she ever cared about Matt."

"This isn't the time for answers."

"He's my son," Magda screamed. "My son. My baby boy. I killed him. I killed my son," she wailed.

"Larry and Bernice ... She's hallucinating. No way Matthew was her son."

"Not now. Not here," Quinn begged. "I need to take care of her. There's a chance ..."

"A chance of what?"

Quinn sat hard in a chair. "The doctor told us if she continues like this, she's going to die. The drinking's taken its toll on her. She can't stand much more. Her body is about done with its abuse. Since we got her clean, this setback is the worst thing that could happen to her. The doctor told me if one of her messed-up pals thought they were doing her a favor, they hadn't. They could have killed her because of the medication the mental health facility had

318

her on. Now, keeping her sober is the only thing that can prolong her life."

"I'm sorry." What else could he say? Magda was a dead woman. He'd never seen her sober. Not one day in his lifetime, and even now, after being safe in a facility, she'd managed to get herself into trouble.

The thought sobered Balaam. How close had he come to death's door to be drawn back to this life by the hand of God.

Balaam sank to his knees and looked up at Quinn. "She's out of our hands, Quinn. Let's give her over to God."

Lyric took her time walking away from her mother's room. She found a quiet place in the corridor. Privacy was in such short demand these days. Even in the midst of the busy hospital, she relished the time with Cade. She bent down. "You okay?"

Cade nodded.

"Cade, Mom's sorry that Grandma hasn't always been very nice."

Cade's lips trembled. "She's nice to me."

Lyric gave the matter some thought. "Yes. I suppose she always has been."

"But she always acts funny around you and Uncle Quinn."

Lyric nodded at the perception of her son. "She's

always been troubled, and I'm thankful that she had you to give her some happy moments. She loves you, and love for Grandma Moxley has always been hard."

"I love her, too."

Lyric tugged his ear. "Don't tell her, but I do, too." She straightened and took his hand in hers. They walked together toward the waiting room.

Pierce's laugh brought her up short.

Warm hands touched her shoulder. "You okay?" Balaam's breath brushed her neck.

She nodded.

"Skipper Playboy," Pierce said. "Can you believe that anyone ever fell for that alias? I thought they wouldn't believe that an agent would be stupid enough to be so transparent. Chief thought I was insane, but it worked."

Balaam tightened his hold on her, and she moved to let him know that he'd hurt her. "Sorry," he whispered into her ear.

"Yeah, Skipper, I can. You're good at what you do, very convincing." Ethan said with no real enthusiasm.

"Look, brother, snap out of it. That raven-haired vixen with those drive-you-wild curls isn't going to look at you. Her husband was a drug runner, a courier. She seems to have a thing for that Brasher character. She has bad taste in men. You're not her type."

"Her husband was our informant."

Balaam had been tense beside her during their conversation. His hold on her shoulder tightened again for

320

a brief second. Then he released her, moving toward the door.

Lyric grasped his arm and shook her head. "Listen."

"He was in it deep, caught red-handed. So what if we used it to get him to turn the tables?"

"A lot of good it did. He turned the tables on us. We have no idea where that list of dealers went," Ethan said, "and they hold the key to everything we need."

"She has them. There's no other explanation," Pierce declared.

"I told you." Ethan's voice was nearly a growl. "She's not lying. She has something else but not what we need."

"What we need to do is pull back from her. Let this thing unfold," Pierce said.

"And what then?" Balaam thundered past Lyric and into the room. "Lyric has nothing in her hands, and she's killed?" He grabbed Pierce by the collar.

Lyric sheltered Cade from the violence. "Bay," she hissed.

"You even suggest putting her in danger one more time, Pierce, and I'll ..."

"Careful, Brasher. Threatening a federal agent is a crime."

"The name's Carter. Balaam Carter. You can call me Mr. Carter." Balaam pushed the man away from him. "You agree with his little plan?" he demanded of Ethan.

Ethan looked between both men then to Lyric. His eyes locked with hers. "At this point, no."

"At this point?" Balaam ground out each word. "At no point. You got it. She won't be placed in the middle of anything."

"Your plan is to sit here and wait for them to make the next move then?" Pierce pressed. "As I understand it, they made a move this afternoon. It missed her head by an inch."

"No. We don't wait on them. I'm your middle man."

"Bay," Lyric reached for him. "No."

He slipped his arm around her waist and pulled her to him. "I'm not leaving you, Lyric. Nothing's going to happen to me. Nathan as much as told me I'd be back working with his old man. Why not let Jessup think that's what I'm doing? I got two federal agents and our favorite sheriff to watch my back. Above all, God is looking out for us. What could happen to me?"

# 19

Quinn looked at his watch. Two o'clock in the morning, and they'd just gotten Momma stabilized, told him she'd most likely live another day. Then they told him the mental health facility wouldn't take her back. Liability, they claimed.

The liability was on them. If he ever learned which of her old pals from The Backslide thought he was doing her a favor, he didn't know what he'd do. He'd have to ask Daniel how they could get copies of the surveillance video of people entering the facility and the sign-in. Everyone who visited had to sign in. But getting past security with a bottle. Someone had to be slick to do that.

He passed the waiting room and peered inside. Lyric was awake, her head against the couch arm. Cade, asleep, leaned on Balaam's shoulder. Since when had he gotten so big.

The boy had grown up without Quinn's notice, and over the last couple of months, he'd showed so much maturity. Quinn's gut twisted. He'd wanted so much different for his nephew. Why had he allowed Momma and Braedon to create this nightmare for all of them?

Goodman's movement jerked Quinn's attention to him. The agent looked in Quinn's direction.

Quinn searched the room. He hadn't noticed Pierce asleep in the chair by the door.

Lyric pushed up and straightened her jeans and shirt before walking toward him. "How is she?"

"Asleep."

"I'd like to go sit with her for a minute. Why don't you go get some fresh air, and I'll join you in a bit?"

Quinn put his hand to the back of his sister's head and pulled her toward him. He kissed her hair. "You don't have to pretend for me. I know you'd rather not be in there with her."

"You're wrong, Quinny," she whispered and stood on her tiptoes. "I had a talk with God today, and as I recall, you have taught and have shown by example that we are to honor our parents."

Quinn widened his eyes. "You talked with…"

"Yeah, and you always told me there was one honest to goodness prayer He would never reject."

Quinn's lips trembled and emotion stung his eyes. He pulled his sister toward him. "Thank You, Lord. Thank You. I've had so many prayers answered in the middle of all this mess."

Lyric turned and looked toward her son and Cade's

father. "You were pretty mad at Bay. You praying for him, too?"

"I've prayed for him every day for so many years I wondered if God had forsaken him."

"If he hurts my little boy, that man will need God's help."

Quinn laughed and wiped at his eyes. "Little sister, I honestly believe that Balaam has never forgotten a thing about you, and he's never seen you live in the fear Braedon caused. He still remembers that formidable temper."

"Well, I learned it from Momma, now, didn't I?" She started past him.

Quinn reached for her forearm. "You learned it from life. Momma's anger was caused by her psychological problems, lost love, and the bottle. When life turned sour on you, the truth is, you were stronger and less angry than Momma. You were staid and purposeful, protecting Cade, Matthew, and me."

Lyric took a shaky breath. "I think he knew. At least toward the end, I believe that Matt learned the truth. That was why he came for me and got himself killed."

Quinn stared at her for a long moment. Then he brushed her face tenderly with his hand. "If not for you..." he mouthed.

"And for you," she whispered back. "Go. Get some fresh air. Bay won't let Cade out of his sight. Momma and I get along fine so long as she's asleep."

Quinn chuckled. "Yes, you do."

Lyric took great care to move the chair beside her mother's bed. She sat with her elbows on the chair arms and her hands folded, but the prayer would not come.

In silence, she breathed in the whiskey or bourbon, whatever the drink that had brought so much devastation to her life. The monitor at the start of the IV running into her mother's arm beeped every few seconds. Outside, nurses scuffled by. One peeped in the door, smiled, and moved away.

Lyric closed her eyes. *Thank You that I never took to the drink. That Quinn and Matthew stayed away from it. And that experimentation thing we did with the other stuff, thank You for making us hate it. Momma was an example of what not to do, and I think it sounds pretty bad to say this, but thank You that we looked into the mirror of her life and decided we didn't want any part of it.*

*I'm sorry, Lord, for what Balaam and I did. Mischief wiled us away, spending hours together doing wrong without thinking of the consequences. I made everything worse by thinking that Brae could make everything right, and I hurt him. I got Matthew killed. Daniel never got to know Matthew as his son. Quinn lost his best friend from the moment I married him, and we both lost our brother. Balaam lost his brother, too.*

She sat with her eyes closed and paused, her heart

aching from the truth. She could have blamed Balaam all along, and she had. She'd never hated him, though, because she knew that if she hadn't wanted to be in his arms, feel his comfort, believe his lies, believe they could live life on the road touring the world, she wouldn't have allowed herself to be beguiled by his boyish charm. Yet, he never showed a selfish side until he'd taken off on her, shrugging all his responsibilities, and leaving her with their son.

She opened her eyes and gasped. *Cade. You gave me Cade.*

The broken heart she'd given to God seemed to rise from the ashes of smoldering pain, and hope filled her.

*Cade has always been here with me, and he has given me joy. He's the reason Momma's anger wasn't allowed to take root in me.* She prayed as if God hadn't known the wonderfulness of the gift He'd bestowed upon her. "You gave me Cade," she said aloud and covered her mouth, looking to make sure she hadn't awakened her mother.

Momma stared at her.

Lyric startled and fought to keep from showing it. "How you doing?" She planted a smile on her face. "I know I upset you earlier. I can leave if you don't want me here."

Momma blinked. "Wasn't you, Lyric Kay." She tried to move her arms, but she was still restrained.

Lyric scooted forward on the chair and brushed her mother's hair from her face. Funny. She couldn't remember ever doing something so simple to the woman who'd given birth to her. "Was it the medication? The alcohol?"

Momma turned her attention to the door. Her face paled, and Lyric followed her stare.

No one. Was her mother seeing demons or contemplating something she didn't want to think about. Matthew's birth or the deaths she'd brought about?

"You're strong, girlie. Always have been." Her mother's fingertips touched the hand Lyric had laid by her side.

A compliment from her mother. A soft touch. Lyric had never known that such actions would make the steel she'd encased around her heart where her mother was concerned, melt, and that she'd actually feel the anger seeping away.

"I don't hate you, Lyric. I know I've said some terrible things to you and Quinny. Tell Quinn I love him. He was so much like his daddy. So gentlemanly. Sweet and kind. I always figured he'd leave me like Quinn, Sr., and I wanted to make sure that I ran him away instead. I couldn't take it if he left me first."

"You should tell him."

Momma nodded. "I should, but I don't think I'll have the chance."

Lyric smiled. "You will. The doctor said you've come through this. If you can stay away from the alcohol, you can have a good life with Quinn and Cade..."

"And you?" Momma raised her brows.

"If you want. I didn't think you'd want..." Lyric

choked out the words. Her mother had only called her strong. She hadn't said she loved her.

"I'd want." Momma smiled.

Another first. A real smile. For Lyric. Just for her.

"I love you, girlie."

Lyric lowered her head and allowed the tears and the sobs to pour forth.

"You asked me a question a while back," Momma squeezed her hand. "You asked me if I'd stand in the shadows if Quinn had died."

Lyric couldn't look into her mother's eyes. Momma could build hope and tear it down as quickly as God had done to Sodom and Gomorrah.

"Lyric," Momma grasped her hand.

Lyric forced her gaze upward. She was a mess, tears and whatnot all over her. Matthew had teased her about her "ugly tear face" on the day Balaam had left her behind, and the remembrance provided the smile she needed to face her mom.

"When Matthew died, and I had to stand back and watch them lower him into the ground, I realized, despite everything I ever said or did, even what I meant for Braedon to do, I had a soul that once loved God. I wanted to be beside you and Quinny, but I'd lost that right a long time ago, just like I lost the right for God to love me. But I swear to you that right now, if I thought I'd lose either you or Quinn, I would be on my knees, and I would beg God to take me instead of you. I'd beg Him to spare you, and I'd tell Him that you never did anything wrong. You never got anything from me or Braedon. That you stood strong and good, and you… that you and Quinn are not to blame for anything I did."

Lyric studied her mother, followed her words. Some meaning was in them, something beyond what she was saying if only because they were not words Lyric ever expected to hear. "God loves you, Momma. He never left you. I never really knew Him until today, but if it's true, and you knew His love once, all you have to do is ask Him. He never left, but you'd have the assurance I can't give to you."

Momma patted her hand. "I'm kind of tired."

Lyric sat back.

"Why don't you let me close my eyes? Maybe I'll have a talk with Him. I'd like to be able to hug my son."

Her mother was dismissing her, but this time, the action came without a sting. She took another quivering breath. "Okay. Quinn's getting some fresh air outside. I'll tell him to come see you."

Momma smiled, but a tear drifted down her face.

Lyric kissed her forehead. "You're going to be okay, Momma. Quinn and I'll help. Cade was just saying how much he loves you. We can be a family."

Momma nodded. "Go…" she whispered. "Tell Quinn I love him."

Lyric walked away, her gaze never leaving her mother until she entered the hallway. She blew her mother a kiss and walked away, a bounce in her step.

What in the world could have changed Magda Moxley so drastically that she wanted to hug Quinn and tell him she loved him?

She hurried down the hall, anxious for her brother to have his greatest wish in the entire world fulfilled. This could only be a gift from God.

Lyric stood back from the automatic doors, debating whether to go outside in the foul weather. The snow was falling, and Quinn wouldn't be out there.

Daniel came from the parking lot, walked toward her, stopped, and looked to his right.

Lyric turned her attention there.

Quinn sat on a covered bench, his head lowered. Daniel started in Quinn's direction, and Lyric moved through the doors.

The temperatures had dropped severely since they'd gone inside hours ago.

"God," Quinn whispered, obviously unaware that they stood near, "this has been one of those weeks where I've gone on the strength of the Word poured into me ahead of time. I'm leaning on You a lot. I haven't even reached much for Your wisdom to fill me so that I can feed your people on Sunday. Thank you for those in my congregation who are standing in for me during this time." He rubbed his face with his hands. "This anger, it's running so deep, like lava in my veins. I'm not used to it, and I need Your help to contain it."

Daniel sat on one side of Quinn and Lyric took the other side. "Maybe you shouldn't try to contain it, Quinn," Daniel said. "Maybe the key is to let it loose. God doesn't say that all anger is sin."

"You preaching to the preacher, now?"

"Just reasoning with him."

"My anger is sin." Quinn tilted back his head and rolled his neck.

"Care to pour a little more of that anger out on me." Daniel nudged him.

Quinn pushed to his feet.

"If I'm the reason, I want to know. I don't want you 'containing' it to spare my feelings. I'm a big boy, son. I'd like to answer your fury—if I have an answer."

"I'm not your son," Quinn released the words to the world. "As much as I always wanted it, I've never been yours."

Lyric's heart actually hurt for her brother. All these years, and he'd held so much on his shoulders: his father's abandonment, his mother's drunkenness and lewd behavior, his sister's wayward soul. No one had ever really been there for him, but Lyric, looking back, could see Daniel had tried to be a father figure to so many.

Daniel's face softened. "You've always been the closest thing I have to a son. I've enjoyed watching the man you've grown into. I always got a kick out of you and those Carter boys, and Matt. They looked up to you. Did you know that? Made me proud."

"I wasn't your son," Quinn repeated, his voice deflating with each word.

Daniel nodded. "I heard you the first time. Maybe I didn't make myself clear. Quinn, I've loved you like a son."

Quinn shook his head and swiped at the tears before they could fall. "No, Daniel. You didn't. You took me back to her. I came to you. I begged you to take me away, but you just fed me and left me with her."

Daniel didn't speak.

"As young as I'd been, I knew better than to show you the bruises she left on me. She pummeled me with a frying pan for no reason that I can remember."

"I knew she hurt you. I didn't know how, but I also knew a little boy who loved his mother no matter what. She never hit you like that again."

Daniel was right, but how did he know? Lyric stared at him, but Daniel's gaze remained on Quinn, who needed him now. "I told her if she ever laid a hand on you, it would be the last time. I didn't need to see the bruises. I saw the pain on your face."

Quinn closed his eyes tight and pulled at his hair with both hands.

"There's more, Quinn. Give it to me? Let's work through this."

Quinn dropped his hands. "Why are you here? Why do you care so much for me? Lyric and Matthew were—"

"I have no other answer for you other than the fact that I think God drew me close to you well before Lyric and Matthew were born. I knew your dad. I know where he is and what he's doing. I know he's left you behind. I wanted to marry your mother so much when you were a little boy all alone. I wanted to adopt you and make you mine. God didn't want it to happen that way. I don't know why, but I trust Him. Just as I trust that my finding out about Matthew too late is a part of His plan, and whatever God's plan, it is meant for good for me and for you." Daniel rubbed his hands together and except for a car driving by, silence around them held sway, as if God listened in on the conversation. "So, you see, even before Lyric and Matthew came to be, way before this time when I learned about your sister and your brother, you were my child. I'm so sorry that I didn't make that clear to you."

Quinn straightened. He stared at Daniel and then fell into him, his arms around the sheriff.

Lyric smiled. The hug was similar to the one Cade had given to Balaam at first sight, and Daniel's actions weren't much different from Balaam's tearful relief.

The automatic doors swooshed open.

"Quinn. Lyric. You need to get inside," Ethan called from the doorway.

## 20

Lyric ran through the hospital, keeping stride with Quinn and Daniel, Ethan leading the way.

Quinn slowed his steps as they neared the hospital room door.

Beside Lyric, he walked like a man condemned to death pacing to the wall in front of the firing squad.

The doctor stepped out into the hallway. He looked in their direction and shook his head. "I'm sorry."

"No ..." Quinn's mournful cry spilled throughout the corridor.

Lyric covered her mouth with her hand and bit back the tears. Daniel moved between them, steadying them with his strong arms on their shoulders.

Quinn stepped out of Daniel's grasp, the first to enter the room.

Daniel still held to Lyric as they rounded the corner.

Quinn fell into the chair beside the lifeless body of their mother, and Lyric fell into Daniel's hold.

Lyric turned to the doctor. "She was fine. I was in here with her. She—she sent me after Quinn. She wanted to tell him something." Lyric's voice climbed in hysterics. "She was fine! She was right here and fine, talking to me. She told me she loved me. She loved Quinn. She wanted to see Quinn. That's why I went looking for him. How? How?"

The doctor gave her a sorrowful look and nodded for Daniel to step outside.

"Quinn needs you. I'll be right back." Daniel kissed her cheek.

Quinn's sobs pounded against Lyric's heart, and she clung even tighter to Daniel.

"Lyric, go to Quinn. I need to find out what happened here," Daniel reasoned as he tugged from her hold. "Do you understand? The doctor wants to share something with me, and you need to be with your brother."

"You said she'd make it." Quinn's voice steadied as he narrowed his eyes at the doctor. "You told me her condition was stable. All we needed to do was keep her away from the alcohol. Something's wrong here. Something's very wrong?"

"Doctor?" Daniel motioned to the door and went with him into the hallway.

Ethan stood back, half in and half out of the room.

Lyric moved to Quinn. She put her arms around him, but her eyes remained on the entrance, ignoring Ethan's presence.

Her mother had turned her attention there while they

were talking. Had the demon she'd seen been Jessup Roy? What was it she'd said? She'd asked her to tell Quinn she loved him, but when they'd talked about God, Momma had said she wanted to give her son a hug. Her words had meaning behind them, and Lyric couldn't grasp them even now. Had she been talking about Matthew? Had she sent Lyric away knowing that someone was going to kill her?

The question hung in the air like a noose over Lyric's head. Momma had said the most unexpected thing: she'd give up her live for them. They weren't to blame. They had nothing. She dug deep into her memory, but the joy of that moment had overshadowed her ability to retain the full conversation.

*You never got anything from me or Braedon.*

Momma had said that. That wouldn't be anything she'd need to address to God, but right in the middle of her show of love, she'd made that declaration. To whom?

Someone had to have been lingering in the hall, a specter of what would come.

Momma had known she was going to die, and she was letting her killer know that she and Quinn had nothing the killer wanted.

Quinn stroked their mother's hand. "I shouldn't have left you. I should have stayed."

Lyric caught Ethan's eye. He stood, his attention obviously on what was being said in the hallway between the doctor and Daniel.

She couldn't trust this man. Had Daniel checked to

make sure that he and his partner were really with the bureau? He wouldn't have allowed them into their lives if not.

Were Ethan and Pierce on the take from some drug lord?

She shivered and hugged Quinn tighter, turning her lips to his ear. "Quinny, I was here with her. She was... she was lovely to me. We had a good talk. We even talked about God."

Quinn sat in the chair still holding to Momma's hand. "What did she say?"

Ethan jerked his attention to them, almost as if he needed to know.

Lyric never lifted her face away from her brother. "I think she saw someone outside her door, and she knew trouble was looming. She said so many wonderful things that I want to share with you."

Quinn turned to face her and away from Ethan. "What makes you think someone meant to harm her?" His words were spoken even softer than hers had been.

"Because in one moment she asked me to tell you that she loved you, and in the next, after telling me that she once knew God and that she wanted to think about her assurance of love from Him, she told me she wanted to hug her son. I thought she meant you, but now I believe the son she expected to hug..." She looked at her mother's face for the first time and saw the faint outline of the beginning of a smile. "...was Matthew." She looked back to him. "And she said something that makes me believe she was talking to someone beyond my sight, someone she thought might harm us, and she told that person that we didn't have it."

"How?" Quinn asked.

Lyric looked toward the door. Ethan was no longer there.

"In telling me what she'd said if she thought you and I were in danger, she declared we never received anything from her or Braedon."

Quinn sat in silence for several long minutes. Then he blinked and reached for her hand. "God really is good even in the midst of tragedies like this one."

She bit her lip and nodded. "I'm beginning to understand that."

Daniel stepped into the room. Ethan stood behind him.

Lyric stepped back away from her brother.

Quinn stood, steadying himself against Lyric. "Someone killed her."

Daniel nodded. "The doctor expects foul play. A nurse checked on Madga after Lyric left. She was fine, but she saw someone she couldn't identify lurking beyond the door, and she believes that person stepped out of the room shortly before the alarms began to ring. I suspect she was smothered."

"Momma would have fought an attacker," Quinn said.

"No." Lyric gripped his arm. "She was very coherent, very aware. She wouldn't have fought if it meant getting her killer away from us. Perhaps she thought if she was silenced, with the information she'd fed to him while speaking to me, that he'd leave us alone. I tell you, Quinn. I've never seen her more lucid then she was when I was with her."

Ethan was standing there, not afraid of being identified. "Jessup?" Lyric asked.

Daniel pulled them both into his arms. "As much as I wish I could pin this on him and loosen some of the pain he's caused all of us, she said she knows Professor Roy. Wasn't him."

His hold on them tightened.

Fear rose deep within Lyric.

Beyond them, Ethan Goodman stood, looking on, and she could swear sympathy filled his eyes.

"Listen to me," Daniel whispered. "Lyric, I need you to remain calm."

Lyric struggled, but his taut arms held her into place. "Lyric, you have to remain calm at what I'm about to say."

Lyric gave a slight nod and braced herself.

"Enemies may be among us, and I need you to stay focused," Daniel's whisper lowered. "I sent security to bring them here. They're not in the hospital. Balaam, Cade, and Agent Pierce are missing."

Lyric dug her fingernails into her father's shoulder to keep the fear from screaming out of her.

## 21

Balaam clung to Cade as the car door was opened. The stranger holding the gun, the one who'd ordered them to move out of the hospital, motioned him to get out. Balaam moved with Cade.

"Nope. Leave the boy in the car."

Balaam continued to push his way out. "Not going to happen. You want me to cooperate, my son stays with me."

"I think you'll wish otherwise."

He probably would, but the driver, whom Balaam recognized from the moment they'd been forced into the car, still sat unmoving behind the wheel. He'd once trusted the man, but not any longer. This turn of events made Balaam sick.

He and Cade stood on the dirt road of the old cemetery. He knew this place well, having spent many a summer night sitting on gravestones and drinking.

Heavy, hard hitting snow, picked up in the wind, pummeled them. Cade shivered beside him as the dampness seeped onto his shirt. They'd been pushed out the door of the hospital so fast without being given the chance for Cade to grab his coat. Balaam hadn't noticed. Until now. He took his jacket off and placed it around Cade's shoulders, managing to keep a hold on him to prevent anyone from taking his son out of his hands.

Two people made their way forward in what was working up to be a powerful winter storm.

"Poppa," Balaam called out.

The thug manhandling the older man was neither friend or stranger to Balaam. Bile rose in Balaam's throat.

He'd allowed this to happen, allowed the creep to get close to them.

Would he ever do anything right?

The ding of his phone caught him off guard. He reached in his back pocket and stared at the message.

Jim Maynard? Odd he'd contact him at this time of night.

SHANE BROWNE SAYS HE'D LOVE TO SEE YOU TONIGHT. HE LIVES IN THE OLD MILLHOUSE ON THE PROPERTY HIS COUSIN'S FATHER USED TO OWN. HE HAS WHAT YOU NEED.

Another text sounded. Daniel this time. One word.

Tom Pierce lunged for the phone, pulling Poppa with him. Pierce snatched the phone and tossed it into the cold, dark depths on the opposite side of the graveyard.

Poppa's face was bruised, and his gaze failed to connect with Balaam. A lump on the older man's temples was beginning to turn colors. When Pierce released him, Poppa slumped to the ground.

Cade fell beside his grandfather. "Grandpa Zeke!"

Balaam bent beside them. He stared up at the wicked smile of Tom Pierce and the smugness of the man beside him. The driver of the car never looked their way.

Poppa shook his head. "Your brother left us with a lot of trouble, boy. I expect you to get us out of it. You hear?"

"Where's the stuff I wanted, old man?" Pierce snarled. "If you didn't bring it, I'll end you right here."

Poppa lifted his eyes off in the distance. "I told you where I'd leave it. I didn't expect someone to want me in the deal. Now that I know you're after my boy here, only fitting I left it on the grave of the man you most likely caused to die."

Pierce yanked Balaam to his feet. "Since it's for you, only fitting you go and retrieve it."

Balaam struggled against the hold on him.

The release of the safety on the other man's gun stopped his fight. Pierce's henchman aimed his weapon at Cade's head.

Balaam raised his hands in defeat and straightened. "I'm gonna need some help. Leave the old man here with my boy. I haven't been here in years until the funerals, and the snow's covering the place."

"Go with him," Pierce ordered. "I'll keep an eye on

these two."

"It's a big place." Henchman looked about him. "And I ain't too fond of cemeteries even in the daylight."

"Afraid the dead might come back for revenge." Pierce laughed then turned a cold, hard gaze on Poppa and Cade. "Boy, you move, and I'll put a hole in your grandpa's heart and one in your daddy's head. You hear me?"

Cade nodded then looked to Balaam.

Something familiar shined from the boy's eyes, and perhaps this would be the only time Balaam would rejoice at the rebellion he saw there.

Balaam started off in the exact opposite direction of his brother's and Matthew's graves. He wanted so badly to turn back and look at the driver of the car, but either Pierce hadn't made the connection or the man was in as much trouble as they were. His reason for being here was beyond Balaam's comprehension, but he was sure he'd soon discover why.

Balaam played at wiping snow from the ground markers and the tombstones. When he was sure he'd led them far enough away, he turned back in the other direction and slowly made his way to the spots he would never forget because each held a piece of his heart. First, though, he led them around and away from Braedon's ground marker, where he was sure they'd find what they were looking to recover. When he got them to Matthew's beautiful granite memorial, he stood for a second, blinking back the tears at the picture staring back at him. Larry and Bernice dearly loved Matthew. Why then—?

He didn't have time for this. Pierce didn't have to say a thing for Balaam to know he was getting restless and paranoid.

"Here's one of the places I thought he meant. He must've meant my brother's grave." Balaam looked around him, as if thinking of the direction to go. "Braedon's over that way."

He started off, Pierce right behind him, and his henchman not too far removed.

Balaam's gaze fell upon the simple metal marker showing this was his brother's grave. The large mason jar lid was partially covered by snow, but the metal glinted in the moonlight as it sat between the graves of Balaam's mother and his brother.

Balaam swallowed hard. Grief tore at him along with the terror of sensing what Pierce had in store for him.

They said what Poppa brought was for Balaam.

They'd made his father bring out the stuff that would set Balaam back or kill him. Balaam wasn't sure which would be worse. *Dear God, not in front of my son. Please, not in front of him.*

"Well, pick it up," Pierce demanded. "I've heard for years that your Poppa's shine is the best in these parts. I'm going to let you enjoy it after you give me what you know I want. Your coming back to town sits just a little too convenient for me. If you don't provide me with what I'm after, I want you to be fully cognizant of what I'll do to everyone you love. Then, just like Magda Moxley, I'll let you drink the remorse away, and if you're lucky, you won't feel the bullet I plan to personally put into your head since…" He tipped his head in Henchman's direction. "… I didn't get the chance to do it to the two buffoons who got in my way, and I couldn't take the chance of killing Magda at the hospital when the booze I gave her didn't work the way I thought it would with any meds they were giving her."

"You kill Magda, and I'll—"

"Too late for your baseless threats." Pierce smiled and tipped his nod in Henchman's direction. "She's already taken care of. I'm sure that Lyric and her brother are mourning her right now. Probably don't know you're missing."

"You mean you ordered this buffoon to do the killing of a law enforcement officer and a man barely old enough to shave and then the coward killed a woman strapped in a hospital bed? All so that you wouldn't take the rap," Balaam challenged.

"No one's taking a rap for anything. Except you. Who knows where you could have been? You used to work for Roy. Perhaps you took up your old job."

The cold had not gotten to Balaam until that moment, but he warmed suddenly at the thought of Jim's text. Pierce had no idea where he'd been or what he'd been doing while away.

Balaam had thought the wording odd, but he

recognized it clearly for what it was. A message from the man who sent the second text that said only TONIGHT confirmed Jim's intent.

They neared the vehicle, and again Balaam's blood ran cold. Had the man in the car been left behind on purpose. Could he have hurt Cade and Poppa?

Pierce spun around, looking and peering into the darkness. He shot his gun three times into the night, and with each shot, Balaam jumped and prayed that the stray shots had not harmed his father or his son.

Pierce kicked in the door of the car. "Where'd they go?" he demanded.

The car door was pushed open. Larry Roberts stood. "What are you talking about? You told me to stay in the car. I did."

"You knew they were here." Pierce lowered the gun at him.

"No," Balaam cleared his throat. "You didn't say anything to him." He nodded at Larry, still not sure if Pierce realized a connection and praying that Larry had helped his son and his father, because if Balaam survived, he'd need a reason to keep from killing his best friend's father.

Balaam turned back to Pierce. "You told your buddy here to watch him, and he was too afraid of ghosts to stay behind."

Pierce's stare hardened, first at Balaam and then at Larry. Then he fired three more bullets, right into the chest of Henchman.

The late shift at the sheriff's office was always light on staff. One officer manned the front desk and the rest were on patrol.

Tonight, that meant they were trying to locate Cade and Balaam. Only Quinn, Lyric, Daniel, and Agent Goodman stood in front of the reception desk. The officer there paid them no heed, though Daniel's angry pacing set every nerve Lyric had on fire. Daniel was afraid, and that could only mean that his hope of finding her son—or Balaam—was nil.

She pressed her closed fist to her mouth and stared at Quinn, who stood facing the front door as if all that troubled them would walk in and right itself or maybe, like her, he feared for Cade out in the mounting storm without the coat she'd found on the couch where she'd last seen him with Balaam.

*Slam!*

Lyric jumped and turned at the same time.

Daniel had Ethan pinned against the soda machine, his feet dangling in the air. "Cross!" Daniel called to his deputy at the reception area as he slipped Ethan's gun from his holster. "Take this and see if it's been fired recently."

Cross hurried as commanded, slipping on a pair of latex gloves as he rounded the corner.

"Daniel, no. He... you... you wouldn't kill my little

boy? Please tell me you wouldn't kill Cade or his father."

Ethan, still dangling in Daniel's firm hold, cocked his head toward her. "Never," he managed to croak out.

"But your partner!" Daniel demanded. "Is he the one or should I be looking for his body, too."

"No!" Lyric gasped and backed up. She turned in Quinn's arms. The thought of Tom Pierce with her boy, whether alive or dead, was too much to take.

Too much loss. So much tragedy. Would this cold dead of winter ever leave and return warmth to their souls?

A freezing breeze fell over her, and she pulled from Quinn's hold. An elderly man, dressed in overalls, a flannel shirt, and a heavy coat nodded at her as if she should know him.

Daniel didn't seem to notice. "What is it, Goodman? Could he be part of our trouble or could he have gotten himself in the middle of it? Because you know, that list you've been looking for, there was a nickname of sorts." Daniel lowered the agent to the ground.

"Nickname?" Ethan shook from Daniel's hold and straightened his clothes.

"Goodman and…?"

"Badman?" Ethan widened his eyes. He paled and leaned against the machine that had been his hanging place only moments before. "My undercover name. Yes, it would be on the list."

Lyric stomped forward.

Daniel held his hand out. "Not any closer," he warned.

She glared at Ethan. "I don't believe you. I think you're part of the drug ring. I heard Pierce laugh about using the alias Skipper Playboy. Was that in the papers, too, Daniel, because when Pierce mentioned it, Balaam went as tight as a high wire?"

Daniel didn't answer. He stepped back as Cross returned. "This gun hasn't been fired recently." He held the gun, bagged in plastic, in his hand.

Daniel nodded. He took hold of Ethan's arm with a sturdy grip. "Cross, you stay here with them while I take the agent back to the interrogation room and make sure he isn't able to leave. With no probable cause, I don't want to read him his Miranda rights and book him into the cell. That could change when I get back here."

Lyric grasped Ethan's jacket before Daniel could lead him away.

Ethan held his ground, his eyes meeting hers. "I swear to you, if I had anything to do with your son's disappearance, my only fault is ignorance. I would rather Tom wind up dead than to be the traitor in my midst all these years. We're too close for me not to have noticed."

"Daniel...?" Lyric released the agent and lowered her gaze to the floor. "I believe him."

Ethan shook his head. "No, Lyric. Daniel's doing what I'd do. He's taking me out of the equation. Keeping you safe. I'll be fine." He lifted his gaze to Quinn. "No heroics, Preacher. She needs you no matter the outcome." He turned and walked with Daniel down the corridor. Before entering the room, Daniel slipped a cuff on the agent's hands.

Ethan wasn't going anywhere.

Perhaps she and Quinn were lucky that Daniel wasn't making them join him.

"Jim." Daniel returned after several long minutes and a muted conversation with Ethan. Then he held out his hand to the older man. "Anything?"

"No response to my text, you?"

"None," Daniel answered.

Jim shook Daniel's hand then turned to Lyric. "You have to be the little lady Balaam was working so hard to get back to. I'm sorry for what Daniel's told me has happened. But I know that if your boy is with his daddy, he's safe." He lifted a hand to Quinn. "We met sometime back. I came to visit Deputy Carmichael and his cousin, Shane Browne. They invited me to church. You were just back from seminary and the congregation had called you as an assistant pastor back then. The church had chosen wisely by calling you to the pulpit. Name's Jim Maynard."

Quinn swallowed hard. "Nice to meet you again, Pastor Maynard. If I'm understanding you, Balaam's been with you. Thank you for seeing to his rehab."

"Balaam was with Jim on his farm. Jim's a retired pastor who has a heart for those suffering with addiction. He sweated the stuff out of Balaam. He's here because Balaam left something with him."

"I haven't even made my apologies to Bay," Quinn muttered.

Jim dug into his jacket and pulled out an envelope.

Lyric widened her eyes. "Is that…" She looked around them. "… what they've wanted all along? Balaam had it?"

Daniel's face softened. "Darlin'." He put his hands on her shoulders. "Braedon put those papers in the hands of your son and told him to hide them and give them to me. He did that before he went to the Backslide. If Jessup or any of his men had seen that happen…"

"Cade never told me."

"He was clutching them like a lifeline when I found him after…"

Anger welled up within Lyric. She wanted to resurrect her husband and kill him all over again. Gone was the peace she'd had during her time with God and later with her mother. Even when doing something right, Braedon still did evil toward Cade.

If Brae were alive, she'd hold the gun and blow him away.

Had she been brave enough to handle her life and the life of her son on her own, if she'd left Braedon to his own devices instead of thinking him her lifeline, her son wouldn't have witnessed what he'd seen, wouldn't have needed an envelope to keep from drowning in the atrocities that would probably leave him with lifelong scars. Her son… her precious Cade would be with her. He'd be safe and warm and loved and… and alive.

*Lyric Kaye.*

She looked to Quinn, but he hadn't spoken. Neither

had the pastor or Daniel. The voice had been a woman's voice, just as her mother had spoken to her before her death.

She covered her eyes with her hand and struggled to keep darkness from invading her senses. She could almost envision herself holding to the sound of her name on her mother's lips. God had tossed her that unlikeliest of lifelines.

As unlikely as her mother telling her she loved her only moments before her death.

The sobs started deep, and she fought to hold them in. She had to cling to hope. To God. He'd tossed her the line. She needed to hold on for all it was worth.

Daniel's phone rang, and he pulled it from his pocket, shaking his head, as if the number were familiar but he couldn't recall it. "Daniel Dixon."

"Sheriff Daniel…" Cade's cry was so anguished and loud, drawing Lyric to her father. "Sheriff Daniel, they got my dad. Grandpa Zeke, he's hurt bad. Can you come?"

"Where are you, buddy?"

Cade's muffled cry was indiscernible to Lyric's ears, and she stood waiting.

"We're on our way. You stay right beside your Uncle Matthew. Don't move. Are you and your grandfather alone?" Daniel waited for Cade's answer. Then he did his best to calm the boy before turning to the older preacher. "Jim, I have to get to Cade first. Balaam used to have a bag of tricks that kept him out of trouble. He's quick up here."

He tapped his temple. "So, he has to be on his own. I get the idea he wouldn't want me saving him before I got to Cade. I hate to ask this of you, but I need you to rush with those papers to the place we had planned. Hopefully, Balaam got our messages." He pulled a key off his chain and tossed it to the older man. "That'll get you inside. If you're able to get there before anyone arrives, pull your car behind the garage. Use the back door to the garage. That key opens all the doors to this place. There's a hatch on the ground inside the garage. Open it up. There's steps to a tunnel leading to the other building and another door. You'll find your way from there. Sit tight, lights off. If Balaam got our hint, I'm sure he'll lead them there as soon as possible. If you believe they've arrived before you, don't chance turning up the drive. Go down the road one click and turn up the dirt path. The folks who lived there are gone for the winter. Hunker down in your truck. You'll hear from me either way. Keep the papers with you. Let's just pray Balaam's still as sly as he used to be, and that I have all this figured out to get him out alive."

Jim nodded. "Understood. I'll be praying the entire time."

"Don't respond to any of my deputies or to any actions outside the place. Only to me. What you have is too important, and you're a treasure to me, old guy. I had one deputy in Jessup's pocket. I'm still ferreting them out. Cross is one I put my trust in. He'll keep Goodman safe."

"We're coming with you," Lyric said, looking at

Quinn.

"Cade, I'm handing your mom the phone. She and Uncle Quinn are coming with me. The only way you move from that spot is if you see anyone coming. When I turn into the cemetery. I'll flash my lights. You'll know it's us. Okay?"

Cade must have answered.

Daniel handed the phone to Lyric. "Cade? Baby, are you okay?"

"I'm cold, but Grandpa Zeke. I can't get him to wake up. He would go to sleep, and I woke him up but he's not doing that anymore, Mom. I remembered his phone, and I know Sheriff Daniel's number. He taught it to me a long time ago."

Quinn's half-chuckle brought Lyric around to gape at him.

He waved her off. "He taught me his number a long time ago, too."

Jim headed toward an old pickup, and Daniel led them to the other side of the parking lot. He dug in his pockets and tossed a set of keys to Quinn. "You two, follow me. Lyric, give me your phone. Let me know if anything happens between now and when we get to him."

Lyric dug her phone out of her pocket and tendered it over to him. "Where's your dad?" she asked Cade as she followed Quinn.

"They took him away in a car. Mr. Roberts told me to help Grandpa behind the big old crypt and not to move."

"Mr. Roberts?" Lyric stared at Daniel who stopped in his tracks for a brief second then hurried to his vehicle.

"They have him, too?" Lyric asked Cade.

"No, Mom. He's driving the car. He's with them, but he told Grandpa that the mean men would kill us when they came back. He didn't want that to happen." Cade sniffled. "For Uncle Matthew's sake, he said. They left a long time ago, and I got scared. That's when Grandpa said he'd tried to make it to where Uncle Matthew was, that Uncle Matthew would keep me safe if something happened to him." Cade wailed. "I don't want him to die, and Uncle Matthew is already dead. I'm scared."

"Honey, we're not far away. We're coming." Lyric held to the dashboard as Quinn sped after Daniel as fast as he could on the slippery roads. "And God has you right where he wants you, okay. Uncle Matthew's not dead. He's in heaven, and I'm sure he's asking God to look after you the same way Uncle Quinn and I have been asking. Shh, baby. Shh."

He'd been so brave, so mature.

"What if Agent Pierce kills dad. He killed the other mean man, Mom. He took shots in the dark, and then he shot the man that was with him. He left him dead on the ground. He's going to kill dad."

"Cade, shh, baby. I know you're scared, but I need you to quiet down." She hated to scare him any more than he was. "They could come back, or he could send someone else. You need to stay down and quiet."

Sniffles were his only answer.

"I'm here," she whispered. "I'm right here. We're coming up on the turn."

Quinn followed Daniel into the cemetery. Daniel flashed his lights off and on.

"Sheriff Daniel flashed his lights."

"There's a car behind him. They're after him." Cade panicked.

"No, baby. That's Uncle Quinn and me. We're in the sheriff's truck. Stay down until we get to you. Don't move."

Daniel pulled off the road.

Quinn parked behind him.

Lyric pushed open her door, ready to run to her frightened son.

Daniel motioned her back and stood behind his own door. He shined a light throughout the graveyard, letting it rest on one area. "Ask Cade if someone was shot."

"Cade said Pierce gunned a man down," Lyric answered.

Daniel motioned Lyric and Quinn to him. "Let me get you to the boy. Then I'll check. He ain't moving. Most likely dead."

Lyric grasped Daniel's arm as they walked forward. "Cade said Pierce has Balaam. He and Mr. Roberts."

Daniel seemed to ignore her. "I have an ambulance on the way for Zeke," he said as Cade ran into Lyric's arms.

"I don't need no ambulance." Zeke sat up but wobbled.

"You old coot," Daniel kicked the old man's boot. "You're getting a ride anyway." He bent down beside Zeke. "Keeping the boy worried about you and his mind off all the other scary things, huh?"

Zeke nodded. "That young'un sure loves his dad. Loves me, too, I reckon." He looked over his shoulder at Lyric as she and Quinn huddled around Cade to keep him warm. "You figured it out yet?" Zeke spoke to Daniel.

Sirens rang in the distance, growing closer.

Lyric moved with her son and her brother closer to Balaam's father. "Figured out what? Do you know where they have Balaam?"

"I got a good idea that Roberts is leading that killer to Roy. Larry came to me early today. Said he'd been involved with Roy's mess from the start—since Roy helped Roberts get your boy and adopted him. Roy's held it over his head all these years. Got it in his head he wanted to own you, too, Daniel. Roberts was real sorrowful, crying about Matthew and Braedon. He said Bernice never knew. Said he was going to take care of Roy, end it all today."

"How is Balaam involved in all this?" Daniel asked.

The *whoop whoop* of the ambulance sounded, and the vehicle stopped. Daniel stood back as the paramedics moved in.

"I think Roberts didn't have it in his plans for Balaam or Cade to be involved. I don't know who that killer is, but he seemed to know Balaam and his weakness for liquor. I think he's a mean 'un, and he's going to try to pin something on Balaam. Simple enough after what Brae went and did." Zeke held his hand out to Lyric. "You've done a good job with the boy here. He was a brave 'un. Took care of me right well."

"I want them to look over Cade, too." Daniel said.

Lyric understood. "If we don't have to, I don't want to go back to that hospital."

"He doesn't look hurt. Did they hurt you, Cade?" Daniel asked.

Cade shook his head, but he pointed. "There's a dead guy over there. Agent Pierce shot him three times."

"Your mom told me." Daniel headed off toward the area where he'd shined his light before. He returned several minutes later as the Amazing Grace night became filled with the sounds of sirens.

"Quinn, let them get Zeke inside. Make them look Cade over, and then you two get back to the station." Daniel held out the phone—her phone.

Lyric handed his back.

He hugged Lyric and patted Quinn on the shoulder. "Straight to the station." He bent down to Cade's level. "Your momma, Uncle Quinn, and I have some news to share with you and Granny Grace. Don't let them do it until I can be there."

Cade straightened his shoulders. "Can Dad be there, too?"

"Never thought he wouldn't be." Daniel messed the boy's hair and headed off in the distance.

The paramedics soon gave them the okay.

Lyric hugged Zeke and talked him into going to the hospital even though they couldn't be with him. He balked at her for trying to give him too much attention, but he let them load him in the ambulance and take him away, agreeing that he'd be safer there than sitting at home with his shotgun, which he should have brought with him and used on that Pierce fellow.

Lyric walked with Quinn toward Daniel's truck, keeping an eye on her father as she went. Out of habit, Lyric scrolled her contacts on her phone. "I wish I had Bay's number." She paused her scroll when she spotted *Cade's Dad* in the list. She shook her head and offered Cade a cautious smile. "Your dad is a sneak." He'd gotten her phone and put the number inside. She hit the phone icon.

As they neared the car, she heard a ringtone: the tune "He's My Son."

Quinn looked around with her and pointed. He held up his hand and made his way from the gravestones, returning with a phone in his hand.

"Dad got a text. Pierce threw his phone." Cade said as Lyric opened the back door and sat inside with him, not wanting one bit of space between them.

Quinn handed her the phone before he started the car. She slid her finger across the screen. Wouldn't it be like Balaam not to put a lock on it? She touched the message from Pastor Maynard, read it, and then looked at the one word from Daniel.

As Quinn drove away, she hugged Cade to her, and prayed, her mind thinking on all that had happened and all she'd heard in such a short bit of time.

*Please let it be over soon. Lord, please keep Balaam as safe as You kept Cade and Zeke. Despite the foolishness, Lord, I still love the idiot.*

**FAY LAMB**

## 22

Balaam rapped on Jessup Roy's door as demanded by Pierce. Larry Roberts stood behind Balaam. Was he oblivious to the fact that only one person could walk out of this situation alive if Pierce maintained control? And Balaam sure meant to keep that from happening.

Dear old Nadine opened the door. Her eyes widened at the gun Pierce pointed at her head.

"Don't…" Balaam growled the word. "I'll tie her up. She won't say—"

"The professor subdued, Mom?" Pierce lowered the gun, and his voice held the most genuine warmth Balaam had heard from the killer.

But Nadine? Balaam had known her when he'd been a courier for Jessup. She'd worked for the professor all those years.

"Not yet, but he has no idea what's coming." Nadine's smile didn't resemble the friendly one Balaam remembered.

Pierce pushed Balaam into the room as Nadine pulled the door back.

The snow dripped off each of them, leaving the professor's carpet wet.

Nadine scurried off and knocked on Jessup's office door. Jessup muttered something, and Nadine went inside. She returned with Jessup on her heels.

He didn't like Nathan's father. He never did, but he didn't wish him dead. Prison was good enough. In fact, prison was what Balaam deserved, too. He'd tried to skate out of it the best he could, but chances were mounting that only two possible scenarios offered him a "Get Out of Jail Free" card: he killed Pierce or Pierce but a bullet in Balaam's head. Pierce had promised that often enough tonight.

Jessup eyed the gun. "Balaam, I'm not sure what this means." The old man cut his eyes to the stairs for the briefest of seconds and then back to Balaam.

"This isn't my deal, Jessup. I'm a pawn in a war between you and Larry here." Balaam glanced up the stairs and quickly back to Roy. His chances of survival had just increased by a fraction of a fraction.

Pierce waved Jessup up against the wall and motioned for Larry and Balaam to join him. He put the gun he'd reloaded while they were in the car up to Larry's temple. "Where's the paperwork?" His cold eyes bored into Balaam. "I know that you and that sheriff are close, and I know you've been the only one he's trusted. I have eyes and ears in places you wouldn't believe."

Balaam breathed a thank You to the Lord for getting Cade away. The soulless man in front of him would have used the boy and dropped him when he was done.

Pierce pressed harder against Larry's temple. Matthew's father winced and, if only for Matthew, Balaam would try to save the man's life. "The papers are hidden. I don't suppose that you'd consider leaving these two geezers here and letting me take you to where they are?"

"Not a chance."

"I could tell you where they are, but you'd never find the place."

"I would." Nadine sidled beside Pierce. "Shoot Roberts if Balaam doesn't fess up, Tommy."

"You could find the place, Nadine, but I doubt you'd know where to look. The snow's coming down pretty heavy now. Be a cold night, especially at a higher elevation, trying to locate where they're hidden."

"Why don't you let me make that decision?" Nadine stood, hands on her hips.

"The old Carmichael property. Abandoned. Neglected. Papers well hidden, even from me."

Balaam didn't miss Roy's slump forward.

"Old? Abandoned? Neglected? Boy, you haven't been out there. Beau and Shane fixed that place up mighty nice. Shane Browne uses it for his studio when he's back in town. Lives in Florida a lot now that he married his dead cousin's widow. The place might be abandoned for the winter, but it's not neglected."

Pierce's face tightened, his rage barely controlled. "Are you lying?"

Balaam remained calm. The Lord had just placed the truth right into his hands and had perhaps given him a little more time. "Only about my knowledge of the place, but I do know that's where they're hidden. I didn't put them there. Someone I know from out of town did. I haven't gone by there since my return. Someone might have followed me."

Nadine left them for a second and returned wearing a jacket and toting a semi-automatic rifle. Jessup's own weapon that sat in the gun cabinet for as long as Balaam could remember. No longer was she the addlebrained, chatty housekeeper. She was a woman who most likely led the largest drug ring in the State of North Carolina right under another drug lord's nose. "March 'em out. I heard the professor say that no-good son of his was coming in to pay a call on Mr. Brasher. Life's gone south for Nathan since he lost his rock star."

Pierce opened the door and marched them outside.

"Get in the car!" Nadine ordered.

Balaam waited for Jessup to scoot inside, noting that the professor looked green and ready to vomit on the floorboard.

Balaam sat in the middle, and Nadine climbed in beside him.

Larry, again, sat in the driver's seat with Pierce up

front, gun at the ready. His phone rang, and he answered. "The old Carmichael place. Is that right?" He turned to look at his mother.

Nadine nodded and patted Balaam's near frozen leg. "Good boy."

"See how it plays out and meet us there. We might have lost the incentive, but I believe he's coming back your way." Pierce smiled at Balaam.

Balaam shuddered and shared a look with Roberts from the rearview. Only God could protect the old man if Cade got hurt.

Beside Nadine, Balaam shrugged his shoulders, leaned back, and tried to relax as if he had no clue of what was going to happen. "You missed your calling, Nadine. You should have worked on Broadway. Instead, you wasted your talents on the drug trade and raising a psycho for a son."

Nadine laughed. "You're wrong, there, Bay. I raised two boys. Tom's the one I'm the proudest of. The other, he's a major source of disappointment. Too stupid and trusting."

Balaam didn't even want to know what that meant, and unless God used a devil to get Balaam out of this jam, he'd never get the chance to ponder the statement.

A lot of people could die in this mess up all because two men in this car hated each other for most of their lives and one was sorry for his actions.

Too bad the remorseful one was the less intelligent of

the two.

Pierce leaned forward and handed the mason jar of Poppa's shine to Balaam. "Might as well start now. It's about all you got to keep you warm since you gave your jacket to the kid."

Balaam didn't lift his hands to retrieve it. "Alcohol lowers your body temperature, genius. You aren't going to find a bunch of hillbillies drinking out in a snow storm. You underestimate us." Balaam tapped his finger to his head and dared to give the killer a sarcastic wink.

Pierce pushed it at him. "Take it. Open the lid. Start drinking."

Balaam stared at him. He'd never been a mean drunk. Not like Braedon. Things might change now. The bottle represented the end of everything he'd fought for over the last several months.

And surprisingly, right now, he'd lost the desire for the taste of it.

Pierce thrust it toward him again. "It'll come in real handy. You won't feel a thing when you kill these two old farts and put the gun to your own head."

Lyric entered the sheriff's department behind Quinn with Cade tucked safely between them.

Quinn halted and Cade drew up short, Balaam's coat was too large for him, and he almost fell.

Lyric slammed into them, pushing them both forward. "What's wrong with you?" she grumbled.

"Where's Cross? The one thing I know about Daniel's department is that the front desk is never unmanned."

Cade shivered and turned his body toward Lyric. The poor kid had suffered so much. Scared was an understatement for all of them.

Quinn held up his hand, commanding them to stay put. He moved to Daniel's office, though the thing was all glass. He started down the corridor that ran behind the desk, stopped, and glanced back at Lyric. Then he bent down for too long.

Lyric moved forward, Cade clinging to her.

Quinn stood. "He's alive. Knocked out cold."

"But who? Why him?" Lyric trembled.

"Because I needed my gun." Ethan stepped out of the interrogation room, his weapon aimed in their direction. "And I need you and the boy."

"Ethan, I don't understand." Lyric tucked Cade behind her. "We're on the same side, aren't we?"

"I need you to shut up. All three of you move this way."

Quinn pivoted toward her.

"If she runs, I'll have to shoot you, Quinn." Ethan must have read Quinn's actions.

Proof they'd allowed him to get too close to them.

"Please…" Lyric begged. "Please don't do this."

Ethan moved down the corridor and stood with enough

space for them to walk by. He reached out and clutched Cade to him, and Lyric struggled to maintain her hold on her son whose wide eyes and trembling lips were enough to suffocate her mother's heart.

She'd done this. All of this had happened because of her. She'd trusted another man who was no better than a murderous thug.

Ethan waved the gun, and they moved down the hall. "Lyric, the handcuffs are still chained on the table. Quinn, sit in the chair. Lyric, put the cuff on his hand."

"Ethan, don't hurt my sister." Quinn wasn't begging. His words were a warning.

Lyric closed her eyes as the cuff clipped into place around Quinn's wrist. "I'm sorry. If not for you…" She leaned against him.

Quinn didn't give her the reply she longed to hear. He stared at Ethan. "I'm praying."

His words sent a jolt through Lyric. Praying? For what? For her? For Ethan to come to his senses? For Lyric to gain a grasp on what was happening?

"I'm praying," Quinn repeated. "Don't cause him trouble, Lyric Kay. Do what he asks you to do and remember that you and Cade are in God's hands."

Momma had been in God's hands, too. Not that she was angry that God had allowed Momma to be taken. She just wasn't ready to go yet, and she certainly didn't want her son put through any more of this.

Anger roiled inside her. If she let it, the part of her

personality she inherited from Magdalene Moxley would pour out of her.

And they'd all be killed at the hands of an agent they had trusted.

"Come on," Ethan ordered. He stepped out of the room and closed the door. Then he walked behind them. "Hold up." He stopped just to the side of the reception desk. With the gun still held on Lyric and Cade, he leaned into Daniel's office and came out with something. "Take that big thing off, Cade, and put this on." He handed Cade's jacket to him—the one Pierce hadn't allowed him to take when he kidnapped her son. The same one Lyric had forgotten when she'd run out to save Cade from Pierce.

Cade obeyed. He slipped his jacket on and reached down and held Balaam's jacket. The look he gave Ethan was pure challenge.

Ethan patted Cade's shoulder. "Good job."

But he still held the gun on them, and he wasn't smiling as he pushed them out the door.

# 23

Balaam withstood Pierce's demand to take the bottle of shine for about as long as Pierce was going to let him. He wrapped his cold fingers around the jar and raised it in a salute.

Larry swerved the car, skidding across the road and back into the right lane.

Balaam fumbled the jar for a second and then allowed it to turn downward, pouring onto Pierce's lap. Oh, man, was that going to put a hurting on the man that Pierce would never forget.

"What are you doing?" Pierce demanded of Larry.

Balaam had to give it to the guy. He hadn't dropped his gun or let his attention sway, but any minute now, the shine was going to burn, and he'd feel like a marshmallow in Hades. Then when they stepped out into the cold, the guy would most likely succumb to hypothermia quickly. Nadine better hope the son she didn't dote on could give her grandkids. Pierce might not be able to by the time this was all over.

"A racoon, a big racoon," Larry said, still staring out the windshield.

Larry pulled down a dirt path and off the road a short way. He parked into what used to be an abandoned watermill.

Nadine climbed out of the car and waved Balaam in her direction. Pierce opened the door for Jessup and waited for him to climb out.

Balaam would have wished for his coat if he knew that Cade was warm and dry somewhere that he didn't need it.

Pierce rounded the car and planted a right hook on Balaam's left cheek. He fell hard against the vehicle.

Balaam leaned against the car. Warmth ran down his face. He swiped the back of his hand and winced. His hand was smeared with blood.

He smiled up at his attacker. "Sorry about that. I got some of Poppa's shine on me when I was younger. I think you've found yourself in between a rock and a hurting place."

"I didn't turn this over on myself." The gun in Pierce's hand shook.

Balaam stared down at the ground, letting the guy think he had him worried. If Balaam still had his long hair, he'd be able to hide the smile he fought to keep from breaking out on his face. Yeah, he'd still like to strangle Larry, but whether intended or not, the man had taken away the one thing that could destroy Balaam—other than a bullet.

Balaam turned away from the fiend. Lye and Formaldehyde tickled Balaam's nose. Poppa hadn't made this batch. He'd often seen his dad stop by the farmer's place down the road, knowing if he hadn't been around to get Poppa's shine, he hadn't had the money and had to by some rot-gut from someone who couldn't care less if harm came to a customer. Poppa often traded the man the nasty liquor for his good stuff. "For the jar," he'd say. He must have done that recently and even though he didn't know Pierce, Poppa was a good judge of character. Clearly, he had a hunch about Pierce, but Balaam's father sure hadn't had any idea the stuff was meant for Balaam.

And Pierce had to be burning in places a man ought not to burn.

Let 'em scorch.

If Balaam had a match, he'd light it.

The snow pelted Balaam as he pushed up. A sensor light flooded the entire watermill in a warm glow, as if an angel hovered above in the frigid air. Balaam had heard via Nathan that Beau had died. Nathan's sister had dated Beau. Shane Browne, Beau's cousin, must have inherited and restored the place. What had Nadine said, he'd renovated it into a studio?

Shane had been forced out of the band by his deputy cousin, forbidden to drive away into stardom. But his songwriting career looked to have taken off, enough to afford his own recording studio. Not that it looked like anyone lived here now.

"Where are the papers?" Nadine snapped.

"I told you. Someone else hid them. He didn't tell me where. I didn't want to know." He hoped God appreciated his ability to speak the truth, though he'd slanted the odds toward himself and away from his captors. Balaam sure needed God now. "We'll have to hunt." He darted his gaze. Shane sure had enough places to keep them busy, but Pierce had obviously inherited his impatience from his mother, and the moonshine had to be adding to the man's angst.

Nadine propped the weapon against her shoulder. She meant business, and her action left Balaam with not much time to overpower her. "Tommy, you take them two idiots up to the barn over there. I'll keep Rock Star with me. We need him alive to finish this up. He can look on the waterwheel and under the bridge here." She stopped for a moment then waved her hand. "This friend of yours, Balaam. How'd he know Shane Browne?"

"From what I understand, he helped Shane get free of your ilk long before I realized I needed to do the same." Movement behind the garage caught Balaam's attention, but he quickly glanced away. Daniel was moving in to position. Balaam fought the sigh of relief that might trigger more suspicion on Nadine's part.

"Our ilk kept you pretty satisfied for a long time, didn't we? And now we're not good enough for you, Mr. High and Mighty Lord of the Stage." Nadine's laugh caught in a swift kick of air that stung Balaam through his clothing.

"I'm not the lord of anything," Balaam quivered in the cold.

The small bridge led over the frozen creek and up a flight of steps to Shane's front door. A nice sheen of very thin ice glinted on the wooden slats closer to the steps leading up to the house. "My buddy who lives here and my buddy who hid the information are pretty good friends. I'm wondering if he had access inside." If he could get her to the ice, she'd be unable to maintain her grip when he went after the gun.

Nadine stared up onto the porch that ran the length of the front of the place. Then she studied the motionless waterwheel at the side. "Search here, and if we have to, we can add breaking and entering to the felonies you're going to commit. Won't matter anyway. Tommy ain't going to let you live to see jail. Get a move on Brasher."

"The name's Carter, Nadine," Balaam said between clenched teeth.

A crunch of tires down on the main road away from the house met Balaam's ears. All movement stopped. The car passed by.

None of them were dressed for a storm of this magnitude and temperatures seemed to still be falling. Even the older woman wore tennis shoes. Balaam's boots at least protected him from losing his toes—for the time being. His fingers were another problem.

"Get a move on, old men. The first one to find what we're looking for dies first at Brasher's hand. Saves you from watching the other go before you and watching me put an end to Brasher's miserable life. Pierce howled with laughter. "Like that would matter to the two of you. Mom says you geezers fight like a couple of little boys. And the liquor won't matter after I get done weaving my heroic story."

Balaam wouldn't remind Pierce that he'd lost his edge over him twice already: first Cade and then the moonshine.

He ducked down as if to look under the bridge. He worked like crazy to make it appear an easy move, but the ground was slick. He got down on his knees, the wet snow seeping into his jeans, his fingers stinging like they'd been asleep for a year.

Nadine's fingernails tapped the metal of the rifle still poised on her shoulder. No doubt she believed her Tommy would kill anyone before they got to her, but she still had her weapon ready to use against anyone threatening her. No need to keep the gun on him. She stepped onto the bridge on easy footing so far.

One more step.

Another.

Another.

Just one more.

Balaam pushed upward, grasping the wooden railing above him and shaking it. He also used it to stay upright, amazed at Nadine's agility.

She pivoted. "Don't trying anything-ang!"

Her foot slid. Her body wobbled. She flailed her free hand in the air, searching for the railing to keep her upright. The gun waved in the air. She fought to keep her balance, but she had a decision to make. Drop the gun and grab the railing or go down and keep the weapon.

Balaam had two choices: duck and make sure Nadine didn't accidentally shoot him, or he could reach over the railing and fight for the weapon. He reached for the rifle.

Nadine tugged it from him, jerking the barrel away and out in front of her.

The blast cracked in the chilled air, ringing through the darkness, and sending a surreal quiet to Balaam's ears.

The recoil sent Nadine off her feet. She screamed and fell backward. Her neck smacked against the railing, and her body thudded to the bridge floor. Her head leaned at an odd angle and a last gasp left her mouth with a puff of white. Balaam pounced, ripping the rifle from her hands.

"Get away from her!" Pierce screamed. "Get away from her."

Balaam lowered the gun at the man who'd threatened Cade's life. He readied himself to die if he had to, but Balaam would kill Pierce before taking his last God-given breath. "I bet the hole I put in you will be bigger than the one yours puts in me. You want to risk it?"

"The one in Larry Robert's head proves you right, but…" Pierce nodded. "Your hands are already all over that murder weapon. My mother will just say she struggled with you."

Balaam turned his gaze to the figure face down out beyond Shane's garage. In the glow of the floodlights, the red blood colored the virgin white snow. He waited for Daniel to make himself known.

Nothing. No movement, no sound.

Pierce continued to delight in the situation. "You're a good shot with a moving target, huh, Mom. If the old geezer hadn't been running away to save himself, you might've missed him."

No use telling the man the truth now. "She's out. No good to you now." Balaam didn't feel one lick of guilt for causing the death of the woman. Maybe later, he'd process it and ask God to forgive him.

Pierce yanked Jessup toward him. As they drew closer, he released the old professor and pulled at his jeans. Poppa's shine was working some magic. Fire and ice had an entirely new meaning.

"Stop where you are!" the voice boomed from the woods at the front of Browne's property. Nathan must have been in the car that had passed. He'd doubled back from that direction. Now, he stepped out into the open, holding what looked like a harmless .22 caliber. From his range, he wouldn't hit anyone.

Stupid move.

The devil was dumber than dirt.

Well, at least he'd shown up, and he'd gotten Pierce's attention.

"Nathan, put the gun away. You'll get yourself killed," Balaam warned without taking his sights off Pierce.

A car pulled into the drive. Its lights shone on Pierce like a spotlight. Balaam kept his aim on the drug lord agent. The car door opened, but Balaam didn't dare take his eyes off his enemy.

"Dad!" Cade's voice was a sharp icicle falling from a height and right into Balaam's heart.

"Get back into the car." Goodman's voice was tight, angered.

"Come here, Cade." Lyric's voice shattered any courage Balaam had.

"Balaam lower the gun," Goodman commanded.

"Glad you finally made it." Pierce smiled. "Brought us our incentive."

Balaam forced his gaze in the direction of the newcomers. Goodman had a gun pointed on him. Lyric must have pulled Cade back into the car, leaving the door open. She sheltered the boy against her, rocking him.

Goodman took a quick look backward and slammed the door so that Balaam could barely see his son and Lyric through the windows. Where was Quinn?

"You have five minutes to find those papers, Carter. Five minutes or my brother and I will make sure your kid dies. Your girl and you will get to watch the life drain out of her son. Then I'll let you put her out of her misery before you put yourself out of yours," Pierce taunted.

Brother? Was Goodman the other son Nadine had

mentioned?

"Drop your gun and get away from the kid and Lyric. And you—get away from my father." Nathan had never shown an ounce of courage in all their lives, and perhaps he was trying to save his father—or maybe his meal ticket, thinking Balaam would return to the stage. Whatever his reasons, Balaam didn't want to see him die.

Goodman kept his sights on Balaam. "Tell your friend to put the gun down, or I'll have to shoot him."

"Nathan, man, we don't need another situation on top of this situation. Put the gun down and run."

Nathan hesitated.

"Put. It. Down." Balaam shifted Nadine's rifle in his hands. His palms were sweaty. He'd have to make a decision. If he killed Goodman for taking aim at Nathan, no doubt, at the same time, Pierce would shoot Balaam, and Lyric and Cade would never survive.

He could have cursed Daniel for not making a move.

Nathan hesitated for a moment, dropped the gun, and dove out of sight. A gunshot shattered the night.

Lyric's scream from inside the car, filled the crisp, cold air with more chill. Balaam jumped.

Pierce laughed. "That'll keep him away from the gun. We'll take care of him later, Ethan."

For now, the devil turned attempted angel was still alive and out of the equation. Balaam's mind swirled with the possibilities of the situation. He'd always been good at getting himself out of a pinch—or taking a fall to get someone out of trouble—but he had too much at stake. He peered toward the car.

Goodman had stepped back and leaned down. Pierce couldn't see him from his angle, but Balaam could hear the tone in his voice, calm and soothing.

Then he stood. "And keep it down in there. One more scream and I'll take you out." He spoke louder, an edge to his tone.

Goodman hadn't fired, hadn't even moved his aim in Nathan's direction. Balaam would bet all he had that Goodman harbored no intention of taking out Roy's son, heir to all of Jessup's domain, competition for other drug dealers.

Balaam shifted his gun more center.

Pierce trained his gun on him. He blinked and stared again. The snow was coming down at a swift and past pace, maybe he hadn't seen correctly. Where had Jessup gone?

Had he run or had Daniel apprehended him? They had the evidence they needed to put all three of these men in prison. Larry, God rest his soul, had fallen victim to Jessup Roy's nefarious actions. And Daniel had never made a secret of his feelings for Jessup. Maybe that had been enough to make the sheriff snap.

Could he be certain that Goodman wasn't actually the "bad man," that he'd used the alias for an undercover sting, learning about his brother's involvement? Or maybe Pierce had let him in on it. Goodman never seemed as callous as Pierce.

Balaam's last nerve sent him into a mode his Poppa, paranoid over revenuers, had trained him in as a kid. He turned, lifted Nadine's rifle, pointing it directly at Pierce's head. "Drop the gun."

"Not going to happen."

Balaam peeled his gaze from the murderous thug.

Goodman's lips snaked up into a smile. He moved his rifle sight to the left of Balaam. "One…"

What was he doing?

"Take the shot, Badman." Pierce's voice was laced with pure anticipation.

"Two…"

Did Goodman want Balaam to kill his brother?

"Three!" Goodman rang out with the shot of his gun. The bullet was close enough to sing into Balaam's ear as it passed.

He swung his sights back upon Goodman. "No. Please no. Please," Lyric's cries wrenched Balaam's heart.

"Drop the weapon!" Daniel stepped from the side of the garage to stand behind Pierce.

Pierce spun around, his forehead meeting the barrel of Daniel's 1911.

"Huh-uh." With his free hand, Daniel wrenched the weapon, pulling it from Pierce's grasp. "You know the drill. Hands up." Daniel stepped back out of the killer's reach, bent down, and tossed the rifle at a safe distance. "Now, turn around." Daniel grabbed one of Pierce's arms, cuffed his hand then brought the other down, subduing him. Then with a swift movement, he kicked Pierce's feet out from under him and left him face down in the snow.

Balaam winced. He'd feel sorry for what was coming to the man at the hand of the rot-gut he'd taken from Poppa.

Daniel gave Balaam his full attention. "Drop it, Bay. Goodman is with us."

The clomp of boots on Browne's porch above them sent Balaam spinning, gun in hand.

Jim stopped his movement, hands raised. "It's me, Bay."

Balaam swung the gun back around toward Goodman.

"Nope!" Daniel shouted. "Nope, boy. You're safe. Your good. We're done."

Balaam didn't back down. "Get away from my son."

Goodman let the gun dangle from his fingers and lowered it to the ground. "We're done, Balaam. They're safe. That's all I wanted. To keep them safe."

Balaam stood, weapon trained on Goodman's head. Balaam's hand on the trigger shook along with his quaking body. "Safe? You brought them here. Lyric and Cade didn't need to see this."

Goodman nodded toward his brother. "He didn't trust me already. Tommy thought I was weak because it took me so long to figure out what he and my stepmother were doing. I'd worked my way into the organization against Nadine's mistrust. If I'd shown up without Cade, they wouldn't have given me time to save you or anyone else."

"Too many people have died because you hid behind

FAY LAMB

your badge to get evidence." The gun in Balaam's hand trembled. He blinked. And blinked again as Goodman's words seeped into him. Then anger swirled around him. Anger like he'd never sensed before. "What kind of a man doesn't know what his brother's up to? How could you not know?"

"Bay," Lyric climbed out of the car, bringing Cade with her. She stepped toward him. "Bay, don't."

"Get. Back. Into. The. Car," Balaam ordered.

"Don't, Dad." Cade begged. "You said you wouldn't go away. You'd stay. If you kill Agent Goodman, you'll have to leave."

Balaam held aim.

"Bay…" With a soft voice, Lyric was trying to soothe the raging hatred building inside of him. "You had a brother who did unspeakable things. Would you have ever wanted to let yourself believe that Braedon could do what he did?"

He took his gaze off Goodman and looked around.

"Quinn?" He could barely get his friend's name out.

"He's fine. Ethan kept him out of harm's way."

Balaam jerked the gun up again. "But not my boy."

"Put the gun down, Balaam." Daniel ordered. "Think of what all of this means to your boy. After Magda got the alcohol in the facility, Goodman came to me with his suspicions. I agreed that he was too close to shutting down some major cartels. Pierce took us all by surprise when he had you and Cade abducted. If you want to blame anyone, you blame me. I let it escalate because I trusted you. I trusted your instincts. They've always been on the money whether you were running from me or protecting others."

The words stopped Balaam's anger and plummeted his adrenaline levels. He lowered the gun, bent, and placed it on the ground. "She said you were a disappointment to her," he said to Goodman before he slunk to the cold, hard ground, all energy drained.

"She told me that from the moment my father died," Goodman countered. "But like you, I had a brother, and I wanted to see the good he did. I only just began to realize he was my enemy."

Cade ran to him and wrapped a jacket around Balaam's shoulder. "You're a hero, Dad." He hugged his neck.

Balaam clutched Cade to him. "No, son. I've never been a hero. I've been a drug addict and an alcoholic. I've disappointed your mother. I even stole her dreams. I caused everything here because I was selfish."

"But you're still my dad," Cade stooped down. "And you came back and stayed. You didn't let them hurt me. You're not a hero. You're my superhero."

Balaam cried against Cade. "God is the superhero, son, but I love you for thinking I could even begin to be a good person."

Icy cold palms touched his hands, and he stared into tear-filled blue eyes. "You are a good person. God put us through all this to prove it to us, and you're not the only guilty one here. I have my share of the blame, but I'd like to put it behind us. Pierce and Jessup are going to jail."

Jim made his way down the steps.

"Careful," Balaam warned. "That's what did Nadine in."

Jim made his way steadily down the icy steps, the infamous envelope in hand. He handed it to Daniel.

"What'd you do with Jessup?" Balaam looked up at Daniel.

A smile crossed the sheriff's lips. He turned back, and Balaam followed his gaze. A deputy was holding firmly to Pierce, and the man was squirming. Balaam thought of telling Daniel the man's problems, but he didn't feel too kindly toward Pierce at the moment. "He's hogtied behind the garage. Nathan's with him. We found some controlled substances in his pocket. Imagine that. I have two good men, ones I can trust with me. They're here for three reasons. I needed them to help control the situation, to take custody of any prisoners who survived this shootout at Browne's corral, and to keep me from killing Jessup Roy and Tom Pierce if I didn't have cause. "Let's get you into the car and get the heater on. Even superheroes need to stay warm, right, Cade?"

"Sounds good to me, Wyatt Earp," Balaam said.

His reward for his joke with a loving cuff upside the head by Daniel, Lyric's laughter—the first he'd heard since he'd arrived—and a beaming smile from his son.

## 24

Lyric shivered despite the fact that the heat was on. The winter storm had picked up. They'd have three to five feet of it by the time evening rolled around, but everyone in her home with her right now would probably sleep through the white wonderland.

Daniel showed Ethan Goodman to Lyric's door. He turned and said his good-byes and headed out. The man had lost his stepmother, and the evidence Braedon had given to Cade, who'd given it to Daniel, who'd sent it to Balaam, would be too much for his half-brother to overcome, especially in light of the bureau's hatred of traitors.

Lyric scooted from her seat between Balaam and Quinn. They were waiting to discuss things until Ethan's departure, but no one had wanted to push him out the door.

"Ethan?" She wrapped her arms around her to ward off the cold and stood on her porch near the door.

He stood, the white snow sifting down on him.

"Don't be a stranger. You did nothing wrong."

"I'm sorry," he said to her for what must have been the fifth time that night. "The bureau always suspected, and I wasn't objective. I really didn't doubt him until the day he arrived, too conveniently, after he took a shot at you in your backyard. He tipped his hand when things began to happen to your mother. When I got the chance to look at his phone and saw that he had Nadine's number, I realized how deep this all went. I thought he'd pushed her from his life like I had done because of her unsavory behavior. That's when I began to I realize how deep this all went. Last night, I needed you and Cade to be afraid. My brother and my stepmother would have known if you hadn't been."

"You did a good job of scaring us, but you also gave me hints that not all was as it seemed. And Quinn was trying to let me know what he'd figured out on his own."

For the first time since the long ordeal, he smiled. "I hoped you'd understand."

"All is forgiven. Please come back for a real vacation. We'd love to see you again."

He nodded. "I think I'll be on permanent vacation unless I can clear myself beyond a shadow of a doubt. From where I'm standing, I look a little shady. But have a good life, Lyric. Don't give up on your dreams."

"If you need anyone to speak on your behalf, you let us know." She returned inside and shut the door.

Balaam held out a blanket, and she slipped onto her spot on the couch, tugging it around her.

Daniel cleared his throat as he touched Grace's

shoulder. "I'm sorry to keep you all waiting. It's been a long night for all of us, especially you, Mom. I'm sorry for all the worry." He stepped to Cade and bent down beside him, wrapping his arm around Cade's shoulders. "We've had a lot of horrible things happen in the last few months, and we have Larry's and Magda's funerals before we can move on, but God has given us reason to rejoice."

"What's going on?" Balaam whispered to Lyric.

She put her finger to her lips, and Quinn shushed him.

"Zeke's doing well at the hospital." Grace scooted forward on her seat. "That's a blessing. But I'm sorry we have to plan two more funerals." She shook her head. "Poor Bernice. She's lost her son and her husband."

Grace didn't know what Larry had done, and she paid little heed to rumors.

"Mom, Bernice will need you, but we want to tell you some news first."

"Okay, Danny Boy." Grace straightened. "I'm ready."

Daniel smiled at Cade. "See this little boy, right here."

Cade turned to look back at Lyric, and she smiled her encouragement.

"Lyric, what's happening," Balaam repeated.

"Shh." She patted his leg.

"I've seen this precious little boy almost every day of his life." Grace leaned forward and pinched Cade's cheek.

"Cade doesn't know this yet because we wanted to tell you and Balaam and Cade at the same time. Granny Grace?"

"Yes…" Grace inched forward.

"This little boy is truly your great-grandson. He's our blood." Daniel pivoted. "And Lyric… she's my daughter. She and Matthew Roberts were twins born to Magda."

Quinn resituated himself.

Lyric leaned forward.

Quinn strained to keep from showing his emotions—whatever they were.

Grace hadn't said a word. Her eyes filled with tears as she stared at Daniel. "I always suspected."

Daniel closed his eyes, and his shoulders fell as if he'd been expecting those words from her. "I never suspected," he admitted like a man who'd done wrong. He released Cade, and the boy moved to his great-grandmother.

Grace pressed her hand to Cade's cheek. "My great-grandson… I always felt that way, but now it's official." She patted his head and stood, wiggling her fingers in Lyric's direction, bidding her to come to her.

Quinn lowered his gaze, staring at his hands pressed in front of him.

"What do you know?" Balaam pushed his shoulder against Quinn.

Quinn nodded. "I'm happy for them."

Lyric stood, moving around her coffee table.

But Grace stood, as if waiting. "Come here," she said to Quinn. "Come here to Granny. I want to hug all my grandchildren at once. God has blessed me so sweetly."

Quinn cleared his throat and looked at Daniel.

Lyric smiled at her brother and waved him forward.

Quinn stood with much effort, trying to control his emotions. He moved into Grace's outstretched arms, and they all embraced. Somewhere in there, Daniel placed a bear hug around them all.

"Sweet Matthew. Dear sweet Matthew," Grace murmured. "I suspect he knew. He came around a lot before the incident, and something weighed terribly on him."

Daniel sobbed, and each of them turned into his embrace.

The front door clicked open and then shut.

Lyric turned.

Balaam had left without a word.

**FAY LAMB**

## 25

Balaam knocked on the door of the Roy's mansion. He waited a long moment before he heard shuffling and then walking.

Nathan finally opened the door. His eyes were glassy. "Come to gloat?" He smirked.

The snow had stopped, but the chill had definitely remained. "Mind if I come in?"

"Yeah, I do as a matter of fact. Say what you have to say and leave me alone." Nathan closed the door a bit more.

Balaam turned and looked at the beautiful expanse behind him. "The place must be a mess. I understand the feds invaded it last night while you were held at the station. Can I help you do anything?"

Nathan shook his head. "Just go away, Balaam. Our business ended the day I walked out of your hospital room."

"I understand you're angry with me for leaving, but what you did last night, that was bravery, and that was friendship."

"I didn't do it for you. I did it for my dad."

Balaam scuffed his feet, thinking of the right words to say, but the wrong ones waited to burst forth. "You didn't care one bit for your father. You used him for the drugs to keep your assets in line. I was no longer an asset to you last night, and you were behind me, not your father, though your diversion probably saved his life, too. I can't really be around you right now because my sobriety is too important to me, but I hope that one day, you and I can be friends. We've been through a lot. I've been looking at all the bad times, but there were some good ones, too, Nathan, and you made me a rich man. I plan to donate a lot to my friend who helped get me sober and to others who do the same thing. The church here—the one Quinn pastors—is going to get some as well."

"And when you're broke and need money...?

"I'm going to earn it in any way the Lord makes possible. I suggest you do the same thing. Get right with God, turn your life over to Him. If you need to talk to me about it, I'll be here."

"I won't. I'm leaving this evening."

Balaam nodded. "You have my number if you need me. I might be going away for a bit, but someone can get in touch with me." He walked away.

Behind him, the door clicked shut, and Balaam doubted he'd ever hear from Nathan Roy again.

Larry Roberts' funeral was a formal one. Daniel and Bernice had met together, and then they'd approached Lyric and Quinn. All had agreed that opening to ridicule Larry's choice of separating Lyric and Matthew from each other and from Daniel and Grace, would be of no benefit.

The man's reputation stood intact, and only those who loved Matthew the most knew the truth. In some way that had united them.

After Larry's funeral, Bernice said she had something for Cade, but she needed a little time. Curious but agreeing, Lyric had hugged her and thanked her for being such a wonderful mother to her brother.

"If I'd known there had been two of you, I would have loved you both." Bernice surprised her. "But when people seek to connive, they always have to find a way to hide it. You were that hiding place. No one ever suspected, least of all me. I'm sorry for what my Larry did, Lyric, but while everything he did was wrong, I know he did it out of love for me. He wanted to place a child in my arms. I longed so dearly for a baby I couldn't have. I can't apologize to you for loving Matthew the way I did—the way I still do. And while I'm a bit angry at Larry, I can't stop loving him either."

"I understand," Lyric admitted. "Braedon and Momma did the unthinkable, and I get so livid at times thinking of all that took place. Then I'll remember a good moment with

Brae, or I'll think of Momma's last moments with me—how she wanted me to go away because she knew she was about to be killed, and she didn't want me to die with her."

"There's good and bad in all of us." Bernice clasped Lyric's hands, facing her. "Sometimes the bad hides the good. Other times the good covers the bad in folks. We choose the part we want to see in them. She gave a gentle shake to Lyric's hands. "Daniel reminded me of the day Matthew almost drowned in the Jordan River. When Larry and I arrived at the hospital, Daniel was there with you. There you sat with Quinn, Balaam, and Braedon, all of you wet and freezing." She wiped at a stray tear. "I screamed at you. I said horrible things to you as I marched past you to get to Matthew. Then Matthew looked up at me with those big blue eyes of his, so much like yours, and he said, "Mom, you shouldn't have said those things. Braedon came in after me, holding to Balaam's hand, who held to Quinn's hand who held to Lyric's. He said you'd wrapped your arm around one skinny tree and refused to let go. The four of you had formed a chain to pull him out of the rushing water. I never had the courage to apologize to any of you, even after I saw your bandaged arm, scraped by the tree, and Daniel told me how very afraid you all had been."

Lyric had never forgotten that day. Up until the latest horrors of her life, she'd had nightmares about Matthew's drowning that day. With all that had happened lately, she'd tucked away that scare, exchanging it for the real-time horrors going on around her.

Bernice shook Lyric's hands again. "Let's hold on to that memory of a heroic Braedon when we're tempted to remember the changes that came about over time."

"But…" Lyric could barely whisper the word. "But I caused those changes."

Bernice shook her head. "Braedon had a few demons chasing him. I suspect he had every intention of doing right by you and Cade. Just like Larry's intentions, in the end, they failed us miserably." Her face softened. "And I need to apologize for keeping you from saying your final good-byes to Matthew. That's something else I've done that will haunt me. I can't change it, but I hope you'll forgive me."

"You had no way of knowing who I was to Matthew. I've learned that. I have a son, and if the same had happened to me, I don't doubt that the shock would harden me in much the same way. Nothing to forgive." Lyric clung to Bernice for a long time without words before she stepped away.

Two funerals in three days, and as suspected, Magdalene Moxley's was sparsely attended. Quinn preached the ceremony. Balaam was beside her, but he bent to give Cade a shoulder to sob against.

Balaam had been too silent for Lyric's liking. Something was going on in the man's brain, and she wasn't sure she would like it when he had his say. Still, she praised the Lord that her son had his father with him.

Zeke Carter rounded out the group. He stood behind Daniel and Grace. He'd reached and brushed Lyric's fingers with his calloused ones. A sign of his silent support.

Quinn opened his Bible and started to read. Several car doors shut, and Lyric turned.

A man, someone Lyric didn't recognize, walked with a woman at his side. Three tall boys, dressed in suits and ties like the man, followed behind. The woman wore a designer dress.

Lyric shared a look with Quinn who shrugged.

As the group drew near, Daniel reached out and shook their hands and thanked them for coming, but he made no introductions as he stepped back beside Lyric.

"Thank you for joining us," Quinn said. He looked down at the page for a long moment before looking up again. His gaze seemed to visibly clash with the older stranger.

Quinn's hands shook as he lifted the Bible. Again, he lowered the book, keeping his hand on the page.

The weather had been nice for Larry's funeral, and though snow had not fallen since the night when both had died, the skies were a weepy sort of gray reminding her of the day of Matthew's funeral.

"God's word has never failed me," Quinn said, his voice strong. "Not once since the man who would claim me as his son..." He nodded to Daniel. "... led me to my Heavenly Father. In essence, what that means is that God has never failed me. No matter what life was for my sister and for me, God was there.

"I've been thinking so much about my mother since her death. Her last few moments, as recounted to me, were a miracle beyond any I've experienced in my life." Quinn smiled at Lyric. "Madgalene Moxley actually said she loved her children—all three of her children."

Quinn hugged the Bible to his chest. "I'd prayed so long and so hard for her to say those words, not to me, but to my sister, who needed a mother's love. And God brought not only the words out of our mother, but they were said in a way and in a situation where we know she meant them. But that wasn't the greatest gift that God gave to me out of everything we've been through. My sister knows the Lord. My friend has returned to the Lord. I dearly hold to the belief that Magdalene shed the demons of her life in her final moments and that one day, I will see my mother in Heaven where I'll hug her and kiss her and tell her that while I never saw much of it here on this earth, I can see the beauty in her soul."

Quinn lowered the Bible. "Psalm 71, staring in verses 12 through 16, says, 'O God, be not far from me: O my God, make haste for my help. Let them be confounded and consumed that are adversaries to my soul; let them be covered with reproach and dishonour that seek my hurt. But I will hope continually, and will yet praise Thee more and more. My mouth shall shew forth Thy righteousness and Thy salvation all the day; for I know not the numbers thereof. I will go in the strength of the Lord GOD: I will

make mention of Thy righteousness, even of Thine only.'"
Quinn reached into his jacket and pulled out a
handkerchief. He ran it over his eyes.

"Our mother wasn't perfect." Quinn chuckled.
"There's no hiding that in this town." He stood for a
moment peering off into the distance.

Lyric followed his gaze. Matthew's gravestone.

"Our Magdalene, unlike Mary Magdalene of the Bible,
will only be remembered as one filled with demons, but we,
her children, her family, know that in God's loving
kindness, in her last moments, the demons were banished
to the darkest corners of hell where Momma often lived
while walking the earth. Those who tried to help her will
understand the miracle God wrought in those few
moments.

"Momma was hanging on the edge of a cliff; she
probably had one hand on one small string of Christ's robe,
reaching up for His help. And He was there. And He took
her with Him.

"So, Lord, Magdalene Moxley's passing will come
with our praise." Quinn looked down at his Bible again.
'Thy righteousness also, O God, is very high, who hast
done great things, O God, who is like unto Thee. My lips
shall greatly rejoice when I sing unto Thee; and my soul,'
and my mother's soul, and my sister's soul, and my friend's
soul 'which thou hast redeemed.'"

Quinn bent down and picked up a handful of dirt. "I
love you, Momma," he whispered the words as he placed

the soil on Momma's coffin.

Lyric bent down and did the same. "Thank you, Momma. I love you, too."

Then Daniel stooped down. He touched Cade's shoulder. "We'll see her again. We have that hope."

Cade nodded and wiped his nose against Balaam's shoulder. Balaam looked and winced but then smiled. Together Balaam, Cade, and Daniel tossed a handful of dirt onto Momma's coffin. "I can't wait to see that pretty smile that's been gone so long," Daniel said.

"I miss you Grandma," Cade sniffled.

Balaam placed his handful and rested his hand on it for a moment. "You were something else, Magdalene. You sure did entertain. Heaven is fortunate to have you. Don't give the Lord too much sass now."

"God bless you, dear," Granny Grace whispered. "Thank you for the blessings you bestowed upon my Danny Boy and me."

In the final good-byes to Momma, Lyric had not seen Quinn step around and greet the family, but when he stood facing the man Lyric had never met, she could not mistake his identity.

Daniel placed his hand on Lyric's shoulder, holding her in place. "Let him have this moment. It's his to do whatever he wishes." He stepped back away from the gravesite and those Quinn joined in conversation.

Oh, how Lyric wished she could be a part of that discussion.

Quinn's face did not give away his emotions. He nodded and spoke in soft tones. Finally, another "thank you for coming," rang out. The man raised a hand in good-bye to Daniel and with a weary smile stepped away. Those with him followed after.

Quinn came to stand with them. "Thank you, Dad," he said to Daniel.

"Quinn, Sr., wanted to come," Daniel said. "He was afraid you'd be angry, but I told him that the young man I knew would welcome the chance to know he did care."

Quinn nodded. "I let him go a long time ago, and he has his own life now. I have three nice stepbrothers and a sweet stepmother, but there's no sense in pretending that we can build a relationship, especially since the man who raised me has been here with me all this time."

Daniel turned and stared as the car drove away.

"I didn't do it to punish him." Quinn seemed to follow Daniel's thoughts. "I did it to set him free. He's carried the burden of leaving me for far too many years. I said he's welcome to contact me any time, and I'd love to hear from him and his family. We'll see what he does with the offer, but God cured that wound with your love, Daniel.

Lyric reached up and gave her brother a tight hug. "Momma would have been surprised at her sendoff, I think."

Balaam scooted around Lyric and Cade and moved to his father.

Zeke stared without words. "Your leaving again, ain't

ya, boy?"

"No, Dad. You're not. You said you wouldn't," Cade cried out.

Balaam smoothed Cade's hair and narrowed his eyes at his dad. "I wanted to tell you in my own way," he turned his gaze to his son, "I have to. Just for a bit. I need to be a little stronger to be the father you deserve."

Cade narrowed his eyes and straightened. "If you leave me, you'll never be the father I deserve. I don't want you to come back." He ran across the graveyard, stopping at Matthew's grave where he fell on his knees.

Balaam started after Cade.

Lyric pushed Balaam away. "No!" She stopped and stuck a finger in his face before hurrying after Cade, sinking down beside him and holding him close.

"Uncle Matthew lied. He lied. He said my dad loved me. I always though he meant Braedon, but he knew it was Balaam."

Lyric had no response. The heart within her broke over Balaam's pronouncement. If she couldn't lasso the pain and disappointment in her soul, how could she help Cade?

Only Balaam could do that, and to do that he'd have to stay, but something had happened, something that made him believe he needed to get out of town.

"Cade." She reached out and touched Matthew's smiling face. "Let's you and me not trust your dad."

Cade stared at her, eyes wide.

"Let's trust our Dad." She pointed to the heavens.

"Your dad here needs to do something. Maybe it's a good reason. Maybe it's a wrong reason. Maybe God wants us to lean on Him and let your dad work out things so that he can be a better dad to you."

Cade blinked. "But…"

"Would you want him to stay with us if his heart was set on leaving?"

Cade shook his head.

"Your dad needs to know you love him no matter what." She touched his nose. "Besides, you got snot all over his shirt, and he didn't even complain."

Cade giggled.

Lyric stood. "Go. Apologize. Tell your dad you love him. Ask him to come back when he's ready, and let's me and you concentrate on trusting the Lord. It's kind of new for me. I need your help."

Cade nodded and ran back. She waited until Cade hugged Balaam to look back at the picture of her brother. "I miss you so, so much, but I hear you've left something for Cade. I can only imagine what it is, but thank you for loving us."

She stood, wiping sand from her overused black dress.

After four funerals in two months, she'd pray for those she loved, especially Zeke and Granny Grace. She never wanted to attend another final farewell as long as she lived.

But if Balaam thought he'd go away without returning to their son, she'd make sure the dress got one more good use.

# 26

Balaam looked around Grace's guestroom, where he had stayed for the last two weeks. He had very little with him when he arrived, and he was taking very little with him now. He folded the last of his shirts washed by Daniel's mother and tucked it into his bag. Balaam had postponed the trip to give Cade a little time to get use to the fact that Balaam needed to leave—for just a while more.

He pulled the zipper closed and looked through the window at the house across the white sheets of snow hiding the road that separated them. Another winter storm had blown through overnight. Cade was standing in the snow, bundled against the elements but wandering as if not knowing what to do with himself.

"Are you sure?" Jim Maynard startled him. He leaned against the doorframe and for the twentieth time since his early morning arrival, he asked Balaam the same question. "I'm not one to tell a person what they need when it comes to their addiction, but you haven't slipped, and you've been here two weeks since that night when you could have fallen hard. My suggestion would be—"

"I didn't slip," Balaam interrupted him, "because I knew that the man wanted me to drink it so he could take me away from them." He pointed out the window. "But I have to be honest with myself. Before I had it in my hands, I could almost taste it. I could smell that prime bourbon seeping from Madga's pores earlier in the evening." He shuddered at the thought. "I wanted the Xanax on that tray in the hospital as badly as I'd wanted it in the hospital in California when I overdosed. Temptation was right there, and I was close. I could have ..."

Jim leaned away from the door. He kicked the heel of one boot against the toe of the other. "You also told me that you distinctly remember an aversion to it when you held it in your hands."

"Because he was going to use it to kill people I cared about."

Jim studied the floor for a moment and then looked up. "Two questions for ya, okay? What's life been like during the last two weeks when you said you needed to give Cade time?"

"I've been busy with him. I've helped Poppa. I've done some carpentry for Grace. I've got the legalities of my royalties going to charities, and I've been deciding what to do with the rest of my life. I've done everything there is to do. The temptation's going to come back. I can't laze around here and do nothing."

"Bay, do you think the temptation is ever going to go

away?"

"I'd hoped it would."

"You spent some good weeks with Constance and me, boy. I know what you're made of. The temptation isn't going to leave you up on that farm. Even during the last week, while you were busy, it sneaked up on you a time or two, didn't it? Tell me the truth."

"Yeah, but…"

"But my farm lies in a dry county, and you'd have had to ask for my vehicle, and I would ask why, and the Balaam Carter I've come to know wouldn't tell a lie to save himself. If you'd have wanted the liquor bad enough, you'd have told me, and when I told you the truck wasn't yours for the taking, you would have walked out of our little valley and down that dirt road, and you'd have found what you wanted."

Balaam continued to watch Cade play in his yard. No, the boy wasn't playing at all. He was walking around, kicking at the snow. His face was tight, and his movements tense. Every once in a while, he'd stare over at Jim's truck.

Both mother and son had to be breathing easy, free of fear, but Cade was controlling rage. Balaam had seen so much of himself in that kid. He'd never miss that emotion.

Balaam closed his eyes. The beautiful stained glass of the funeral home had stood before him. He'd walked around the outside, even seen beak-nosed Mr. Parsons peer out the slender curtain at the right of the old home's heavy wooden door. Balaam had kicked the grass with his tennis shoes. His nostrils had flared, and his breath had come in short gasps. His momma was gone, and she wouldn't be coming back.

"Bay?" Jim broke into his thoughts.

"You're saying you think I'm strong enough to beat the temptation."

Jim chuckled. "Nope. I'm saying you're strong enough to lean on the Lord for your strength to deny temptation, and I think you have two pretty strong reasons to avoid it. Add that to the amount of prayer I'm sure the Lord hears with your name uttered in the petitions, I think staying is what you need. Don't tempt temptation. Best it."

"How do I keep busy? I don't have a trade."

"I suggest you use it to get that songwriting career in order. I feel strongly that the Lord is leading you there. I've even placed a call to Shane Browne. He's waiting to hear from you. Daniel has the key to his studio. Shane said you can go there, even suggested that a routine of eight-to-five would help."

Balaam stared across the way. Lyric had barely talked to him since her common sense had pushed through his desires to kill Ethan Goodman. They'd shared a few moments during the funerals, sticking close to one another, but once the dead had been buried, it seemed their future had been placed six feet under as well.

Of course, Poppa's reading him aloud like an open book hadn't helped.

Too many people had died in that kid's life, and now

one of the living ones was leaving him, as far as the boy knew.

So many had lived, and God had brought him back to his son and to the woman he loved, but Balaam was stymied by fear.

Cade stooped to pick up snow in his gloved hands. He pounded at it, forming it into a nice, tight, possibly damaging weapon. Jim's truck was probably the target. He'd hate to make his son apologize and then to work off the damages.

"Excuse me." Balaam grabbed his jacket and threw it on as he passed his friend and went through Grace's home. The screen door slammed behind him, and as Balaam pushed his way through the heavy white snow, Cade stared up at him with narrowed eyes filled with disappointment.

Balaam slowed his pace and did his best to seem controlled, unworried. "Whatcha doing?"

Cade stared at the packed ice and back to Balaam. "Why?" His lips trembled and a tear tracked down one cheek.

"Why what?" Balaam held out his hands for the nicely packed snowball, as if he had no idea what bothered his kid.

Lyric opened her door and stood in the small opening, as if she feared what he would say to Cade, who had yet to answer Balaam's question.

"Why what?" Balaam repeated.

"Why are you leaving?" Cade moved to hurl the

411

snowball into the yard, away from objects or persons. Balaam smiled. The kid hadn't inherited everything from him.

"Am I leaving?" Balaam looked to Lyric, not missing the fact that Cade had jerked his attention to him.

"Is there any reason you need to leave?" She brushed back those luscious raven curls of hers, a challenge forming in the set of her face, the glare in her eyes.

"I put you in danger. All our lives, that's what I've done. I came back to save you all from something I started years ago, and we ended up facing down death. Pierce was within a few minutes of killing you both."

Lyric stepped to the edge of her porch. "You think you're a savior?"

Balaam blinked. Had he talked to her about his thoughts, his remorse about the idol he'd become to so many disillusioned people. "No... I... It's just—"

"You're no more a savior, Bay, than you are responsible for all that's happened." She moved down a step. "Matthew and Quinn were the only innocent ones in all of this. The rest of us were pieces on a gameboard for Jessup Roy. Momma was a pawn. Daniel was a target, Larry was a fool..." She shook her head as if to clear emotion. "But he loved Matthew. I can't stay angry with him. Matthew loved him." She wiped at the tip of her nose, which had begun to redden, a sign that the holding back of tears might be causing it to sting in the cold. "Braedon allowed himself to be used for what? For greed." She turned and looked back at the house. "We've moving out of here as soon as I can get it on the market and sold. I thought he'd put in some honest work to buy the land and the materials, but I'd blinded myself to the truth about the Carter boys because I thought you two were the answers to all my dreams and my problems. I didn't care that their poppa was a moonshiner, and no matter how much Zeke pretends the government has no say in his business, he's a criminal. He's made money off the suffering of others just as much as Jessup Roy has done. Brae, too."

Balaam lowered his head.

Cade inched closer to him. Why did his son have to hear all the ugliness about their lives after seeing what it had caused? Little boys shouldn't be burdened with such things. They needed to be in Little League with their dad coaching or sitting on the sidelines. They needed to toss a football around in the yard, they needed…

Tuesday.

Balaam swallowed hard. Today was Tuesday.

He should be eating ice cream at Grace's shop with his son, sharing memories of a good man. He'd already failed in that promise.

"I firmed everything up with Nathan. I'm out of the rock star business."

"What business you planning to go into?" Lyric took another step down. "Jessup Roy is in jail, and since Daniel helped clear Ethan, they're working to make sure the state gets a good flushing out of its drug lords. No courier work there."

This was the old Lyric. The spitfire he'd loved to spar with. She was coming out of the shell his brother had tucked her into. "Well, I don't plan to do any more work to help Satan destroy souls."

Cade peered up at him. He blinked and moved closer. "She wants you to stay," he whispered. "Give her the right answers, Dad."

Balaam could have laughed, but he held it in, peering up at Lyric who stood her ground on that bottom step. "Jim Maynard says that Shane Browne turned his life around. He's writing music. I've been writing some, too. I found that heavy metal was a little easier to pen because no one can understand the lyrics, and they don't have to make sense because someone will read something different into them anyway." He shrugged. "Shane's in Florida, but Jim said he placed a call to him to see if I could contact him. I'd like him to see the songs I've written to let me know if I can transition into music that glorifies the Lord. I thought I'd never want to pick up a guitar or any instrument again, but I've been talking to God. If I can stand on a church stage and share my music and my testimony, then perhaps I can save…"

Lyric held up her hand.

He nodded. Temptation was going to have a tough job getting past her to him—if she would have him. "Perhaps God can use the story of all I did against Him to bring others to Him."

Lyric stepped down onto the snow. "I haven't really played a lot since you left, but do you think there might be room in your new dreams for a piano player and another songwriter? I'll practice. I won't embarrass you." She smiled.

Balaam stared at her. Could she really be saying what he thought she was saying? She'd forgiven him enough to trust him with her dreams again? "Can I give you my answer in about an hour?"

Lyric tilted her head, the smile disappearing. She gazed at Cade and back to him. "Please," she whispered the plea.

"It's just that it's Tuesday." With each word, the emotion within him welled. "And Tuesdays were made for ice cream. That's what Matthew said, and I promised Cade that every Tuesday we'd share an ice cream in his Uncle Matthew's memory. I want to start today. I'm not going anywhere. Even if you told me to leave, I'm staying put."

Lyric covered her face with her hands and bent forward. Great choking sobs fell from her.

Balaam had hurt her without even intending to do it. He moved toward her.

She stepped back.

"Yes, Lyric. Oh, Lord, let her know the depths of my answer. I want you beside me. You and Cade. Always. Do you want me?"

Cade slipped his hand into Balaam's.

"So much has happened. You don't need to make

promises to me," he pleaded with Lyric. "Just say there's a chance."

Lyric turned her tear-stained face to the sky. "Oh, Lord, let him know the depths of my answer." She reached for his hand and her son's hand. "I want you both beside me always, but we need to take it slow, Balaam. No pressure. One day at a time. We need to seek counseling with Quinn." A devilish grin he'd remembered from her youth turned her face into pure joy for him. "I want you to ask my dad for permission to court me. And that's what we'll do. Court. No going on dates alone. No Shepherd's Rock."

"Oh, there will be Shepherd's Rock."

She stared at him, her mouth open. "We will not…"

"Trust me. What you think I'm saying is not what I'm saying."

She nodded. "And we'll wait for my father and for Quinn to tell us when they think we're ready."

Balaam nodded. "Okay. Face big, bad, sheriff dad, kiss my girl in front of a chaperone." He tugged Cade to his side. "Can I kiss my girl?"

"Not now." Cade smirked. "Let's go to Granny Grace's for ice cream."

Lyric giggled. "He's good. He's real good. I'll fix dinner. You two go have dessert first. Invite Granny Grace to eat with us. I'll call Daniel and Quinn."

"When you call him," Balaam leaned close to her. "Call him *Dad*. I think he'd like that." He pecked her cheek with a quick kiss.

"Dad!" Cade laughed. "No fair."

"Okay. Let's go." Balaam laughed. "Of course, I need to borrow Mom's car."

Lyric went inside and returned, keys in her hand. "Be careful."

"Mom?" Cade asked. "I know that Uncle Matthew meant Tuesdays were made for ice cream for him and me and now for Dad, but I want you to come this time with me and Dad. Uncle Quinn, too."

Lyric beamed. "I'd like that very much. But I might cry a little. Is that okay?"

Cade nodded. "It's okay if we all cry. Uncle Matthew would want us to be happy, but once he told me that to know how it feels to be truly happy, you might have to have been truly sad."

Balaam didn't wait for the ice cream. The tears came unbidden, and he didn't even try to stop them.

If Matthew had only known…

Lyric's eyes ran with happy tears as Balaam recounted for Cade, who'd never heard the story before, how they'd tormented a hornet all summer long. "One day, Horace had enough of us, and he zeroed in on Matthew and chased him into Poppa's tool shed. Horace kept buzzing us, but he didn't take aim. When Matthew, thinking it was safe, opened the door, Horace divebombed him and stung the fire out of him."

Cade leaned back in his chair and laughed.

"Well, sounds like a party over here." Granny Grace came from her office. "Mind if I join in?"

Balaam stood and pulled out a chair for the older woman, but she held up her hand. "We need to pull two more seats around this table. Daniel and Bernice are joining us."

Balaam dragged two chairs from a nearby empty table.

Lyric wiped her eyes and laughed a little more at Balaam's memory. "Remember that old bike Quinn found and dragged to our house. We fixed that thing up the best we could and rode it all around, sometimes three of us on it at one time."

Quinn looked down and rubbed the knee of his jeans over where Lyric knew a scar existed. "We were taking turns going up the hill and cutting back down and around the creek. When it came my turn, I was riding along and suddenly I tilted forwarded. Before I flipped over the handlebars, I saw the front wheel rolling down the street."

Balaam laughed. "I never told you, but that was probably my fault. During my turn, I hit a rock and skidded. I was sure after that happened to you that I'd knocked an already decrepit bolt free."

"As I recall, the only one who took my accident seriously was Matthew. The rest of you turned into a pack of hyenas, guffawing at my bloody knee, skinned up elbows, and scraped face." Quinn put on a façade of bitterness.

"I don't feel sorry for you at all. I was the one who ran for the pop fly and fell into the sewage at the end of the field," Lyric bantered.

Balaam had taken a bite out of his ice cream. He nearly spit it out with his laughter. "Yeah, that was pretty funny."

Lyric had never been able to share her memories with her son, and this time with him was a real treat. The giggles and laughter were a precious gift.

"I bet even Uncle Matthew laughed at that." Cade snickered.

Lyric gave him a playful push. "Yes, he did."

"They weren't the only ones." Granny Grace giggled. "They came tromping by my house," she reached toward Cade and touched his hand, "and your momma, she was fit to be tied. I had the boys hose her off in the front yard and made her come in and take a shower while I washed and dried her clothes. She was so fired up, she wouldn't let a one of them in the house with her."

Lyric smiled at the memory. "That's the day I sat in your living room and plinked on your piano. You offered me free lessons."

"Yes, I did, because what you were doing was more than plinking. You had a natural talent." Grace stared out into the store for a long moment. When she looked back, she seemed to be lost in some other time. "Did Matthew ever tell you that after you started the lessons, he came by my house every week during the spring and summer and every two weeks during the fall until it snowed?"

Lyric shook her head. "I know he mowed your grass. I asked him what you paid him, and he said a million bucks. He was always joking like that. He'd never tell me the truth."

Grace's eyes softened as she looked at Lyric. "I suppose to him what I did was worth a million dollars, though I told him it wasn't necessary."

"What did you do?" Quinn asked.

"Matthew never let me pay him for the work he did, and he worked hard." She put her hand to her chest. "Lyric, he took care of my yard because he wanted to thank me for giving you the piano lessons."

"Oh," Lyric put her hand to her mouth. She looked to Quinn. "Oh, Matthew," she whispered. "He never told me."

"He wouldn't." From behind her, Bernice spoke. "I never knew why he insisted on mowing your grass until now, Grace." Matthew's mother wiped her eyes. "He was such a good boy. Naturally so, wasn't he?" She looked to Daniel who stood beside her. "A lot like his real father."

Daniel didn't speak, but the look on his face said enough.

"Hey, boy!" Cade jumped from his seat, and for the first time, Lyric noticed the black lab Bernice had on a leash inside the store. The dog wasn't too old but yet he wasn't a puppy.

Daniel took his hat from his head. "Bernice wanted to see Cade. I hope it's okay if we join you."

"Sure, Danpa." Cade said.

"Danpa?" Daniel held a chair for Bernice and took one beside her.

"Grandpa, Danpa." Cade shrugged. "And Aunt Bernice."

Bernice gasped at the endearment.

"I'm sorry…" Lyric started.

"Oh, no." Bernice smiled. "I lost my entire family, and Cade just reminded me what I'd gained because of Matthew's friendship, his loyalty, and his love."

"Is this what I think it is?" Lyric asked, pointing to the well-behaved dog that Cade continued to lavish his affections upon.

Bernice nodded. "Daniel didn't think you'd mind, and I hope my trust in him is well placed."

Lyric didn't know what to say. "Sure," slipped between her lips.

Bernice leaned down and petted the dog, who looked up at her. "Cade, Uncle Matthew had planned on giving you a gift, but he had been waiting for the right time. The vet who bought Uncle Matthew's practice allowed the techs to take care of him for me because… well, I was having a tough time with Uncle Matthew's death." She dug into her jacket pocket and came out with an unsealed envelope. "The girls also found this in Matthew's office when we were getting it ready for the new vet to take over the practice. They gave it to me, and I'm ashamed to say I held on to it all this time, but somehow I couldn't let them give your gift away."

Cade stared at the envelope with his name on it and then handed it to Balaam. "Would you read it?"

Balaam held it. "Are you sure?"

Cade nodded.

Balaam slid the card out and read silently before looking up. Cade moved to stand beside him. "Uncle Matthew says, 'Cade, meet Chester. I knew he belonged to you the moment he was brought into my office as a runt of a litter not expected to survive. I fought for him because, well, I intended for him to be yours, and I wouldn't want anything to get between you and Chester. Every time Chester gives you a big old lick on your face (which he'll do all the time), I want you to remember, even when I forget to tell you, that I love you more than anyone in this whole world has ever loved anyone. Well, that's not true. Cade, God loves you more. But still, I do love you, and I want Chester to remind you of that love. Be good to him. He almost didn't make it, and I suspect Chester's been anxious to meet you because I've told him about this terrific little boy that can do all things because he loves God, and that this little boy will always love him the way I have always and will also love you. Uncle Matthew.'"

Balaam brought the back of his hand to his lips, holding the card between trembling fingers.

Cade bent beside Chester, wrapping his arms around

the dog without hesitation. For the first time since the dog arrived, he became animated., swishing his long tail across the floor. Then he licked and licked Cade's face until the boy cried for mercy. "Uncle Matthew was right," the little boy rang out with such glee that the adults around him laughed.

Balaam caught Bernice's gaze and smiled. "Thank you," he mouthed and Lyric nodded in agreement.

For a long time, they watched until the dog and the little boy tired.

"Daniel and Quinn, I have a question to ask you." Balaam asked while watching Cade play.

Both men stared at him.

"Quinn, Lyric has asked me to seek counseling with you and her. I need to be accountable for so many things, and I'd like it if you'd do that for me—for us."

Quinn didn't smile. "You aren't going to do things the way you did before."

"I've told him that," Lyric smirked. "We're both asking for accountability."

"And Daniel, Lyric and I aren't planning to get married tomorrow, next week, maybe not next year, but I'm asking your permission to court your daughter, as in no dates alone, always with a chaperone." Balaam rolled his eyes toward Cade. "And we'd like to trust you and Quinn to tell us if or when you might think we should marry."

Daniel smiled then held out his hand. "Thank you for the privilege of allowing me the chance to do that, Bay.

You have my permission to court my daughter."

Balaam moved to Lyric and helped her to her feet. "You didn't say, but there's a question I should have asked you from the beginning. May I assume a true role as Cade's father?"

"You have…"

"No, Lyric, I haven't. I let you both down. I don't deserve any mercy from either of you. But I want to take on the responsibility as his dad. Of course, I'm not going to go against your wishes. We're not married. I'm on the outside looking in, but I'd love for you to let me in to help you bring him up as God intended from the start."

Lyric bit her lower lip, but the smile burst forward. She hugged him to her, her arms around his neck. "Try to skip out on us again. Just try."

Balaam rubbed his nose against hers. "We have some sadness to put behind us, but we have a future of happiness ahead. Let's dream together and ask Matthew's Compass to point the way."

"Matthew's Compass was God," she whispered, her lips touching his.

"I know that now."

"And so do I. She leaned against him, her lips touching his. He pulled her to him, and she remembered what they'd once shared.

Waiting for Daniel and Quinn's permission was going to be murder—no wait. She'd had enough of that. Torture. She'd be tortured by thoughts of his being hers every night, but this new man that Balaam had become—he'd be well worth the wait. She pressed deeper into the kiss.

"Dad!" Cade laughed. "Mom!"

"Son!" Daniel picked up Balaam by the scruff of his jacket and turned him to face his unsmiling fatherly face. "That type of kiss doesn't work in courting at this stage."

"Yeah, but it'll give me something to look forward to."

FAY LAMB

# Epilogue

*Two years and three months later*

Balaam stared across the mountain. Mists of thin clouds moved across the greenery. A world of color had begun to unfold, including the plentiful bluebells he'd dreamed about here on Shepherd's Rock. The sky had turned from dark to pink to Carolina blue while he'd been here.

In homes nestled around the peaceful park, the smell of burning fireplaces blended in the air, reminding him of his childhood and how much he and Braedon had looked forward to the first time the fireplace would be used. Pretty soon, the firewood wouldn't be burned until fall.

The morning had been chilly, as most spring mornings were in Western North Carolina, but the warmth was beginning to move out the chill. Balaam bent down and wiped at the clean black shoes, removing blades of grass.

Just yesterday, he and Quinn had sneaked up to this

spot and mowed a patch—just enough to accommodate the family, which now included the Maynards and his former boss and new business partner, Shane Browne and Shane's three children, and his wife, Abra.

Earlier, as the sun crept over the mountains, the men had helped Balaam set up the chairs and the arch that Shane said had been used during his marriage to Abra.

Shane wrote and performed music for children. He was also a popular wholesome country music and Christian songwriter with many awards. He'd chosen his performance stage for children because of the same temptations Balaam faced daily. Balaam and Lyric worked with him on many songs, getting their names recognized and gaining the trust they needed to earn because of his prior musical antics and stanzas. Soon, without Shane's goading, Balaam and Lyric's songs were being sung by the same popular artists who loved Shane's work and some who'd approached Balaam and Lyric to add a song or two to an album. He and Shane worked alone and together, but Shane had asked him to work with him as a business partner.

The old watermill where danger had found them hadn't been Shane's home since he'd married Abra. They'd moved into the old Carmichael mansion in town and spent their time between Amazing Grace and Abra's hometown in Florida. The watermill had been converted into a studio Shane dubbed Watermill Music. Before Balaam collaborated with him, Shane only opened the studio to artists when he was in town. Balaam had learned from Shane how to produce music, which added considerably to both their income since Balaam moved back to Amazing Grace. Balaam worked hard so that Watermill Music could produce some of the best music.

Then Shane had suggested that Balaam and Lyric record an album, mostly older hymns, tweaking the sound just a bit for a younger audience and adding in a few of their own, never-heard tunes. Balaam fought it at first, but Shane nudged him on. And Lyric, who had renewed her piano lessons from Granny Grace, urged him forward. Lyric had played piano, Balaam the bass, Shane his guitar, and Cade had picked up the drums—a natural. With everything planned, Shane surprised Balaam and Lyric by inviting a few well-known musicians. The end product was the first work that Balaam treasured. The instruments produced a beautiful sound where the beat never overshadowed the words and took away the depth of their meaning.

And the sales had taken off.

Balaam shunned the concert stage, except for church venues, and God was still using Balaam's and Lyric's testimonies to draw people to Him. When Lyric spoke of the years of growing up without a father or a mother who showed her love and then ended with the powerful message of the love God had showed her through Quinn, and Matthew, and Daniel, and Grace, people sobbed.

Then Lyric would look out at the people before her, no

matter how large or how small the crowd, and she'd proclaim, "I wouldn't have it any other way, because today I have something for you to hear, a message for you to receive, a message that only God could have given me because He brought me through all that's gone before.

"What's your message? Is the Holy Spirit whispering to you and telling you that you're not perfect and you need Christ? Well, I'm not perfect either. But Christ has brought me through—has brought Balaam and me and our son through. He will do the same for you."

Lyric's words were a part of his soul now, even as he stood alone here on Shepherd's Rock. He'd told Lyric they'd see this place again. She had no idea where they planned to marry. He'd taken over the where and asked her to plan the colors, the clothing, and the reception—which would be held at the reception hall of the church.

Balaam was alone now, dressed and waiting for the wedding party and the guests. He'd returned back to Quinn's place where he'd been staying and dressed quickly, wanting time here with God to comprehend all that God had restored.

He sat hard in the first blue padded chair of the first row, reserved for Granny Grace, and he stared out around him.

When he'd almost died nearly two years and five months before, he'd thought his memory of this place, of what he'd done to Lyric, a dream. He'd grown to understand, though he'd never told a soul, that God wasn't going to let him die that night. The dream of this place where he saw Lyric once again and Cade for the first time had been a promise to Balaam. A do-over. The winds tearing him away from them had surely been God telling Balaam all that he'd lose if he didn't bring his heart back to God.

Balaam had taken the challenge, and every day, he woke with a new drive to walk God's path.

Two years and three months of counseling alone and with Lyric had taught him that God had His reasons for everything, and Balaam didn't have to understand them. He simply had to trust. Realizing that God allowed things to happen—and sometimes Balaam's own actions had brought about those horrible things—had been the hardest truth to grasp.

Then Quinn had reminded Balaam of the renovations he and Lyric had done to the home Braedon had built. Folks thought them crazy to practically tear a perfectly fine house down and rebuild, but Lyric decided she didn't want to move. With the renovation over—paid for at their own expense without blood money—they'd decided that however he had purchased the land, Braedon had inadvertently given Lyric and Cade the gift of living close to Granny Grace. Lyric had innocently remarked that the renovations were a lot like a renewal of the soul. You had to get rid of some of the old things in your life—whether they were good or bad—so that you could see that God had so much better waiting for you.

He was marrying one smart woman, and today they would begin their lives together in that home. Of course, they had a honeymoon planned in Paris, but that flight left the next day.

Down the hill, out of Balaam's sight, the sound of car doors shutting brought him from his pondering. "Thank You," he uttered the two words with all the emotion he could place behind them. "Thank You for Your grace and Your goodness I do not deserve."

Lyric took deep breaths to keep the tears from falling. The convoy of three cars and a truck pulled alongside the park road.

Shepherd's Rock. Balaam hadn't mentioned the place in the two years since he'd asked her dad for the opportunity to court her and possibly marry her someday.

Dad had his left arm hooked with her right and Granny Grace walked with her hand on his right. They stood and let the wedding guests pass. The only one who would stand with her during the wedding was her new—and her first— female friend that Lyric could remember—Abra Carmichael. And fast friends they'd become. She worked with Abra, an interior designer, through the antique store Granny Grace had tendered into Lyric's hands. Abra consulted with Lyric often on ideas for both the North Carolina homes and the Florida homes where her designs were sought after. Lyric stayed busy with both the store and the music career she shared with Balaam.

Quinn touched her cheek as he walked past, and she smiled. Balaam's best man had become his best friend, and for that, Lyric was grateful. Quinn's date, an aide he'd met at the mental health facility while Momma had been there, smiled as she passed. Cade held her hand and turned back to offer his mom a bright smile. He'd waited for this day as long as Lyric had, and he chose to sit beside his Granny Grace and Danpa, after Daniel walked her down the aisle, to watch the ceremony.

Shane Browne, carrying a guitar case, herded his three children, two boys and a girl, up the rise. The Maynards followed after, both kissing her cheek and saying, "God bless this day."

Jim would officiate the ceremony.

Balaam's father, moving slowly, wrapped callous hands around hers. "Take care of my boy, darlin'. Neither of them deserved you, but I know he loves you—like I loved his momma." He bowed his head then looked up. "I love you, too."

He'd never said that to her before, and the emotions overwhelmed her. "I love you, too, Poppa."

Word had gotten around that Poppa had given up his still, trashed it. For Balaam's sake. Apparently, it happened sometime within that two weeks when Lyric feared Balaam would leave her and Cade. They never spoke about it, but Balaam's relationship with his father had grown close.

Lastly, Bernice Roberts, soon to be Mrs. Daniel Dixon, came to stand before her. "You're a beautiful bride," she whispered. "Isn't she Daniel?"

"Thank you for the compliment," Lyric said. She leaned forward and hugged her. "When you marry my dad," she whispered, "I hope you'll let me call you *Mom.*"

Bernice stepped back, tears in her eyes. Then she reached and hugged Lyric even tighter. "How I longed to hear again those words spoken on my child's lips. "Thank you." She stepped back. "Daughter." Then she reached for Grace's hand, and they walked up the steep rise slowly, Zeke with them.

Abra moved to the rise where the wedding party could see her. The wind caught her light blue knee-length taffeta-filled skirt on her Maid of Honor dress, and she held it down. "Take your time." She turned back to speak but then faced ahead.

Left alone with her father, Lyric ran her hand down the sleek silk of her soft, baby blue wedding dress. The silk crossed at her hips and a chiffon train flowed down her right side.

Her never-tamed curls had grown out, and the wind caught them.

Her father reached out and tucked them behind her ear. "I bet you're wishing you'd decided on a veil." He smiled.

"Granny was right. This dress stands alone." She swirled the train. "But why in the world did she let me keep the train if she knew we'd have to walk through the grass?

Balaam did let you in on his secret, right?"

"On day one of the countdown." Dad touched her face.

She leaned into it. Since the day Balaam had suggested calling Daniel *Dad*, she'd used nothing else, and Quinn had quickly picked up on it.

Her father brushed a soft caress against her cheek. "Your granny said she saw the stars in your eyes the moment you showed her the pattern, and she wouldn't have taken it away from you for all the stars in the sky. Besides, she's a wise woman, and she said you'd never remember any trouble on this day. You'll only remember the look on your groom's face."

"My bouquet?" she said.

Daniel hurried back to Bernice's car they'd driven here because "it wouldn't look nice for the bride to show up in a pickup truck," as Granny and Bernice had insisted.

Daniel handed her the artificial white rose bouquet tied with a ribbon the same color as her dress. "Are we ready?"

"No," she whispered, afraid saying it too loudly would cause the tears to stream like a raging river. She'd promised herself she wouldn't cry. Balaam would never let her live down having racoon eyes on her wedding day.

"No?"

"Thank you," she said a bit louder. "For being my dad—always. For being Quinn's dad." She swallowed hard. "So many kids in this town have received your love. Tough love, kind love, concerned love, and sometimes you've stood between us and death and stared it down. You had faith in us when others didn't. God gifted Amazing Grace with you Sheriff Daniel Dixon. There are a lot of kids now and in the past who have been looked after by you, but Matthew and I were the lucky ones, because though you didn't raise us, I've come to understand that we inherited a lot from you. But I'm so thankful that Quinn and me, and now Balaam are the only ones who can truly call you our father."

Her dad wiped his eyes. He pointed upward. "To God be the glory and the thanks for that. I'm proud of you, Lyric. You never gave up on anything but your music, and now even that is back."

"Frozen Notes," she said.

Her father shook his head. "What?"

"That's what Balaam said one day recently. He said that he thanked God that my notes were frozen and that I hadn't made the same mistakes he had made."

"Well that lunatic of wisdom is waiting to marry my only daughter. I think we've made him fidget long enough."

As if on cue, Shane began to play, "Only God Could Love You More."

Since Balaam had read Matthew's note to Cade telling their son that only God could love Cade more, Lyric had known this would be her wedding song.

Abra turned back for permission to start, and Lyric nodded and smiled.

Though Shane didn't sing the words, as they crested

the rise, the song rang in Lyric's heart—so appropriate for her and Balaam.

She stepped carefully with her father down the mown aisle separating the two rows of chairs. When asked who gave this woman to this man, her father said, "Her granny, her brother, and I do."

She smiled at Quinn who'd been standing beside Balaam, until her groom stepped forward, then at Granny. Then she kissed her father's cheek. "Thank you, Daddy," she whispered, handed Abra her bouquet, and reached out to hold Balaam's hands.

Jim nodded to them, and as Shane began to play the chords to the song Lyric had walked the aisle to, Balaam sang the first words. At the chorus, Lyric joined in, fighting back the emotions she saw mirrored on Balaam's face. This moment, encompassed by this song had seemed so long in coming. In reality, God had timed it just right.

Their paths had kept them apart because of their own unwise decisions, but now, they were together, and they would always cling to each other with God at the center of their marriage—as the head of their family.

When the song ended, they faced Jim Maynard.

The spoken vows were a blur. The rings were exchanged, and before Lyric could take in the diamond-filled wedding ring, Balaam's lips claimed hers and her feet left the ground. He swung her around and around.

"Whoo-ee! It's about time!" Poppa gave the hillbilly shout.

"Ain't that right?" Balaam set Lyric down, making sure she'd found her footing before releasing her.

When they turned, hand in hand, to face their family and friends as Mr. and Mrs. Balaam Carter, she recalled Granny Grace's wisdom. All she could remember of most of the ceremony was Balaam's handsome face so filled with emotion and love for her.

He squeezed her hand and smiled at her, his blue eyes still filled with that love and something more—desire. He took a deep breath and looked heavenward before turning to her again and brushing a soft kiss against her lips. "A wise person with a north-pointing Compass once told me that no matter how far or how fast I ran away from Amazing Grace, there were two things I could never do." He touched her cheek with his warm hand.

"What two things were those?" She leaned into his touch.

"I could never outrun God's love for me or my love for you."

Lyric placed her hands on both sides of his face and kissed his lips. "And he told me the same thing about God and you. Aren't you glad God chased us to the same place?"

Balaam leaned back and held her in place with the growing desire she saw on his face. "I think our family is waiting for us to leave the altar."

Lyric pressed her lips against his and smiled. "They can be patient because it took us such a long time to get here. I want to savor every second as your bride."

**If you enjoyed *Frozen Notes***
**please consider returning to the**
**Amazon page and leaving a**
**review for the author.**

## *About the Author*

Fay Lamb writes emotionally charged stories with a Romans 8:28 attitude, reminding readers that God is always in the details. Fay donates 100% of her royalties to Christian charities. Currently, Fay will be donating her royalties from the second quarter of 2017 through December 31 (royalties paid March 31), to Samaritan's Purse Relief Fund to aid victims of Hurricane Harvey and Irma and any other relief the organization feels necessary.

Fay's fourth book in the Amazing Grace romantic suspense series, *Frozen Notes* brings to a close stories of intrigue and suspense and reveals to her readers the secrets of one of the series reoccurring characters from the first three novels, *Stalking Willow, Better than Revenge,* and

*Everybody's Broken.*

Fay is also the author of The Ties that Bind Series, which includes *Charisse, Libby, and Hope.* The fourth story in the series, *Delilah*, will be coming soon.

Fay's adventurous spirit has also taken her into the realm of non-fiction with *The Art of Characterization: How to Use the Elements of Storytelling to Connect Readers to an Unforgettable Cast.*

Readers of Fay Lamb's fiction can look forward to her Serenity Key series, with her epic novel *Storms in Serenity* set for release in early 2018.

Fay loves to meet readers, and you can find her on her personal Facebook page, her Facebook Author page, and at The Tactical Editor on Facebook and on Goodreads. She's also active on Twitter. Then there are her blogs: On the Ledge, Inner Source, and the Tactical Editor.

## Letter from the Author

Dear Readers:

I want to take this opportunity to thank you for visiting Amazing Grace, a fictional town clearly etched into my imagination from the moment I stumbled into the quaint Western Carolina mountains. My hope is that you have enjoyed your visits here.

Throughout the writing of this series, I have been dealing with a burden that many of my generation are facing: the horrors of Alzheimer's Disease. No, not my own, but someone I love dearly. I have gone from times of tremendous joy with this loved one where we tootled all across the mountains on adventures to places we knew how to find, some we expected to find, and others we stumbled upon and made perfect memories—for me. This loved one is the person who introduced me to the laid-back mountain lifestyle, and she is now the one who can no longer enjoy it due to the confusion of the disease.

Many of you have shared the laughter and tears of this journey in social media as I struggled to deal with the loss of someone who is sitting right in front of me. I laughed at the miscues and cried at the missteps. I grumbled at the pain of suddenly being unloved by the person she has become and sometimes not like that new person in front of me and not liking myself very much. Many of you have been there with me whether you are new to this series or whether you have been with me from the beginning. You, dear readers, have kept me sane. You are the ones who gave me the reason to write, and in writing, I found sanity in a world out of my control. I envisioned you opening the pages on this book and others in the series, and I found purpose and the courage to go forward. That purpose allowed me to escape into the world of Amazing Grace and the characters I have come to love. When the books were published, I then began to interact with my readers, all of whom are real-life characters in one extreme or the other, and therein lies the beauty of friendships. We all have a measure of crazy, and that's what makes life fun—and makes for great fictional characters.

So, to you, those who have opened the pages of my stories and have gotten lost in my world of suspense or intrigue, those who encouraged me by declaring you were waiting for the next novel, and those of you who simply let me know that you were out there praying for me, cheering for me, laughing and crying with me, you have my utmost appreciation. You are all wonderful gifts from God, and you are never taken for granted by this woman who gets to pour words onto paper and fill the imaginations of others with characters and settings and plots and conflict all from my overflowing noggin.

By our Heavenly Father and by you, I have truly been blessed.

Fay

# Get the Whole Amazing Grace Series

Bitterness, a stalker, and a neighbor to die for. What's a girl to do?

Trailed by a stalker in New York City, Willow Thomas, a young ad executive, scurries back to her small North Carolina hometown and the lake house where ten years earlier a scandal revealed her entire life had been a lie, and a seed of bitterness took root in her soul. The cocoon of safety Willow feels upon her arrival home soon unravels when she meets opposition from her family, faces the man she left behind, and the stalker reveals he is close on her heels.

Can Willow learn to trust God to tear out her roots of resentment, reunite her family, ferret out a deadly stalker, and to rekindle the love she left behind?

"... if we kill him, our family will be safe ..."

Michael's fiancée, Issie Putnam, was brutally attacked and Michael was imprisoned for a crime he didn't commit.

Now he's home to set things right.

Two people stand in his way: Issie's son, Cole, and a madman.

Can Michael learn to love the child Issie holds so close to her heart and protect him from the man who took everything from Michael so long ago?

The walls have ears … and voices.
Voices that threaten …

Abra Carmichael's husband, Beau, has been murdered. She begins to realize that the man she loved was never who he seemed. Beau's secrets endanger Abra, their twin sons, and everyone who loved him. When Abra's life and the lives of their boys are threatened, she flees to Amazing Grace, North Carolina, and to Beau's family--people she never knew existed until the day of Beau's funeral.

For six years Shane Browne, an award-winning songwriter had both wished for and dreaded the return of his cousin. Beau's departure from their small hometown left behind his family and his inheritance, a grand Victorian with its legend of secret passages, which lay empty. Empty until Abra moves to Amazing Grace, into the house Beau willed to her only weeks before his death. Shane finds himself deeply drawn to Abra and her sons, desiring a future with them and his daughter.

But the danger follows Abra to the peacefulness of the North Carolina mountains. Abra and Shane are both threatened, and Abra claims to hear noises deep within the walls of the old home. Shane will do everything possible to keep Abra and her boys safe, even if that means revealing secrets of his own that will completely shatter Abra's already broken heart and destroy his relationship with everyone he loves.

# *Recent Releases by Write Integrity Press*

*Secrets never stay hidden.*

James Evers turned his back on a life of power and privilege to carve a place in the world for himself. Now that he's finally discovered his niche as a small-town sheriff and found the woman he wants in his future, a past indiscretion struts in on high heels and sends his newfound love fleeing headlong into peril. His mission: neutralize old enemies, defuse new threats, resolve past mistakes, settle family disputes, and—most importantly —find and rescue his woman from terrorists before the unthinkable happens.

What would you do if you discovered,
by accident, no less, that the
President of the United States was
attending your daughter's wedding
in less than two weeks?

Panic. You'd panic, I tell you.

That's what the parents of the bride,
Pastor Hugh Foster and his wife
Melanie, did. Talk about a faux pas!

Well, good luck with all that,
Pastor Foster.

Oh, and Heaven help the president.

**Thank you
for reading our books!**

**Look for other books
published by**

Write Integrity Press
www.WriteIntegrity.com